THE REUNION
&
THE SECRET OF CYPRIERE BAYOU

New York Times Bestselling Author

JANA DELEON

ISBN-13: 978-0-373-69719-9

THE REUNION
Copyright © 2013 by Harlequin Books S.A.

The publisher acknowledges the copyright
holder of the individual works as follows:

THE REUNION
Copyright © 2013 by Jana DeLeon

THE SECRET OF CYPRIERE BAYOU
Copyright © 2012 by Jana DeLeon

PLEASE RECYCLE
THIS PRODUCT IS RECYCLABLE

Recycling programs
for this product may
not exist in your area.

HARLEQUIN®
www.Harlequin.com

Printed in U.S.A.

CONTENTS

THE REUNION

CAST OF CHARACTERS

Joelle LeBeau—The social worker specialized in helping women escape situations of domestic abuse, but her job was not without risk. One man will do anything to find his wife, whom Joelle helped hide. When she finds out that her stepfather died and the terms of her inheritance require her to spend two weeks at her childhood estate, it seems like perfect timing for her to disappear.

Tyler Duhon—He's back from the Middle East and attempting to gain his footing in the civilian world. His father, William, has other ideas. William wants Tyler to play bodyguard to the last of the LeBeau heirs. Tyler knows his father wouldn't ask if it wasn't important, so he can't say no. But he hopes the time passes quickly and the heiress doesn't bring as much trouble down on Calais as her sisters did.

Victor Brant—The abuser wants to find his wife in the worst way possible, and he's not going to let up on Joelle until he does exactly that. But did he follow her to Calais, or is someone else responsible for all the odd things happening at the LeBeau estate?

Mayor Dupree—The only time the old windbag isn't gossiping is when he's sleeping or eating, but does he know even more about Trenton Purcell and the situation with the inheritance than he's saying?

Bert Thibodeaux—Purcell promised the trucker he'd get a new rig when Purcell died, but the money wasn't Purcell's to give away and he knew it. The trucker is beyond angry, but is he angry enough to try to get revenge on the legitimate heirs?

Doctor Picard—The now-deceased physician had treated the heiress's mother over twenty years ago and had clearly been hiding something all these years. Was his secret worth killing over?

To my husband, Rene.
We've come a long way, baby!

Chapter One

The woman stared out the second-story window of her mansion, looking across the overgrown driveway and down the lonely dirt road that led into town. Where had her children gone? Two were here before, then there were none. But the third...the third had never returned. Did she not know how much her mother loved her? Did she not know that only the thought of seeing her again kept the woman tied to this place?

A tear slid down the woman's cheek as the house began to fade away.

"I grow weak. Come to me, soon. Before it's too late."

JOELLE LEBEAU STOOD next to her ancient Honda Accord, certain it was totaled and not even wanting to think of replacing it. The two Jackson, Mississippi, policemen documented the vandalism, one with pen and paper and the other with a camera.

It was only 6:00 p.m., but the fall sunlight was already fading, leaving the parking lot behind the Office of Social Services building dim. Joelle had been working late, as usual, when she heard a noise outside. By the time she'd removed her pistol from her desk drawer

and peered out the back door into the parking lot, the vandal was already gone.

But he'd managed to do so much in so little time.

Every tire had been slashed and all the windows were shattered, leaving shards of glass littering the parking lot and the interior of the car. The windshield had a huge crack in the center that splintered out in every direction, and a message in dark red paint sprayed across it.

Destroyer.

That one word left her no doubt who had done the damage, and if she'd had trouble guessing, the note on the dashboard cinched it.

Give me what's mine.

One of the officers stepped up next to her. "You said you had someone in mind for this?"

She nodded. "Victor Brant."

The officer made a note. "Is he a client of yours?"

She almost laughed at the thought of the abusive, narcissistic Victor Brant admitting he needed help. "No. His wife is."

"And I take it Mr. Brant is unhappy with that?"

"He's unhappy with anyone who doesn't bow down to his every word or whose thoughts differ from his own. He's the worst type of abuser—successful, good-looking and adored by his colleagues and in his community."

"So you're saying it would have been unlikely that people believed Mrs. Brant when she said her husband was abusive."

"She wasn't believed. The police were dispatched twice to their home. Both times, they declined to even take Mr. Brant in for questioning. In fact, the last time all they did was schedule a round of golf with Brant the following week at his country club."

The officer frowned. "The Jackson Police Department?"

"No. The Brants' estate is in Willow Grove. It was their local department. The mayor is Mr. Brant's first cousin. The chief of police is his uncle. Are you getting a clear picture?"

"Yes, ma'am, and I don't like it, but I can assure you that neither the mayor of Jackson nor the chief of police are interested in playing flunky to Mr. Brant. If he's responsible for this threat, he will be prosecuted. What I don't understand is this note."

He held up the note in a plastic baggie. "What do you have that he thinks belongs to him?"

Joelle took a deep breath and blew it out. "His wife."

The officer's eyes widened. "Excuse me?"

"In addition to my counseling job at the crisis center, I volunteer with an organization that helps women… quietly relocate, let's just say."

"An underground railroad?"

Joelle held in her frustration at the officer's obvious displeasure. Dedicated, honorable law enforcement professionals didn't like the vigilante-like tactics that the underground railroad organizations often used, but they had yet to offer a solution when their own departments couldn't keep women safe.

"There were no children," Joelle assured him. "And Ms. Brant left only with the clothes on her back and a watch that belonged to her mother. What we did was in no way illegal."

"Maybe not, but it's still not the usual way to get divorced."

"Look," she said, unable to control her aggravation any longer, "if any of us thought for a minute that Ms. Brant could simply file and get a divorce, like normal

people do, she'd be staying at a Hilton, not hiding in a ten-by-ten room, afraid to even look out a window. Victor Brant said he'd kill her before he let her go. We have no reason to think he's lying."

The officer sighed and shook his head. "Assuming all of that is true, you haven't solved the problem. You've simply momentarily shifted Brant's focus from his wife to you. What makes you think you're any safer than she was?"

Despite the somewhat warm temperature of the fall evening, a chill passed over her and she crossed her arms across her chest. What he said was entirely correct, but it wasn't something she wanted to dwell on at the moment. When she'd decided on this profession and her volunteer work, Joelle invested time and money into her own safety. She lived in a well-lit condominium with a good security system. She spent at least an hour a week at the gun range and was a black belt.

"I'm safer, because I'm more qualified to handle this," she said finally. "It's my job to be prepared for these kinds of threats."

The officer didn't look convinced, but he closed the notebook and handed her a card. "If you receive any more threats, please contact me immediately. And be careful, Ms. LeBeau. Even the best trained among us can be gotten to. Can we give you a ride home?"

"No, thank you. A friend is coming to pick me up."

He nodded and climbed into his car with his partner. Joelle watched them exit the parking lot, then cast one more baleful glance at her junkyard-bound automobile. Sighing, she turned toward the office building, and when she did, she caught sight of movement out of the corner of her eye.

She spun around to peer at the Dumpster that rested

in the corner of the parking lot against the fence. Nothing moved now, but she was certain something had just a second before.

You let that cop spook you.

Blowing out a breath, she hustled toward the back door of the office and let herself inside. Likely, it had just been an alley cat. Two or three regularly hung around the Dumpster, looking for an easy meal.

She pulled the dead bolt on the back door and hurried to the front of the office. Lisa would be here any moment to pick her up, and she didn't want her waiting too long. Her friend was an incredibly nice woman but a bit prone to dramatics and quite fearful of everything. Joelle had omitted the truth when she'd asked Lisa to give her lift, only citing car trouble as the reason for needing help.

As she walked through the office, she grabbed her purse from the desk where she'd dropped it earlier and continued through the reception area. As she approached the frosted glass door, a shadow moved in front of it and she drew up short.

The shadow stood for several seconds and Joelle dipped her hand into her purse and gripped her pistol. Then the shadow rapped on the door, causing her to jump.

"Anyone here? It's Myer's Courier Service. I have a package."

She hesitated just a second before releasing her pistol and stepping up to the door to unlock it. Myer's had delivered packages to the office many times before, but they usually made deliveries before the office closed for the day.

Peering out a tiny crack, she was relieved to see the

same tall, skinny young man who always delivered. She pulled open the door and smiled at him.

"Hello, John. You almost missed me."

John handed her a legal-sized envelope and produced a clipboard for her to sign. "I know I'm late," he said, flushing a bit. "I had a flat tire and it took longer to change it out than I thought it would."

"Well, I'm glad you're fixed now. How's Janey doing her first semester of college?" John's sister had volunteered at the crisis center her senior year of high school.

"She'd doing fine. She's working with disabled kids two days a week after class."

Joelle smiled. "That's great. Tell her we miss her and good luck."

"Yes, ma'am," he said and left.

She closed the door and placed the package on the secretary's desk, but as she started to walk away, the name on the package caught her eye. Joelle LeBeau.

Frowning, she picked up the package again. It was unusual for her to receive a courier delivery. The secretary usually dealt with all incoming paperwork and orders. She glanced at the return address and sucked in a breath.

Calais, Louisiana.

She studied the return address more closely. What in the world would an attorney in Calais want with her? She was only four years old when her mother died and she was sent to live with distant cousins in Mississippi, but certain moments of her childhood on the LeBeau estate were etched in her mind, with recall so vivid it was as if she were watching it take place on a television. For years, she'd tried to convince herself to visit Calais—to confront her stepfather, the man who cast

off the three sisters—but every time she approached the entry for the highway to New Orleans, she drove past it.

Not ready to face those vivid memories yet.

She tore open the envelope and pulled out a letter, already certain she didn't want to hear anything her stepfather had to say. If Trenton Purcell was on his deathbed and begging forgiveness, she'd raise a glass and toast, but she'd never accept an apology for what he did.

As she began to read, her pulse ticked up until she could feel it beating in her temples. Her evil stepfather was dead. He had been much older than her mother, so Joelle knew the day would come sooner than later, but she'd never expected to be notified of the event.

Then she read the second paragraph and sank down onto the desktop, her knees weak. It was all theirs. The estate, the fortune—everything her mother and her mother's ancestors had built—it all belonged to Ophelia LeBeau's three daughters. Purcell hadn't been able to control the fortune after his death.

She continued reading and frowned. In order to inherit, she had to spend two straight weeks on the estate, to be verified by the local sheriff. Her two sisters, Alaina and Danae, had already completed their two weeks and were anxious to meet her.

A wave of excitement rushed over her, then a flash of anxiety. All these years, she'd wanted to meet her sisters, but hadn't even known where to start looking. Now they were waiting for her at their childhood home—waiting for her to come fulfill a rather bizarre inheritance request so that they could finally claim their birthright.

But that meant not only returning to Calais, but staying in that house. The house with bad memories.

A mental image of her vandalized car flashed

through her mind. Maybe leaving Jackson for a couple of weeks wasn't a bad idea. It might give Brant a chance to realize that the Jackson Police Department wasn't for sale like the one in Willow Grove. She had plenty of vacation coming. In fact, she hadn't taken more than a day off at a time since she'd started working at the crisis center over five years ago.

A horn honked outside and she stuffed the letter into her purse and swung the strap over her shoulder before hurrying out of the office. She'd call William Duhon, the attorney who'd sent the letter, first thing in the morning. Then she'd call her boss to say she was taking a long overdue vacation…for the long overdue purpose of addressing her past.

Chapter Two

Tyler Duhon stared in dismay across the café table at his father, William, Calais's resident attorney. Not even Johnny's absolutely stellar banana pudding could sweeten Tyler's disposition toward what his father had just asked him to do.

"No way," Tyler said. "Look, I promise I'm not going to be lying around on your couch all day for months on end. I'll be starting my own security firm as soon as I get all the permits and approved formation documents."

William pushed his empty bowl to the edge of the table and took another sip of coffee. "I'm not worried about my couch. Your mother picked it out and I never liked it much—all those roses. And I'm well aware of your business pursuits as I filed the corporate formation documents for you last week."

"Then what's your angle?"

"I don't have an angle. What I have is a spooky, partially repaired old house that has three deaths attached to it in as many months, and an heir who needs to occupy that house for two weeks in order to gain back everything that was stolen from her. I'd really like her to have an easier go of it than her sisters did."

Tyler frowned. The happenings surrounding Trenton Purcell's death and the subsequent arrival of two of

Ophelia LeBeau's daughters had set off a chain reaction of threats, break-ins, stalkers and eventually, three deaths—one murder and two in self-defense. But the facts paled in comparison to the sheer amount of disturbance that had rocked the sleepy bayou town.

"I'm not sure what you think I can do," Tyler said finally.

"You plan on opening a security firm, don't you? I expect you can protect the heiress and her assets. I'm not expecting you to do so for free. The estate will be happy to cover the cost of on-site security—in fact, in light of recent events, they're requiring it."

Tyler shook his head. "I'm opening a firm, but I'm not going to do any of the face-to-face work. I'm focusing solely on hardware and administration. I'll hire some of my military buddies for the groundwork."

William scrunched his brow. "You plan on sitting behind a desk all day? You'll be bored within a week."

I don't think so.

"If I get bored," Tyler said, "we'll go shopping for a new couch. Mom's been gone for years. It's time you got some manly furniture in the place."

William studied him, and Tyler forced himself not to squirm under his father's scrutiny. Apparently, his attempt at levity hadn't distracted his father for a moment. Tyler had never been able to hide anything from the shrewd attorney, who seemed to possess the ability to read minds. And more than anyone, his father knew how much Tyler hated sitting still—hated concentrating on paper and numbers and words. He was smart, but it had been a struggle to get him out of high school. He'd sit in class almost twitching with anxiety, wanting desperately to jump out a window and run until he sated his body's always-demanding call to action.

It's why he'd joined the Marine Corps as soon as he graduated.

The Marine Corps had immediately recognized that Tyler was able to sit still long enough to take a flight to where they needed him for action. Beyond that, and you risked a fidgety bored adult, carrying a weapon and expertly trained at using it. When Tyler wasn't on maneuvers in the Middle East, he worked in the villages alongside the occupants, helping them rebuild their homes. He hadn't sat behind a desk since high school, and he already knew he was going to be bored.

But you rarely saw people die when you sat behind a desk.

And that was the bottom line. He'd seen too much sadness, too much tragedy, and he needed to get away from it all. Which was why he was digging in his heels over the issue with the heiress. The last thing he wanted to do was sit all day in that monstrosity of a house with some fainting violet of a woman.

"I don't know what happened overseas," William said quietly, cutting into his thoughts. "I'd like to think that someday you'll tell me. But I wouldn't ask this of you if I had other options. The reality is, you're the best person for the job and I need the best. This woman's safety is on my conscience. I can't rest if she's not protected."

Tyler held in a sigh, knowing he'd just lost the fight, but determined to give it one last parting shot. "What about Carter? He's definitely capable, and his mother would make him do anything for you."

William nodded. "Quite true, which is why Carter was tasked with verifying the daily presence of all the heirs. But Carter is Calais's sheriff, and lately, that job is more than full-time. Not to mention that he has a new

fiancée who lives with him, and it would be highly in-
appropriate for him to move in with her sister—even
if only for two weeks and for the purpose of protect-
ing her."

Tyler's parting shot faded into the distance, and he
let out the sigh. If anyone but William had tried such a
line on him, he would have accused them of attempt-
ing to guilt him into doing what they wanted, but that
was something his father would never do. Which was
why Tyler knew William was telling the truth when he
said the woman's safety weighed on his conscience.
His father was a good man—the best, actually—and
he wasn't afraid to care about people.

Even if it cost him in the long run.

"Fine," Tyler relented. "I'll do it. But only for the
two weeks the estate requires her to be there. If she
wants to stay and redecorate or open a knitter's colony
or something, she's on her own. And I have no intention
of sitting and staring at her all day. You want me in the
house, that's fine, but I want to talk to the contractor
and get a list of things I can work on while I'm there."

William beamed at him. "Thank you, Tyler. I'm sure
Zach can provide you with plenty of items that need
attention."

Tyler nodded. Zach Sargent was the contractor Wil-
liam had hired to make repairs on the house, but he'd
had other reasons for coming to Calais. Zach's father,
a funeral director, was one of the many people Purcell
had paid off, and Zach took the job in order to figure
out exactly what his father's attempted deathbed confes-
sion and the large cash deposit had entailed. Zach hadn't
gotten the answers he'd hoped for, but he'd formed a
relationship with the youngest of Ophelia's daughters
and had moved back to New Orleans, with her in tow.

He returned to Calais on weekends to continue repairs on the house.

"You don't know how relieved I am that you'll be my eyes and ears in that house," William said.

"Why? Surely, it's all over now."

William's smile faded away and he shook his head. "Much of Purcell's evil intentions and those who carried them out have been exposed, that's true."

"But?"

"But I still have a bad feeling about all of it."

"Of course you do. Purcell was a hit man for the New Orleans mafia who romanced Ophelia LeBeau for her money and a safe hiding place when his own employer put a hit on him. Then he killed her and sent her kids away like they were department store returns. I've got lots of feelings about it myself, and trust me, all of them are bad."

"We don't know for certain that Purcell killed Ophelia."

"Then what was he paying all those people for?"

William nodded. "Oh, we're certain Purcell was paying for silence, and I'd guess it's exactly as you say and he killed Ophelia, but we still can't prove it. And with everyone on his payroll dead, there's no one left to ask."

"And that's exactly my original point—all the bad guys are dead."

William stared out the plate-glass window of the café and looked across the street into the swamp. Finally, he looked back at Tyler and leaned across the table.

"I don't think they are *all* dead." William's voice was barely more than a whisper. "The swamp is wrong. You don't even have to enter it to feel it. Something is still out of balance, and I don't think the swamp will rest until it churns up all its secrets."

If it were anyone else speaking or if his father were talking about anywhere else but Calais, Tyler would suggest he needed professional help. But the swamps of Mystere Parish were different than any place he'd ever been. Although he'd been surrounded by them his entire childhood, and had traipsed through them thousands of hours, Tyler had never felt at ease in the dense cypress trees and foliage.

It was as if the swamp itself was alive.

Certainly, the swamp comprised lots of living things, but it was something more than that—as if the swamp were a separate living entity, with its own agenda. At times, it was pleasant enough, but he'd never found the atmosphere relaxing, even though parts of it were beautiful. At other times, it had been oppressive, the weight of it pressing in around him.

That oppressive weight had always aligned with something tragic, usually death.

If the swamp was out of balance, then something was still very wrong in Calais. Given that the only recent tragedies all centered on the LeBeau estate, Tyler understood why his father was so anxious to ensure that Ophelia's middle daughter was offered the best protection he could provide. The swamp wouldn't return to a peaceful state until a reckoning had occurred.

"What do you think is wrong?" Tyler asked.

"I don't know, and that's what bothers me the most. But we may get some answers soon."

"How's that?"

His father looked at him, his expression sad and haunting. "We're exhuming Ophelia LeBeau tomorrow."

Chapter Three

As she pulled through Calais, Joelle studied the old buildings, looking for something that appeared familiar. The weathered brick buildings were typical of any old small town, but none of them sparked even a twitch of memory. The café caught her interest as she pulled by, but only because she planned to spend her two weeks allowing others to cook for her. She hoped the food was good, as it appeared to be the only option.

Her stomach rumbled as her thoughts turned to food, and she realized it was well past lunch. She'd almost stopped several times, but each time she pressed the accelerator and continued down the highway, anxious to get the long drive over with. Unfortunately, she had arranged to meet the attorney at the house in about ten minutes, so eating would have to wait a bit longer.

As soon as she passed the last building on Main Street, she pulled a paper with directions from her purse. She'd gotten this far without referring to the attorney's instructions, but when the directions started including items such as "turn right at the giant oak tree," it was time to pay attention. The last thing she wanted to do was to get lost in the swamp.

She turned to the right at a four-way stop, directing her car onto a semblance of a road. The economy rental

she'd acquired before leaving Jackson was no match for the bumps and holes that mostly made up the dirt trail that led to the house, and she gritted her teeth as the dashboard rattled. She swerved to miss a huge hole, but her right front tire caught the edge of it and the entire car dropped. Cringing at the sound of the bottom of the car sliding across rocks, she clenched the steering wheel and leaned forward to get a better look at the road.

The cypress trees that lined both sides of the road grew thicker, creating a canopy above the road that blocked most of the sunlight from entering. If she hadn't known any better, she would have sworn it was late evening rather than mid-afternoon. Surely, the house couldn't be much farther.

Fifteen minutes later, she rounded a corner and the house burst into view. Continuing her slow creep around what remained of the circular driveway, she looked up at the place she'd spent the first four years of her life, waiting for that spark of recognition to hit. She was disappointed when it never came.

A new pickup truck was parked in front of the house, and she pulled up behind it and parked, figuring it belonged to the attorney. She jumped out of the car and stretched her aching legs and cast a glance back at the car. She'd rented the economy vehicle to try it out, thinking she might purchase the same model to replace her totaled Honda. The tiny car would be a huge benefit in the city, where she rarely drove more than twenty miles in one stretch, but after hours on the road, she was well aware of just how cramped her long legs were in such a compact space.

Her suitcases could wait until after she'd spoken to the attorney, so she headed up to the front door. When she raised her hand and knocked, the door inched for-

ward just a bit. She pushed the door open and stuck her head inside.

"Mr. Duhon," she called out. "It's Joelle LeBeau."

She waited a bit, expecting the attorney to appear or at least respond, but only her own voice echoed through the giant entry. Deciding the attorney must be off in a part of the house where he couldn't hear her, she stepped inside, then drew up short. A twinge of something—some tiny flicker of recognition—flashed through her, but as soon as she tried to grasp it, the flicker disappeared.

The entry was massive, like the entry of a hotel or museum. The giant spiral staircase was centered toward the front and she peered up to see the balcony running around the entire second floor, doors to various rooms lining the upstairs walls. The first floor of the entry was littered—there wasn't really a better word—with decorative columns and tables, all housing art, china and glass that seemed to have no consistency of era or country of origin.

To the left, a wide hallway led away from the entry. Patches of sunlight streamed from the room at the end of the hallway and onto the stone floor. Figuring the hallway led to a family room or kitchen, she took off to the left, hoping to locate the attorney.

The kitchen and breakfast nook were in sharp contrast to the rest of the house and had her smiling. Clearly, someone had put in long hours on this room and it showed—the gleaming cabinets, polished countertops and fresh coat of paint made the room a cheery retreat from the gloomy entry. Giant windows formed the far wall, along with a single door that led onto an overgrown patio.

She gazed around the room once more before ready-

ing herself to continue her search for the attorney, and that's when she realized the patio door was partially open. Now understanding why the attorney hadn't heard her call out in the entry, she stepped outside and looked up and down the long stone patio. Shrubs and brush had grown right up to the edges, and vines climbed the stone columns and trailed across the ground, but it was clear that someone had recently started clearing the brush away.

Following a trail of small branches and leaves, she walked to the far end of the patio and saw the tiny path that led straight into the swamp. The remnants of foliage continued down the path, but Joelle hesitated before stepping off the stone patio. Something about the swamp bothered her—more than just the dim, creepy appearance.

She was just about to head back inside and wait for the attorney when a voice sounded behind her and she jumped, her foot slipping off the edge of the patio and onto the path several inches below. She struggled to maintain her balance, but the drop was just enough to send her crashing into the brush at the side of the trail.

As soon as she hit the ground, she scrambled to get up, fighting the thick vines that she'd brought down on top of her. Suddenly, she felt someone grasp her arm and tug her completely to her feet. A branch slapped her across the face and her eyes watered, so the only thing she could make out when she was upright was a tall man with dark hair.

Brad.

Instantly, a mental image of her ex-boyfriend flashed across her mind, and just as quickly, she sent it scurrying to the recesses where it belonged. Brad was long gone and old news.

She blinked a couple of times and the man came into focus, but this young, incredibly gorgeous and seriously ripped man couldn't possibly be the aging attorney she'd talked to on the phone. The scowl on his face was just further proof. The attorney had been kind and cheerful. This man looked like those attributes were not part of his makeup.

"I hope you're not always this jumpy," he said. "A fall in the horror funhouse could bring more than just vines crashing down around you."

A blush ran up her neck and onto her face, and she felt a flash of heat wash over her. "Maybe if you didn't go sneaking up behind people, you wouldn't startle them."

He raised his eyebrows, looking almost amused at her accusation. "I'm wearing work boots, and I was hardly tiptoeing across that patio. Hell, people back in town could hear me coming."

"Really? Then maybe you should tell them why you're trespassing on private property."

He sighed. "You must be Joelle. My father owes me big-time for this."

Joelle narrowed her eyes at him. "Exactly who is your father?"

"William Duhon."

"Oh," she said, momentarily taken aback that the pleasant gentleman she'd spoken to on the phone had produced such a surly son. "Your father was supposed to meet me here. Is he on his way?"

"He's not coming."

"What do you mean? He's supposed to provide me a key to the house and go over any of my questions concerning the estate requirements."

"Well, you got me instead." He pulled a giant iron

key from his pocket and handed it to her. "That's the front door key. I'm having keys to the patio and back door duplicated and will pick them up this afternoon."

"Am I supposed to meet your father at his office?"

If possible, he looked even more aggrieved.

"No. I'm supposed to take you to meet him for an early supper at the café, after I get you settled in."

She stared. Was he joking? The last thing she intended to do was get in a car with Mr. Personality.

"I'm sure I can find my way back to the café, the same way I found the house," she said. "I don't need an escort."

"My father says you do, and unfortunately for me and you, so does the estate. During your two-week stay in Calais, I will go wherever you go."

"That's outrageous! Neither the estate nor your father can mandate who I spend my time with."

"No, but they can insist you maintain personal security at all times, and they have."

"What in the world for? To protect me from the clutter and dust I saw in there? The only risk to my safety so far has been you, and I'm supposed to believe you were assigned to protect me?"

He clenched his jaw and she could tell she'd insulted him, just as she'd intended.

"Well," he said, "I managed to sneak up on you in broad daylight wearing construction boots, right? I'm guessing that makes my observation skills a sight better than your own."

He whirled around and strode away from her.

"I'll get your things out of your car," he mumbled as he left.

Joelle stared behind him wondering if the entire world had gone crazy.

I will go wherever you go.

She stiffened. Surely that didn't mean he was staying in the house with her. Granted, she had her apprehensions about staying in the spooky, rambling mansion alone, but if the choice were Mr. Personality or the ghosts, she'd definitely take the ghosts.

TYLER STALKED AROUND the side of the house to the front where Joelle's car was parked. She'd left it unlocked, which surprised him at first given that his father said she was some sort of social worker, but then she probably figured no one was roaming this far out in the swamp looking to lift items from a car.

If only she were right. Then he'd be sitting on his dad's couch watching television instead of fending off insults.

Likely, no one would lift items from her car, but if his father's instincts were correct, someone was still roaming around the estate. At least this time, a full-time security detail was on-site and prepared for battle. Tyler wasn't about to let someone get the better of him in his own neck of the woods.

He grabbed two suitcases from the backseat of the car and carried them inside, still trying to figure out how he was supposed to manage two full weeks around Joelle LeBeau. When his father told him Joelle was a social worker, Tyler had formed a mental picture of some motherly-type woman—probably heavyset—and with a kind smile.

The tall, curvy Creole beauty he'd pulled out of the bushes was the last thing he'd ever expected and, certainly, the last thing he wanted. Gorgeous, endangered women were part of a past he intended to put far behind him, which was precisely the reason he wanted to

sit at a desk until he passed out from boredom. During his eight years in the Middle East, he'd had enough excitement to last a lifetime.

During the last twelve months, he'd had enough beautiful women to last ten lifetimes.

Chapter Four

Joelle looked across the table at William Duhon, as charmed by the aging attorney as she was frustrated by his son. Clearly, Tyler hadn't inherited any of his father's charisma. Her private security detail hadn't spoken a word during the entire drive into Calais, and after arriving at the café, had opened his mouth only long enough to tell his father that he needed to pick up some supplies at the general store and would meet them back at the café in an hour or so. William appeared a bit embarrassed by his son's behavior, but just nodded and directed her to a booth in the far corner.

"I apologize for the rather unconventional meeting location," William said, "but I recall you saying when you called from New Orleans that you hadn't stopped to eat. I figured we could accomplish two things at once."

Joelle took another bite of sirloin steak, smothered in gravy and onions, and said a silent prayer of thanks that she hadn't stopped for fast food on the way to Calais.

"It was worth the wait," she said.

William smiled. "Johnny's mother was the best cook in Calais. When he opened this place, it was with the intention to use only her recipes, and he's kept it that way for thirty years."

"If it's not broken…"

"Quite so. Johnny's made a good business here. Most everyone has at least a couple meals a week at the café. Make sure you save some room for banana pudding. That's the dessert special today."

"Banana pudding?" She looked down at her plate. "Maybe I'll take half of this home for supper. I may have to start jogging while I'm here."

William pointed out the plate-glass window to a building across the street. "I'm convinced that this café is the reason the seamstress shop stays in business— letting out waistbands and such."

"It probably won't come to that. My brief glance at the downstairs of the house provided a mental list of things to do that is as long as the Mississippi. I won't have any problem getting my exercise in."

Quite frankly, the state of the house had surprised her more than anything else she'd heard so far. She never expected that her stepfather would keep it up, but he'd been dead for months. Surely, the estate could afford to hire a cleaning service.

"Can I ask a question?" she asked.

"Of course. That's what I'm here for."

"Can the estate hire someone to help with the cleaning? Even if I worked on it full-time for two weeks, I couldn't put a dent in it."

William sighed. "The big services in New Orleans won't travel this far out for the job, especially with no hotel to place the crew in. I've hired several local women, but they never last more than a day."

"Why not? Surely, jobs are hard to come by here."

"Absolutely, and they could all use the money, but they were too afraid to continue working."

"Afraid of what?"

"They claim they saw a ghost."

Joelle stared. "You're serious?"

"Yes." William frowned and hesitated a moment before continuing. "There's been some unpleasantness surrounding the house."

"What do you mean?"

"Your sister Alaina had a stalker who tried to kill her. Sheriff Carter Trahan, now Alaina's fiancé, shot and killed him in the front drive of the house."

"Oh, my! Alaina is all right, though?"

"She's fine. After all that was put to rest, we hoped Danae would have an easier time with her two weeks, but a different set of problems surfaced."

William took a deep breath and blew it out before continuing. "I don't know how to say this in a good way, so I'm just going to lay out the facts. Your stepfather used estate money to buy assets and then sell them. He had the authority to use estate money to purchase investment property—such as art—but could not request cash withdrawals outside of a small living allowance."

"So that's why we still have an estate to inherit," Joelle said, one of her questions answered. "I wondered about that."

William nodded. "Danae accepted contract work with the estate to go through all the paperwork in the house, and she located some of Purcell's personal accounting records. The records show large cash receipts, which we think are from the sale of the assets acquired using estate money, but they also show large cash disbursements."

"I thought he became a hermit after we left. What was he purchasing?"

"Part of the money spent was on you girls."

"Us? I doubt that. Purcell hated us. Even as young as I was, I could feel it."

"No doubt you're right." William paused for a couple of seconds and frowned. "Your adoptive parents passed away, correct?"

Joelle nodded. "They were already in their fifties when they took me in. They'd never been able to have their own children, and even though they knew it would be a struggle at their age, keeping up with such a young child, they knew it was their last chance at being parents."

William's expression softened. "They were good people, then?"

"The best. Of course, I would rather have been with my mother and sisters, but given the circumstances, I couldn't have asked for a better place to go."

"I, uh, don't want to do anything to diminish your opinion in any way, but it appears that Purcell paid each family twenty thousand dollars to take you girls in."

Suddenly, something Joelle had never understood clicked. "My college fund."

"What do you mean?"

"My adoptive parents didn't make a lot of money. I always assumed I'd need loans to pay for college, but they established a fund for me when I came to live with them. I've seen the records. They opened the account with twenty thousand dollars. I always wondered where it came from."

William's relief was apparent. "That's wonderful. Just wonderful."

"You said part of the money was spent on the families that took us in. What else did he pay for?"

"I apologize in advance, because this is most distressing, but we suspect he paid for silence. So far, we've discovered payments to the man who pronounced

your mother's death and the funeral director in New Orleans who handled her burial."

A wave of nausea rolled over Joelle as William's words clicked in her mind. "No, you're not saying…"

"I'm so sorry to have to tell you this," William said, "but we think Purcell killed your mother to get control of her money. He probably didn't know that the terms of the estate would prevent him from taking control of the cash."

Her chest felt as if an entire city block had been dropped on it. She tried to concentrate on controlling her breathing, but every intake of air felt as if a burning dagger stabbed her lungs. Her mind slipped to the past and she steeled herself for the vision that would surely come.

"Are you all right?"

William's voice seemed far away, and it took her several seconds to force herself back to the present— back to Johnny's Café in Calais. She couldn't afford to slip into the past, especially not to the dark place. Not if she had any intention of making it the two weeks she needed to fulfill the estate requirements.

She took a big drink of water and nodded. "I'm okay. It's just shocking."

"It is," William agreed. "I still have my moments when I think it all must be a mistake, but the facts all seem to point that way, especially as one of the men Purcell paid kidnapped Danae and tried to kill her."

Joelle's heart dropped once more at the thought of her baby sister kidnapped and fighting for her life. "I can't believe it. It's like something out of a movie."

"Perhaps, if it's a horror movie. Of course, there's quite a bit more research to be done as we try to get to

the bottom of things. Danae is still going through household records…there's something else."

Joelle stiffened, not certain she wanted to hear anything else. If William's hesitation was any indication, then what he was about to tell her wasn't going to be any better than what she was already trying to absorb.

"How much more can there be?"

"This is a big one, I'm afraid. Given that there's mostly only circumstantial evidence and hearsay as to Purcell's crimes, your sisters requested that your mother be exhumed."

Joelle stared. "They're hoping to find evidence of murder. After all these years, is that even possible?"

"Anything's possible, although it's probably not likely. But Alaina and Danae felt they had to try everything. They would have waited for you to make the decision but, at the time, I had no idea how long it would take to locate you."

Joelle waved a hand in dismissal. "I don't mind any of that. I agree with their choice. I want answers as much as they do."

"That's a relief. I'm sorry to dump all this on you the second you arrive. Your sisters planned to tell you everything when you met, but I asked them to allow me to speak to you instead. I didn't want your reunion marred by all this unpleasantness. I want you girls to focus on getting to know one another again."

Joelle smiled at William, his thoughtfulness such a departure from the people she normally dealt with. "Has anyone told you how wonderful you are, William?"

The attorney blushed a bit. "Just doing my job."

"We both know you're doing far more than that. I remember you said someone would verify my presence

on the estate each day. Will you be doing that or will Tyler report to you?"

"Actually, Carter Trahan has an agreement with the estate to perform the verification duties for all three of you. Given everything that's happened, he's also busy trying to investigate Purcell and those who may have been on his payroll."

"Carter is the sheriff, right?"

William nodded. "And will become your brother-in-law next year."

Joelle struggled to wrap her mind around it all. Two sisters, a future brother-in-law, a potential fortune and a sulking bodyguard. Only the bodyguard ruined the perfect picture.

That, and kidnapping, and attempted murder.

Before she could change her mind, Joelle launched into her next set of questions. "Your son…Tyler…I get the impression he's not overly happy with his job."

William sighed. "I noticed his manners weren't exactly up to par when you arrived. I apologize that he didn't provide a warm welcome."

"He's a grown man. You don't need to apologize for him."

"In this case I do, as I'm responsible for putting him in a position he didn't want to be in. Given everything that has happened with your sisters, the estate insisted on twenty-four-hour, on-site security for you, and I put pressure on Tyler to provide it."

"After everything you've told me, I completely understand the estate's position, but why Tyler? If he doesn't want to do it, why did you pressure him to?"

"Because he's the best man for the job," William said simply. "Tyler was a securities expert for the Marine Corps. He kept entire military bases safe while ferret-

ing out the secrets of the enemy. If he can't protect you, I'm not sure anyone can."

Some of Tyler's stiff, direct approach to things now made sense. "He was in the Middle East?"

William nodded.

"How long?"

"Eight years. He arrived back in the States only two weeks ago. He's starting a private security firm as soon as the formation documents are approved by the state."

"Well," Joelle said, processing all this new information. "I suppose tolerating a bit of a grouch is a small cost for the level of protection I'm getting in return."

William gave her a small smile. "He wasn't always this grouchy. His time overseas changed him, but he won't talk about it."

The attorney sighed. "I'm sure he saw horrific things. Hearing about them on the news is bad enough, but to see it firsthand and then feel some level of responsibility because it happened…I imagine it's a lot of weight for any man."

Instantly, Joelle's training kicked in and she slipped directly into psychologist mode, momentarily chiding herself for making something personal when that was rarely the case. "I'm sure you're right. So what can I do to make the transition easier?"

"Communicate your plans with him and don't try to fight his presence, even though I'm sure it will feel awkward and inconvenient at times. Allow him to do physical labor. He's not made for sitting behind a desk, although he thinks that's what he needs to do. Movement keeps his mind focused and his body ready for action. He's been that way his entire life."

Joelle nodded. "He was clearing brush from the back patio when I arrived. Now that I think about it, I sup-

pose it was a two-point process—he worked off some energy, and the more brush that's cleared away from the house, the easier it will be to see someone approaching."

William's expression softened and his eyes misted up just a bit. "Your mother would be so happy to see how you girls turned out. Despite all the obstacles placed in your path, you're all self-confident, intelligent and compassionate. She couldn't have asked for more."

A blush ran up her neck at William's compliments. "Thank you. It's so nice to finally talk to people who knew my mother, and I can't wait to meet Alaina and Danae."

"They're visiting this afternoon?"

"Yes. Alaina was in New Orleans on business, but she is going to pick up Danae and they'll both be here late this evening. They have to be back in New Orleans tomorrow, so we're planning a slumber party."

"How delightful!"

Joelle nodded, hoping the attorney was right. More than anything in the world, she wanted to meet her sisters, but the reality was, she was nervous. Based on everything she'd heard, Danae and Alaina had already formed a close bond. What if they didn't like her? What if the passage of time had removed that connection between them?

She took a big sip of water and told herself to relax. Her sisters were alive and well and spending a night with her catching up. In two weeks, all of them would inherit everything that was temporarily stolen from them.

Nothing or no one was going to put a damper on her happiness.

TYLER PICKED UP a bag of chocolate chip cookies and a six-pack of beer and set them on the counter in the gen-

eral store. The owner, Samuel, was tied up in the back helping a man load his new lawn mower onto his truck, so Tyler leaned back against the counter and grabbed a hunting magazine to flip through while he waited.

"Only two weeks out of the Corps and you already have bachelor shopping down," a voice sounded in front of him.

Tyler looked up at a grinning Carter Trahan.

Despite Tyler's general disgust at his current predicament, he couldn't help but smile as he shook Carter's extended hand.

"I'm sorry I missed you when you came by my dad's house," Tyler said.

Carter waved his hand in dismissal. "You're working on your business stuff. I'm working on solving ancient murders. I knew we'd run into each other eventually."

"I guess it's hard to go too long without seeing someone in a town as small as Calais."

Carter nodded. "It's certainly a different pace than New Orleans. I imagine you're in an even bigger culture shock, relocating from a war zone halfway across the world."

"It's been…interesting. Sometimes I still have these moments of panic, where I think there's something I was supposed to do that I didn't."

"I know exactly what you mean. Between the caseload and the constantly increasing paperwork requirements, New Orleans cops are to the point of needing personal secretaries to keep up."

"Do you ever miss it?"

"I did a little at first. It was too slow, too quiet and I think I spent a lot of time feeling guilty because it was too easy."

"Trenton Purcell's death seems to have changed all that."

"You got that right. If anyone had told me before I came here that this much crime—running this far back—could happen in a place like Calais, I would have laughed. It's hard to believe one man can cause such a ripple of crime that lasted past his own death."

Tyler nodded, thinking about everything his father had told him about the situation. "My dad told me you found out Purcell was a hit man and probably took up with Ophelia for a place to hide."

"Yeah, at first I thought Purcell married her figuring he could get Ophelia to move away from Louisiana, but with everything I know now, I'm guessing he planned to kill her from the beginning. He wouldn't have known about the will. He probably assumed he'd get everything when she was gone. When I think about everything those girls lost because of him…"

Tyler felt a flicker of guilt over the terse way he'd handled meeting Joelle. She and her sisters were the living victims in the middle of this mess. She certainly hadn't asked for her mother to be murdered and for her stepfather to send her off to strangers. He'd been so busy worrying about his own needs that he hadn't really stopped to consider how difficult this must be for her—for all of them.

"Alaina and Danae are fine, right?" Tyler asked. "I mean…considering everything that's happened."

"They are both incredibly strong women," Carter said, and Tyler could hear the admiration in his voice. "Most people would have crumbled under the stress of the discoveries alone, much less the attempts on their lives. But those two just got mad and more determined."

Tyler smiled. "You have to admire that."

"Definitely. It helps that they have each other. They're thick as thieves. You'd never know they spent most of their lives apart."

"Hopefully Joelle will fit as well with them."

"I don't think they're going to give her a choice. Your dad tells me he's got you on security detail."

Tyler sighed. "I tried to get out of it, but you know Dad."

Carter laughed. "Oh, yeah, I know your dad. Between him and my mom, I could be talked into most anything. This whole mess started for me when your dad asked me to play hall monitor. I ended up with a kidnapping, three deaths and a fiancée."

Tyler winced at the fiancée part of Carter's statement. "I'm not looking to acquire any of those on my Calais service record, especially the last one."

Carter grinned. "And you think I was? Have you met Joelle yet?"

"Yeah, she arrived this afternoon. I brought her to town for a meeting with my dad at the café."

"So how does she look?"

Tyler shrugged, not about to go into details of the delicious Joelle with Carter. "She looks like a woman."

Carter's grin widened. "That good, huh?"

"I didn't say anything like that."

"You didn't have to. I know both her sisters, and I know that look. I used to wear it. Joelle is a knockout and that pisses you off even more."

Tyler sighed. "Remind me again why we're friends?"

Carter laughed and clapped Tyler's back. "Because I keep you honest."

"Is that even possible?" A man's voice boomed from behind them.

Tyler turned around as Mayor James Dupree stepped up to him, his hand extended.

"It's good to have you home," Mayor Dupree said. "I know your daddy must be relieved."

"Yes, sir, I imagine he is." Tyler shook the man's hand and hoped that he had an appointment that didn't allow him to hang around for long. Mayor Dupree was a marathon talker and had never once said anything even remotely interesting.

"Good to see you, Carter." Mayor Dupree nodded. "How's that pretty fiancée of yours doing?"

"She's fine, sir," Carter replied and rolled his eyes at Tyler as soon as Mayor Dupree looked away.

"Good, good," Mayor Dupree said and studied Tyler again. "So what will you be doing now that you're home?"

"I'm opening a security firm. Maybe city hall can use my services."

The mayor laughed. "Well, we're still holding council meetings at the café, so you'd have to wait until we build a city hall. I hope you have some other clients in mind, as that might be a while in coming."

"Actually, I'm doing some work for my dad."

"The LeBeau estate?"

"Yes."

The mayor shook his head. "That has been such an unfortunate set of circumstances. I never would have imagined such things could happen in Calais."

Carter cleared his throat. "I thought you and Roger Martin were friends from way back. I would have figured you'd know if he was plotting things with Trenton Purcell."

Mayor Dupree sighed. "I wish I had known. Maybe

I could have talked him out of it. Maybe all this would have turned out differently."

"Maybe," Carter said. "You know, I'm pretty sure Purcell had more than just Roger on his payroll. Since you were around then, maybe you'd have an idea who I should take a closer look at."

"I wish I did, and I'll be sure to let you know if I think of something. Well, I've got to run. You two stay out of trouble." He gave them a nod and hustled out of the store quicker than Tyler thought his flabby frame would allow.

Tyler stared after him and frowned. "Should I be happy he didn't stick around and talk us to death, or suspicious and wonder why?"

"Number two."

"Any particular reason other than him being friends with Roger?"

"Yeah. If Joelle doesn't make her two weeks, the city of Calais inherits millions' worth of LeBeau assets."

"You think he knows that?"

"Do you?"

"The way he left… Wow, all that money and under the control of the good mayor," Tyler said, a whole new train of thought opened up with that bit of information. "My dad really needs to learn to talk more about things that matter."

Carter smiled. "Come on, I'll buy you a root beer float and we can talk about your ideas for security now that you've seen the house, and I can try to fill in any blanks that William might have left."

Tyler checked his watch but figured his dad and Joelle would probably be a while longer. Besides, the general store had an old-fashioned soda fountain with the best root beer floats in the South, and he did have

some things he wanted to run by Carter after seeing the house. His friend had suggested a casual planning meeting over a drink, but Tyler could tell Carter was worried, and Carter Trahan was the last person to go off on a tangent.

Maybe his dad was right. Maybe it wasn't over.

Chapter Five

Joelle pushed her feet against the floorboard of Tyler's truck, wishing he could navigate the bumpy road at a faster pace. She'd been finishing up with William when her cell phone rang with Alaina's call. Her sisters had forgotten to call when they left New Orleans and had lost cell service not far outside of the city. By the time she'd gotten a signal again, Alaina was only ten minutes from Calais.

Instant panic set in with Joelle. She hadn't had time to assess supplies at the house, much less get to the general store to fill in the gaps. And what about the sleeping arrangements? Were the linens clean or was that one other job she'd already fallen down on? She assumed at least one bedroom was suitable for habitation but they needed more than one.

William had immediately clued in to her distress and calmed her down by assuring her that her sisters were well aware of the living conditions and their only requirement was seeing her. Joelle appreciated William's kind approach to her crisis, but that didn't solve the problem of upbringing, and Joelle's adoptive mother had been a real stickler for manners. No way could she allow people in her home—or what would be her

home for the next two weeks—without attempting to be a good host.

They'd left the café and headed to the general store to see if Tyler was ready to leave. Even though William had already assured her she didn't need to provide anything for Alaina and Danae, Joelle picked up the best bottle of wine they had before hurrying out to jump in Tyler's truck.

Now she wished she would have bought crackers and dip—something to pick at while drinking the wine. Something to keep her hands busy while she had her first conversation with her sisters since they were all children.

Tyler looked over at her and frowned. "Are you nervous?"

Surprised that he'd even spoken, much less at the question, Joelle had to think a couple of seconds before responding.

"Yes," she finally admitted. "It's all a bit overwhelming and surreal. Not just that I will finally be reunited with my sisters—which I thought would never happen—but with everything that's happened surrounding our stepfather's death."

"I guess Dad filled you in on everything at lunch?"

"Probably not every detail, but I got the overview. As a social worker, I always think I've heard everything. Then occasionally, I'm still blown away at the things human beings will do to one another."

"I know exactly what you mean."

The sadness in his voice had her studying him for a moment, then she remembered—marine. "I guess you saw your share of horror overseas."

"We all did."

His speech was slightly abrupt, leaving her no doubt that his military service was something he didn't wish to talk about. Another piece of her softened toward him, because she understood that on a level that people who didn't deal every day with the horror of human behavior would never understand.

"I don't know why I'm so nervous about seeing my sisters again. I mean, I'm excited but also nervous."

He was silent for several seconds, and Joelle wondered if he'd even heard what she said. Or maybe he decided the conversation had gotten too girlie or too psychological.

"Maybe because you're afraid you won't fit with them," he said finally.

She stared at him, surprised at his intuitiveness. "Yes, I think you're right."

"Everyone needs to be where they belong—whether that's the place they live or a person they're with. But I don't think you have anything to worry about."

"No? Why is that? Have you met my sisters?"

"I haven't yet had the pleasure, but I've heard plenty about them from my dad. He thinks they're the best things since cable television came to Calais. My dad likes most people, but he admires few. No one has said anything yet, but I'm going to guess that he's planning on having Alaina take over his practice in Calais. She's already doing some work for him."

"Your dad is very sweet, but he also knew our mother, so it might make him a bit biased."

"Maybe, but Carter Trahan didn't know your mother. He's marrying Alaina and vouches for Danae. Carter and I have been friends since the crib, and trust me when I say a more shrewd human being has not been invented."

"I wish I would have gotten to the general store before he left. I'm looking forward to meeting him."

"He'll be keeping tabs on you for the estate, so I suppose you will soon enough."

Joelle held in a smile. Tyler was so direct and practical. On a normal day, she dealt with so much fabrication and drama that his what-you-see-is-what-you-get style was refreshing.

"So what do you plan on doing while we're conducting our Sisterhood Reunion?" she asked.

He frowned. "Staying out of the way."

His dismay was so comical that she couldn't hold in the laugh, but as he rounded the tree line and turned onto the circular drive in front of the house, she froze. The SUV in the driveway had a bumper sticker for a New England university. It had to be Alaina's car.

"They're here already," she said, her voice barely a whisper.

Tyler parked next to Alaina's vehicle. "I'm going to take a walk around the perimeter. I'll be around if you need me."

He jumped out of the truck and took off at a decent clip around the side of the house. Joelle's nervousness ticked up another notch as the only person she had any connection with fled. Not that she blamed him. It was an uncomfortable situation for her and she was one of the parties involved. Anyone else would feel even more uncomfortable, especially men, who, in her experience, tended to avoid questionable social situations anyway.

Grabbing the bottle of wine and her purse, she took a deep breath, then climbed out of the truck. The front door was open a crack, and she pushed it the rest of the way and stepped inside. Voices echoed down the

kitchen hallway and she started that way. The voices sounded happy and excited, which helped her nerves a bit, but when she reached the threshold of the kitchen, she paused.

What if they hate me? What if I hate them?

She said a silent prayer, then stepped around the corner into the kitchen.

A tall, thin woman with long black hair pulled back in a ponytail stood in front of the refrigerator, her back to Joelle. A shorter, curvier woman with shoulder-length black hair stood at the counter, arranging cheese and crackers on a tray.

They were so busy chatting, they didn't hear her enter.

"Hello," she managed.

Immediately, all activity ceased and they both whirled around to stare at her. Joelle sucked in a breath as she looked at the tall woman.

Alaina.

She'd always looked like their mother. Joelle could remember that now. For a split second, all three of them held in that position, then they rushed over to her.

"Joelle," Alaina said as she stopped in front of Joelle, studying her face. "I remember now. You look like our father."

Alaina teared up and threw her arms around Joelle.

"I never thought I'd find you two," Alaina said. "It's a dream come true."

All of Joelle's nerves slipped away as she hugged Alaina. It all came flooding back to her—the love and admiration she'd always had for her big sister. It was as if the years fell away and they were right back in step.

"My turn," Danae said, clapping her hands.

Alaina laughed as she released Joelle, who turned to look at a smiling Danae.

"The dimples," Joelle said. "I remember them."

Danae's smile widened and she wrapped her arms around Joelle, tightly squeezing her.

"I'm so glad William found you," Danae whispered.

"Me, too," Joelle said.

"This calls for a toast," Alaina said.

Danae released her and they both looked over at their big sister, who was pouring champagne into beautiful crystal glasses.

"I cleaned some of the crystal to get ready for this moment," Alaina said. "Please don't tell me you don't drink."

Joelle laughed. "I'm not a professional, but at the moment, I can't think of anything more perfect than champagne."

Alaina smiled and her whole face brightened, her happiness so clear. "You haven't had Danae's cheesecake yet. I bet it's more perfect than champagne, but she was cruel and wouldn't let me try a piece before we left."

Danae blushed a bit, clearly pleased with Alaina's praise, and Joelle felt her chest tighten as if her heart were expanding inside it. All the anxiety and doubts she'd felt were wasted emotion. These women were so comfortable...so right.

She took the glass of champagne that Alaina offered her and watched as Alaina lifted her glass in the air.

"To sisters," Alaina said. "To us."

"To us," Joelle and Danae repeated and they clinked their glasses together.

Joelle couldn't remember any moment in her life more perfect than this one.

TYLER MADE HIS way around the back of the house, pushing through the dense undergrowth, looking for any sign that someone else had passed this way recently. If Carter and his father both felt things weren't right on the LeBeau estate, then Tyler had no doubt they were right. If someone was prowling around the estate, he wanted to get a handle on it now and try to keep things from getting as out of hand as they had with Alaina and Danae.

So far, he'd turned up nothing. The house appeared tight as a drum. One window downstairs was broken, but it was boarded up. The rest were nailed shut. Danae's fiancé, Zach, the contractor making repairs to the house, had made sure everything was sealed tight before he returned to his regular workweek in New Orleans and so far, Tyler hadn't found a single thing the contractor had left undone.

Tyler knew the front door was the questionable point. It was a huge wooden double door, ornately carved, likely ridiculously expensive, and was equipped with ancient hardware complete with giant iron keys like those you'd see in a horror movie. In anticipation of Joelle's arrival, he'd ordered some security equipment, but it hadn't arrived until today. As soon as he finished his perimeter walk, he'd start setting up the equipment, beginning with the alarm on the front door.

When he rounded the corner for the side of the house containing the long patio, he paused, staring into the brush. Something looked off. He stepped into the trees and pushed through the foliage, working his way around a forty-foot-square region. On the surface, everything appeared normal, but the telltale signs of recent passage were visible to someone as skilled in tracking as Tyler was.

Some of the broken branches could be attributed to the storms that had swept through the area lately, but the depressions in the ground cover were the result of being trod upon. The ground cover was too dense to make out an actual footprint, but the size of the indentations was too large for any of the creatures that would normally roam the woods, except maybe bear. And if a bear had passed this way, Tyler would see far more damage to the branches.

He followed the depressions and the broken branches about twenty yards into the swamp before turning around. Someone could have traversed the swamp from any number of locations surrounding the house, and may have walked hundreds of yards or even miles to throw someone off the track. Likely, the tracks would come out on one of the many dirt paths that led through the swamp, easily reachable by an ATV. As most everyone in Calais owned or had access to an ATV, that didn't narrow the suspect pool even a bit.

Turning back, he tried to track the depressions toward the house, but they seemed to end about twenty feet from the patio, which made no sense. Tyler could understand if a stalker had a viewpoint to simply observe the comings and goings of the house in order to plan a strike. The military often watched from one vantage point but attacked from another. But from this vantage point, all he could see was the corner of the house and a bit of the patio. No window or door offered a view inside, except for the small pane of glass on the exterior door off the laundry room. But he couldn't see in that pane from his current position.

Deciding he wasn't going to figure it out standing there, he made a mental note to keep an eye on this location and continued back to the patio. The stone patio

didn't leave any opportunity for tracks, so he checked the windows and scanned the nearby brush, but the only tracks he saw were his own from when he'd hauled away brush earlier that day.

As he made his way down the patio toward the kitchen, he heard the high-pitched voices of the three sisters. The excitement was clear in their tone, and Tyler was happy that Joelle's reunion with her sisters seemed to be going so well. He'd had no doubt that would be the case, but he understood why Joelle was nervous. It was a whole lot to absorb, especially some twenty-five years later and after living so long as an adult with no family to speak of.

He had a key to the patio door that led into the kitchen, but didn't want to startle them by letting himself in, so he rapped on the glass panes and waved when they whirled around. Joelle hurried to the door to let him in while her sisters stood there, clearly waiting for an introduction.

"Guys," Joelle said, "this is William's son, Tyler—my personal bodyguard."

They both smiled and the taller one walked over to extend her hand. "I should have known," she said. "You look just like your father. I'm Alaina."

"Nice to meet you," Tyler said. "You look like the pictures I've seen of your mother."

Alaina beamed and Tyler understood why his old friend Carter had gotten himself tied down. Alaina Le-Beau was gorgeous and, according to his father, brilliant. And from limited exposure, he'd already gathered she had personality to boot. Triple threat. Carter had made a good choice.

"You must be Danae," he said and extended his

hand to the youngest of Ophelia's daughters. Danae was shorter and curvier than Alaina, and looked like a combination of Alaina and Joelle. Perhaps she'd taken after both parents, while Joelle looked more like their father. Not that it mattered. Apparently any combination of those genes produced good-looking women.

Danae shook his hand and smiled. "It's nice to meet you. William talks so much about you. We're thrilled that you'll be checking up on Joelle. We worry about all of this, and it's too much for Carter to handle alone."

"Oh, he's not checking up," Joelle said. "He's living here, going with me when I leave the house. For all I know, he might be sitting guard outside the bathroom when I shower."

A flash of Joelle standing naked and wet under a shower stream bolted through his mind, and he felt his chest constrict. Instantly, he forced the image from his mind. The last thing he needed was to imagine Joelle— or any other woman—naked and vulnerable.

"I don't think it will come to that," he said. "Well, if you ladies are okay in here, I'm going to start installing a security alarm on the front door."

"That's a great idea," Alaina said.

Danae waved a hand over the counter, which was loaded with food. "Do you want to eat? We brought a feast with us."

"Not right now, but I will take you up on that later if you don't mind."

"It's ready when you are," Danae said.

"Thank you for installing an alarm," Joelle said. "I know we'll all feel better sleeping here tonight."

Tyler gave them a nod and walked out of the kitchen.

"Stand outside the bathroom?" Alaina said. "I'd

totally let him stand next to the shower and hold my towel."

They all laughed, then he heard Danae say, "You're awful. Entirely correct, but awful."

He smiled as he went to the entry to retrieve his equipment. Even the strongest man's ego couldn't ignore such compliments from beautiful women. He'd almost slowed for a moment, wondering if Joelle was going to comment, but decided it was information he didn't need.

Alaina and Danae were safe to admire. They were both attached to good men, but Joelle was risky. Granted, for all he knew, she could have a man back in Jackson, but he doubted it. She had a nervousness about her that seemed like a lack of recent socializing.

Maybe it's just me.

The thought crossed his mind and he frowned. True, he wasn't the most pleasant of people to be around, and he could have been a lot nicer when they'd met. He probably owed her an apology for his boorish behavior, but he wasn't likely to offer one. Less said, soonest mended was pretty much his motto.

He grabbed the box and removed the alarm. What he needed to do was focus on the job. Because he knew from firsthand experience what happened when he got sidetracked.

That was something he never intended to do again.

HE WATCHED THE house from the safety of the swamp. The women occupied the kitchen, clinking champagne glasses and eating hors d'oeuvres. They thought they had it all, but they were wrong. If it was the last thing he ever did, he was going to get what was coming to him. What he was due.

The man was somewhat of a concern. He had that

posture that screamed military and a bulge at his waist that spelled concealed weapon. Right now, he could see the man, installing a security alarm on the front door.

What a waste of time.

Chapter Six

Joelle trailed up the enormous circular staircase with her sisters, studying every inch of the house, looking for something recognizable. When they reached the landing, she stopped short at the painting of her mother, directly in front of her. She took a hesitant step forward and touched the painting with her fingertips.

"This was here before," she said.

"You remember," Alaina said. "I didn't at first, but when Danae and I came across the picture tucked in one of the downstairs rooms, it came back to me. The painting hung here for as long as I can remember. The hook was still in the wall. So we dusted it off and put it back where it belongs."

Joelle looked over at Alaina. "You look so much like her. I remember being jealous of you, even at such a young age. Mother was the most beautiful woman I'd ever seen and I wanted to look like her, too."

Alaina smiled. "You were always wearing her shoes. You'd find the highest set of heels in her closet and come shuffling down the hall. Mom was always afraid you'd fall and hurt yourself."

Joelle laughed. "She had a pair of shiny red ones that were my favorite."

Joelle turned back to the painting. "I remember this

necklace." She ran a finger over the diamond necklace that circled her mother's neck. It had been her mother's prize piece and was always kept under lock and key.

"I wonder what happened to it," Joelle said.

Alaina shook her head. "I imagine Purcell sold it. Danae and I have poked into every area of the house. We've found some pretty things—some of them nice quality—but nothing of high value."

"But what about the art in the entry? Some of it looked valuable."

Alaina nodded. "I thought so, too, but upon closer examination, they appear to be reproductions. Good reproductions, but not near the value of the real thing. My guess is Purcell cleaned out anything that would bring him a fistful of cash."

"You're probably right." Joelle looked over at Danae, who wore a pensive look.

"Are you all right?" Joelle asked Danae.

"I'm fine," Danae assured her, but Joelle could tell something was bothering her.

"Danae doesn't remember," Alaina said quietly.

"Oh!" Joelle's heart went out to her sister, who had been no more than a toddler when she was sent away.

"We're staying in our old bedroom," Alaina said. "It's the only room big enough for three beds and I didn't want us split up—not in this house. Danae..." Alaina looked over at Danae and bit her lower lip.

"I haven't gone in that room yet," Danae finished. "If I go in our room and don't remember anything, then I'm afraid I never will."

Joelle reached out and took Danae's hand in hers. "Then Alaina and I will remember for you."

Alaina took Danae's other hand in hers and nodded. "Absolutely."

Danae sniffed and smiled. "You guys are the best."

"We know," Alaina joked. "Now, let's go see that room."

They walked down the hall, hand in hand, until they reached the doorway. Alaina stepped inside first, then Joelle followed. A flood of recognition washed over her. The furniture was different, but the wallpaper was the same dusty-rose pattern that she remembered. In the corner sat the old wooden school desks that she'd spent hours at, coloring and learning her alphabet and numbers.

She looked back at Danae, who still lingered just outside the doorway. "It's okay," she said.

Her younger sister took a deep breath, then closed her eyes and stepped inside the room. Joelle and Alaina each moved to her side and waited as she slowly let out the breath and opened her eyes. She scanned the room and Joelle could tell that nothing was clicking. Her heart broke for her little sister, who wanted so badly to remember.

Danae stepped away from them and walked over to the desks. She lifted the top of the first desk and pulled out a pink plastic comb. Suddenly, she spun around, her eyes wide with excitement.

"Mom used to comb our hair with this." A single tear fell down her cheek. "It's faint—almost like I dreamed it—but I remember. I remember."

Joelle's heart was practically bursting with happiness for her little sister. On the surface, it didn't seem like a lot, but Joelle understood how monumental it was for Danae. She stepped over beside her and ran one hand over the scarred desktop.

"I wonder how many hours we spent at these desks," Joelle said to Alaina.

"Hundreds," Alaina replied. "Thousands, maybe."

A memory, so vivid it seemed like a movie running through her mind, came to Joelle in a flash. She squatted down and reached underneath the seat. She didn't expect to find anything but an empty cubbyhole, and when her fingers brushed against soft velvet, she gasped.

"What?" Alaina asked. Her eyes widened. "No. It's still there?"

Danae stared down at the purple bag in Joelle's hands. "That's a Crown Royal bag. Were you two child alkies?"

Joelle laughed. "No, but we loved purple and we begged for the bag. Mom said no for so long, which I totally get now, but it made no sense then."

"We harassed her," Alaina agreed. "Open it."

Joelle pulled the drawstring on the bag and turned it over. Gray rocks tumbled out onto her palm.

"Rocks?" Danae raised her eyebrows.

"Joelle loved to play in the dirt in the driveway," Alaina said, her eyes bright with the memory. "We built roads and forts and fences for our plastic ponies."

"Purcell hated it," Joelle said. "He thought little girls should sit silently and be pretty, not play in dirt, and especially not track it inside."

"But Mom didn't care, and let us do it anyway," Alaina said. "One time Joelle got sick—I don't remember with what—and she had to stay in bed. It was beautiful weather and she was so mad that she couldn't go outside with me. Mom and I went outside and picked up rocks. She told me to hide them in my pockets so that Purcell wouldn't see. Then we hurried upstairs and she pulled out the purple bag to put the rocks in for Joelle."

"She told us to keep the bag and the rocks hidden so

we wouldn't get in trouble for having either of them," Joelle said. "We played with them all day, and then I hid them in the cubbyhole. I'd completely forgotten."

"You were well enough to go outside the next day," Alaina said. "So it was business as usual."

Danae smiled. "I know I'll never remember things like the two of you, but I'm so glad you're here to tell me about them. The way you describe things, I can picture them in my mind."

Alaina sniffed. "It seems so strange to me, that I had almost no memory of this place when I first returned, but the longer I'm in Calais, the more I remember. I don't know why I'd forgotten so much."

Joelle glanced at Alaina, who gazed around the room. She wondered, too, why Alaina had no memories before. Being two years older, Alaina should have more memories than Joelle, not fewer. If Joelle had to guess, something had caused Alaina to shut her childhood off—to compartmentalize it and file it away where she didn't access it. In Joelle's line of work, she saw a lot of that, but usually only following a great trauma.

Joelle couldn't help but wonder if Alaina would ever remember the thing or things that prevented her from clear recall.

Alaina reached for Danae's hand and gave it a squeeze. "I promise I'll share everything with you. More of the past returns to me every day."

Joelle froze for a moment, then recovered. Certainly, she wanted to share with her sisters, but she wasn't ready to share everything. Not yet. Not until she knew more about her mother and Purcell, and not until she had a better idea why Alaina couldn't remember more.

Joelle stepped over toward the closet and ran her fin-

gers across three holes in the wall, remembering what William had told her about Alaina's attacker.

"Bullet holes," Alaina answered her unspoken question.

Joelle spun around. "Are you okay to stay in here?"

Alaina nodded. "It's our room…our house. I want us to reclaim everything. This seemed like the best place to start."

"Then I say we haul the champagne up here and christen it."

Alaina smiled. "Sounds like a plan."

They hurried back down to the kitchen to refill their glasses. As Alaina poured, Joelle's cell phone buzzed. She frowned as she reached for her purse and pulled out the phone. She had a text message, but not from a number she recognized. She punched the button to read the text and gasped.

Give me what's mine.

Her fingers tightened on the phone so hard they hurt. It couldn't be.

"What's wrong?" Danae asked.

"It's nothing," Joelle said, not about to let Victor Brant spoil their night.

Danae glanced over at Alaina, who raised her eyebrows. Clearly, neither of her sisters believed her for a moment.

"You may as well give up trying to keep things from us," Alaina said. "Danae is as street-smart as they come, and I've made witnesses cry in the courtroom. You're not going to get anything past either of us."

"You shouldn't even try," Danae said. "You're our sister. Your problems are our problems."

Joelle looked at both their faces and sighed. If they were anywhere near as stubborn as she was, they weren't going to let this go. She may as well tell them and get it over with.

"There was an incident before I left Jackson," Joelle said, then told them about Brant and his threats.

"Why haven't the police picked him up?" Alaina asked.

"Because I can't prove it was him, but I know it was, if that makes any sense."

Danae nodded. "Makes perfect sense. So do you think this Brant is capable of destroying more than a car?"

"No one can ever be certain, but if I had to guess, then I'd say yes. That's why I agreed to come right away. I talked it over with my boss and the Jackson police, and everyone felt my leaving town would give him time to cool off."

"Does he know where you are?"

"No. Only my boss and the Jackson police know. I didn't tell anyone else." She frowned. "This is a new phone. Only my boss, the police, you two and William have the number. How did he get it so quickly?"

"I assume it's unlisted?" Alaina asked.

"Yeah. In my line of work, that's the norm."

"Carter will be by here soon," Alaina said. "You need to tell him about this…about everything."

"He's bluffing," Joelle argued. "He doesn't even know where I am. How could he come after me?"

"He got your phone number," Alaina said. "If he could get that, he could get the rest."

IT WAS ALMOST dawn when more glasses of champagne and soda than Joelle could count sent her shuffling

down the hall to the bathroom. She and her sisters had sat up in the bedroom, talking through the wee hours of the morning until none of them could stay awake any longer. Carter had been and gone hours before, promising to follow up with the Jackson police and to let her know the next morning what their thoughts were.

Tyler had taken everything in when she'd explained the situation to Carter, but hadn't said a word. Then the two men had spoken for some time outside at Carter's truck, and Joelle had no doubt they were comparing notes and formulating a plan to keep the womenfolk safe. At any other time, the feminist in her might have found it annoying, but the genuine concern kept her from feeling anything but grateful that such capable men had her back.

Wincing as a floorboard creaked, she glanced at the bedroom where Tyler was staying. It had unnerved her a bit that a mere wall would separate them, but he wanted to be in hearing distance, just in case. The door was pulled mostly shut, leaving only a thin crack with moonlight streaming through it.

She was almost to the bathroom when her foot brushed across something hard and cold. The dim glow from the entry lights illuminated the balcony, and she could see something shiny on the floor. As she bent over to pick it up, she realized it was a quarter. She clasped her fingers around it and looked up before straightening. From that position, she could see through the balcony banisters down into the massive entry.

A flash of pain came over her and in an instant, twenty-five years slipped away.

Mommy was crying again. She cried a lot since the bad man came. He'd married Mommy but he wasn't Daddy.

Daddy was in heaven with the angels, but Joelle wished he would come back. Mommy and her and her sisters needed him more than the angels did.

The bad man yelled at Mommy again and Joelle ducked lower, clutching the banisters with her small hands. If the bad man saw her, he'd spank her like he did last time he caught her watching them. Spying, he called it, but Joelle didn't know what spying meant.

She wondered for a moment if she should go get Alaina. Her older sister hated when she woke her up in the middle of the night, but she wouldn't mind being awakened if it was to protect Mommy. Alaina was older. She would know what to do.

As she gripped the banisters and started to rise, the bad man raised his hand and slapped Mommy across the face. Unable to help herself, she cried out, telling Mommy to run. Instantly, the bad man whipped around and pinned his gaze on her. She knew she should run but she was frozen in place, as if nailed to the floor.

The bad man started toward the stairs, but Mommy grabbed his arm, trying to prevent him from going after her. He pushed Mommy and she crashed down on the floor. Joelle sprang up from the balcony and ran to the bedroom, locking the door behind her like Mommy had taught her and Alaina to do.

She ran across the floor and jumped into her bed, pulling the covers up over her head. The bad man's footsteps echoed in the hallway outside of their room. She lowered the covers just enough to see the door. The doorknob jiggled and she heard the bad man say a curse word.

Joelle clenched the covers tighter, and wondered why Alaina didn't hear the bad man—why she didn't wake up and tell Joelle what to do. It seemed like forever, but

*finally the jiggling stopped and she heard the bad man
stomping away from their room. When she couldn't
hear his footsteps any longer, she grabbed her blanket
and crawled under her bed, where she remained the
rest of the night.*

JOELLE BOLTED UP so quickly, she staggered backward.
When her hands met with the wall, she leaned back
against it, trying to catch her breath. Her heart pounded
in her temples and her chest ached with every rise and
fall.

She'd had the visions as long as she could remem-
ber, but never had she had one that played out at such
length and in such detail. Never had she remembered
her stepfather coming after her, or her sleeping under
her bed. Never had one of the visions brought the sheer
panic she now felt—anger, certainly, but never panic.

She pushed herself off the wall, knowing that it
would be no use to attempt to go back to sleep. Maybe
she'd finish up in the bathroom and head downstairs
to make coffee. As she reached for the bathroom door,
a squeaking sound carried from downstairs. Immedi-
ately, she froze. It had sounded like a door opening, but
surely she was mistaken. The front door had an alarm
and all the other doors had new locks that Carter had
installed. There was no longer any chance that random
Calais residents were wandering around with keys to
the other doors, as Alaina and Danae told her had hap-
pened when they first got to town.

Deciding she must have been mistaken, she pushed
the bathroom door open and that's when she heard the
squeaking sound again—this time louder.

Before she could even think about waking Tyler, he
rushed out of his bedroom and ran straight into her,

knocking her to the floor. It only took him a second to realize whom he'd crashed into, then he cursed and hauled her up from the floor the same way he'd pulled her out of the brush the day before.

The girls' bedroom door flew open and Alaina and Danae bolted into the hall, both clutching pistols. Tyler took one look at them and raised his eyebrows.

"I'm not sure whether to be impressed or afraid," he said.

"Definitely afraid," Alaina said as they lowered their weapons. "What happened?"

"I heard a noise," Tyler said, "and rushed out to investigate, but only managed to tackle your sister. Was it you who made the noise?"

"No," Joelle said. "I was just about to wake you. It came from downstairs. I dismissed it as an old house creaking the first time, but the second time, I'm certain it was a door opening or closing."

Tyler cursed again, then ran downstairs, and it was only then that Joelle realized he had a nine millimeter in his hand.

"Unbelievable," Joelle said. "I'm the only one in this house who doesn't sleep with their hand on a loaded gun. And I'm the social worker."

"This house," Danae said, "is *why* we sleep with our hands on loaded guns."

"Should we go after him?" Alaina asked.

"He probably won't appreciate it if we do," Danae said, "but that's not going to stop me."

Danae took off after Tyler with Alaina only a step behind. Joelle stared after them for a moment, then ran to catch up. At the bottom of the stairs, they peered into the dim light, trying to figure out which direction

Tyler had gone, but there was no movement or noise to guide them.

Just as Joelle was going to suggest they call for him, the light in the kitchen came on, illuminating the hallway. Alaina motioned to Joelle to get behind her, and she and Danae lifted their pistols and walked down the hallway.

"Stop!" Tyler's voice boomed from the kitchen when they reached the archway.

Alaina stopped short and Joelle had to grab her shoulders to keep from running into her.

"What's wrong?" Alaina asked.

"I don't want you to ruin evidence," Tyler said.

Alaina's eyes narrowed and Joelle knew her sister had slipped into attorney mode. She'd seen that look so many times in court.

"What evidence?" Alaina asked.

"I'm not sure yet, but I rigged the downstairs after you guys went to bed. I wanted to get to the bottom of things."

"Rigged how?" Joelle asked.

"I sprinkled powder across some thresholds and in front of exterior doors."

Danae nodded. "To see if someone passed there. Smart."

"And someone passed through the kitchen?" Alaina asked.

Tyler squatted down and inspected the floor in front of them. Joelle could barely make out the fine powder scattered on the stone tile.

"It doesn't look like anyone passed this way," he said, "or through the patio door."

"What about the door off the laundry room?" Alaina asked.

"I was going to check there next," he said.

"We'll come with you," Danae said.

He paused and Joelle knew he wanted to tell them to stay put, but he was far too smart to argue with three angry women, two of whom were toting guns.

"Hurry up, then," he said as he rushed past them and back to the entry.

The laundry room was at the end of a hallway off the back of the huge entry. It took ten seconds to get there and only one glance at the floor to see that Tyler's trap had worked. Right in front of the exterior door was a single footprint, stamped in powder.

The dead bolt was pulled back in the open position. Tyler turned the doorknob and pulled the door open. Joelle sucked in a breath. "He left through this door, but how did he get in?"

Tyler closed the door, locked it and pulled the dead bolt back into place. The frustration he felt rolled off of him.

"I don't know, but you can bet I'm going to find out."

Chapter Seven

Gray, gloomy skies presided over the cemetery in New Orleans where Tyler stood with his father, Carter, Joelle, Alaina, Danae and her fiancé, Zach, waiting for the medical examiner to direct his staff to open the LeBeau family crypt and remove Ophelia LeBeau's coffin. William had already provided the key to the crypt, courtesy of the LeBeau estate attorney's office in New Orleans.

Tyler stood back a bit from the rest of them, wishing things had not come down to this—wishing the sisters had chosen to leave the exhumation to professionals used to dealing with such sordid things and not chosen to stand there, waiting. Their first glimpse of their mother, after twenty-five years, was going to be shocking, and despite the fact that they were all strong, intelligent women, Tyler didn't think they were ready for it.

The medical examiner opened the crypt and directed his staff to the correct vault box. Tyler could see the assistants pulling the coffin out of the box inside and noticed that the sisters shifted so that they stood close together. As the assistants carried the coffin out of the crypt, it started to mist.

The medical examiner had come prepared for such a disruption and directed his staff to the easy-up tent placed to the side of the crypt. The staff placed the cof-

fin on the ground under the tent, then stepped back so that the medical examiner could take over. He pulled on a mask and stepped up to the coffin, placing a crowbar under the lip. One of the assistants moved into position behind him, ready to take the required pictures to document the exhumation prior to transport.

He saw the sisters take one another's hands and looked over at Carter, who glanced back at him, the worry on his face clear as day. Prior to returning to Calais, Carter had been a homicide detective with the New Orleans Police Department. He'd seen bodies in various states of decay. In the Middle East, Tyler had seen every possible atrocity one could imagine and many one couldn't stretch the mind to think of.

But these three women hadn't seen anything like what the two of them had.

Tyler watched Joelle as the medical examiner clenched the crowbar, preparing to open the coffin. He shoved the crowbar down and the wood splintered, a loud crack echoing across the cemetery. Joelle winced and swallowed, but all three girls held fast. The medical examiner set the crowbar on the ground and reached out one gloved hand to lift the coffin lid.

Everyone leaned forward except Tyler, who had returned to Calais to avoid exactly this kind of sight. Instead of looking at the coffin, Tyler watched Joelle—the only sister without a fiancé—ready to be by her side in a second if she needed him.

He heard the sound of the coffin lid slamming back, and then everyone gasped. Joelle threw her hand over her mouth and stumbled backward into Tyler, who clutched her shoulders to steady her and peered over to see if anything was out of the ordinary.

What he saw was an empty box.

EVERYONE BUT THE medical examiner and his staff was crowded inside Zach and Danae's one-bedroom condo in New Orleans. Joelle stood near the fireplace, looking at framed pictures of Zach and Danae. The smiling Zach in the photos looked completely different from the shaken and pale Zach they'd brought home. Joelle didn't understand why Danae's fiancé had taken this so hard, but it was something she'd ask Alaina about later.

The bedroom door opened and William, who'd been inside with Danae and Zach, stepped out.

"Are they okay?" Alaina asked.

"They're fine. Zach is understandably upset, and Danae is trying to reassure him that none of this casts light on him."

Joelle frowned. "I don't understand."

William nodded and walked over to stand beside her. "I didn't have time to cover all the details in our meeting the other day, but our friend Zach came to Calais looking for answers of his own. His father was the funeral director that your stepfather paid off. He attempted a deathbed confession but all Zach understood was your mother's name."

"Oh!" The implications of everything William said rolled over Joelle like a tidal wave. "But Zach didn't have anything to do with that. He's as much a victim of Purcell's actions as we all are."

William smiled and gave her arm a squeeze. "Of course he is, but he can't help feeling responsible on some level. After all, his father was part of something that hurt the woman he loves. Don't worry about Zach. He just needs some time to process all of this, and seeing you all is harder at the moment."

"We should go," Tyler said. "Give him some space."

Alaina nodded. "I'll just tell Danae we're going."

She slipped into the bedroom and was back out a minute later.

"Danae said to tell everyone thank you and that they'll be in Calais this weekend," Alaina said.

William, who'd ridden to New Orleans with Tyler and Joelle, looked over at Carter. "If it's all right, I'd like to ride back to Calais with you so that we can discuss what needs to happen next, from a law enforcement and legal perspective."

"Of course," Carter said.

Joelle trailed out of the building, not entirely comfortable with spending the two-hour drive alone in the truck with Tyler. Although he'd been pleasant enough the night before when the girls had their sleepover, he'd gone right back to silent and closed off after discovering evidence of the intruder. He'd remained silent through the entire exhumation process, and Joelle didn't relish the long, boring, uncomfortable drive.

The first twenty minutes passed in exactly the manner Joelle expected—she tried not to fidget and Tyler stared straight out the windshield, not saying a word.

Finally, he looked over at her. "Are you all right?"

"Yes. Your truck is quite comfortable—almost like riding on my couch."

She could see a smile hovering around his lips, but it didn't quite break through.

"Thank you," he said, "but that's not what I meant. I'm talking about the exhumation."

"Oh, well," she said, trying to formulate a good response to a question she hadn't yet answered for herself. "I'm all right, but I don't know what I think about it."

"You've had an awful lot to wrap your mind around in a short amount of time."

"True, but at least I have the education and experi-

ence to handle crisis. I can't imagine what your average person would do in my situation."

"Sit in a corner crying or run screaming from the town, is my guess."

"I've actually considered both, but neither seemed overly productive."

Now the smile broke through. "I tell you what—I give all you ladies credit for being tough. When your sisters ran out of the bedroom last night, wearing pink pajamas and packing guns, it gave me a bit of a start. Then the more I thought about it, the bigger kick I got out of it."

"I got a kick out of it, too. It's nice to know my sisters *really* have my back."

"Did anything else happen…before you heard the noise?"

Joelle stiffened, somewhat taken aback. "No," she lied. "Why do you ask?"

He shrugged. "You were pale and your hands were shaking as if you'd had a recent shock."

Instantly, Joelle's mind leaped back to the vision she'd seen looking through the banisters. Tyler was far more perceptive than she'd given him credit for if he'd picked up on her reaction. But no matter how pleasant things seemed at the moment with the hunky bodyguard, her childhood flashbacks were something she wasn't ready to share with anyone—not even her sisters.

"I think I was just unnerved," she said finally. "You know, big spooky house…things that go bump in the night…and after hearing everything that happened to Alaina and Danae, I suppose my imagination is working overtime."

"Hmm," he said, but didn't look the least bit convinced.

She looked out the windshield, mentally running through the morning's events. "What do you think it means?"

"The empty casket?"

"Yeah. The medical examiner was quite clear on the fact that the casket had never been opened. So it's not like Purcell could have sent someone to steal the body after the fact. And since the serial number inside the casket matched the burial records, I don't see how the entire casket could have been switched."

"Unless someone made up plates for the replacement casket that matched the records, or switched the casket before the burial."

"But why?" she asked. "She was going in the crypt. No one suspected foul play. Why take such a risk?"

"Just to be certain that nothing could ever be traced back to him? Honestly, I don't know. Purcell was a hit man for a mob family. It's hard for a person with morals to get into that mind-set."

"But Carter is trying to."

Tyler nodded. "Carter takes his job seriously, and with you three involved, it's personal. He won't give up—no matter how long it takes."

"You trust him," Joelle said, a bit surprised that the cagey bodyguard had such absolute faith in someone other than himself.

"I've known Carter my whole life. Him, his mother and my father—I've never seen any of them do or say something without someone else in mind. Carter would never talk about it, because he'd consider it bragging and therefore rude, but my dad told me he received several commendations when he was a detective in New Orleans."

"Then it looks like I'm well protected. Your father

told me you have quite a collection of medals yourself."

Immediately, Tyler stiffened and his jaw flexed. "My dad shouldn't talk about things he doesn't understand."

Even though she knew she'd hit a nerve, Joelle couldn't help saying, "He's proud of you."

Tyler stared out the windshield for several seconds before responding. "Maybe I'm not proud of some of the things those medals were given for."

Joelle stared at him, his words hitting her like a tidal wave. It was easy to watch the news footage from the Middle East on the television and shake your head, but had she ever once thought about the extent of mental and emotional damage that was inflicted on those simply doing their job?

In her own work, she'd done things during crisis situations that she would never have done under normal circumstances. She'd hit people, broken major traffic laws and effectively kidnapped children to remove them from dangerous situations. She'd never regretted a single action she'd taken to save a woman or a child, but sometimes the extent of her anger during the fray disturbed her. It gave her a clear understanding of how much humans were capable of when placed in volatile situations.

Given Tyler's length of time overseas, the things he'd seen probably made a day at her job look like Disneyland.

And she'd just opened her big mouth and brought it all back to the forefront of his mind.

Idiot.

She slumped back against the truck seat and focused her mind on the first project she intended to work on

at the house. Every time she opened her mouth, she made things between her and Tyler more uncomfortable. Maybe it was time to be quiet.

Chapter Eight

Tyler managed to endure the rest of the drive to the mansion in calm silence but it was a strain. Why had his dad brought up his medals? Tyler understood that William was proud of him, but the last thing he wanted people doing was thinking him a hero, when he knew the truth. And the very last person he needed thinking him a hero was a woman with a dangerous job and living in a dangerous situation.

He'd already played that game and lost.

From now on, no more personal conversations with Joelle. He'd be polite, but no one claimed being buddies with her was part of the job he was hired to do. Talking to her always brought him back around to things he'd come back to Calais to forget.

He checked all the windows and doors in the house as soon as they arrived, then went back outside to do another perimeter search, desperately needing to work off some pent-up energy. Also, he was determined to discover how the intruder had gained access to the house. If he couldn't prevent access to the structure, how was he supposed to protect Joelle? The last thing he needed was something to happen to the heiress on his watch.

As he walked around the side of the house, scanning the ground for any trace of recent passage besides his

own, his mind rolled through the conversation they'd had on the ride back from New Orleans. When he'd run out of his bedroom the night before, something had startled Joelle. Something besides the noise she heard downstairs.

The expression on her face went far beyond simple fear and crossed right into haunted. He'd seen that look on so many soldiers—young men who weren't prepared well for the atrocities they would face or the things they'd be asked to do. Joelle had seen or heard something that forced her to remember something particularly horrible. So horrible she couldn't control her body's reaction to it and refused to discuss it.

Alaina is starting to remember more....

Something his dad said during a recent discussion ran through Tyler's mind. William had said that despite being the oldest of the sisters, Alaina didn't have much memory of her childhood at the LeBeau estate. William thought she'd blocked it out because the death of her mother and being sent to live with strangers was so traumatic for a six-year-old girl. But since returning to Calais, Alaina's memory was starting to return, and Carter hoped that at some point, her memories might help them unravel what happened to her mother.

Joelle was only four when she was sent away, but even someone so young could have memories, if they had produced great emotion. Overwhelming happiness and extreme fear would be enough to imprint on a four-year-old. Based on Joelle's expression when he came out of his bedroom, he was betting on fear.

The question was, were the memories always present, or like Alaina, had something come flooding back since she'd returned to the house?

Either way, she'd clammed up as soon as he asked.

Maybe he'd mention his suspicions to Carter, who would tell Alaina. Perhaps if Joelle knew her sister was remembering, she'd be willing to tell her secrets to Alaina.

As he rounded the corner to the patio side of the house, he looked into the swamp toward the clearing he'd seen the day before. Dark clouds were starting to form overhead, and he knew he had little daylight left before the rain began, so he stepped into the swamp to see if he could discern any more details of passage.

At the edge of the clearing, he hit pay dirt. Where leaves had been the day before, now a patch of loose dirt remained, and at the edge of it was the front half of a shoe print. Without making a cast, there was no way to be certain, but it looked like the same size and shape as the print he'd lifted from the laundry room.

He followed the trail into the swamp for about a hundred yards before stopping. It wasn't safe to leave Joelle unprotected. He'd wait until Carter was available to keep watch, then he'd track the intruder to his getaway point. It probably wouldn't tell them who the intruder was, but it would be one more thing in their arsenal of knowledge.

As soon as he got back inside, and if he had any service left on his phone with the storm moving in, he'd order outdoor video cameras with motion detectors. Someone had used this path twice that he knew of. He'd stopped at a supply store in New Orleans on the way to the cemetery and picked up some cameras to place inside the house. Maybe if he didn't catch them inside, he could catch them outside. Either way, a picture or video would put the entire thing to rest, quickly and easily.

He headed back to the house and as he stepped on

the patio, his cell phone rang. It was Carter, so he answered, happy service hadn't dropped yet.

"I'm glad I caught you," Carter said. "With the storm coming, I didn't figure I would."

"I expect service will go anytime now. What's up?"

"I talked with the Jackson police. Brant is MIA. He left his house three days ago and no one has seen or heard from him since."

"That's not good."

"It gets worse. The Jackson police ran his credit cards and one of them was used last night at a hotel and restaurant in New Orleans."

Tyler cursed. "And I suppose there's no legitimate reason for him to be in New Orleans?"

"No family or friends, and his secretary says they don't have any business interests or contacts in New Orleans that he would need to see. Besides, if it was legitimate, his secretary would know where he was. She's been trying to reach him for two days with no luck."

"Have the police tried triangulating his cell phone?"

"Not yet, but I asked them to. They're supposed to call me when they get something."

"Good, let me know."

Tyler waited several seconds, but no response was forthcoming. Then his phone beeped twice and he looked at the display and sighed. No service. And he hadn't gotten a chance to tell Carter about his theory on Joelle's childhood memories.

He glanced overhead and saw that the clouds had almost covered the sky and grew darker by the second. He needed to finish his outside rounds and get inside. Ordering the night-vision cameras would have to wait until the next day. The rain wasn't supposed to clear out until the next evening, but his dad had Wi-Fi, and

if he headed into town early enough, he could probably catch Carter at the café.

He worked his way down the patio, but didn't see anything out of place, then let himself in the patio door and into the kitchen. Joelle was nowhere in sight, so he figured she was upstairs. He started across the kitchen when suddenly, the pantry door flew open.

If his reflexes had been any slower, it would have smacked him directly in the face, but he got his hand up in time to stop it.

"Oh!" Joelle cried out as she stepped around the door. "I'm so sorry. I didn't know you were there."

He struggled to control his aggravation. "What are you doing hiding in the pantry?"

"It's not a pantry. Well, at least, not like any I've ever seen. See?"

She pushed the door completely open and he peered inside. Joelle was right. It wasn't like any pantry he'd ever seen, either. It was approximately eight feet wide and at least ten feet long. Shelves lined one wall from top to bottom. On the other side rested cabinets with a stone countertop as well as another set of counter-tops above. At the opposite side of the pantry was another door.

"Where does that go?" he asked.

Joelle stepped through the pantry and opened the other door. "It's filled with junk now, but with that chandelier, I'm going to guess this was the formal dining room. I think that's a butler's pantry."

"What the heck is a butler's pantry?"

"Wealthy people often had a room connecting the kitchen to the formal dining that the staff could use to prepare the food for service. That way they didn't walk up and down the main halls of the home carrying trays."

"Like the servants' stairs that lead from the upstairs directly to the kitchen and the laundry room?"

"Exactly. The premise was that the servants' work should be visible everywhere, but not the people themselves."

"Sounds like a lot of pompous nonsense to me."

"My great-grandparents—or maybe even someone before that—built the house. My guess is it's what they were used to. But I agree with you, it seems an odd way to live—with people roaming your house all the time."

"You don't remember servants from when you lived here before?" Tyler asked, hoping to get some idea of the extent of Joelle's childhood memories.

Joelle frowned and she shifted her glance down before answering. "I don't really remember much. I think I was too young."

"Really? It seems like something should register, even at four. You don't even remember your mother?"

Her face softened a bit and she nodded. "Sometimes, but it's not clear. More like glancing at a photograph or a tiny video clip. It's usually gone as quickly as it appeared."

"Carter said Alaina started to remember things after she returned to the house."

"That's what she said the other night. I did remember a couple of things when I walked into our old room, but it was still like the others—snatches of the past."

Tyler studied her closely, but she appeared to be telling the truth. "Carter said he's hoping that Alaina will remember something that can help him with the investigation."

Her eyes widened. "Really? I don't see how…"

"For instance, we know your stepfather paid off peo-

ple—it's possible Alaina could have seen some of those people meeting with him. If she remembers anyone we haven't already identified, it might help us figure out who's still accessing the house and why."

"Oh. I'd never thought of it that way, but it still seems such a long shot, a child that young being able to not only remember a face but extrapolate it to that person now."

"You work with kids who've been through traumatic experiences a lot," Tyler continued to push. "Surely you've seen cases where they saw something so bad that they pushed it to the back of their mind, only to have it resurface later on."

She frowned. "And you think Alaina might have seen something so bad that she blocked all her memories of her childhood here?"

Tyler shrugged. "I'm no psychologist. You'd be able to answer that question better than me."

She was silent for a couple of seconds, and he could tell she was trying to formulate a response. Finally, she put her hands up in the air and said, "It's certainly possible, but I can't say whether it's something Alaina is experiencing. At least, she hasn't said so to me."

She glanced out the window at the dark clouds. "I guess I better go to the laundry room and get the lanterns and flashlights that Alaina told me about."

Tyler watched her as she hurried out of the room. He hadn't been mistaken. For just a millisecond, that same haunted expression he'd seen on her face the night before had flashed by. If he hadn't been watching closely for it, he would have missed it entirely.

Alaina may not be experiencing a recollection of something traumatic, but he'd bet any amount of money that Joelle was.

CARTER TOSSED HIS cell phone on the kitchen counter and looked over at Alaina, who was spooning chicken gumbo into two bowls.

"No service?" she asked.

"I've got service on this end, but my guess is there's none left at the house. Not with this storm moving in."

Alaina nodded. "I had my share of that problem. I wish we could have gotten a landline installed before Joelle came, but William said it would take months. She didn't want to wait, but I wish she had."

Carter took the bowls of gumbo from Alaina and placed them on the breakfast table. "My guess is Joelle wanted to get away from Brant. It's a smart thing to do—leave town for a couple of weeks and give him a chance to cool off and wise up."

Alaina set two glasses of tea on the table. "Except that it doesn't appear he's done either."

"No," Carter said, still unhappy over the Jackson Police Department's report on Brant. "Well, if he makes the mistake of coming to Calais, we'll be ready for him. First thing tomorrow, I'll circulate a picture of him to every businessman and otherwise sane individual in Calais. If anyone sees him, they'll let me know."

"Someone from the outside can still get to you," Alaina said quietly.

Carter wrapped his arms around his wife and kissed the top of her head. "In your case, we didn't know we were looking for an outsider, much less who he was. Joelle's situation is different."

Alaina leaned back and looked up at him. "Is it? Someone's still gaining access to the house, and I seriously doubt that's Brant. Not this soon, and not without avoiding detection. Whoever is entering that house has an agenda and a way in we've yet to figure out. And

that means Joelle is in just as much danger as Danae and I were."

"We're better prepared this time," Carter assured her. "We know he's out there. We know some of what happened and we're uncovering more every week. And Tyler's there. She's got full-time, on-site, ridiculously qualified security, *and* I trust him."

Alaina studied his face for a moment, still not appearing convinced, but finally she nodded. "I know you're doing everything you can, and because Tyler is William's son, I trust him, too, even though I don't know him that well."

"But?"

She blew out a breath. "But after today, I just don't know what to think anymore. I'm starting to think that we've only scratched the surface of my stepfather's sins."

"You may be right."

Alaina's eyes misted up and she sniffed. "What did he do to her, Carter? Where is my mother's body?"

Carter pulled his fiancé to his chest and hugged her tightly. "I don't know, but I'm going to find out. If it's the last thing I ever do."

Chapter Nine

Joelle set the lantern on the nightstand next to the twin bed she'd claimed as hers the night before. Rain had been falling steadily for a couple of hours, but apparently, it hadn't gotten bad enough to cut off power. Still, having the lantern in easy reach made her feel better.

After fleeing from Tyler and his questions, she'd gathered bad-weather supplies, then spent the rest of the evening wandering from room to room, digging through the contents, and marveling over the beautiful art and paintings shoved in piles, boxes and closets. According to Alaina, most of it probably wasn't worth much, but some of it looked fantastic. If her sisters didn't mind, Joelle intended to ask if she could keep a couple of the items. She would purchase them, if needed.

She'd found a particularly lovely painting of Alaina as a baby tucked behind a buffet table in the formal dining room. Even though she couldn't have been any older than six months in the portrait, Alaina already favored their mother. Joelle had eased the painting out from behind the buffet and leaned it against the door to the butler's pantry. As soon as she got an opportunity, she'd inquire about getting the piece professionally cleaned.

Tyler had gone back into silent mode and had spent the entire evening installing motion-activated cameras

around the house. With no wireless internet available, he had to hard-wire the devices. Joelle had heard a lot of mumbling as he tried to decide where the wire would be least visible. As she didn't have the skill set to offer any aid, she went quietly about her business and tried to stay out of his way.

After several dust-filled hours, she'd finally stopped poking through things, and her thoughts turned to a long overdue shower. She was on her way down the hall to the bathroom when she heard a knock at the front door. Frowning, she glanced at her watch. Seven o'clock. The storm and the gloomy house made it feel later than it was, but still, who would be out in the middle of the swamp in a storm?

She hurried down the stairs and arrived at the front door the same time as Tyler, who'd come from the kitchen.

"Wait," he said and pulled out his pistol. He opened the door a crack and peered outside, then opened it wide and motioned someone inside.

The man was on crutches and looked to be a hundred years old. He pulled back the hood of his rain slicker and looked straight at Joelle. Tyler must know the man if he'd let him inside the house, so she gave him a polite smile. Then something in her clicked.

"Amos," she whispered. "Is it really you?"

The old man broke out in a grin. "You remember?"

Given the crutches and his obvious frailty, she was afraid to hug him, but she leaned over and gave the old caretaker a kiss on the cheek. "Of course I remember. You had all those wonderful tools."

"You liked my nail gun the best, but your mother wouldn't let you use it. You pitched a righteous fit over it, if I remember correct."

Joelle smiled. "I'm sure your memory is fine, although I don't relish recalling any of my somewhat spoiled behavior. Please come into the kitchen and sit."

"Can't right now. My niece is out front waiting to take me to a cousin's in New Orleans. I have a doctor's appointment tomorrow so they can check my foot. They're thinking they might have to reset it, so I might be gone a couple more days. But I promise you, when I get back, we'll sit down and have us a chat."

"I'm looking forward to it," Joelle said. "Take care, Amos, and thank you so much for dropping by."

Joelle watched as the caretaker navigated the stone driveway and hopped into a sedan, then Tyler closed the door and drew the dead bolt into place.

"He seemed ancient when I was a child. I can't believe he's still alive," Joelle said. "How old is he?"

"I'm not sure even Amos knows, but my dad says he has to be in his eighties at least."

"He was the caretaker. I remember following him around—little snapshots of Amos fixing the toilet or repairing the driveway."

"He's still the caretaker—or was until he broke his foot."

Joelle stared. "He's been here all these years? Why in the world did he stay?"

Tyler's expression softened. "He said he was waiting on you girls to return."

"Oh!" She covered her mouth with her hand as her eyes watered with potential tears. "That's so lovely… and sad. I'm glad he was still alive to see us return."

"Me, too."

All the events of the day rushed in, overwhelming her, and Joelle choked back a sob. "Well, I was about to jump in the shower."

Tyler nodded. "Go ahead. I have some things to finish up here, then I'll need one myself."

She hurried upstairs and hopped in, almost weeping with relief as the steamy water ran over her tired, filthy body. Forcing her mind to a blank slate, she felt her muscles start to loosen. No doubt, she could stand here for hours—or until the hot water ran out—but that probably wouldn't be fair to Tyler, who'd earned his hot shower as much as she had. She lathered up her hair and body and rinsed, then dried off, pulled on her robe and headed into her bedroom.

Now, squeaky clean, she had a completely different dilemma—bra or no bra. Normally, after-shower time was her favorite part of the wardrobe day. Everything restrictive came off and comfortable worn clothes went on, but normally, she wasn't bunking with a bodyguard.

A hot bodyguard.

She shook her head, not about to let her mind dwell on the fact that she was locked in a spooky old house, completely cut off from the rest of the world, and her protector was the most attractive man she'd ever seen up close and personal. Fortunately, his personality dimmed any carnal thoughts she might have had if the circumstances had been different, and that was a really good thing. The last thing Joelle needed was a random fling with a man who clearly had issues with intimacy.

Sighing, she pulled a sports bra out of her suitcase. It was a reasonable compromise and would allow her to venture downstairs to fix something to eat without feeling cheap and loose. Given her luck lately, she might need to sleep in it. A mental visual of fleeing the house in the rainstorm and being collected by Carter or his deputy came to the forefront of her mind. Probably be-

cause she'd seen it played out over and over in late-night suspense movies.

Of course, in the movies, the sexy hero always rescued the beautiful heroine and then gave her a passionate kiss, which led to them living happily ever after with a cottage and a golden retriever. She sighed again. And that's exactly why movies were fiction. She dug into her suitcase again and pulled out a book. Sleep wasn't easy for her under the best of circumstances and she'd packed several books, figuring on long, sleepless nights.

She glanced down at the title, then pulled the rest of the books out and scattered them on the bed. Romances. Every single book. She was batting a thousand. Where was a nice boring literary work when you needed it? She scooped all but one of the books up and tossed them back in the suitcase before zipping it and placing it in the corner next to the bed.

The remaining book, she placed on the nightstand next to the lantern. The beds all contained rumpled covers from the night before. After their dash downstairs, no one had felt like going back to bed, so they'd sat in the kitchen, drinking coffee and trying to ready themselves for the exhumation. Joelle pulled the sheets and blankets straight on all three beds and placed the pillows neatly against the headboards, wishing her sisters were joining her again tonight.

It was such a big room for one person.

Last night, with all three of them in there, it had seemed so much smaller, so cozy and intimate, but tonight it almost felt institutional, not dissimilar to the orphanages she frequented. She thought briefly about moving to one of the smaller rooms, but except for the one Tyler occupied, none of the others had been cleaned. The last thing she felt like doing this late was tackling

cleaning one of those cluttered, filthy rooms, especially given that she'd already showered.

First thing tomorrow, she'd find a better location and get it ready for occupancy. A single bedroom wouldn't feel as lonely. But now, it was time to rustle up dinner.

As she walked down the hall, the door to the bathroom swung open and Tyler walked out, a wave of steam following him. He wore only sweatpants, and his ripped chest and abdomen still glistened with moisture. She was struck momentarily silent as she took in every single perfect inch of him.

When she realized she was assessing him like a twenty-ounce porterhouse steak, she yanked her gaze up to his face and saw a hint of a smile lurking behind his otherwise blank expression. A blush ran up her neck because she'd been caught ogling him.

"I was, uh," she stammered, "I was headed downstairs to fix something to eat. There're leftover finger sandwiches, crackers and stuff from last night. I know Alaina stocked the refrigerator with meat and stuff, but I was afraid to start cooking lest the power go out in the middle."

You're rambling.

She clamped her mouth shut as his smile broadened. Damn him! He was actually enjoying her discomfort. That was *so* not the behavior of a movie hero.

"Leftovers are fine," he said finally. "Let me grab a shirt and some shoes and I'll join you."

She watched him as he walked away. His backside was just as impressive as the front. As he started to walk into his bedroom, he glanced back and grinned. She whipped around, holding in a groan, and ran straight into the kitchen, where she opened the refrigerator door and promptly stuck her head inside.

What in the world has gotten into me?

She hadn't behaved that way since she was an awkward teen—far, far in the past. Now she was a successful, educated woman who'd had at least one serious relationship and several semi-serious ones. Yet, here she was, almost thirty years old and acting like she was fifteen and he was a star from *Twilight*.

The night just kept getting longer.

THE LIGHT SHINING in her eyes awakened Joelle, and she put one hand up to shield herself as she leaned up in bed. Her book lay beside her, long since forgotten when she nodded off reading it. Assuming she left the lamp on, she turned to the side, and froze when she saw that the lamp didn't emit even a hint of a glow. She bolted upright, trying to ascertain where the light came from, and finally found the source in the far corner of the bedroom.

And that's when panic set in.

The light shimmering in the corner was tall—at least five feet from the floor to the top of it—and as it grew brighter, it began to take shape. Joelle fixed her gaze on it, afraid to even blink, and gasped as the lines of light grew solid and formed the outline of a human body.

I'm dreaming.

It wasn't a bad idea, except for the part where she was positive she was awake.

I'm imagining it.

Also not a bad idea, except for the part where she had twenty-twenty vision and was completely sane.

She reached for her pistol, resting on the edge of the nightstand, and gripped the cold metal in her hands. It seemed silly given that the corporeal being was any-

thing but human, but the weight of the gun made her feel better.

The light seemed to pulse, and then the figure in the center sharpened once more and Joelle gasped.

Mother!

There was no mistaking those high cheekbones, the wide-set eyes and the big smile. Her long hair seemed to billow around her, as if caught in a breeze. Her long white gown rippled along with her hair as she drew closer to the bed.

"You came," her mother said. "I was afraid you wouldn't find your way back here. I waited for you."

A sob broke through and Joelle dropped her hands, letting the gun fall out of her grasp and onto the bed. "I'm so sorry. I didn't know."

"I waited for you, but I grow weak."

The light started to drift back from the bed and Joelle sprang up and hurried to the end of the bed. "Wait! Please don't go. We're trying to find you. Do you know where you are?"

The ghost looked confused for a moment, then gave her a sad look. "I'm here. And then I'm not. I grow weak, but I waited. Now, you need to go."

"Go where?"

"Away from here. It's not safe. I'm tired."

The light began to fade and Joelle reached out one hand. "Please don't leave me."

"I'm here. Sometimes. And then I'm not. I'm here…"

And with one last flicker, the light disappeared completely, casting the room into complete darkness.

Joelle jumped out of bed and ran to the corner, waving her hands around. The hair on her arms stood on end from the electrical charge, but otherwise, no indication remained that something had been here before.

She went back to the bed and flopped down on the end of it. No one would believe her. With all the stress she was under, everyone would assume she dreamed it, or imagined it, or drank heavily. Heck, if she was someone else and heard this story, she'd think the same thing.

Now that the light was gone, the room was so dark, she couldn't even see her hand in front of her face. She'd fallen asleep with the lamp on, so she assumed the power had gone out sometime during the night. She glanced at her watch and saw it was 3:00 a.m. Way too early to be awake, but she seriously doubted she'd be able to go back to sleep. Maybe she'd suggest to Tyler that they purchase a generator and spotlights and do all the work at night and sleep during the day.

Yeah, he wouldn't think that was strange at all.

She crawled across the bed and picked up the lantern, but couldn't even see well enough to light it. Thankful she'd brought the lantern and a flashlight, she picked up the flashlight and clicked it on. The beam of light cast directly at the paned-glass patio doors that led onto the balcony off the bedroom.

At first, the light reflected across the glass, causing a glare. Then her vision sharpened and she saw a masked face staring through the door at her.

Chapter Ten

A bloodcurdling scream sent Tyler vaulting straight up out of bed, grabbing his pistol on the way. He bolted down the hall to Joelle's room and tried to open the door, but it was still locked from the inside. Cursing himself for telling her to draw the inside dead bolt, he banged on the door, yelling for her to open it and hoping like hell she was in a position to do so.

He was just about to start kicking it open when he heard the dead bolt slide back. Joelle threw open the door and pointed to the balcony.

"He was there," she said, her voice breaking, "looking through the door."

Tyler rushed across the room and threw open the patio door, Joelle close behind. He took her flashlight and leaned over the railing, shining it on the kitchen patio. The stone patio wouldn't leave any indication that someone had passed, but he could see branches broken at the edge of the patio where the swamp began. Maybe the damage was from the storm, but it was possible it was from something else.

"Come with me," he said and ran down the hallway.

He looked back as he skipped down the stairs two at a time, figuring he might need to slow down so that Joelle could keep up, but either fear or excellent con-

ditioning had her keeping pace. Satisfied that she was still in sight, he took off at a dead run as soon as he hit the entry floor and rushed out onto the kitchen patio.

Shining the flashlight into the brush at the edge of the patio, he saw the signs that something big had passed through here and without regard to covering its passage. He directed the light to the ground and saw the clear print of a hiking boot where the rain had washed the leaves away, leaving a patch of mud.

If Joelle wasn't there, he'd take off into the swamp after him, but he couldn't leave her unprotected. Purcell's death had already unearthed several people with hidden agendas at the estate. He had no reason to assume only one man was left to carry on business now, or that multiple people were acting independently of each other. Carter had already said that since the start of the events, he'd always felt that whatever was going on was more organized than it seemed.

Luring Tyler away from the house might be just what they wanted to do.

"Let's get back inside," Tyler said.

He waited until Joelle hurried into the kitchen, then pulled the patio door shut, sliding the dead bolt back into place. Even under the cover of the balcony, the steady flow of rain had blown across them, leaving them both damp.

A stack of folded towels and rags sat at the end of the breakfast table and Joelle pulled two off the top and handed one to him. "I never got around to putting them up last night," she said as she ran the towel across her face.

"You're not the housekeeper. I don't expect you to clean up after everyone," he said as he lit the lantern on the kitchen cabinets. The light started small, then

grew into a large flame, casting a dim yellow glow across the kitchen.

She shrugged. "Someone's got to do it, and sometimes doing mundane things helps my focus."

Tyler wiped his face and arms and nodded. He understood exactly what she meant. He'd spent countless hours volunteering for hard labor because he needed to work out a security problem that he hadn't found a good solution for. Manual labor unlocked his creativity in a way sitting and pondering never did.

He looked over at Joelle as she wiped her arms with the towel and his eyes locked on her thin white T-shirt, currently clinging to her otherwise bare breasts. Before she looked up, he managed to avert his eyes, but no way was he going to be able to get that image out of his head.

Joelle was quite simply the most beautiful woman he'd ever encountered.

He held in a sigh that his mind had finally admitted what his body had known from the first moment he'd met her. Why couldn't she have been the ugly sister? Wasn't every family supposed to have one? Instead, all three of Ophelia LeBeau's daughters looked as if they'd stepped off the pages of magazines, and with seemingly no effort if the amount of time they spent getting ready the prior morning was any indication.

Life simply wasn't fair.

Growing up in Calais, he'd dated pretty girls, nice girls and girls with great personalities, but in the years he'd been away, all of the ones who were "wife material" had settled down with Calais boys or moved away to capture bigger fish. He'd expected his return to Calais to be "safe" in far more ways than just physically, especially since according to reports from William,

the only single women in Calais were newly widowed grandmothers.

His dad had conveniently forgotten the LeBeau sisters in his statement. Or maybe it had been a deliberate oversight.

Tyler knew his father wanted to see him paired up and happy, as he and Tyler's mom had been for so many years before she passed away. But that sort of life wasn't on Tyler's radar. Not now. Not ever. Which was why staring at beautiful women's essentially naked breasts was something he had absolutely no business indulging in.

"What happened, exactly?" he asked, trying to get his focus back on track.

"I woke up…and the room was dark. I'd fallen asleep with the lamp on, so I figured the power was out. I turned on the flashlight so that I could see to light the lantern and that's when I saw him."

"Did you recognize him?"

She shook her head. "He was wearing a black mask. When I screamed, he vaulted over the railing."

"Was he trying to get in the room?"

Her eyes widened. "I don't know. I guess that makes sense, right?"

"But you didn't hear anything?"

"No. I think that's why it was such a shock when I saw him. Is it important that I didn't hear anything?"

He shrugged. "I'm just trying to figure out what woke you up at three a.m. and bothered you enough that you wanted to turn on the lantern."

"I…I don't know. I'd fallen asleep with the lamp on, but when I woke up, it was so dark…" She rubbed the towel across her already dry face and looked down at the floor.

"Yeah, that's what you said." Tyler would bet anything he had that she was lying. But why? What did she have to gain from keeping things from him when his only objective was to protect her?

"Are you sure that's all?" Tyler asked. "Because you don't strike me as the kind of woman who is afraid of the dark."

She looked back up at him and he could see the hesitation in her eyes.

"I can't do my job effectively," he said, "if I don't have all the facts."

She shook her head. "You'll think I'm crazy."

"Trust me, after everything my dad's told me, I will not think you're crazy. There's an explanation for everything happening in this house. We just have to find it."

He hadn't convinced her completely, which made him even more curious as to what she was hiding. She pulled at the bottom of her T-shirt for a couple of seconds, then finally sighed.

"I'll tell you, but can we make some coffee and change clothes first? I'm not going to be able to go back to sleep and I want to make sure my head is straight before I try to explain it to you."

"Sure," he said. "You go ahead and change. I'll put the coffee on."

He watched her as she trailed out of the kitchen, wondering if whatever had awakened her tonight was the same thing that had scared her in the hallway the night before. Either way, he planned on pushing that issue, as well.

Now was not the time for secrets.

JOELLE SNAGGED A dry shirt and a sports bra and hurried back to the bathroom. She'd pulled her long hair back in

a ponytail before she'd headed to bed, but she released it now so that the thin sheen of rain that covered it would dry more quickly. As she reached for the hem of her T-shirt, she glanced in the mirror and groaned. The thin white cotton was just damp enough to be completely sheer. She may as well have been standing shirtless in the kitchen.

This is what you get for taking off the sports bra.

She tugged off the damp garment and wiped her body with the towel to remove any remaining moisture. It wasn't enough that she had to go downstairs and tell Tyler she'd seen a ghost—who'd talked to her, no less. But she had to do so with the knowledge that he'd seen half of her practically naked.

Pulling her bra and dry shirt over her head, she marveled at his self-control. He'd never given any indication that she was essentially half-clad. Not a single flicker, wide eye or half smile. He either had the self-control of an android or he wasn't interested in what he'd seen.

She took another critical look at herself. Considering she was being stalked and haunted and had just learned her mother's body was missing from her grave, she thought she looked pretty good. Her body was a combination of Alaina and Danae. She'd gotten Alaina's height and Danae's curves. It was a good combination and one she knew attracted male attention. And although she didn't have her mother's fine bone structure like Alaina, her face was nice. Her hair—thanks to a genius hairstylist—was stellar.

Definitely android.

And completely unfair. She'd practically drooled at his bare chest the night before and he hadn't returned the favor. Okay, rude *and* unfair.

She ran her fingers through her hair to fluff it out

some, then tossed the towel over the shower rod and headed downstairs, unable to think of a good reason to delay the conversation she had no desire to have.

Tyler hadn't changed clothes, but then his T-shirt was black, not see-through, and even if it had been, those rules didn't apply to men. He poured two cups of coffee when he saw her enter the kitchen.

"How do you take it?"

"Normally with lots of sugar and cream, but I think I'll go with black."

"Black it is," he said and carried the mugs to the breakfast table.

She dropped into a chair and took a sip of the hot, steamy liquid. The bitter taste gave her a momentary shock, but she figured it would also keep her sharp. Her story wasn't going to go over well with Tyler. He was a no-nonsense sort of guy, and what she was about to say was definitely nonsense. At least, that's what she'd think if she hadn't seen it herself.

"So," he said. "You were going to tell me what woke you up?"

"I'll tell you, but you're not going to like it."

"I didn't figure I would, but that doesn't eliminate the need for hearing it."

"Fine." She took a deep breath and then proceeded to explain her awakening to the light—how it changed form to become her mother—how it spoke to her.

She had to give him credit. He listened intently, never interrupting and without so much as a raised eyebrow. If roles had been reversed, she'd have been looking for a psych referral form a long time ago.

"And then the light just faded away," she finished.

Tyler stared at her for a long time, slightly frowning.

"I told you that you'd think I was crazy," she said, unable to keep the frustration out of her voice.

"I don't think you're crazy," he said quietly.

"No, you probably think I dreamed it or imagined it due to stress or something."

"I think you saw exactly what you say you saw."

Her jaw dropped a bit and she stared at him, looking for any indication that he was humoring her, but his expression was completely serious.

"I just want to be clear. You believe the ghost of my mother came to visit me and spoke?"

He nodded. "You seem surprised."

"Surprised is the understatement of the decade. I'm completely blown away. Do you know what I would tell anyone who tried to pass off a story like that to me?"

He smiled. "That they were crazy?"

"For starters. Should I even ask why this doesn't freak you out?"

He shrugged. "I've seen a lot of things I couldn't explain. There's a lot of myth and legend buried in Mystere Parish swamps. Some people believe the swamp itself is a living, breathing entity and that it sometimes comes alive if things are out of balance."

"People believe in a swamp god?"

"No, people believe the swamp is a force of nature that will act to change things it doesn't like."

"Who believes this?"

"My dad, for starters. Me, Carter, Carter's mom… truth be known, probably everyone who's lived near the swamp their whole lives believes it, even though some wouldn't admit it."

Joelle leaned back in her chair and stared at him. "I can't believe it. Here I am all worried about what you

think, and you're telling me straight out that I saw a ghost."

"You're not the first to see her."

She sat straight up again, jostling her coffee. "What?"

"Alaina and Danae have both seen her, and Danae's fiancé, Zach."

She sucked in a breath, her mind racing with this new bit of information. "Why didn't they tell me last night?"

"Maybe because you would have thought they were crazy? I'm just guessing that it's not the kind of conversation sisters want to lead off with after a twenty-five-year separation. I'm sure they were planning on telling you soon—might have today—but the exhumation kind of put a kink in things."

"Hmm." She couldn't come up with any viable comment.

"Did you see her that first night?" he asked. "Right before you heard the intruder?"

"No," she said quickly.

"Then what did you see, and don't tell me nothing. You had that same look then as you did when you let me in your bedroom tonight. Something spooked you."

She clenched her hands and stared down at them, not wanting to share such a horrible memory. Not wanting to repeat it out loud. "I remembered something from my childhood. No ghosts—just the recollection of a child."

"Why did it scare you?"

"I was standing on the balcony. I was supposed to be asleep, but I was peeking through the banisters and looking downstairs at my mom and Purcell. They were arguing. He…he was an evil man. I felt it long before I knew any of the things he did."

She looked up at him. "I don't like remembering my

stepfather. It's almost like he's right there with me all over again. He always scared me."

She watched him closely. His expression softened and she relaxed a bit. He'd bought her story. Not that it wasn't true—Purcell had always frightened her—but she hadn't told him everything. Hadn't told him that she was sure Purcell had physically abused her mother their entire relationship. How could she share such a personal thing that didn't matter to anyone any longer, except her? Joelle knew how normal people viewed abused women. Most blamed the victim for the abuse, not bothering to try to understand the dynamics in play. William said everyone in Calais had loved Ophelia. Joelle wasn't about to do anything to change that.

Tyler sighed. "I would say he can't hurt you now, but that's not exactly true. I wish I could say something that made it better. I guess the only thing I've got is that you can be certain Purcell didn't win. He didn't get the money. He had to remain hidden in this house for the last third of his miserable life, hustling family heirlooms to pay people for silence. I guarantee you, that's not what he planned."

Joelle gave him a small smile. "That does make me feel a tiny bit better. Do you think that's why my mother's ghost haunts the house—because Purcell killed her?"

"It would be as good a reason as any."

"You said Alaina and Danae saw her. Did she talk to them, too?"

"I heard it all thirdhand through my dad, but according to him, she didn't speak to Alaina but she did to Danae."

"What did she say?"

"She kept repeating 'so close.'"

Joelle frowned. "So close? What does that mean?"

Tyler shook his head. "No one knows. It could be a lot of things."

"Or it could be nothing."

"What do you mean?"

Joelle took a minute to think of a good way to explain what she'd felt during her interaction. "She seemed confused...like she wasn't sure how she got here, and she also said she's weak. Maybe she's not strong enough to appear and manage coherent thought."

He blew out a breath. "I suppose anything's possible. If it requires a lot of effort for her to appear, she may be using all her energy and focus just on that."

Another thought flashed through Joelle's mind and she crossed her arms and shivered. "Or maybe she's lost in limbo somewhere...because her body is lost."

Tyler placed his hand on her arm. "She's not lost. She's just not readily visible. We're going to figure all this out."

"I know you believe that, and I want to, but it all happened so long ago. What if it's not possible to unravel it all?"

She reached for her cup of coffee, eager to feel the warm cup between her hands. Tyler never answered her, and that pretty much said it all.

Chapter Eleven

It was barely 7:00 a.m. when Tyler dropped Joelle off at Carter's house to talk with Alaina. He waved from the truck and headed into town, hoping to catch Carter having breakfast at the café. The list of things they needed to discuss was growing by the second, and the steady drizzle was preventing any contact by phone.

Carter was perched on his usual stool at the counter, and looked a bit surprised when Tyler slid onto the seat beside him.

"Morning, Tyler." The waitress, Sonia, smiled at him as she slid a cup of coffee in front of him. "Saw you on the sidewalk and figured you'd be wanting a cup. You hungry?"

Tyler looked over at Carter. "You eating?"

"Am I breathing?"

Tyler grinned and turned back to Sonia. "I'll take the special."

Sonia made a note on her pad and stuck the ticket up next to the grill, then hurried into the café to refill coffee cups.

Johnny, the café owner, turned from the grill and winked at Tyler. "Looks like you lost your boyish charm."

Tyler laughed. "Apparently so."

"What do you mean?" Carter asked.

Johnny grinned. "Sonia used to chase after him so hard he stopped coming in here with his daddy for a good month. Heck, I figure he went into the marines as much to get away from Sonia as to have a job."

Carter smiled. "She was dating a guy in New Orleans—even moved there for a while—but apparently it didn't work out and she landed back in Calais a month ago."

"Yep," Johnny said. "One of them numbers guys—finance, stock…something like that. Never sounded like a good fit to me. Sonia's a great gal, but she's more of a *Field & Stream* type than *Wall Street Journal,* if you know what I mean."

Tyler nodded at Johnny's accurate description.

"Worked out fine for me, though," Johnny continued, "as Danae gave her notice and claimed her fortune. Anyway, I got some stock to get in the refrigerator before it spoils, then I'll start your breakfast."

Johnny paused for a moment, then looked a bit embarrassed. "I don't usually say things like this, but it's good to see you two sitting here again."

"It's good being here again," Tyler said.

"Absolutely," Carter agreed.

Johnny gave them a nod and headed through a door to the back room of the café.

"You're up and out early," Carter said, as soon as Johnny was out of hearing distance.

"Been up for hours. The out part is recent."

Carter's eyebrows went up. "Any particular reason you've been up for hours?"

"More than one, and that's part of the reason I'm here." Tyler gave Carter a recount of the night's events, only leaving out the part about Joelle's sheer breast dis-

play. It had certainly made an impact on Tyler's night, but it wasn't relevant to the investigation.

Carter's scowl told Tyler everything the good sheriff thought about the situation. "You check for tracks off the patio?"

"Yep, but I lost them ten yards in when the ground cover got too thick to leave prints. The storm caused too much damage to the foliage to tell the difference after a while. It was easy to see where he barreled into the swamp, but my guess is that he slowed up when no one pursued him and got more deliberate about his path choice."

"I'm sure you're right. So what do you make of this ghost thing?"

Tyler shook his head. "I was going to ask you that question. You know more about it than I do, and heard some of it firsthand."

"You're sure Joelle saw her mother's ghost?"

"I don't think she imagined it. She was wide awake when she let me in the room, and something got her out of bed or she wouldn't have seen the intruder to begin with."

"And the ghost told her to leave the house?"

"Yeah. Said it wasn't safe."

Carter blew out a breath. "Which we already know, but why now? It wasn't safe before but she didn't try to warn off Alaina or Danae."

Tyler remembered Joelle's thoughts on the ghost. "Joelle wonders if the spirit is completely aware—like maybe the energy it takes her to appear leaves her confused on other things."

"If that's the case, it's damned inconvenient."

"No kidding."

"Any ideas on what to do about it?"

"The ghost? Heck no. The Marine Corps didn't offer training for that problem. On the security end of things, I got the inside cameras hooked up. With no internet, it's not as easy to cover a lot of area. Hiding the wiring presents some challenges. I think we're fine as long as he enters at night, but if he comes in during the day and looks closely, he may pick up on the cameras."

"Any progress on entry?"

"None, and it's really bugging me. The house is locked up tight. Every window is nailed shut. The dead bolts are pulled on the patio and laundry room doors, and the front door is equipped with an alarm."

"But yet, he still got in night before last."

"The front door didn't have an alarm then," Tyler pointed out.

"Yeah, I know, but the front door angle is too simple." Carter blew out a breath of frustration. "I've had this feeling all along that I'm missing something. That it's right under my nose and I haven't seen it yet. Do you know what I mean?"

Tyler nodded. He knew exactly what Carter meant because he felt it, too. Like every second he spent in that house was a second where he was at a disadvantage.

"I'll keep looking," Tyler said. "He can't hide forever."

"I'm glad you're there, man. I hate to admit it, but I'm running out of ideas. A fresh look by someone with a different perspective might open an avenue I hadn't considered."

Tyler nodded, pleased with Carter's faith in him. When they were in high school—Tyler the quiet freshman and Carter the football-star senior—he'd always admired Carter and wished he could be more like him. He'd managed to develop a more outgoing personality

and his own level of high school success before graduating and leaving for the Marine Corps, but his high opinion of Carter Trahan had held fast.

"So how are other things?" Carter asked.

"What other things?"

Carter grinned. "C'mon, I've seen Joelle. You're a red-blooded American man, spending every waking hour with her at arm's length. Don't tell me you haven't noticed she's a looker."

The last thing Tyler was going to admit to Carter was that he'd noticed entirely too much about the way Joelle looked. "Aren't you marrying her sister?" he asked.

Carter laughed. "That doesn't mean I'm blind or dead, or that I'm too dazed to know a deflection when I hear it."

"No deflection. I'm just there to do my job."

"I see. It's all a professional thing."

"Exactly."

"Uh-huh. It was a professional thing when I agreed to verify the heirs' presence for the estate, and I ended up engaged to the first one I met."

Tyler studied Carter for a moment. He was the last guy Tyler had ever imagined would be cozied up with a fiancée. According to William, they were about to break ground on a bigger house and possibly acquire a golden retriever. It was so incredibly domestic for the man he'd once thought was a superhero. But the strangest part of it all was how happy he looked about the entire thing.

"You're really happy," Tyler said.

Carter smiled. "Seems strange, right? If anyone had told me a year ago that I'd be back in Calais and living with a woman I planned to marry, I'd have called them crazy. But yeah, I'm happier than I've ever been."

"It doesn't seem strange—this pace after working for the New Orleans Police Department?"

"Not lately," Carter joked, "but all Purcell business aside, it felt slow and dull for several months. Then I started developing a rhythm. I think my body and mind needed time to decompress."

Tyler considered Carter's words. Maybe his friend was right. Maybe he just needed some time to adjust, and then everything would feel right.

"You feeling restless?" Carter asked.

Tyler nodded, not the least bit surprised that Carter had picked up on his state of flux. Everyone swore that Carter's mother, Willamina, was darn near psychic, and most thought Carter had inherited his mother's ability to read people.

"I don't know why, though," Tyler said. "I couldn't wait to leave Calais when I graduated high school. I did a good job for the Marine Corps—more than my share of overseas tours—and I have no regrets about leaving the military."

"But?"

"It's hard to explain."

Carter took a sip of his coffee. "You feel like you can't get firm ground beneath you. Like no matter where you go or what you do, you don't fit."

Tyler stared. "Yeah. That's it exactly."

Carter nodded. "I felt that way when I came back. My mom says it's because humans are always looking for a constant, and life doesn't have any. She thinks that when we accept that everything changes and that the only thing we have control over is ourselves, that the feeling of restlessness goes away."

Tyler mulled that theory over for a minute. Finally, he shook his head. "Your mother is a genius."

Carter laughed and clapped Tyler's back. "Don't tell her that. She doesn't need any more people in this town telling her how great she is."

Tyler smiled, a tiny inkling of what his life could be starting to creep through his closed mind. "Sorry, but I've always thought she was the bomb. I'm unable to hide it. Hey, did you ever wonder why our parents haven't hooked up?"

Carter's expression changed from laughter to slightly mortified. "No, I never wondered that. I don't ever put 'hooked up' and thoughts of my mom in the same realm."

"That's because she's your mother and a lady, but if William were your dad, what would you think?"

Carter's brow scrunched for several seconds, then he sighed. "I guess I'd be wondering why he wasn't chasing my mother. But can we leave that up to them? I love your dad, but I don't want the visual."

Tyler smiled at Carter's obvious discomfort, but the question was one he'd wondered about for quite some time. Both his dad and Willamina had been widowed for a long time, and neither had established another relationship that he was aware of. They'd known each other since they were kids, seemed to enjoy each other's company and planned to stay in Calais the rest of their lives. It was the perfect fit.

"Maybe I'll ask my dad about it sometime," Tyler said.

"Ha. Do that and you'll be inviting your dad to point out that you're currently living with a drop-dead gorgeous heiress. He spent some time trying to convince me that I needed to settle down. Pointed out every single woman under fifty, like I didn't already know them all."

"You're kidding? Wow, I guess I'll leave that door shut, then."

"He'll get around to it anyway. He's just waiting for an opportunity."

"He can get around to it all he wants, but it's not going to happen."

Carter took another sip of his coffee. "So you said."

JOELLE CLIMBED OUT of Alaina's car in front of the prettiest house she'd ever seen, not even the constant drizzle able to diminish its loveliness. It was Southern, with white siding and bright white columns across the front. The landscaping looked like something from the White House grounds and nothing she'd expected to see in the middle of the swamp.

"Isn't it beautiful?" Alaina said as they walked to the front door. "Willamina should have been a professional landscaper."

"She did all this herself?"

Alaina nodded. "She hires local teens for some of the manual labor, but the design is all hers."

"It's amazing."

Alaina grinned. "Wait until you see the back."

"Are you sure this is okay? It's really early to visit someone, especially when she didn't even know we were coming until ten minutes ago."

"If Willamina found out you were at my house and I didn't bring you to meet her, she'd never let me live it down. Besides, I'm fairly certain she's a vampire. I've never once caught her sleeping."

Alaina rang the doorbell and a couple seconds later, an attractive, silver-haired woman opened the door and waved them in. She gave Alaina a hug, then turned to Joelle with a big smile.

"You look like your father," Willamina said. "He was a handsome man, but I think his features look even better on a woman. You're absolutely gorgeous."

Joelle flushed at the compliment, not used to people being so direct.

Willamina smiled. "And I've embarrassed you. How delightful!" She threw her arms around Joelle and squeezed her.

Joelle hugged her back, surprised that her discomfort level was quickly subsiding.

"It's a pleasure to meet you," Joelle said when Willamina released her. "Alaina has told me so many good things about you."

Willamina beamed at Alaina, and Joelle could tell how much Willamina adored her future daughter-in-law. "Alaina is a real treasure. I couldn't have picked a better woman for Carter if I'd done it myself, and don't think I didn't consider it."

Joelle smiled at the thought of Willamina pushing a woman on Carter. That would be a battle worthy of box seats.

"I have quiche and blueberry tarts ready in the kitchen, and I've set up the patio for breakfast. We're having mimosas and I don't want to hear a single complaint about calories."

"Woo-hoo!" Alaina said as she headed off to what Joelle assumed was the kitchen. "You'll never hear me complaining about champagne for breakfast. Wait until you taste her tarts, Joelle."

"We better hurry," Willamina said, "or she'll drink all the good stuff." She linked her arm through Joelle's and guided her through the house to the huge kitchen off the back. It had miles of granite countertops and top-of-the-line appliances. Huge windows and patio doors

allowed light to stream inside, making the entire room bright despite the fact that the overhead lights weren't even turned on.

"This is beautiful," Joelle said. "Your entire home is beautiful and the landscaping is the best I've ever seen."

Willamina beamed. "Thank you so much, dear. Cooking and planting are my two biggest loves."

Alaina picked up a tray of tarts to carry outside. "It's a good thing she loves manual labor, because with her cooking, a sedentary lifestyle would be killer. I've had to add an extra two miles to my daily run just to keep the pounds off."

Joelle picked up the champagne glasses and followed Alaina out on a huge covered patio. It overlooked the well-manicured backyard that covered a couple of acres before ending at a line of cypress trees that formed the edge of the swamp. She could hear running water nearby and figured a bayou ran just past the line of cypress trees.

It was as lovely as the woman who cared for it, and Joelle understood why Alaina had insisted she meet Willamina.

"So," Willamina said after they'd taken their seats and dug into the truly incredible quiche. "Alaina tells me that Tyler Duhon is your personal bodyguard."

"Yes, ma'am."

"Please, call me Willa. I'm not old enough to be ma'am yet. I've known Tyler since he was born. He was a beautiful baby, and seems to me that hasn't changed."

Joelle laughed. "Are you calling Tyler beautiful?"

Willamina smiled. "Heavens, no. You can't say that about grown men, even if it's true. What I would say is that he's a fine specimen and just as handsome as his father was back in the day. Tyler's got a much bet-

ter body than his father ever did, though. I suppose the military did that."

Alaina snorted and grabbed her napkin. "I totally got champagne up my nose. Willa, you're awful!"

"I suppose he is quite attractive," Joelle acquiesced.

Willamina shook her head. "Don't play dumb with me. I know you've got better eyesight than that. Please tell me you've gotten a glimpse of him in some state of undress."

Joelle felt a blush creep up her neck and Willamina hooted.

"I knew it," Willamina said. "Tell all."

Joelle was completely mortified, but knew she had to say something or Willamina would never let her off the hook. "I saw him when he came out of the shower last night. I hate to disappoint you, but he was wearing sweats."

"Ah, but he wasn't wearing a shirt." Willamina nodded at Alaina, who just smiled at her future mother-in-law. "So is he a finely tuned machine under that cotton?"

"He definitely works out."

Willamina rolled her eyes. "I can see that with the clothes on. Give an old widow a thrill."

Joelle sighed. "He's absolutely perfect. In fact, I've never seen anyone with such a perfect body except in magazines."

"And they're airbrushed," Alaina pointed out. "So that makes Tyler even better."

Willamina nodded, then patted Joelle's arm. "See, that wasn't so hard."

Willamina's obvious delight was so clear that Joelle couldn't help adopting the lighthearted mood. These were good women—one of them her sister. If

she couldn't speak honestly with them, she couldn't with anyone.

"I didn't want people to get the wrong idea," Joelle said, trying to explain her hesitation.

"Honey," Willamina said, "I've got all kinds of ideas for the two of you, and none of them are wrong."

"No!" Joelle stared. "I have no intention—"

"Neither did I," Alaina said and smiled. "And you see how that turned out."

The last vestige of holding out fled from her and Joelle laughed. "You win. I took one look at his bare chest and my mind went places it had no business going. His backside is just as perfect, by the way. But even if I was interested in a relationship, I get the idea that it's the last thing Tyler wants."

"Why is that?" Alaina asked.

"He's distant. Don't get me wrong, he can be very nice and surprisingly intuitive, but the instant I try to turn the conversation to anything personal, he clams up and bolts."

The smile faded from Willamina's face and she nodded. "William is worried about him. I have to agree that he's not the same man who left here eight years ago, but how could he be? We can only imagine the atrocities he faced overseas. He needs some time to shed the worst of them, but that doesn't mean he's not still a red-blooded man."

Joelle's mind flashed back to several hours before, when she'd stood in the kitchen, her damp T-shirt leaving nothing to the imagination. "I don't know about the red-blooded part," she said, then told them about her grossly embarrassing T-shirt mishap.

Willamina waved a hand in dismissal. "That's just manners. If he had stared, his mother would have

popped straight up out of her grave and given him the what for."

"Maybe," Joelle said, but she couldn't shake the feeling that his failure to respond like the average male was due more to disinterest than manners.

"You aren't serious with anyone, right?" Alaina asked. "I mean, the other night, you said you were single, but you seemed to hesitate when you said that."

"I'm single," Joelle assured her. "I guess I'm still a bit aggravated because that's the case."

"Was there someone before you came here?" Alaina asked.

"Yes. Brad. We met in college and dated for over five years. I thought we were on our way to white picket fence territory, but apparently that hinged on whether or not I'd change jobs."

"What difference does that make?" Willamina asked.

"Brad never understood why I took a master's degree in psychology and chose to become a social worker. He pictured me with a private practice, maybe even a home office, and couldn't understand why I'd put myself at risk to help battered women and children. When I started volunteering with the underground railroad, it was the final straw for him."

"Good riddance, then," Willamina said. "You're providing an incredible service for people in awful situations. How can that be a bad thing?"

"Intrinsically, it's not. But Brad worried about my safety, as well as his own or that of our kids, in the future. He's not wrong, really. There's always the element of risk that an abuser will take things to a personal level. Look at Brant."

Alaina sighed. "No, he's not wrong. I've seen enough horror in the legal system to know that the danger is

very real. But people live with it all the time. Every law enforcement officer, every member of the legal system—"

"Every politician," Willamina interjected.

"Got that right," Alaina agreed. "They're all at risk and yet most of them marry and have families and live without anything untoward happening."

"I know," Joelle said, "but it was still his choice to make, as it was mine to choose to remain doing a job that gives me purpose."

"I still say he was a fool," Willamina said. "That's my choice to make."

Joelle smiled, marveling at how comfortable she felt with Carter's engaging mother. Willamina was everything she wished for the women she helped—strong, independent, intelligent and not the least bit afraid to speak her mind.

"You would be a great influence on the women I work with," Joelle said.

"Me?" Willamina seemed surprised. "Oh, I don't think so."

"She's right," Alaina said. "If Jackson wasn't so far away, you could do group therapy with them. Just talking to someone with your fortitude might make a difference."

Joelle nodded. "Maybe you won't have to come as far as Jackson."

"What do you mean?" Willamina asked.

"Ever since I talked to William, I've been doing a lot of thinking…about what happens when this is over and the estate is distributed. I think I'd like to open a home for women, where they could live with their children while they learn a job skill and transition into a

new life. Give them a safe place to stay and the training they need."

Willamina's eyes misted up. "That's such a wonderful thing to think of."

"What else am I going to do with all that money? I'm not the private-island-and-servant kind of gal."

And it gives me a chance to use my mother's money to help other women in situations similar to hers.

But Joelle wasn't willing to talk about her childhood memories, so she left that part unsaid.

Chapter Twelve

It was almost lunchtime when Tyler pulled through the circular drive in front of the house. Looking up at the depressing structure, Joelle sighed, already missing the company of Alaina and Willamina, who were thoroughly interesting and entertaining.

"We didn't have to leave Calais," Tyler said, apparently cluing in to her less-than-enthusiastic demeanor.

"We have to come back sometime. And it's not as scary during the day. Depressing...but not scary."

They climbed out of the truck and hurried inside before the drizzling rain soaked them. Joelle shrugged off the light jacket she wore and headed to the kitchen, Tyler close behind. She draped her jacket over one of the kitchen chairs, then pulled open the refrigerator and grabbed a bottled water.

"Would you like one?" she asked Tyler, who stood in front of the patio door, staring out into the swamp.

"No, thanks. This rain has ruined any chance of my tracking the man you saw last night," he said with a sigh. "Any prints he may have left were washed away."

Joelle could practically feel the frustration coming off of him. Tyler was a man of action. Certainly he'd had to exercise patience with his work with the Marine Corps, but the feeling of being trapped here added to

the helplessness that Joelle felt about the entire situation. Perhaps Tyler felt the same.

"So what are you planning on doing today?"

He turned around to look at her. "First, I'll check the laptop and make sure we didn't have any activity on the cameras while we were gone."

She froze. "Surely he wouldn't come inside during the day?"

Tyler shrugged. "He could have been watching when we drove off. Or he could have already been inside and heard us leave. Carter thinks that someone was listening to their conversations when Danae was here. The timing of things was too perfect to suspect otherwise."

"He ran away last night," she continued to argue, completely uncomfortable with the idea that he might be in the house with them at this moment. "We would have heard him if he came back in."

Tyler shook his head. "Not if he has another way in—one we don't know about. Carter is convinced there's an alternate entrance to the house, and I'm inclined to agree. I don't think someone's been able to slip unnoticed through the front door all this time."

She frowned. "If he has a way in, then why was he on my balcony last night?"

"I don't know," Tyler said, looking a bit uncomfortable. "Maybe he figured you were locked inside and wanted to assess who was in there with you. He might be willing to risk an attack on one person, but that first night, there were three of you in there."

"Oh." She immediately realized what Tyler was too classy to say—that the intruder was trying to determine if she was sharing a room with Tyler. "So how do we find the entrance?"

"Give me a minute," Tyler said and hurried out of the

kitchen. He returned shortly with the laptop he had hidden in one of the front rooms and wired to the motion-activated cameras.

He placed the laptop on the kitchen counter and opened it up. "If he's been inside since I rigged the cameras, I thought they would give us a starting point for finding the entrance."

Joelle moved next to him and watched as he brought up the surveillance software. "Two saved files," she said, her pulse ticking up a bit.

"Nine a.m. for the first video. I hope it's not mice," he said and clicked on the first file.

As soon as the video feed opened, Joelle sucked in a breath. "It's him!"

She leaned forward, trying to make out the grainy infrared video, and saw a dark figure emerge from the kitchen hallway into the entry. He looked upward and then continued ahead until he fell out of sight of the camera.

"Can you zoom in on his face?" she asked.

"Already working on it," Tyler said as he froze the video as the intruder stepped into the entry. He highlighted a section on the video and tapped the mouse pad to expand it.

Tyler cursed as the grainy feed came somewhat into focus. "He's wearing a mask. I figured as much after what you saw last night, but I hoped he'd slip up and remove it when he was inside."

He started the feed again and she pointed at a blur on the screen just before the intruder disappeared behind the camera. "What was that?" she asked. "That blur?"

"Let me see if I can slow it down to get a better look."

He backed up the feed a bit, then inched it forward frame by frame until the intruder was right below the

camera. "I still can't make it out. Let me slow it down some more."

He backed the feed up again and moved it forward at an even slower speed. This time, he managed to capture the blur as it was right in front of the camera.

Joelle's eyes widened. "Oh, wow!"

The vulgar hand gesture was grainy, but there was no mistaking it.

Tyler cursed and closed the feed. "He knows the cameras are there."

"But how?"

Tyler shook his head. "Maybe he was inside when I rigged them. Maybe it's because I'm staying here and he was looking for something like this."

"Does everyone know what you did in the service?"

"My dad, Carter, Carter's mom and your sisters for sure. I don't think it's common gossip, but I suppose someone could find out if they tried."

He clicked on the second feed and watched as the intruder walked back down the hall to the kitchen.

"We know he didn't come through the patio door," she said. "So how did he get in? How did he leave? There's no other way out of the house that way except the patio door. Could he have taken the servants' staircase upstairs and left that way?"

Tyler shook his head. "I have a camera pointing at the hallway where that staircase emerges."

"Well, he didn't go into the kitchen and disappear into thin air!"

"No, but he could have walked through the butler's pantry and worked his way around the back side of the house from the formal dining room. The camera doesn't cover that area of the house."

A wave of disappointment washed over her at their

failure to narrow down the possibilities, then suddenly she remembered something. "Come with me," she said and hurried out of the kitchen and around the entry, taking the long way to the formal dining room.

Her pulse quickened as she pointed to the painting of Alaina that she'd unearthed the day before. It was still leaning against the door to the butler's pantry. "I propped it up there yesterday. He couldn't have come through that door without knocking down the painting."

"He could have easily propped it back up afterward."

She sighed. "You're right."

"Let's check again, just to be sure." Tyler walked over to the door and slid the painting to the side. He walked inside the pantry and studied the wall that ran along the exterior of the house. Shaking his head, he pulled open the cabinets and peered inside. "There's no exit here. He can't walk through walls."

She blew out a breath of frustration and slid over to peer inside the cabinets. As she moved, her left foot banged into something small and hard and she stumbled into Tyler. He reached out to steady her, but she caught her balance and took a step back to flip up the end of the rug.

"Holy crap," she said as she stared at the iron ring secured to the wooden floor.

Tyler pulled the rug from the floor and tossed it in the dining room. The clear outline of a trapdoor stared back at them. He reached for the ring and pulled the trapdoor up, exposing a narrow set of wooden steps that led straight down. Joelle hurried into the kitchen to snag a flashlight, and he shone it down the stairs.

Joelle peered down into the dark hole, thinking it was the last place she wanted to go. "I guess we have to go down there, right?"

Tyler grabbed the lantern from the kitchen and lit it, then handed Joelle the flashlight. "I'll go down first with the lantern. Wait until I tell you to come down. If the steps are rotted…"

He didn't finish but she understood the score. She needed to remain up top in case a call for an ambulance was required. She leaned over, watching as Tyler slowly descended the narrow stairs.

"The stairs are good," he called out when he got to the bottom. "Just be careful. They're narrow."

Joelle tucked the flashlight in her back pocket and, taking a deep breath, stepped down. She clutched the ridges of the trapdoor until she got low enough to grab the railing, then ducked under the edge of the floor. The railing stopped halfway down and Tyler reached up to offer his arm. She held his arm with her right hand, just to keep herself steady, and negotiated the rest of the stairs.

When she got to the bottom, she looked around, somewhat surprised at the size of the room. It was probably twenty feet square with a dirt bottom. At some point, an attempt had been made to finish out the dirt walls, but it wasn't complete. Two walls were covered in paneling, but the other two only contained two-by-four framing.

"I didn't think people had basements in this area. Isn't it below sea level?"

He nodded. "It's not common, that's for sure. But I don't think this is a basement—I mean, not like what you and I know as basements."

She frowned. "It's under the house and surrounded with dirt. What else could it be?"

"A root cellar. The house is over a hundred years old."

Suddenly Joelle understood. "And they didn't have refrigeration then, so they stored perishables underground. That's why the entrance is in the butler's pantry."

Tyler walked slowly around the room, taking in every square inch. When he got back around to Joelle, he shook his head.

"I don't see why anyone would come down here now. It's empty except for that stack of unused lumber."

"Maybe someone used it as a hiding place. I bet you could hear everything said in the kitchen from down here."

"I guess it's possible he could have held the edge of the rug when he pulled the door down. Then no one would have seen it if they passed through here. Still, it's a big risk. There's nowhere to hide if anyone came down here."

"Desperate people do desperate things," she said. "I see it all the time."

Tyler studied her for a moment, then nodded. "I guess you do. Well, there's nothing else to see here, so let's get back upstairs."

Joelle started up the stairs, disappointed that yet another promising lead had turned into nothing. Short of the intruder dropping down a chimney like Santa Claus, she had no clue how he was getting inside the house. She knew Tyler wouldn't stop looking until he found the answer, but what could happen in the meantime? What if someone shot at her through the walls as they had Alaina? What if she couldn't scramble and get away as fast as her marathon-running sister had? Joelle was in good shape, but she definitely wasn't a sprinter.

As she stepped into the kitchen, she felt her cell

phone vibrate in her jeans pocket. Hoping it was Alaina or Danae, she pulled it out, then frowned.

"What's wrong?" Tyler asked.

"Unknown number."

"Answer it," he said and stepped close to her. When she put the phone to her ear, he leaned in so that he could hear.

"Hello," she said.

At first, there was only silence, then they could hear someone breathing. Finally, the phone beeped and she looked at the display.

"The call dropped," she said.

"Or he disconnected. It could have been a wrong number."

Joelle nodded, but something told her it wasn't a wrong number. Something about the breathing had hit a nerve, and somehow she knew it wasn't as simple as a wrong number.

Then the phone vibrated again.

"It's a text," she said and pressed the button to open.

Return what's mine, or maybe I'll take something of yours.

She sucked in a breath so hard it made her dizzy. Tyler put his hands on her shoulders to steady her and looked down at the phone.

"There's something attached to the text," he said.

She blinked twice to clear her vision, then accessed the attachment. As soon as the first picture came into view, she gasped. It was a picture of Danae walking down the sidewalk in front of Zach's condo in New Orleans. She scrolled to the next picture, then the next, her heart pounding harder in her chest with every image—

picture after picture of Danae in New Orleans. Then the images shifted to Alaina, and Tyler cursed.

"That's in Calais," he said.

In a daze, Joelle scrolled through the pictures of Alaina entering the general store, getting in her car at Carter's house and walking into the café. When she got to the last image, she dropped the phone.

"No!" she cried.

It was a picture of her, Alaina and Willamina, sitting on Willamina's back patio.

Unable to stand the stress any longer, she burst into tears. Tyler immediately wrapped his arms around her and pulled her to his chest, hugging her tightly. She clutched him, feeling as if she were drowning, and sobbed as she'd never done before.

Tyler stroked her hair and whispered, "It's going to be all right."

Finally, she slumped against him, her body spent. She stayed there for a while, relishing the comfort of his strong arms around her, until she mustered the strength to regain control. Then she looked up at him. "I'm sorry," she said.

"Don't you dare apologize. Anyone in your position would be upset. I'm a half step away from losing it myself."

His expression was a mixture of sympathy, worry and frustration, and Joelle's heart leaped at this man's honor and heart. He may not have wanted this job, but he would risk anything to protect her and her family. In all her life, she'd never met anyone like him, and she doubted she ever would again.

He looked down at her and lifted one hand to wipe a tear from her cheek. "He will not hurt you or your sisters. I won't let that happen."

"I know," she said and believed every word.

He stared at her a moment more and his expression shifted from frustration to something else…something she hadn't seen before. A shiver of excitement ran through her as she realized he was going to kiss her. Before he even lowered his head, her lips were already tingling, waiting for his touch.

When his lips brushed hers, her knees went weak and she had to lock them in place. She slid her arms around him, the feel of his strong back beneath her fingers sending a thrill through her already-stimulated body. He deepened the kiss, and a rush of heat passed over her as she prayed that this was only the beginning.

"Anyone home?" Carter's voice boomed from the entry.

Immediately, Tyler broke off their kiss and released her, then rushed out of the kitchen without so much as a backward glance. Joelle stared after him, not sure whether to be angry that he could switch gears so quickly or angry at Carter for interrupting something that could have gotten very interesting.

What she knew for certain was that a little taste of Tyler Duhon was not nearly enough.

Chapter Thirteen

Tyler strode away from the kitchen wondering what the hell he was thinking. Strike that. He knew exactly what he'd been thinking, but couldn't believe he'd allowed such a slip in self-control. The last thing he ever intended to do was hook up with a woman with a dangerous job, much less a client. He'd done it before and it had ended tragically. He wasn't about to risk that again.

Joelle was beautiful, intelligent and built like a pinup girl—which was exactly his type—and if she'd been an accountant and not his client, then he would have told Carter to come back in a couple of hours. But reality painted an entirely different picture and right now, he was thankful his friend had interrupted before he carried things too far.

"I'm glad you're here," Tyler said. "Joelle just got a call and texts that you need to see."

"From Brant?"

"It has to be." Tyler waved him toward the kitchen.

As he stepped inside, his gaze went immediately to Joelle. She stood in front of the refrigerator, drinking a bottled water, and a tiny blush crept up her face as he walked up to her.

"Hi, Carter," she said.

Tyler felt a pull of sympathy as she tried to force a smile, but didn't quite achieve it.

"Show him the texts," Tyler instructed.

She passed Carter the phone and they both watched as Carter scrolled through the feed. His jaw clenched tighter with every new image until Tyler wondered if his teeth would break. When he got to the last image, he cursed and placed the phone on the kitchen counter.

Tyler watched as Carter paced the length of the kitchen twice but wisely kept silent while his friend worked out his personal—and completely justified—anger.

Finally, Carter stopped pacing and ran one hand through his hair. "How is it that he's gotten all these photos in Calais and not a single person has seen him? I have every business owner and trustworthy person in town on the lookout. None of them have seen him."

He picked up the phone and scrolled to the picture of Alaina entering Johnny's Café. "These were taken on Main Street. How could he get close enough to take these pictures and yet no one saw him?"

"Maybe sitting in a vehicle with tinted windows?" Tyler suggested. "He could be farther away than we think and using a telephoto lens."

Carter scrolled to the picture taken at Willamina's house. "This one was taken from the property line, not thirty yards from where you were sitting. He could have easily picked you off with a rifle from that location."

"I don't think he wants to kill me," Joelle said. "If I'm dead, I can't tell him what he wants."

"No," Tyler said, "but he could kill one of your sisters to make you talk."

Carter blew out a breath and Tyler knew his friend had already gotten to that possibility.

Joelle's eyes widened and her jaw dropped. "I don't know why I'm surprised. I know he's capable of hurting someone, but I hoped the pictures were just to scare me."

"And they may be," Carter said, "but we can't assume that."

"Just out of curiosity," Tyler said, "but do you even know where Brant's wife is?"

Joelle shook her head. "It's one of the ways we protect the women. I deliver her to another person who delivers her to someone else. I have no idea how many hands she passes through before she arrives at a safe house. It's set up that way to protect the victims."

"And clearly it does," Tyler said, "but it doesn't do much for the volunteers. Have you ever had something like this happen before?"

"Nothing like this. We've had husbands show up at the center where I work yelling threats, and a couple of them have grabbed me, but nothing ever escalated beyond that. Usually when the police get involved, they back off."

"Either Brant is supremely arrogant to think he won't get caught or he's not sane. This definitely escalated beyond simple threats."

Joelle's eyes filled with tears. "This is all my fault. I brought that monster to Calais and put my sisters in danger." Suddenly, she straightened up. "I'll leave. That will get Alaina and Danae out of danger."

"No." Tyler issued the directive without even thinking.

"Tyler's right," Carter said. "It wouldn't change anything. Brant is already aware of your sisters. He would still use them to get to you no matter where you go.

What I don't understand is how he found out about them so quickly."

"He's smart," Joelle said. "Scary smart, and he has a whole fleet of private investigators at his fingertips. His wife showed us some of his records. He pays them a fortune and they'll do anything for him."

"It wouldn't be that hard to find out information about the estate," Tyler said. "Not if someone was looking."

Carter sighed. "No, probably not. So the question is, what can we do to protect them?"

"Yep," Tyler said, "and I'm up for any and all suggestions you have."

"Any luck on finding out how he's getting in the house?"

Tyler frowned. "No, and even worse, he knew the cameras were there. Gave me the one-finger wave when he went under the one in the entry."

Carter slammed his hand on the counter. "He's always one step ahead of us. Over two months I've been investigating and I'm no closer to knowing how now than I was then."

"That's not true," Tyler disagreed. "You've found out that Purcell was paying people for his dirty work, and you've already identified two of the Calais residents who were part of it. Granted, they're both dead, but two months ago, you didn't even know who Purcell really was, what he was up to and that anyone from Calais was involved."

"And despite two dead, I have to assume someone else from Calais is still in the thick of it," Carter said. "Someone knows their way around this house entirely too well."

"I've been over every room in here—both floors—

and checked the windows and for any exterior passage-
way. They're all secure. With all the clutter, he could
easily hide once inside, but I still have no idea how he's
getting in."

"What about the attic?" Joelle asked. "Is there any
way he could get in through the roof?"

Tyler shook his head. "I checked it first thing. The
attic stairwell is at the end of the hall on the second
floor above the laundry room, but I padlocked the door
to it that day. No one is getting through there unless
they can walk through walls."

"It almost seems like he can," Carter said.

"Do you want to take another look at everything?"
Tyler asked. "Maybe if we go over it together, we'll
think of something we haven't individually."

Carter threw his hands up in the air. "I'm willing
to try anything. First, I want to call Alaina and Danae
and give them a heads-up, and I'll need to borrow your
phone, Joelle, so that I can forward this information to
the Jackson police."

"Of course," Joelle said.

"Give me a minute," Carter said and stalked off to-
ward the front of the house.

"What do you want me to do?" Joelle asked.

Tyler looked at her, then immediately shifted his gaze
out the patio windows. With the taste of her cherry lip
gloss still lingering on his lips, the question was one he
couldn't answer honestly, especially as he didn't want
to be honest with himself. Finally, he looked back at
her, trying to keep his thoughts on his job, where they
belonged.

"I don't know. I mean, I guess do whatever you
would have done otherwise—just carrying your pistol."

She sighed. "The real irony is I came here thinking

I would avoid having to carry my pistol around inside my own house."

His heart ached for her, but he was glad Carter was just down the hall. If they were alone, he'd put his arms around her to comfort her, and he had a really good idea where that would go.

"We're going to figure this out."

She nodded, but he could tell she wasn't convinced. "I'm going to start sorting stuff in the downstairs rooms. I've spent a little time picking through it, but I need to start separating the good stuff from the garbage."

"I figure we'll start outside, so keep the doors locked and your phone on you as well as the pistol. I'm going to see if Carter is ready."

It took every ounce of control he had to leave her in the kitchen. It bothered him to see such a normally strong woman at the point of breaking, and it made him angry that evil men had put her in this position. He would figure out what was going on at the estate.

But he wasn't about to audition for the role of white knight. Not again.

HE WATCHED FROM his hiding place at the edge of the swamp. He'd seen the man and woman come out of the butler's pantry and made his call when he had a clear view of her through the kitchen patio windows. He wanted to see her response—her fear. He needed to remind her what he was capable of. She thought she already knew, but she had no idea. His bitch of a wife had no idea, but she would.

They both would, very soon.

JOELLE WATCHED AS Carter and Tyler exited the front door, and she locked it behind them. She checked her

pistol for the third time that morning and slipped it into her waistband. Her cell phone was already tucked into her jeans pocket, so she headed into one of the back rooms to start digging through the stacks.

She'd already assembled some cardboard boxes that William had delivered and set them in the entry in different sections—keepsakes, donation, potential valuables and trash. She'd spent some time poking through stuff the previous days, but there was no way she could keep track of everything unless she started organizing it.

The first room she went in had a stack of boxes against the far wall and a chest of drawers against another wall. The closet looked as if it was going to spit its contents out onto the floor—assuming it could find a bit of open floor space.

She opened the first box and a flurry of dust flew up in her face. Coughing, she took a couple steps back and leaned against the wall. Who was she fooling? Her head wasn't in this. And despite her fear of Brant and absolute conviction that he was capable of hurting her or her sisters, her mind wasn't dwelling on him, either.

It was stuck on Tyler's kiss.

From the look on his face, she'd known it was coming, so it wasn't surprising on a momentary level. But now, after the fact, she was surprised that he'd ever gotten around to such a thing. At first, she'd thought Tyler didn't like her in the least, despite the fact that he didn't even know her. She could tell he resented her presence.

After talking to his father, she realized that his issues were internal, and he would have felt the same about anyone in her position. So it definitely wasn't personal, but it was still hard not to take his brusque attitude that way. Then when things intensified, he'd dropped the

aggravated attitude and stepped instantly into professional mode, surprising her with an occasional bout of personal interaction. But even then, she was still well aware of the emotional wall he'd erected.

William thought Tyler had seen so many atrocities overseas that he needed time to decompress and work through them, and she was certain William was right. Given Tyler's specialty and the length of his time spent in a war zone, a certain level of PTSD should be expected.

But she'd always gotten the feeling that it was somehow more personal than that. That the wall he'd erected was specific to her, and not in place with his father or Carter. Maybe now, she knew the reason why. Clearly, Tyler was attracted to her. She hadn't mistaken his expression when he kissed her, but she'd understood his expression when Carter interrupted them, as well.

She wasn't surprised at the kiss, but he was.

He'd lost control—let down that wall for just a second and allowed her in, and that scared him so much that he'd fled when Carter interrupted. Seconds later, the wall was back in place, strong as ever and just as impenetrable.

Sighing, she pushed herself off the wall. She had no business dwelling on Tyler and his love life. He'd already made it clear that he didn't want to become involved and, realistically, it wasn't a good idea for her either. When all this was over, they would sell off the estate, dole out the money, and the sisters would continue the lives they'd already started. Now those lives would include one another, but Joelle didn't think for a moment that any of them were going to change directions simply because they'd found one another or become wealthy. All the money did was allow them to

easily pursue things they'd always been working toward anyway.

And Tyler Duhon was not one of the things she'd been working toward.

Her mind said it; now, if only her body and heart would comply. Despite the standoffish attitude that was in place most of the time, Joelle was drawn to him in a way she never had been to another man, not even Brad. Tyler was an alpha male in every way, but she knew that beneath that bravado lay a kindness and empathy that made him even more attractive. She'd seen that side of him peek out a couple of times and knew that Tyler was so much deeper than the layers of absolutely perfect muscle that physically defined him.

When it came to the possibility of relationships, Tyler may as well be another ghost in the house—showing himself just enough to give her a taste of what he had to offer, but not sticking around long enough for her to touch something solid. Likely, he would remain that way the entire two weeks, then she would leave, and they would have polite exchanges when they happened to run into each other after that.

Depressing, but probably accurate.

Sighing, she reached into the box to lift out a stack of clothes, and then she heard the sound of glass breaking. Instantly, she froze, trying to figure out where the noise had originated. It sounded like it came from the direction of the kitchen.

She stepped out into the entry and listened again, but only silence surrounded her. Maybe Carter and Tyler came in the patio door and dropped something. She pulled her cell phone from her pocket, then swore. The one bar of signal that had been present earlier was gone.

She removed her pistol from her waistband and

headed for the kitchen, creeping down the hallway, both hands clutching the pistol in front of her. She stopped right before the entryway to the kitchen and listened again, but no sound came from the room. Maybe she'd been wrong. Maybe the noise hadn't come from this direction at all.

She inched around the wall and peered into the kitchen, but it was empty. Shaking her head, she stepped around the corner, chastising herself for creating a fright when there was no reason for one.

That's when he grabbed her.

He'd been standing against the wall right next to the door just out of her field of vision when she'd peered inside—in a perfect position to grab her arms and shake the pistol loose. She screamed as the pistol fell from her hands and slid across the stone floor.

He yanked her around to face him and she stared right into the face of the devil—Victor Brant. One look at the .44 Magnum he held to her head and the smile on his face, and her fear turned to terror. This was it. She was going to die in this house at the hands of a male abuser.

Just like her mother.

"Where is she?" he asked.

The calm politeness in his voice made her blood run cold. He wasn't human. At least, not in any of the good ways humans ought to be.

"I don't know where she is," she said.

His fingers dug into her arm and she winced. "Liar!"

Her heart pounded so hard in her chest that she thought it would break, but a sliver of anger replaced some of her fear. "I'm sure your flunkies looked into it. You know how this works. I passed her off. I don't know where she is."

His lips thinned and he narrowed his eyes at her. "You can find out. And you will."

Before she could reply, he pulled her into the butler's pantry.

"Open the trapdoor," he said.

She hesitated, trying to scramble for an escape plan.

He shoved the barrel of the gun into the back of her head so hard that her scalp ached. "Don't play dumb with me. I saw you go into the cellar with that man you're shacked up with. Had a real clear view through the patio windows."

She leaned over and pulled open the trapdoor.

"Get inside, and don't even think about fighting or I'll shoot you right here, then go after your sisters."

Everything she'd been taught told her to fight with her attacker and at least you leave a body that can be found—but what had her creeping down the stairs and into the cellar was her sisters. Brant was probably going to kill her, but maybe she could stall long enough for her sisters to get to safety. Carter had called them earlier to warn them. Surely, they were working out every possible precaution.

When they got to the bottom, Brant motioned her toward the tiny space under the stairs. "Get in there," he said.

She stepped in the cubby under the stairs, not even able to stand upright because of the low support beams, and looked back at Brant, her mind whirling with possibilities. What in the world was he going to do? If he killed her down here, it might take a long time for Tyler and Carter to find the body, and they would definitely go looking for her when they came inside and found her missing.

She cursed herself for her stupidity. The longer they

spent looking for her, the more time it gave Brant to go after Alaina and Danae. When she'd come into the cellar, she'd thought she was buying her sisters time, but she'd forgotten that she was buying Brant time, as well.

Now she crouched there, waiting for the shot that would end it all—would destroy so many lives—but instead, he picked up a piece of plywood and propped it and covered the opening to the cubby. With only a tiny bit of light streaming into the cellar from the butler's pantry, the cellar was already dim. But with the plywood covering the cubby, she was pitched into total darkness.

Chapter Fourteen

A wave of dizziness passed over Joelle as she heard Brant hammering the first nail into the plywood, and she struggled to keep from passing out. It wasn't a lack of air, as the steps and the opening had plenty of cracks, even with the plywood in place. It was fear. She took a deep breath and slowly blew it out, trying to keep herself from dwelling on the fact that he planned to leave her here, boarded up in this empty cellar.

Think! There has to be something you can do about it.

But what? Given her black belt, she could definitely kick and normally, the half-rotted piece of plywood in front of her wouldn't have taken her seconds to plow through, but crammed into a space where she couldn't even extend her legs made it impossible.

The hammering went on for what seemed an eternity, but finally, it stopped and she heard Brant breathing on the other side of the sealed opening.

"Give me what's mine," he said. "Or the next body I board up won't be breathing and it won't be yours. I'll give you some time to think about it."

A second later, she heard his footsteps above her, and then the trapdoor slammed shut. Panic coursed through her. For all intents and purposes, she'd been

buried alive. The urge to scream was overwhelming, but she managed to choke it back. It would just use more air and energy, and she was too light-headed. Besides, she needed to save her strength to get out before Brant could get to Alaina and Danae.

She turned sideways and placed her shoulder against the plywood, then leaned away from it as far as possible and slammed her shoulder into the wood. Pain shot through her arm and up her neck, but the plywood didn't budge. She took a deep breath and tried again. The wood bent out a bit, but she didn't hear a single splinter. Nerves in her shoulder set off, sending shock waves that felt like fire shooting down her arm. Involuntarily, she grabbed her arm and squeezed it, trying to stop the pain from moving farther down, but it moved right past her grip and into her hand.

Brant had secured the plywood well. Too well. And she couldn't get her leg in place for a good kick without risking breaking her ankle or foot.

He'd won.

He'd closed her off from her protectors, both of whom were here with her instead of protecting her sisters. And that was the part that bothered her the most.

She slumped against the wall and slid down until she collapsed on the dirt floor. There was nothing left to do now but cry.

TYLER OPENED THE front door and punched in a code for the alarm. He and Carter had spent almost an hour inspecting every square inch of the outside of the house—banging on it with hammers, poking at it with pry bars—and digging through the brush surrounding the house for signs of passage. They'd come up with exactly nothing.

"You want something to drink?" Tyler asked.

"I'd love a whole bottle of scotch or a case of beer," Carter replied, "but that won't help us find answers. I'll settle for water or soda, if you've got it."

"I'm out of ideas as to how else he'd get in," Tyler said. "Unless he's living inside the house and never left, I've got nothing."

"Yeah. I do think someone was in here while Danae was working in the house. They had to have overheard conversations we had in order to make the moves they did. But I always assumed the front door was the weak link. You've eliminated that possibility with the alarm."

"We're missing something," Tyler said as he stepped into the kitchen. His shoes crunched on something and he stopped, staring down at the broken glass that littered the floor.

"Where's Joelle?" Tyler asked, his pulse ticking up a notch. "Did you see her in the entry when we came in?"

Carter frowned. "No, and I didn't hear her either, which is strange. You'd think she would have come out to talk to us when she heard you turning off the alarm."

"Joelle!" Tyler yelled, trying to keep from panicking. "Something's wrong. No way Joelle would leave broken glass all over the floor."

"Maybe she cut her hand and went upstairs to clean it off," Carter suggested.

Desperate to cling to any normal and safe explanation, Tyler nodded, even though it didn't feel right. "I'll check," he said and dashed into the servants' staircase in the kitchen.

Taking the stairs two at a time, he prayed that Joelle was upstairs, wrapping a bandage around her finger. He burst out into the upstairs hallway and yelled Joelle's name again before looking in her bedroom. Empty. He

ran to the hallway bathroom as Carter stepped out of the stairwell.

"It's empty," he said to Carter, panic now setting in full force.

Carter immediately sized up the situation. "Whatever went down started in the kitchen. Let's go back there and figure out where to start looking."

Tyler nodded and ran back downstairs. People didn't disappear without a trace. They would find something to help them track Joelle.

If it wasn't too late.

Tyler pushed that thought from his mind. He had to focus on the mission. He couldn't afford to start thinking of the potential costs. Or casualties. He rushed into the kitchen and this time went around the counter to avoid stepping in the glass. Carter was right behind him.

At the edge of the counter, Tyler bent over and picked through the glass. "The bottom of the glass is here, which is probably where it broke. It scattered evenly in all directions, so it was probably dropped rather than thrown."

"I agree," Carter said. "Was any of the glass tracked outside of the splatter?"

"Yeah, toward the servants' staircase, but that could have been me."

"Nothing else? Joelle is wearing tennis shoes. They wouldn't pick up the glass like our boots."

Tyler leaned farther over until his face was only inches from the floor, looking for even a glint of light reflecting off of glass. His heart fell as he covered foot after foot of the stone floor without a single spec of glass. Then something caught his eye—a tiny shard several feet away.

"That way," he said, pointing toward the breakfast

nook. "Only a single piece but well outside of the range it would have scattered from the drop."

Tyler walked to where the shard lay and checked again, but this time, he couldn't locate another piece of glass. "Nothing else," he said and glanced across the breakfast nook.

"Wait!" He jumped up and hurried over to the dark object underneath the table. His heart leaped into his throat as he reached under the table and drew out Joelle's pistol. He held the gun up to Carter, whose eye's widened.

"Damn it!" Carter said and stepped over to the patio door. "It's open, and the storm's moving in. We won't have light for much longer."

"Start trying to find tracks," Tyler said. "I'll grab some flashlights."

Tyler ran to the butler's pantry where they'd left the flashlights earlier. He grabbed them from the counter, but when he turned to leave, his boot hung on the rug. Drawing up short, he stared down at the ugly, rumpled rug, certain he'd left it flat and even.

He looked out the patio windows where Carter was disappearing into the brush just off the kitchen. He should be out there, but something kept him from moving. It would only take a minute to make sure no one was down there.

Before he could change his mind, he yanked open the door and ran down the stairs, shining his flashlight across the black room. Nothing. Disappointed, he turned to leave and his light flashed across the stairs. He froze, certain that piece of plywood had not been nailed up there before.

"Joelle," he called out.

"Tyler!" Joelle cried out as she started banging on the plywood. "Get me out of here!"

The sheer panic in her voice launched his anger into the stratosphere. He dropped the flashlight and grabbed a pry bar from the tools in the corner, attacking the plywood with everything he had. It only took two pushes before the plywood splintered and popped off the framing.

He threw the plywood on the floor and reached out as Joelle leaped into his arms. Her entire body was shaking and he worried that she would go into shock.

"Are you hurt?" he asked.

"No," she whispered between sobs.

He held her tightly, overwhelmed with relief that she was safe, mixed with insurmountable anger at what Brant had done to her.

"Let's get out of here," he said when the sobs finally wound down a bit. "Carter went outside looking for you."

She sniffed but allowed him to pull back from her. Her face was puffy and her eyes bloodshot, but she didn't appear to have any physical injuries. Tyler knew, though, that the emotional ones were harder to overcome.

"Can you walk?" he asked.

She nodded.

"You go first. I'll be right behind you." He fell in step close behind her. She was a little shaky walking up the stairs, but he was right there if she started to fall.

She crawled out of the trapdoor and slumped onto the pantry floor. He climbed out and reached down to help her into the kitchen, where he sat her in a chair. The clean laundry still sat folded at the end of the break-

fast table, and he grabbed a blanket and wrapped it around her.

"I don't want you to go into shock," he said. "Keep this wrapped around you."

He pulled her pistol from his waistband and placed it on the table in front of her. Gripping her shoulders with both hands, he leaned over and looked her straight in the eyes. "I've got to go outside and get Carter."

"Hurry," she whispered.

He ran outside and down to the end of the patio where he'd seen Carter enter the swamp, yelling out his name. A couple seconds later, he heard someone running through the foliage, then Carter burst through a drapery of vines and skidded to a stop on the patio.

"Inside," Tyler said and hurried back inside, Carter right on his heels.

Tyler locked the patio door behind them and gave Carter a rundown of how he'd found Joelle. Carter knelt beside her and took her hand in his.

"Are you all right?"

"Yes, but you have to go!" Joelle straightened up in her chair and Tyler could practically feel the tension rolling off of her. "It was Brant. He said he'd go after Alaina and Danae. You have to protect them."

Carter pulled out his cell phone and cursed when he saw there was no signal.

"Go," Tyler said. "I'm going to get Joelle to Doc Broussard. If the cell phones don't work in town, I'll call dispatch from Doc's office and arrange a place to meet up."

Carter was already halfway across the kitchen before Tyler even finished speaking.

"I don't need the doctor," Joelle said.

"That's not your call to make, it's mine. I know you

have a lot of experience with crisis, but you're usually on the other side of the desk, so no arguing. Besides, do you have any idea what my dad would do to me if I didn't get you medical attention?"

Although it was the truth, he'd said it to make her smile, and he gave her credit for the effort. He extended his hand down to her and helped her up from the chair. She was still a bit unsteady, but she no longer shivered, which was a good sign.

"Do you have service yet?" Joelle asked as they exited the house.

He checked his cell phone display. "No, but I promise I'll check in with everyone when we get to Doc Broussard's."

Joelle nodded and wrapped her arms across her chest. She seemed steadier, but she was so pale, and although Tyler wanted to make sure nothing was physically wrong with her, he was more worried about her mental health.

No matter what, they had a long night ahead of them.

Chapter Fifteen

Carter paced from one end of the sheriff's department office to the other so many times, he thought he'd wear a hole in the old carpet. Alaina perched on the end of the lobby couch, exchanging glances with Thelma, the gray-headed dispatcher.

"What?" he asked on his tenth pass, as Alaina looked at him, eyebrows raised.

"We're just wondering whether to get you a drink or extra bullets, or perhaps call for new flooring."

He threw his arms up in the air. "Hell if I know. I've never been at such a loss. I'd tell all of you to get out of here and go to Mexico, but Brant won't stop there. He'd just move on to me or Zach or Tyler or even worse, William or my mother."

"You think it's that bad?" Alaina asked.

"He dragged Joelle into the cellar and boarded her into a wall while Tyler and I were right outside. A cellar with one exit, and he took the time to nail plywood in place. We could have walked in at any minute and he'd have been trapped down there. That's not sane."

"No, it's not," Alaina agreed. "But what do we do? I'll bet I've been through every possible solution you have, including having all of us move in to that blasted house until this is over."

"He'd just launch a stick of dynamite through a window and get us all."

She sighed. "I got around to that, too. Face it, Carter, the best thing we can do is what we're already doing. Stay put and stay aware. Did you find how Brant got in the house?"

"I didn't even take the time to look. I was too worried about getting word to you and Danae and I had no signal, as usual."

"The caretaker's cabin and the rental cabin are still uninhabitable, right?"

"Yeah. Zach hasn't had time to address them at all, and his crew can only get so much work done over the weekend. With all the problems at the main house, I don't think they've done anything on the cabins."

"So Joelle has to stay in the main house or leave and start her two weeks again some other time. Maybe that's what needs to happen. Maybe she needs to get out of Calais long enough for you to find the entry point."

"No," Joelle's voice sounded in the doorway and Carter whipped around as Alaina jumped up from the couch and rushed over to hug her sister.

"Sit," Alaina insisted and guided Joelle to the couch. "What did Doc Broussard say?"

"He says I'm lucky," Joelle said, her voice breaking a bit. "I was in a bit of shock when I got there, but he gave me a shot of something and a bottle of something else."

Alaina nodded. "Antianxiety meds, probably. Don't be afraid to take them. You, of all people, know how difficult this is going to be for you to process. Promise me, you will take your own advice when it comes to taking care of yourself."

Joelle's eyes misted up and she leaned over to hug Alaina. "I promise," she said as she released her.

Alaina leaned back and narrowed her eyes. "What's wrong with your shoulder? You're holding your arm funny."

"I tried to break down the plywood. It's not dislocated or anything but Doc Broussard said it's going to be black and blue by tomorrow. It's pretty sore."

Alaina rose from the couch and grabbed her purse from the dispatcher's desk. "You guys catch up on everything. I'm going to run to the general store and pick up an ice pack and a heating pad. You'll need both. I'll be back in a sec."

"Alaina," Carter said, and she paused in the doorway. "Be careful."

She gave him a single nod before hurrying outside.

"So what's the plan?" Tyler asked.

Carter shook his head. "I've alerted the Jackson police and the state police, but neither of them have the manpower to send backup—at least, not until next week. So we're on our own until then. If you want to leave—"

"I don't," Joelle interrupted. "Location is irrelevant. I'd rather stay where I'm surrounded by people who care about me."

"Good," Carter said. "I wish there were other options for living quarters, but if you want to meet the inheritance requirements, you're going to have to stay in the main house. After that last storm blew through, neither of the cabins is fit for living."

"Don't worry," Tyler said. "I have some ideas about securing the house, at least at night. And from this point forward, Joelle will not be leaving my sight."

"I have to shower," Joelle said with a small smile.

"Then I'll be standing outside the bathroom door with my pistol…or two."

"And my first day here, you said it wouldn't come to that."

Carter smiled. "Think you can put that 24/7 guard plan on hold for thirty minutes or so?"

"Why?"

"I'd like to have another chat with Bert Thibodeaux. I still think he knows more than he's telling me, and maybe if we explain that assault and kidnapping could be part of the deal, he'll give something up."

"And why do you want me there?"

"A second set of eyes. I've missed the boat so many times on this mess that I'm starting to second-guess myself."

Tyler looked over at Joelle, the hesitation on his face clear as day.

"Go," Joelle urged. "I'll be fine. I'm sitting in the sheriff's office in broad daylight. I couldn't get safer if I tried."

He studied her a couple seconds more, then Thelma stood up behind the dispatcher's desk and pumped a sawed-off 12-gauge.

"Don't worry," she said with a broad smile. "I got you covered."

"Is that even legal?" Tyler asked.

Carter patted him on the back. "I didn't see a thing."

TYLER WAS LOST in thought on the drive to Bert's place, trying to put together all the pieces and at the same time, formulate a plan to ensure that Brant—or anyone else—didn't get to Joelle. It was all jumbled together in his mind, and every avenue of thought he started down led to a dead end or more questions.

Finally, he sighed and looked over at Carter. "I un-

derstand why you've been so frustrated over all of this. I mean, I thought I understood before, but now..."

Carter nodded. "In all my years as a detective in New Orleans, I never had a case with so many moving pieces, and so many hidden ones. And never a crime that stretched back twenty-five years, implicating people along the way."

Tyler shook his head. "It's impossible to determine what's happening because of Brant and what's happening because of Purcell."

"It's always been that way. With Alaina, at first, I thought everything was about the estate, and I was wrong. With Danae, at first, I thought she might have brought trouble with her, and I was wrong. Now I'm sure it's both, but it doesn't put me any closer to catching Brant or exposing the rest of Purcell's crew, much less their intentions."

"And you think Bert is part of Purcell's crew?"

"I know he was insofar as he was one of Purcell's errand boys. He picked up the valuables Purcell bought with estate funds, then hauled them back to New Orleans for sale. Purcell promised him a new rig when he died, but Bert got screwed on that like everyone else Purcell made promises to. Bert tries to claim ignorance on anything beyond his trucking service, but I've always thought he was lying. He thinks Purcell owes him, and he's definitely capable of trying to collect after the fact."

"So you think he knows something, but the question is, what? And is it relevant to anything else we're worried about?"

"Exactly."

Carter pulled his truck up in front of Bert's cabin and

parked it behind the man's semi. "His pickup truck's here," Carter said. "That's a good sign."

They walked to the front door and Carter pounded on it a few times. "Open up, Bert. It's Sheriff Trahan."

Nothing stirred inside and Carter frowned. "Look in that window and see if you see anything."

Tyler walked over to one of the front windows and attempted to peer inside. The dirt and grime cut the field of vision, but he got a decent view of the man's living room. "Looks like a pigsty."

"Yeah, I got a peek around last time I talked to him. He's not winning any awards for housekeeping."

"There's a red lace bra hanging from a lamp." He straightened up and shook his head. "Some women really have no taste at all."

Carter laughed. "Clearly."

"Maybe he's fishing," Tyler said. "That pier doesn't look in much better shape than his house, but it's probably good enough for a boat launch."

"Yes, probably so," Carter said and pounded on the door one last time. Finally, he sighed. "I'll try again later."

As they turned to walk away, the door flew open and Bert glared at them.

"Waking me up is getting to be a habit with you, Sheriff," Bert said, his scorn clear when he said the word *sheriff.*

Carter gave him a fake smile. "I don't want to be here any more than you want me here."

"Then why don't you do us both a favor and stop coming." He started to close the door, but Carter put his hand on the door to stop him.

"It's not that easy, Bert. I got problems in Calais, and I think you know something about them."

Bert crossed his arms over his chest and smirked. "That right. Let me guess, you got another rich bitch on your hands whining about keeping her and her money safe."

A rush of anger passed through Tyler and he itched to punch the man right in his smug jaw.

"What I've got," Carter said, "is a stalker, a kidnapper and someone who breaks into houses and assaults women."

"Sounds like a real problem. Maybe you should stop hassling me and do something about it."

"I am doing something about it. Any of those descriptions fit you?"

Something flickered in Bert's eyes, but it was gone as quickly as it appeared. Bert dropped his hands. "Look, I already told you all I did for Purcell was cart stuff up and down the highway to New Orleans. I don't know nothing about kidnappings and beating up on women, especially rich bitches."

"Who says the assault was on a rich woman?"

"Please. Everyone in Calais knows the sheriff's department works for the LeBeau sisters."

Tyler glanced at Bert's shack. "A woman with money might come in handy."

"Yeah," Bert said. "That worked out well for Purcell. Don't worry about me. I make my own money."

"Like Roger and Jack?" Carter asked. "Making money the Purcell way got them killed. If you know anything about that, you need to tell me now."

Bert sneered. "You afraid I'm in danger, Sheriff?"

"Maybe."

"Well, don't worry your pretty little head about it. I can take care of myself."

He stepped back and slammed the door.

"I see what you mean," Tyler said as they climbed into Carter's truck.

"He's hiding something, right?"

"Yeah. I'd bet on it. But we already know Victor Brant, not Bert, attacked Joelle."

Carter nodded. "But did you see his look when I mentioned the assault?"

"It bothered him, but I can't figure why."

Carter sighed. "I can't help thinking if we knew the answer to that question, we'd be halfway to solving all of this."

Tyler looked at Bert's cabin in the passenger's mirror as they drove away and saw curtains on the kitchen window slide back into place. It was clear to Tyler that Bert was nervous about something. He only hoped Carter figured out what it was before someone else wound up dead.

JOELLE PULLED THE T-shirt over her head, wincing as she lifted her right arm up and caught sight of it in the mirror. It was throbbing a little and she could see a light purple shade was already setting in on it. By tomorrow, she had no doubt it'd look like her entire biceps had been caught in a vise.

She pulled her wet hair back with a clip, not about to bother with a blow-dryer, and slipped her feet into flip-flops. When she pulled open the bathroom door, she drew up short for a second, then remembered that the armed man standing outside the door was Tyler.

"Sorry," he said as he caught sight of her. "I didn't mean to startle you."

She waved a hand in dismissal. "I knew you were out here. I don't know why I'm so jumpy."

"Don't you?"

She sighed. "I guess those meds aren't doing much."

"They're doing enough. We don't want you drugged beyond the point of reaction."

The thought of being so out of it she couldn't move and wouldn't even care held a sliver of appeal, but Joelle knew Tyler was right. She had to be able to run or fight or whatever else may be called for.

"What about you?" she asked.

"What do you mean?"

"I assume you'd like to take a shower. How do you intend to do that if you're not letting me out of your sight?"

"I've been thinking about that. I know this will be uncomfortable for you, but I thought I'd put a chair in the bathroom. You can sit with your back to the shower."

She stared. "You want me to sit in the bathroom with you while you shower? Are you going to shower with your gun?"

"No, but there's a shelf at shoulder height right outside the shower. It will be within easy reach."

A million reasons why this was a horrible idea ran through her mind. A million reasons to choose from and all she had to do was select one.

"That's okay," he said. "I'll just wait until tomorrow when Carter can guard you."

Great. Now she felt guilty. Tyler had spent half the day tromping around the swamp, with unseasonably warm temperatures and humidity that made you sweat indoors, much less outside. She wasn't about to send him to bed dirty, itchy and sweaty.

"Fine," she said. "I'll file my nails or something."

"Thanks," he said, and the grateful look he gave her made her feel guilty for hesitating.

He dragged a small chair from one of the bedrooms

into the bathroom, then squeezed by to the shower. "Close the door and lock it," he instructed as he pulled her pistol from his waistband and handed it to her.

She closed and locked the door, then pulled the chair up a bit to allow him more room to undress. The bathroom was tiny, and with the two of them and the chair, the floor space was almost gone. She set her gun on the edge of the sink, next to the chair, and grabbed her makeup bag.

"Ready when you are," she called out as she slid onto the chair, her back to the shower.

The water came on, and then she heard the sound of clothes falling on the tile floor. She pulled her nail file from her makeup bag, trying to force her mind from thinking about Tyler and his perfect chest and back. Then she heard a zipper and knew he'd removed his jeans. She'd bet the entire LeBeau estate that his legs were just as impressive as everything else on him.

Her compact rested at the top of her makeup bag—almost daring her to take it out and open it up. She shoved it to the bottom of the bag, chastising herself for high school thoughts, but couldn't stop the sliver of disappointment she felt at her lack of adventure. Sighing, she began to file her nails.

She was about to spend the entire night in a twin bed not two feet away from the man. The last thing she needed was to go to bed with a clear mental picture of exactly what rested beneath those covers.

When Tyler had told her they would be sharing a room from this point forward, she'd protested, but his argument was sound. The patio off her bedroom was a security risk. It was smarter to move into Tyler's room, which had no patio and only one window with no trees offering access. The problem was, Tyler's room was

tiny—maybe ten by ten—and even though she had a separate bed, they were so close that she may as well be sleeping alongside him.

Still, although she'd never admit it, she did feel safer knowing he would be so close she could reach out and touch him. He'd placed her bed against the wall on the opposite side of the door. If anyone came inside, they'd have to go through Tyler to get to her. Of course, if she wanted to go to the restroom in the middle of the night, she'd have to practically climb over him to get out.

The thought of climbing over Tyler led to a whole other set of images, and she bent her file against her finger and it flicked over her shoulder. She leaned over and felt the floor behind her, still facing the door, and finally, her fingertips touched the edge of the elusive board. She leaned over a tiny bit farther to get her fingers on top of it and realized too late that she'd completely miscalculated her balance.

The chair tipped a tiny bit to the side, then the legs slid across the tile floor, sweeping the chair out from under her.

Chapter Sixteen

Joelle crashed onto the floor, groaning as her left shoulder hit the hard tile. Great, now she'd have two purple arms tomorrow. She could wear a muscle shirt and double as Barney.

In the excitement of the fall, she didn't realize that the shower had shut off, but now the quiet of the bathroom seemed to echo around her. She closed her eyes for a second, wondering what in the world she'd done to deserve this.

Just get up and stand in the corner until he's dressed.

That sounded reasonable, so she opened her eyes, preparing to rise, and a giant foot appeared in front of her.

"Are you all right?"

Tyler's voice sounded above her and she held in another groan. Her mortification hadn't been this high since she'd ripped her gym shorts during square-dancing class in eighth grade.

"I'm fine," she managed.

"Let me help you up."

The "No" was still on the tip of her tongue when his hands slid under her arms and he pulled her straight up to a standing position. She clenched her eyes again,

praying that when she opened them, she would find it had all been a really bad dream.

"You can open your eyes," he said. "I'm wearing a towel."

Definitely not a dream.

She opened one eye and saw him standing directly in front of her, wearing nothing but a towel and a sexy grin.

"If I'd known sitting in the bathroom could be so dangerous, I would have gotten you shoulder pads."

"I dropped my fingernail file," she said, cringing inwardly at how incredibly lame she sounded.

"And the potential of seeing me naked was so horrible that you risked breaking your arm instead?"

"No...I mean...I..." She clamped her mouth shut, unable to fathom any response that didn't implicate her one way or another.

He stepped closer to her and she could feel the heat coming off of his skin. A flush ran through her from head to toe as an overwhelming desire to touch his bare chest came over her. Then he lowered his lips to hers and all apprehension melted away. Lost in his kiss, she ran her hand across his chest, feeling every square inch of his perfectly toned body.

He put his arms around her and pulled her body next to his. That's when she realized his towel had slipped to the floor, and the reality of being pressed against his completely naked body sent a chill through her. Moving his lips from hers, he trailed kisses down her neck and she moaned.

Then without warning, he swept her up in his arms and carried her out of the bathroom and into the bedroom, where he placed her on one of the twin beds. She looked up at him, marveling at his physique. Even the

scars that graced his skin made him more masculine, more attractive.

"Protection?" she asked, praying that he had some.

He nodded and reached into a nightstand for his wallet. While he was otherwise engaged, she shrugged off her T-shirt, yoga pants and undies. Her body trembled as he moved into position over her, lowering his lips to hers again. He entered her in one fluid motion and she gasped, digging her fingernails into the soft skin of his shoulders.

Her body felt as if it were on fire, starting at her center and flaming out through every square inch of her. She clutched his back and moaned as he set the pace. The last thing she could remember thinking before he sent them both over the edge was how much she wished this moment would never end.

THE TINY BED didn't leave much room for two grown adults, but Joelle didn't mind the narrow space one bit. Her body pressed against Tyler's, their hot, bare skin touching from head to toe. Satisfied as she'd never been before, she laid her head on his chest and closed her eyes, relishing the moment.

"I didn't want to get involved with you," Tyler said quietly.

"I know."

"You did?"

She looked up at him and smiled. "You don't exactly do subtle."

"No," he said with a laugh. "I guess I don't."

"You plan on telling me why, or are you still keeping secrets?"

He ran his fingers across her hair and sighed. "There are things I've experienced that I don't plan on ever

telling anyone, but since this one sort of involves you, I guess I can give you the basics."

Joelle pushed herself up on her elbow so that she could look directly at him, surprised he'd agreed so easily. "I'd love to hear anything you want to share, and I promise not to push for more."

He nodded. "There was a woman—a specialist in my line of work—that I met on my third tour of duty. She was brilliant and beautiful, and I was a little surprised when she wanted me."

"I'm not surprised."

He smiled and leaned over to kiss her, then straightened back up, and his smile faded. "Unfortunately, she took risks. Don't get me wrong—it was our job to take risks, but she took it to a whole other level. A level that put her in more danger than she needed to be. Our commander came up with an idea. It was far-fetched but if it worked, it would have given us a huge tactical advantage."

"You didn't want to do it."

He shook his head. "It went against protocol and all good common sense, but she was enthralled with the idea of gaining such an upper hand. I tried to talk her out of it, but she was already invested. So I agreed to partner with her as security detail."

Before he even said the words, Joelle knew what they would be. Her heart fell as he took in a deep breath and stared up at the ceiling. Finally, he looked back down at her.

"We walked into a trap. In a matter of seconds, I was living my worst fear."

The pain in his eyes was so clear that her heart ached for him. She placed her hand on his chest. "I'm so sorry," she said.

"I couldn't save her. It was my job to keep her safe, and I failed."

"It wasn't your failure," she said, although she knew he wasn't ready to accept that. "You were against the mission from the beginning. If they had listened to you…"

"I shouldn't have agreed to go."

"Would that have prevented her from going?"

He sighed. "No."

"Then there's nothing you could have done, but I understand how much that bothers you, truly I do."

He nodded. "I guess you probably do."

"It's an awful feeling…to see something horrible coming and not be able to change it. You're constantly internally screaming at people to give you control so that you can save them."

"But people rarely do."

"No."

"How do you keep doing it? Keep trying to help people when you know so many of them are already lost?"

She shook her head. "I guess I focus on the ones we save."

"Yeah," he said, but she could tell he wasn't convinced. "Anyway, that's why I avoided getting involved with you. I didn't want to care for someone who voluntarily put herself in a position of danger, and your job definitely qualifies."

"I understand," she said, "but I'm glad you changed your mind."

She moved closer to kiss him and he wrapped his arms around her, pulling her naked body against his. And within minutes, he began the slow pace that would send them both over the edge again.

TYLER PULLED ON his jeans the next morning, looking down at Joelle, who was still asleep in the narrow bed they'd shared. Shared, and darn near destroyed if his ego was to be believed. He'd been attracted to her from the moment he laid eyes on her, but even his imagination hadn't come close to what it had been like to make love to her. And that was saying a lot, given that he had a fairly good imagination.

She stirred and looked up at him with a lazy smile. "What time is it?"

"Almost eight o'clock. We slept late."

"Well, most of the night wasn't about sleeping...."

He laughed as he sat next to her and leaned over to give her a kiss. "Well, there is that. How's your arm?"

"Which one?"

He smiled, fondly remembering her tumble onto the bathroom floor. After all, it had kicked off the best night of his entire life. "Both."

She glanced down. "Stiff and certainly not the most attractive, but not as bad as I thought they'd be." She reached up to touch his face with her hand. "I'm glad you changed your mind about dangerous women."

He shrugged. "I cheated, really. I mean, once the Brant issue is solved, you're free and clear. Your two weeks will end and you'll get the mother lode of cash from the estate. You can spend the rest of your life doing anything you want—reading, traveling...spending sleepless nights with security experts."

Her smile slipped away and she sat up. "I...I'm not planning on quitting my job."

"Sure you will. Your job's in Jackson and your family is here. Besides, you won't have to work, much less at something so difficult and dangerous."

"It's true...I have already thought about moving

closer to Alaina and Danae. We have so many lost years to make up for and it will be easier if I'm close. But, Tyler, you have to know I don't have any intention of leaving my profession. I want to help women. What I do makes a difference."

Tyler jumped up from the bed and practically ran from the room. "This was a mistake."

Before he'd even made it to the doorway, the tears spilled over Joelle's cheeks.

Chapter Seventeen

Tyler dropped Joelle off at the general store and watched as she walked inside with Alaina before heading down the sidewalk for the café. The ride into Calais had been silent and uncomfortable, and he welcomed an hour away from Joelle and all the problems she brought with her.

He slid onto a stool at the café without even looking at Carter. He waved a finger and Sonia slid a cup of coffee in front of him, then wisely set off across the café with her pot and her smile. Clearly, she understood that the smile part would be wasted here.

"Women trouble?" Carter asked.

Tyler choked on his coffee and Carter slapped his back.

"Everyone says your mom is psychic," Tyler said once he could breathe properly. "Did you inherit the ability?"

"You don't need to be psychic to know that look. I've worn it myself."

"Women troubles? You?"

"Hey, I'm engaged to a LeBeau sister. Do I have to say more?"

Tyler took another drink of his coffee. "Clearly, you

and Zach got the rational sisters. I got stuck with the stubborn one who won't listen to reason."

"Oh, man." Carter laughed. "You really don't know Alaina very well, do you? I'm not going to speak for Danae because I'm not the man sleeping with her, but I'm going to go out on a limb and guess that Zach would find that statement as amusing as I do."

"I... Who said I was sleeping with her?"

"Dude, you don't care how stubborn they are unless you're sleeping with them. So what kind of 'reasonable' advice did you give Joelle that she's not interested in taking?"

"I suggested she change careers because the one she has now is too dangerous."

"Whoooooooo, boy, you've put your foot into it big-time."

"What's wrong with wanting her to be safe? Or, for that matter, what's wrong with my not wanting to be involved with a woman who has a dangerous job?"

"Asks the guy who's starting a security firm."

Tyler frowned. "I'm not going to do fieldwork. I'm going to run the company and work with hardware."

"Uh-huh."

Tyler threw his hands in the air. "You sound just like my dad."

"William's a smart man."

Tyler huffed, then looked over at a grinning Carter. Unable to help himself, he smiled.

"I'm not trying to give you a hard time," Carter said. "I know how it feels to be at odd ends career-wise, not really sure what you even want for a future, and then to have it all clouded with stalkers and an incredible woman. I met Alaina at the time of my life when I knew less about myself and what I wanted than I ever had."

"Then how did you know you were supposed to be with her?"

"Because no matter what future I imagined for myself, I couldn't come up with one where she wasn't in it."

Tyler forced his mind to imagine himself five years from now—running a successful security firm, with a little cabin on the bayou somewhere in Calais, maybe a golden retriever. Then the door to the cabin opened and Joelle stepped out.

"Crap," he said.

Carter clapped him on the back. "The bar's not open for several hours. Let me buy you breakfast."

As he waved for Sonia, Carter's cell phone rang. He glanced at the display and frowned. "Carter," he answered.

Tyler watched his friend's face as it grew tight, his jaw flexing. Something was wrong.

"I've got to cancel breakfast," Carter said.

"What's wrong?"

Carter glanced around the café, then lowered his voice. "A fisherman pulled a body out of the east side bayou."

Tyler sat up straight. "Who is it?"

"The fisherman didn't recognize him." Carter studied Tyler for a moment. "Joelle's with Alaina, right?"

"Yeah, they're picking out paint or something over at the general store."

"I'll call Alaina and tell her to stick close and stay in Calais. If you don't mind, I'd like you to come with me."

"Sure," Tyler hopped off the stool and tossed some money on the counter for the coffee before hurrying out after Carter.

If the fisherman didn't recognize the body, that meant one of two things—either it was too badly dam-

aged to identify or it was someone the fisherman didn't know, such as Victor Brant.

Tyler hoped for option number two.

As JOELLE AND Alaina wrapped up their paint shopping and made their way out of the general store, Alaina's cell phone rang. As soon as she answered, Joelle could see a shift in her sister's demeanor, but Joelle couldn't extrapolate the problem from only Alaina's end of the conversation. By the time she hung up the phone, Alaina was frowning.

"What's wrong?"

"That was Carter. He said there's something he needs to check out and he's taking Tyler with him. He wants me to stay with you and says neither of us should return to the estate without them."

"He didn't say what they were doing?"

"No, but I could tell he was worried by the sound of his voice."

Joelle shook her head. "Maybe they're checking up on a suspect. I'm sure they'll let us know as soon as they finish."

"I'm sure you're right. Come on. We may as well kill some time over coffee."

Joelle slid into the corner booth at the café across from Alaina, trying to maintain her composure, even though her heart was completely broken and her pride was annihilated. So far, she'd managed to keep Alaina from figuring out something was bothering her, and that was fairly impressive given Alaina's track record as a trial attorney.

They had no sooner slid into the booth than a pretty young woman stepped up to them with a pad of paper.

"'Morning, Alaina," she said.

"Good morning, Sonia," Alaina replied and waved a hand at Joelle. "This is my sister Joelle."

Sonia smiled. "Guess this means you're all here now. That's nice. Can I get you some breakfast?"

"I'll just have coffee for now," Joelle managed.

"Me, too," Alaina chimed in.

Alaina glanced back as Sonia walked away, then looked over at Joelle. "You going to tell me what's bothering you? Please don't make me work for it. I didn't sleep all that well."

"Me, either."

Alaina gave her a sympathetic look. "Are you too stressed staying in the house?"

"Yes, I'm stressed, but that's not it." Joelle paused as Sonia pushed cups of coffee in front of them. "I saw something that first night I stayed in the house. I didn't say anything to anyone, but Tyler got it out of me."

Alaina nodded. "Tyler told Carter and Carter told me."

"He said you and Danae saw things, too."

Alaina dumped some sweetener in her coffee and stirred. "By things, do you mean our mother's ghost?"

"Is there more than one?" Joelle tried to joke, but her delivery lacked enthusiasm.

"Yes, actually," Alaina said, completely serious. "I saw two different spirits. One was definitely Mother. Danae saw her, too."

"And the other?"

Alaina shook her head. "It didn't look like anyone, but it felt like pure evil."

Joelle sucked in a breath. "Purcell?" she whispered.

"That's what I think."

"Wow. I hope I don't see him. I don't even like remembering him."

Alaina frowned. "I can't remember much about him at all. Things about us girls and Mom are coming back, but Purcell is always like a shadow—like he's offstage when I'm remembering. Is that how it is for you?"

Joelle shook her head. "Unfortunately, no. Some of my memories of Purcell are very vivid, and none of them are pleasant."

Alaina reached across the table and squeezed Joelle's hand.

"Well, isn't this a pretty picture?" A man's voice boomed beside them.

Joelle looked up at a beefy man, probably in his sixties, who smiled down at them.

"Mayor Dupree," Alaina acknowledged. "Have you met my sister Joelle yet?"

The mayor extended his hand to Joelle. "I should have known such a lovely young lady was one of Ophelia's girls. It's a pleasure to meet you."

Joelle shook his hand and studied his face. "Nice to meet you, as well," she said.

"Is something wrong?" the mayor asked as he released her hand.

"No." Joelle realized she'd been staring. "I'm sorry. It's just that you look familiar, but I can't imagine when I would have seen you before."

"Oh, well, Johnny's my brother. Some say we favor each other, so that's probably it."

Joelle glanced over at the café owner, but didn't really see much resemblance.

"I didn't know Johnny was your brother," Alaina said. "Carter really needs to do a better job filling me in on everything."

Mayor Dupree laughed. "Well, we're half-brothers, so different last name. My daddy passed and then

Mother remarried to Johnny's dad. Joelle, if there's anything I can do while you're staying in Calais, you let me know."

"Thank you," Joelle said. "I will."

The mayor walked across the café to talk to Johnny and took a seat at the counter.

"I guess Johnny got all the brains in the family," Joelle said, "since his brother went for politics."

Alaina laughed. "I'm so glad someone feels the same way about politicians that I do."

"Politicians are the people who keep trying to cut funding at my job so that they can drive fancier cars or have more expensive vacations. It's hard to like people who only think of themselves."

"Isn't that the truth? So getting back to our previous discussion—what did you see?"

Joelle told Alaina about seeing Ophelia's ghost and her theory that she might be too weak to properly communicate.

Alaina slumped back in her seat. "That makes sense as much as anything else about this does. You know, if someone had told me six months ago that I'd be sitting in a café in a tiny bayou town, trying to psychoanalyze a ghost, I'd have called them insane."

"Me, too."

"I wish she'd tell us something concrete."

"Like where her body is?"

Alaina frowned. "That would be a really good place to start. It's all so gruesome, and for a trial attorney to make a comment like that, it's pretty bad."

"This time it's personal."

Alaina gave her a small smile. "You're right. That makes all the difference. So are you going to tell me what else is bothering you?"

"What do you mean?"

"Come on. You have that faraway, slightly disconnected look. I mean, you're in the conversation for the most part, but I can tell that part of you is dwelling on something else. Let me take a stab at it—man problems?"

Joelle sighed. "Am I wearing a sign?"

"It's not so hard to figure out. I've seen Tyler and I've worn that same look before. So what happened?"

Joelle didn't think she'd want to talk about it, not even to her sister, but once she started talking, she poured out everything that had happened the night before and that morning.

Alaina listened without interruption until she finished, then shook her head. "William was certain Tyler was holding in something big—something preventing him from moving forward the way he should be. What a horrible thing to have happen, especially to someone who will feel responsibility even when there was none."

"I know. I wish he'd talk to William, but if it's all the same, I'd prefer if you don't repeat any of this."

"Of course, but I hope Tyler talks to his dad or someone else soon. That's a lot to carry around with you."

"It is, and I understand completely how bad he must feel, but that doesn't mean I will give up my work for him. Not that he's asking me to—he just stormed out and hasn't said a word since."

"I understand how much your work means to you, and I'd be the last person to tell you to change careers. From what I understand from Carter, Tyler isn't the kind of person who would expect it, either. I think he's got a lot of anger and grief he needs to work through, but if he really cares about you, he'll come around."

"If he really cares…" Joelle shook her head. "I was

engaged to Brad and he still walked away from me over my work. Maybe I should give up and get a bunch of cats."

"No way am I letting you do that."

"Still holding out hope for a happily ever after?"

"No. I'm allergic."

Joelle laughed. "So am I. Then I guess I'm doomed to a lonely existence free from cat hair."

"Give him some time."

"I guess I don't have a choice. I still have to finish my two weeks, so neither of us is going anywhere." She sighed, the thought of the long day stretching in front of her. "I'm not looking forward to sitting cooped up in that house all day with him. The drive into Calais was incredibly uncomfortable."

"Then I'll come back with you. I mean, once the menfolk allow us back in our house." Alaina grinned.

"I can't ask you to do that."

"You didn't. I'm volunteering. I don't have any client work today and it's high time I got back to helping out around the house. I've got a list of purchased assets from the estate accountant that I've been trying to match to objects in the house, but so far, I've come up empty. I have located quite a few through auction houses, though, so it reinforces our belief that Purcell was selling assets to keep cash coming in."

Joelle felt the tension that had been squeezing her all morning start to melt away. A day working alongside her sister was exactly what she needed to get the ground back underneath her.

"That would be great," she said and smiled.

"Good. Then let's get some breakfast. If Carter and Tyler aren't back by the time we finish, we'll head to my house and work there until we can return to the es-

tate. I've got a whole box of paperwork that I'm going through for Danae."

Joelle nodded as Alaina waved Sonia over to get their order.

She'd have a pleasant breakfast with her sister, then help her sort through estate paperwork. With any luck, the day would be much lower on the excitement scale than the one before.

CARTER LOOKED AT the body lying on the bank of the bayou and compared it to the image on his phone. "Looks like Brant," he said, and showed Tyler his phone with the picture of Brant on it.

Tyler didn't have to take a long look. The man's square jaw and crooked nose in the image were identical to the waterlogged corpse. "At least cause of death isn't a mystery."

The bullet hole in the center of the man's forehead left no doubt as to what had ended Brant's stalking and wife-beating career.

"Yeah," Carter said. "That only leaves the who and the why, but at least it should offer Joelle some comfort."

Tyler nodded. "When I left the Middle East, I never wanted to see another body again, but I have to admit that seeing this one doesn't make me feel anything but relief. Sometimes I wonder what happened to my empathy."

"Hazard of the job." Carter waved at the paramedics who had parked near the dock and were coming down the bank with a gurney.

Tyler watched as they stuffed Brant's body into a black bag and zipped it shut.

One less threat to worry about.

That was true enough, but someone else was still

entering the estate, so they weren't in the clear. Then there were his feelings for Joelle.

And that was the biggest threat of all.

Chapter Eighteen

Alaina and Joelle sat at the kitchen table in Carter's cabin and combed through the stack of records they'd taken from Purcell's office. Frustrated by the tedium and lack of pertinent discovery, Joelle tossed a stack of papers on the table and sighed.

"There's nothing here," Joelle said.

Alaina looked as skeptical as she felt, but apparently was not ready to admit defeat. "There's got to be something," she said. "Someone, or more than one someone, is breaking into that house for a reason. Someone besides Brant."

"But you already said you haven't been able to find anything on the asset list the estate accountant sent you. Maybe it's just someone else worried we'll find their name in one of Purcell's payoff notations."

"Maybe, but then why not simply pour gas all over Purcell's office and set it on fire? That's what Roger Martin intended to do." Alaina shook her head. "I've just got this feeling that something else is going on."

"Okay, then let's change tactics. Can I see the asset list? Maybe that will give us a clue."

Alaina pulled a folder out of her briefcase and passed it to Joelle. "The items that I've already tracked to auc-

tion houses or art dealers are highlighted in yellow. The rest are unaccounted for."

Joelle flipped through the papers, noting that a good two-thirds of the assets were already highlighted—at least a hundred assets located. "You located this many already?" Her sister's research skills were nothing short of amazing.

"It's not that difficult when you're a fairly well-known attorney and start throwing around words like 'felony theft.'"

Joelle knew Alaina was understating the amount of effort that had gone into tracking down that many of the estate's valuables. She couldn't even imagine the number of phone calls and subtle threats it had taken.

"Some of the things Purcell managed to acquire are amazing," Joelle said as she scanned the list.

"The list of things pre-Purcell is even more impressive. Flip to the end."

Joelle turned to the last page in the folder, her eyes widening at some of the descriptions. "I haven't found any of these things in the house."

"They were probably some of the first to go."

"Seems like it would have been easier for him to just disappear again. I mean, why stay in Calais, closed up in that house, scamming the estate to pay off blackmailers? I don't get it."

Alaina nodded. "I thought the same thing at first. But I think that over time, Purcell started to lose it. I think he stayed for a while thinking he'd make enough money on the sale of estate assets, but once he paid off his helpers, there wasn't much left."

"So he started the buy-and-sell game."

"Exactly, but I think the longer he stayed in the house, the more unstable he became until finally, he

was trapped there with his own dark deeds staring him in the face every day."

Joelle looked at the list of assets again. What Alaina said made sense. Purcell thought he had everything planned to collect a fortune and disappear—probably to another country where his mob buddies couldn't find him. He must have grown more desperate with every failed attempt to get out of Calais, and more psychotic with every moment he was forced to remain hidden away in the swamp.

The page she'd turned to only had three missing items on it—a vase, a set of silverware and an entry that simply said "diamonds."

"I guess this was Mother's necklace?" Joelle asked, pointing to the diamonds notation.

"That's what I assumed. It was the only jewelry listed. Apparently none of the women in our family tree went in for glitter and flash."

"How come it doesn't have an estimated value?"

Alaina shook her head. "I assumed it was because it had never been appraised."

"Probably not. She was so young. Death would have been the last thing on her mind. I guess it's foolish to hope we'll ever find a trace of it."

"My guess is he removed the stones and sold them—melted down the gold."

Bastard. The word echoed through Joelle's mind and she turned her attention back to the paperwork in an attempt to drown it out. She flipped to the next page, then frowned. "A necklace is listed on this page. No other description, but it's got a value of thirty thousand. If the diamond listing was Mother's necklace, then what is this?"

"Let me see." Alaina took the list from her and

checked the notations. "I worked on the items so sporadically, I must have missed this. That's some shoddy work."

"You've had a couple of things on your mind besides tracking down stolen property."

Alaina frowned. "I don't remember Mother wearing any other jewelry except the necklace, and that was rare, but then my memory isn't all that reliable. She had a wedding band from her marriage to our father, but I don't think she even had that when she was married to Purcell. I suppose we could call the estate accountant and ask."

"Might as well tie everything down as much as possible," Joelle agreed.

Alaina grabbed her cell phone off the coffee table and dialed the accountant, then put the phone on speaker.

"Leonard, this is Alaina LeBeau," Alaina said when the accountant answered.

"Hello, Ms. LeBeau. What can I do for you today?"

"I'm working on the asset list with my sister Joelle, and we had a question for you."

"I'll be glad to provide any answers that I have."

"Great. On page eight, you have a necklace listed, but on page seventeen, you have a listing that simply reads 'diamonds.' We can't remember our mother owning any valuable jewelry other than her diamond necklace, so we're a bit confused."

"Yes, the necklace listing is for the teardrop diamond necklace I've seen your mother wearing in photographs. I assume that's the one you remember?"

"Yes, that's right. So then what are the diamonds in the other listing, and why don't they have a value assigned?"

"They're a bit of speculation, if you ask me, although

the senior partner who has managed your mother's estate for the last forty years assures me they exist, or existed. The story is that your great-grandparents, or some other relative far up the line, acquired some uncut stones reported to be of very high value. The senior partner always assumed that some of them were used to make the necklace your mother wore, as it was a gift from her parents on her eighteenth birthday. But for all we know, the uncut stones never existed, or they used all of them for the necklace and no more remain."

"We've found no record of such stones in the paperwork we've been through so far," Alaina said. "But thank you for the information. If we find anything that seems to confirm the stones' existence, we'll let you know."

"Thank you very much, Ms. LeBeau. I hope you and your sister have a lovely day."

Alaina disconnected the call and looked over at Joelle. "What do you want to bet those stones do exist—or existed?"

"I was thinking the same thing. Uncut diamonds are definitely something Purcell would stick around for, but he must not have found them, or he would have left."

"Maybe Mother wouldn't tell him where they were. Maybe that's why…"

Alaina didn't finish her sentence, but she didn't have to. If Purcell killed Ophelia in a fit of rage over the diamonds, that would explain the cover-up.

"Do you think that's what the others are looking for?" Joelle asked.

Alaina shook her head. "How would they even know about them? Purcell would never have told anyone because he'd want them to himself, and if a rumor about

them ever floated through Calais, William or Willamina would have heard it."

"Do you think they existed?"

"Maybe…probably, but maybe it's like the accountant said and they were used to make Mother's necklace."

Joelle sighed. "I suppose that's more logical than thinking a fortune in diamonds has sat undiscovered in the house for decades."

"Another potential lead blasted to shreds. I don't know how Carter does this type of work every day. I thought being a lawyer was hard, but this is simply exhausting."

"It does give me a new appreciation for law enforcement."

"Well, I guess it's back to the paperwork and hopefully a new lead. I have a client meeting tomorrow morning in New Orleans, then I'm going to pay Danae a visit and help her work through some more of the documents. I'll fill her in on the diamond angle so she knows to pay special attention to anything that might mention them."

As Alaina reached for a stack of papers, the front door to the cabin opened and Carter and Tyler walked in. Alaina jumped up from the couch to give Carter a hug. Joelle's heart ached a bit as she watched Alaina wrap her arms around Carter and kiss him gently on the lips.

The look of absolute adoration on Carter's face was so clear, and while Joelle was thrilled for her sister, she couldn't help but want the same thing for herself. Carter was a wonderful man, and he and Alaina were perfect for each other. Before she'd seen them together, Joelle had assumed talk of soul mates was a plot device for

romance books, but looking at her sister and Carter, she knew she was wrong. It was possible to have your own happy ending.

She glanced up at Tyler, who stood just inside the doorway. He stared at his friend and Alaina, an odd expression on his face, as though he was trying to make sense of it all. He glanced over at Joelle, but when their eyes met, he immediately looked away. Joelle's chest tightened and another trickle of disappointment ran through her.

"I didn't even hear you pull up," Alaina said when she released Carter.

"Too engrossed in your work," Carter said. "How's it going?"

Alaina filled them in on the diamond theory.

"Doesn't sound like much," Carter said.

"No," Alaina agreed. "We figure it was enough for Purcell, but we can't think of any way the others would have heard about them."

"They certainly wouldn't have from Purcell."

"That's what we figured. So whoever is breaking into the house is probably looking for something else."

Carter nodded, but Joelle could tell that he wasn't really focusing on the conversation. The tension he'd worn when he first entered the cabin was back, and she wondered if whatever was bothering Carter was part of the reason Tyler seemed even more distant that usual.

"So what were you two doing?" Alaina asked.

She tried to keep the question casual, but Joelle could tell that her sister had sensed something was wrong.

"I got a call this morning that a fisherman found a body washed up on the east bank."

"Oh, no!" Alaina said. "I suppose it's pointless to

ask if it's someone you knew, as the town has less than five hundred people. I'm sorry, Carter."

"I'm not. The body was Victor Brant."

Joelle sucked in a breath as the room started to spin. Alaina rushed over to sit beside her and put her arm across her shoulders.

"Breathe deeply," Alaina said.

Joelle let the breath slowly out and some of the dizziness began to subside. Finally, she found her voice. "You're sure it's him?"

Carter nodded. "He hadn't been in the water very long. It was easy to identify him from the photo I passed around. The coroner will do an official identification, of course, but as far as I'm concerned, it's official."

"I can't believe it," Joelle said, her voice barely a whisper.

"It's true," Tyler finally spoke. "I saw him myself and have no doubt it's Brant."

Weeks of tension began to slip from Joelle as she began to realize all the implications Carter's announcement carried. "I'm safe," she said.

"Safe from Brant," Tyler said. "But someone is still entering the house, and given what happened to Alaina and Danae, we're not about to let up on the investigation or the security."

"Tyler's right," Carter agreed. "Don't get me wrong—this is a major improvement for you, Joelle, but we're not about to assume the house is safe. We can't take the risk."

Alaina nodded. "Tyler, if you don't mind, we'd like to do some work at the estate today. We were just waiting on you to return."

"That's fine," Tyler said.

"I can't join you yet," Carter said. "I've got to go talk

to the state police and sort everything out with Brant. Joelle, if you know how to get in touch with Brant's wife, now would be the time. The police are going to want to talk to her."

"I will call my point person. They give all the women a prepaid cell phone when they go under. She'll be able to fill her in. Should his wife contact the Jackson police?"

"Yeah. As far as I'm concerned, it's an open-and-shut file. I don't need anything from her. I sent them your statement on Brant's attack yesterday, but they're probably going to want to talk to you in person at some point."

Joelle nodded. That was one conversation she looked forward to having.

It was almost nine o'clock when Joelle, freshly showered, pulled on yoga pants and a T-shirt and propped herself up against the wall in the little twin bed that she and Tyler had shared the night before. Alaina and Carter had stayed late, all four of them working through the house, looking for anything that might provide them a direction for investigation. Alaina and Joelle made spaghetti and garlic bread for dinner and they'd had a pleasant, if not overly dynamic, meal before Alaina and Carter headed home.

Tyler hadn't stood guard outside the bathroom door this time, but she knew he was close by. Now he stuck his head in the bedroom.

"I'm going to shower."

"I don't need to sit in there with you again, do I? I mean, with Brant dead…"

"The immediate danger to you is probably gone. I think you're fine staying in here. You've got your pistol, right?"

She lifted her book from the nightstand, exposing the pistol underneath.

"Good," he said. "Lock the door behind me. I'll knock when I'm done."

He pulled the door closed behind him and Joelle jumped off the bed to push the dead bolt into place. The entire time he'd been talking, Tyler had barely looked at her. She'd hoped with some time passing and Brant's death, that Tyler might loosen his stranglehold on his opinion of her job, as Alaina thought he would. But apparently, he was going to need more time than she'd hoped.

She walked back to the corner and flopped back on the bed. Who was she kidding? Twelve hours wasn't enough time for some people to make up their mind on positioning the toilet paper over versus under, much less change their mind on major life decision points like what kind of woman they wanted to have a relationship with.

What she needed to do was focus on her blessings—and they were many—instead of dwelling on things she couldn't have. Take Brant, for example. Joelle's contact had called her back after relaying the information concerning Brant's death to his wife. The woman had collapsed in tears of joy, and the other rescued women she lived with cheered. That was a victory. It was a shame that they lived in a world that required someone to die in order to let someone else live out their life free of terror, but at least this time, the victim was the one still standing. It had turned out the other way more times than Joelle wanted to remember.

She glanced down at the romance novel lying beside her and sighed. It seemed everywhere she looked a woman was getting a bright future—Alaina, Danae,

and always in fiction. When she'd come to Calais, she'd hoped to get her family back, and she had. The money was a huge plus, but not the most important thing, although it was going to allow her to help so many more women than before. What she hadn't expected was to find a man who tugged at her heart the way Tyler did. Somewhere in the midst of all the chaos, she'd tumbled headfirst for the sexy marine, and now, the thought of moving forward without him made her heart ache.

The shower went off in the next room and she grabbed her book, determined to appear collected and aloof. No way would she spend the entire night staring at Tyler like a lovesick puppy. She was going to read her book until she couldn't keep her eyes open any longer, then for the first time since she'd arrived in Calais, she was going to get a good night's sleep.

The knock on the door startled her for a second before she remembered Tyler had her bolt herself in. She jumped up and slid the bolt back, then hurried back to her bed without even a backward glance at Tyler. The bookmark was on page eighty, so that's where she started, but if she was being honest, she couldn't remember a thing about the story. Still, she was determined to look busy, so she focused on the words and started to read.

It lasted about two seconds.

Tyler stood with his back to her, his hair still damp from the shower. He had on sweatpants but no shirt, and one look at his marvelously cut back had her hands itching to touch every inch of him as she had the night before. He bent over to retrieve a T-shirt out of his suitcase, and she held in a sigh.

It was going to be a very, very long night.

He pulled the T-shirt over his head, then sat on his

bed with his back against the wall, clutching a file folder. Joelle had heard him request some police records from Carter, and the stamp on the outside was a dead giveaway. Apparently, Tyler intended to do some night reading, as well.

Fine.

She pulled the pillow behind her back to a more comfortable position, then dove back into her book. Before she knew it, her eyes were drooping—the events of the day finally catching up with her—and she dropped off to sleep.

SHE WASN'T SUPPOSED to be out of bed, but Joelle loved the still night air of the house—loved roaming around its vast open areas and dozens of nooks and crannies when no one else stirred. Things were reversed, she thought. If she could stay up all night and sleep all morning, life would be perfect.

Well, as perfect as it could be with him in the house.

She'd begged Mommy the night before, and that was something Joelle never did. Begging was for little girls with no manners, but she'd abandoned all training and begged Mommy to make the bad man leave. Mommy had hugged her and cried and whispered that she wanted to make him leave, but she couldn't just yet. She'd asked Joelle to be patient like the big girl Mommy knew she was.

Tonight, Joelle had crept into the attic. In all the ancient trunks, the attic held untold treasures—dresses and shoes from so long ago, you could only see them in books. Joelle loved trying on the beautiful layers of satin and lace and standing in front of the dusty mirror to try to figure out what she'd look like when she was older. She hoped she looked like Mommy, as Mommy

*was the most beautiful lady in the world. Alaina al-
ready looked like Mommy and it made Joelle jealous
of her older sister.*

*She had no idea what time it was when she crept out
of the attic staircase and onto the second-floor land-
ing, but it had been dark outside for some time. She
paused at the edge of the hallway and peeked around
at the balcony. All she had to do was scurry down one
side of the balcony and she'd be at the hallway to the
bedroom. Then she was in the clear.*

*The balcony was empty and silent, so she slipped
around the corner and hurried down the carpeted run-
ner in the center of the wooden flooring. But when she
was halfway to the safety zone, she heard the front door
open and hushed voices echoed up from the entry. Im-
mediately, she dropped on her hands and knees so that
they couldn't see her if they looked upstairs. She recog-
nized one of the voices as the bad man. The other voice
was low and raspy.*

*She waited, hoping they'd move off to the kitchen
or one of the formal areas on the first floor, because
if they came upstairs, she was caught for sure. No way
could she make it across the balcony, down the hall and
into her bedroom before they climbed the stairs. Pray-
ing that the wooden floors didn't squeak, she started
to crawl toward the hallway, staying as far away from
the balcony as the carpeted runner allowed.*

*She'd only made it a couple of feet before she heard
Mommy. The fear in Mommy's voice made her freeze
again. Joelle knew Mommy was afraid of the bad man,
but she'd never heard her sound like this. Something
was wrong—even more wrong than usual.*

*She crept to the edge of the balcony and lay down
flat, peering over the edge. Mommy was standing next*

to the bad man near the front door. All she could see of the raspy man was his legs as the rest of him was hidden by the staircase.

"You'll tell me or you'll pay," the bad man said.

"I don't know," Mommy cried, her voice shaking.

"Lying bitch," the bad man said and struck Mommy with his hand, knocking her to the floor. "Grab her!"

Joelle saw hands reach from behind the staircase and clutch Mommy's shoulders, preventing her from rising—preventing her from escaping. The bad man pulled something from his pocket and poked Mommy in the arm with it. She struggled, but couldn't get away. Then she went completely limp and her eyes rolled back in her head.

Joelle began to scream and everything went black.

"JOELLE, WAKE UP!" The voice sounded above her and she bolted upright, then clutched her head as a wave of nausea ran through her.

"Can you hear me?" Tyler's voice registered somewhere in her frantic mind, and she looked up at him and nodded.

He dropped onto the bed next to her and gathered her in his arms. She clutched him, her heart pounding so strongly in her chest she swore she could hear it echo in the dead silence of the room. Her mind spun with what she'd seen—what she'd remembered.

Tyler pushed back from her and studied her face. "Are you all right? You started screaming and I couldn't wake you."

"I remembered something—something horrible."

"What?"

She sucked in a breath, her heart pounding in her temples and making her head swim.

"I saw Purcell kill our mother."

Chapter Nineteen

Tyler placed a cup of coffee in front of Joelle along with cream and sugar, then he took a seat next to her at the breakfast table. It was only 5:00 a.m. when Joelle had startled him out of bed, but one look at her wide eyes and pale skin and Tyler knew she wouldn't be able to sleep again anytime soon. Her terror-filled screams had sent him hurtling back to a past he'd been trying to lock away, and his pulse still beat stronger even twenty minutes after he'd sprung up from his bed, certain someone was killing her.

After her statement, she'd collapsed in tears, then after gaining a bit of composure, locked herself in the bathroom for a bit. When she'd finally emerged, Tyler suggested they head downstairs for coffee and to talk. With all the overhead lights on, the kitchen would be bright and cheery, and Tyler wanted her to wind down enough to tell him what she'd remembered.

Her hands shook as she added sugar to her coffee and Tyler's guilt over adding a shot of whiskey to it melted away. His anxiety grew with every second she continued to stir, staring blankly into the cup, but finally, she pulled the spoon out and lifted the cup to her lips.

When she took the first sip, her eyes widened and she looked at him.

"Whiskey," he said.

She nodded and took another long sip, then she lowered the cup and frowned.

"I can get you something else," he said.

"No. That's not it." Her brow creased and she took another sip, then stared at him. "The milk."

He jumped up from his chair. "I'll get the milk."

"No!" she said.

He sat back down, completely confused.

"I'm sorry," she said. "I don't want milk. I remembered something about milk. Every night before bed, Purcell made us a glass of warm milk. He claimed it made you sleep better, but I never liked it. It always tasted bitter to me—like the coffee did."

"You think Purcell doctored your milk?"

"It would make sense, right? He usually left the room long enough for me to dump it out, but Alaina always drank it. When I started remembering things that happened when I was roaming the house at night, I wondered why none of the fights woke Alaina up, but whiskey would explain that, right?"

Tyler clenched his jaw at the thought of Purcell drugging his stepdaughters so that he could abuse their mother. Truly, there was no end to the evil he'd brought into their lives. "It may also explain why her memory is so foggy despite her being the oldest."

Joelle's eyes widened. "You're right." She shook her head. "For a bodyguard, it seems you've spent a lot of time helping me work through my childhood issues."

"It's all part of the same service," he said and gave her an encouraging smile.

"Well, the service has been exemplary. And you've been very patient, fixing me coffee and coddling me, but it's time I tell you what I saw."

"Were you dreaming?"

"Yes, but I'm certain that what I saw really happened." She paused for a second and stared out the window into the darkness, then looked back at him. "I didn't tell you everything about the last time I remembered something from my childhood."

"I had a feeling that was the case, but I think you need to tell me everything now."

She nodded. "That night in the hallway wasn't the first time I remembered what I told you about—the argument between my mother and Purcell. I've carried that with me for as long as I can remember, but being here and recalling it made it feel so much worse."

He nodded. It made sense that being back in the house would make everything seem more vivid.

"He hit her," Joelle blurted out, almost as if she had to get it out before she changed her mind. "I saw him hit her so hard she fell and then just stayed there, huddled up and crying while he stood over her and screamed."

Tyler's jaw involuntarily clenched and anger coursed through him as he processed her witnessing her mother's abuse so young. "I'm sorry. No one should ever have to see such things."

"That's the reason why..."

"Why, what?"

She looked directly at him, her eyes filled with tears. "Why I do the work I do. I couldn't help my mother, but if I can prevent another child from living that nightmare, then I have to do it."

A rush of regret ran through Tyler as he remembered his harsh words to Joelle about her profession. Her choice of profession was so personal, and he'd used her doing the right thing as a reason to prevent her from entering his life. Shame followed the regret, and he tried to

push it down. For all those medals he had locked away in a box, he was a coward.

"I can't quit," she said. "Even if I wanted to, my conscience wouldn't let me."

He put his hand over hers. "I shouldn't have assumed you would. What you're doing is important. I was selfish to think you'd give it up simply because I was too afraid to deal with my own issues."

The relief on her face was so clear that a second wave of guilt washed over him. He'd let his own inability to deal with his past allow him to try to force someone else into a neat little box just so he could feel better about caring for them.

He gave her hand a squeeze. "What did you see in your dream?"

She took another drink of coffee, then began to talk. He listened intently—his pulse increasing with every word—as she described in horrifying detail what she'd seen looking down from the banister.

When she finished, he blew out a breath. "You didn't see the other man?"

"No. I just heard his voice."

"Raspy…could it have been Amos?" As soon as the words left his mouth, he hated saying them, but now was not the time for sentimental thoughts. Every angle must be explored.

Her eyes widened. "No! No way."

"You're one hundred percent positive that it couldn't have been him?"

"Of course…well, I'm sure…." She clasped her hands over her mouth. "Oh, no. I can't be positive, but surely it couldn't be. Amos loved us girls and our mother."

Tyler nodded. "That's what we've all thought, but he's been in the perfect position to know everything

that goes on in this house, including knowing about any valuables that Purcell acquired."

"But his foot is broken," Joelle argued, refusing to buy into Amos being a bad guy. "He couldn't have been out on my balcony or strolling in front of your cameras."

Tyler frowned. "No, none of those could have been him, but he could be working with someone else."

"I hate this! Suspecting people who claim they care about you."

She was so distressed that he rose and pulled her up from her chair to hold her. They stood there, arms wrapped around each other for a while, and when he finally released her, he placed his hands on both sides of her face and lowered his lips to hers. She responded with such passion, and his heart swelled with emotion.

"Are you sure about this? About us?" she whispered when they finished the kiss.

"It may be the only thing I'm sure about."

She broke into a smile so beautiful it made him feel warm all over. He wasn't about to fool himself into thinking it would be easy. A lot of unresolved issues lay in the back of his mind, just waiting to resurface at the most inconvenient times. If he wanted to move forward, he was going to have to face them all.

But for the first time in years, he thought it might be possible.

ALAINA TOSSED A stack of paper in the recycle box and stretched before flopping back onto the recliner. She and Danae had been sitting in Zach's living room, sorting through LeBeau estate paperwork for three hours. They still hadn't unearthed anything that gave them a clue as to who else Purcell was involved with or what

exactly had happened to their mother, and not even a hint of information on the elusive diamonds.

"How's Zach?" Alaina asked. She'd been waiting for Danae to offer the information, but either her sister was dense or being protective. Alaina didn't believe Danae was capable of being dense, so the second option was the most likely.

Danae glanced over at her, then back down at the coffee table. "He says he's all right."

"But you don't believe him?"

Danae shook her head. "He's better than before but the guilt is eating him up. Every day that passes and we don't know what happened to Mother's body, it's like adding five pounds to the weight he's already carrying."

"He's not responsible for what his father did. None of us think that."

Danae gave her a grateful smile. "I know, and deep down, so does he. But I'm afraid of what will happen if we never find the answers. I'm afraid of what he'll become if he lives his whole life under this shadow."

"Oh, baby sister." Alaina rose from her chair and sat next to Danae on the couch to give her a hug. "We're not going to let that happen."

Alaina released her and grabbed a stack of paper. "I have a good feeling about this stack." She divided the stack in half and held half out to Danae.

Danae laughed and grabbed the papers. "You've said that about every stack for the last three hours."

"Those were practice runs."

"Eternal optimist."

"Nope," Alaina said as she scanned the first page. "Desperate realist."

Danae laughed and started reviewing the papers. Alaina scanned the first sheet for large dollar amounts,

then finding none, flipped it over and started on the next sheet. She trailed her finger down the yellowed paper, expecting that this was another page of house supplies and gas bills and suddenly she froze.

An entry for twenty thousand dollars—the same amount Purcell had used to pay off others.

She looked to the left, hoping the entry was legible. Her heart leaped in her throat when she saw a single last name.

Picard.

"I found something," Alaina said, her voice cracking. "Look."

Danae leaned over to view the paper. "It's the same twenty thousand," she said, the excitement clear in her voice. "Do you know anyone in Calais with the name Picard?"

Alaina slowly shook her head. "I'm mentally running through everyone, but I don't think I've ever heard of someone by that name in Calais. How about you?"

"It doesn't ring a bell, and I'm sure I met everyone when I worked at the café."

"But it sounds familiar." Suddenly, Alaina bolted off the couch. "I got it!"

Danae jumped up beside her. "Who?"

"The family doctor. Doc Broussard said our mom took us all to her doctor in New Orleans—the doctor her parents had always used. I'm almost positive Doc Broussard said his name was Picard."

Danae flopped back down on the couch and grabbed her laptop. She tapped in a search, and Alaina leaned over to see the screen.

"There's a Dr. Richard Picard in New Orleans," Danae said and clicked on a link. "But it looks like he's retired."

"That would be reasonable. If he was our grand-parents' doctor, he can't be young. What about a home address?"

Danae tapped again and came up with an address in a wealthy historic district. "No telephone number. Do you think Carter's friends at the New Orleans Police Department would be willing to get it for him?"

"Probably, but I don't know that it's a good idea to call. You can't see someone's expression over the phone, and even scheduling an appointment would let them know you're coming."

"So you're thinking just show up and have Carter flash a badge?"

Alaina smiled. "It *is* really handy sleeping with a cop."

A knock on the condo door interrupted them and Alaina went to open it.

"Speak of the devil," she said as she gave Carter a kiss.

"What did I do now?" he asked.

"Nothing yet," Alaina said as Danae jumped up from the couch to give him a quick hug. "It's what you're going to do."

He narrowed his eyes at them. "You found something."

"Oh, yeah," Alaina said and she and Danae showed him their work.

"So what are we waiting for?" Carter asked. "Let's pay him a visit."

Alaina jumped up and down and clapped her hands. Danae checked her watch and groaned. "I have class in half an hour, and we're having a test. Go, then come back and tell me everything!"

"Of course," Alaina said and grabbed her purse.

Fifteen minutes later, Carter steered his truck up a huge circular drive and parked in front of a plantation-style house with white columns and blue shutters. They walked to the front door, and Alaina bit her lower lip as Carter rang the doorbell.

Within seconds, an older lady wearing light blue scrubs opened the door. "Can I help you?"

Carter showed her his badge and her eyebrows went up.

"I'm Sheriff Carter Trahan from Calais and this is Alaina LeBeau. I'm conducting an investigation and need to ask some questions."

"The police? I can't imagine what anyone in this household would have to do with the police."

"It's an old matter," Carter said, "and one that I'd like to put to rest. Can we speak to Dr. Picard?"

"I'm sorry," the woman said. "You're about five years too late for that."

Alaina's hopes fell. "Perhaps Mrs. Picard could help us. Do you care for her?"

The nurse nodded. "I'm sorry to disappoint you, but Mrs. Picard can't even help herself. She's in the late stages of Alzheimer's. Most days, she thinks she's back in grade school. By the time he passed, she'd already forgotten the doctor, and they'd been married over forty years."

"Oh, that's so sad," Alaina said.

"Yes, ma'am, it is. I wish I could help."

"Thank you for your time," Carter said and he put his arm around Alaina as they walked away.

"Wait!" The nurse hurried down the sidewalk after them and grabbed Alaina's arm. "Did you say your name was LeBeau?"

"Yes. Alaina LeBeau. My mother, Ophelia, was a patient of the doctor's."

"All these years… I never thought…" she said, her eyes wide. "I better explain. Dr. Picard died of pulmonary disease, but it took a while to happen. Toward the end, he gave me an envelope and said if anyone by the name of LeBeau came looking for him, I was to give them the envelope."

Alaina sucked in a breath. "And you still have it?"

The nurse nodded. "I stuck it in the desk drawer and forgot all about it. I figured it was the ravings of a dying man. I never actually thought someone would come. Let me go get it."

She hurried back inside and Alaina clutched Carter's arm, unable to control her excitement. "Maybe he felt guilty like Zach's dad. The letter might explain everything."

"Let's not get our hopes up just yet," Carter warned, but Alaina could tell he was as excited by the potential as she was.

It seemed like forever, but was probably only minutes before the nurse hurried back out with the envelope. She handed it to Alaina and smiled. "I hope it has the answers you're looking for."

Alaina clutched the envelope as the nurse walked back into the house and shut the door. She looked up at Carter. "I'm afraid to open it. What if it doesn't say anything? What if he was out of his mind and he stuffed his grocery list in here?"

"Then we'll keep going," he said. "I'm not going to quit until we have answers to all of your questions. Every single one."

She smiled at him, her heart swelling with love and pride for the man she was going to marry. She'd never even known a man like him existed, much less that she'd find him and he'd want to be with her.

Her hands shook as she tore the corner off the enve-

lope and slipped her finger inside to tear it open. For a second, she worried that it might be empty and all of this buildup would have been for nothing, but a single sheet of paper lay inside.

She pulled it out and unfolded it, her heart pounding as she looked at the shaky cursive, then she began to read it out loud.

To whoever comes for this letter,
Twenty years ago, I did a horrible thing. The reason why I did it is unimportant and doesn't excuse my actions, so I won't go into it.

I helped Trenton Purcell get rid of his wife, Ophelia LeBeau.

I have regretted it every day since I deposited the money, but by then it was too late. If I'd confessed, I would have been stripped of my medical license and my wife and kids would have lost everything. I couldn't make them suffer for my bad decision, so I said nothing.

But it's eaten away at me like a cancer.

I knew he was going to send her to Eleanor, but I didn't think he would leave her there. I'm sorry for what happened to her children and to her. If I could go back and change things, I would. Every day, I ask God to forgive me, and every day, I am worried that he can't.

My sin was too great.
Richard Picard

Alaina clutched the letter and read it again silently. Finally, she looked up at Carter, more confused than ever. "He didn't say he helped Purcell kill her. He says they sent her to Eleanor…but who is Eleanor?"

"You haven't run across that name in any of the documents you've helped Danae catalog?"

She shook her head. "I don't know anyone named Eleanor."

"Maybe the nurse knows."

They hurried back to the front door and rang the bell again. The nurse seemed surprised to see them again.

"Is everything all right?" she asked.

"In the letter that Dr. Picard left," Alaina said, "he said he sent my mother to Eleanor. Do you have any idea who that is?"

"Eleanor isn't a person, dear. It's a sanitarium."

Thoughts of tuberculosis raced through Alaina's mind. "What was wrong with her?"

The nurse gave Alaina a sympathetic look. "Eleanor Roosevelt Sanitarium cares for the mentally ill."

"Oh!" Alaina's hand flew over her mouth.

"Thank you, again," Carter said as he placed his arm around Alaina's shoulders and led her back to the truck.

"He had her committed and then told everyone she'd died," Alaina said as she stared out the windshield. "That's why there was no body in the casket. That's what he paid them to cover up."

Carter pulled out his cell phone and called information to get the number for the sanitarium. He put the phone on speaker as it dialed.

"Thank you for calling Eleanor Roosevelt Mental Treatment Facility. Can I help you?" the receptionist asked.

"Yes, I'd like to inquire about a patient you had there twenty-five years ago."

"Mrs. Anderson has been in charge of medical records for over thirty years. If anyone can help you, it will be her."

"Great. Can I speak to her?"

"She's on vacation and doesn't return until the day after tomorrow, but I can make you an appointment for then. Is ten o'clock okay?"

"That's great. My name is Carter Trahan, and I'll have some family members with me."

"Okay, Mr. Trahan, I have you down for ten o'clock."

"Thank you." Carter disconnected the call. "Looks like we have to wait a couple of days."

"I know. At first, I wanted to scream, but this way is better. This way, Danae and Joelle can go with us. Just in case…."

Carter reached over and squeezed her hand. "Just in case."

ALAINA COULD HARDLY contain herself as she rushed to the front door of the estate and fumbled with her key.

"Don't open it," Carter yelled from behind her. "The alarm is probably set."

"Oh, I forgot." She slipped the key back in her purse and banged on the door, hoping Tyler and Joelle were somewhere they could easily hear. A couple seconds later, the door opened a crack and Tyler peered out, then he stepped back and they hurried inside.

"We have news," Alaina said. "Where's Joelle?"

"She's in the kitchen. We were just about to fix some sandwiches. Are you interested?"

"That would be great," Carter said. "We didn't stop on the way back from New Orleans. Alaina was in too big a hurry to get here."

Tyler raised his eyebrows. "This must be good."

"Oh, yeah," Alaina said as she hurried down the hallway, silently willing the two men to get the lead out.

Joelle stood at the counter, putting lettuce on tur-

key sandwiches. She looked up and smiled when she saw Alaina. "I thought I heard your voice," Joelle said.

Tyler and Carter stepped into the kitchen behind her and Alaina grabbed Joelle's hands, unable to hold her news in any longer.

"We found something," Alaina said, then explained what she and Danae discovered and her and Carter's visit to the doctor. She pulled the letter out of her purse and handed it to Joelle. Tyler stepped behind Joelle and read over her shoulder.

"Wow!" Joelle said. "This makes so much sense now."

"It does?" Alaina looked surprised.

Joelle nodded and told them about her dream. "So the needle wasn't used to kill her. They sedated her."

"That fits with everything," Carter said, "but I'd still like to know how Purcell got her committed. You can't just drop someone off at a mental institution and claim they're sick when they're not."

"I think she was cracking," Joelle said. "The stress and abuse could have put her over the edge. And there's something else…something that I can't prove, but I believe happened."

Joelle told them about her suspicion that Purcell had spiked their milk each night.

"You were always able to stay up later than me," Alaina said. "I could barely get in bed before I was out."

"Exactly," Joelle said. "So if he was doing it to us, why wouldn't he have done it to Mother?"

"As despicable as it sounds," Alaina said, "I've seen it before in child custody cases where one parent wants to make the other look incompetent. If Purcell drugged our mother to the point that she seemed incoherent and erratic, all he'd need was a doctor's assessment and

a couple of credible witnesses to say she was behaving irrationally. He paid for the doctor's assessment—he could have paid for witnesses. If he made a case for child endangerment, it would have been enough to commit her."

"But why?" Joelle said. "Why keep her alive?"

Alaina shook her head. "It sounds like he wanted something and Mother wouldn't tell him what he wanted to know."

"The diamonds?" Joelle said.

"It's possible. Maybe Purcell thought there was more than just her necklace, and he didn't believe her when she said she didn't know. He might have figured that locking her up would make her tell."

Joelle stared at Alaina, her eyes wide. "Then what happened to her after that? I mean, she died at some point or she wouldn't be haunting us, but I always assumed she died here since she appears here."

"Maybe he brought her back here at some point and killed her then."

"That could be. Did you tell Danae and Zach?"

Alaina nodded. "We went by Zach's place before heading back to Calais. We wanted to tell him in person that it didn't look like his father was involved in a murder. He's still not happy about his father's decision to bury an empty casket, but I think he's relieved that it's a lesser sin than what he feared."

Alaina looked out the kitchen window, all the day's events running through her mind. For the first time since she'd arrived in Calais, she finally felt that they were on the right track—that they were finally going to get the answers about everything that happened so long ago.

Suddenly, she froze. "There's something out there."

"Where?" Carter asked, shifting immediately into cop mode.

"In the brush about twenty feet from the house. It was big and moved quickly."

"Bear?" Tyler asked.

"Unless it was walking on hind legs and thinner than the average bear, no."

Carter pulled his pistol from his waistband. "Let's check it out," he said to Tyler, then turned to Joelle and Alaina. "Keep the doors locked and your weapons ready."

The two men rushed outside and Alaina locked the door behind them, already worried about what lurked in the swamp. "Do you have your pistol?" she asked Joelle.

"It's upstairs on the nightstand."

Alaina pulled her pistol from her purse. "Run up and get it. I'll wait in the entry where I can see the balcony."

Alaina followed Joelle to the entry and watched as she hurried up the stairs and into one of the bedrooms. By the time she heard the footsteps behind her, it was too late.

A cloth covered her mouth and nose, a hand pressed against it and an arm wrapped around her back. She struggled for a second, then everything went black.

Chapter Twenty

Relief coursed through Joelle when she saw her pistol on the nightstand where she'd left it that morning. She grabbed it and rushed out of the room.

"Got it!" she yelled down at Alaina.

Her own voice echoed back at her and she drew up short and peered over the balcony. Her heart caught in her throat as she scanned the entry. Alaina was nowhere in sight.

"Alaina!" she called down.

Nothing.

Maybe something happened outside. Maybe Alaina went to help Carter and Tyler.

Clutching her pistol, she inched toward the staircase, scanning below her with every step. There was no sign of Alaina anywhere and no sound echoed up from the entry. She leaned over the railing, trying to look down the kitchen hallway.

When she rose back up, she felt cold metal press against her scalp.

"Drop it," he said.

She let her pistol slide out of her hand and onto the carpeted runner. His voice sounded familiar, but she couldn't place it.

"Now," he said and coughed. "Turn around. Slowly."

Terror coursed through her as the raspy voice from her nightmare rang through her head. It was him. The man who'd helped Purcell attack her mother. The man who'd held her mother down while Purcell drugged her.

Her feet seemed to move involuntarily. She didn't want to turn, but she couldn't keep herself from doing it. She clenched her eyes shut until the gun pressed directly into the center of her forehead, then opened them and stared at the man who'd helped ruin her childhood.

Mayor Dupree!

"I don't understand," she said. "Why would you help Purcell?"

He lowered his pistol and took a step back from her. "The oldest reason in the world—money."

"Fine. That was twenty-five years ago. You got away with it. Why bother with me now and risk exposing yourself?"

His eyes narrowed at her. "Because when you talked to me in the café with your sister, you recognized me. It was only a matter of time before you remembered why."

"I never saw you that night. I only heard you."

He sighed. "Then I guess this is going to be a waste of a bullet."

As he lifted the pistol up toward her head, she screamed.

TYLER AND CARTER hurried through the swamp to the spot Alaina had indicated. Two clear footprints stared up at them from the soft ground.

"This way," Tyler said and headed through the swamp in the direction the steps pointed. As he ran through a thick set of brush, his feet connected with something heavy and large and he grabbed hold of a tree trunk to keep from falling.

Carter slid to a stop behind him and they looked down at the crumpled body of Bert Thibodeaux.

Tyler immediately dropped down and put his fingers to Bert's neck. "He's alive."

Carter stooped and helped Tyler roll Bert over onto his back, then Tyler tapped his cheeks. "Bert. Wake up."

The burly truck driver stirred a bit, then bolted upright.

"Oh, my head," Bert said and clutched his head with both hands.

"What happened?" Tyler said.

"What does it look like? Someone cracked me on the head."

"Did you see who did it?"

"No. He came up behind me."

"You're in a lot of trouble, Bert," Carter said. "A lot of things have gone wrong in this house and I can put you on the hook for all of them if I want."

Bert's eyes widened and for the first time, Tyler saw a glimmer of fear in them. "I haven't hurt nobody. That ain't my thing."

"Then maybe it's time you tell me exactly what your thing is. Or I can haul you in now."

Bert studied Carter's face for a while, and Tyler wondered if the stubborn trucker was about to clam up again, but apparently he figured out that Carter wasn't joking about pinning everything on him.

Finally, he sighed. "I was looking for the diamonds."

Carter's eyes narrowed on him. "How did you know about the diamonds? And don't tell me Purcell told you, because I'm sure he took that secret to the grave hoping to find them himself."

Bert looked down at the ground. "Roger Martin told me. I don't know how he found out."

He was lying. Tyler would bet anything on it, and one look at Carter's face told him his friend didn't buy it either. But what was Bert hiding now?

Or who?

It hit Tyler like a shock wave—the red lacy bra suddenly stringing everything together.

"Sonia," Tyler said. "It was Sonia who told you."

Bert's eyes widened and Tyler knew he was right.

"Johnny said she dated a numbers guy. What do you want to bet it was the estate accountant," Tyler said. "She did it for the information and always intended to come back here to you."

One look at Bert's face and Tyler knew his guess was correct.

Carter whistled. "That's one even I didn't see coming. How have you been getting in the house?"

Defeated, Bert inclined his head toward a set of brush to their right. "Same as always. Through the tunnel."

Tyler stared at Bert for a moment as he remembered the footprints near the house but not leading up to it and the small clearing he'd discovered that first day. The clearing they were standing in now. "The cellar. It connects to the cellar in the butler's pantry."

Tyler pulled the brush and a huge tangle of dead vines came away, exposing a wooden door. "Brant must have seen someone use it. That's how he got in before."

Carter nodded. "And that same someone put a bullet in him before he could make matters worse. And likely cracked our friend Bert here on the head."

"Well," Bert said, "whoever it was is in the house now. The door was still covered with dirt when I got here."

"Get out of here and have your head looked at," Carter told Bert. "I'll be by later to take your state-

ment. Don't even think of leaving town or you'll have more trouble than you'll ever work your way out of."

Bert knew when he was defeated. He gave Carter a single nod and hoisted himself up from the ground. They watched as he stumbled through the brush back toward the house, still clutching his head.

Tyler pulled back the wooden door and peered inside. "It's not deep," he said and climbed down the ladder into the pit. Carter pulled a penlight out of his pocket and dropped it to him.

"I'm going to circle around and enter through the front door so maybe we can corner this bastard once and for all. Be careful when you get to the cellar. He could be in there waiting for you."

Tyler gave him a nod and directed the penlight down the tunnel. The tunnel was so narrow only one person could fit through it at a time, and he had to duck a bit to keep from scraping his head on the ceiling. The entire thing was composed of chopped stone, and Tyler wondered briefly how long the tunnel had been there. The craftsmanship of the stonework led him to believe it was very old.

He hurried down it, careful not to bang his head against the ceiling. It shouldn't take long to reach the cellar entrance given the proximity of the trapdoor from the house. As he rounded a corner, he drew up short. A door made of thick wooden planks and steel belts was directly in front of him.

He pressed his ear against it, but couldn't hear anything. That didn't mean the room was clear, though. Gripping the penlight with his left hand and pistol with his right, he pressed his shoulder against the door and eased it open enough to peer inside. He cast his penlight across the cellar, but didn't see anyone.

Relieved, he stepped out of the tunnel and into the cellar, then turned back to look as the door swung shut. The cellar side was finished with a sheet of paneling that blended perfectly with the rest of the wall, explaining why he hadn't noticed it before. He shone the penlight around the edges of the paneling, now able to make out the outline of the door.

Clever.

He headed up the cellar stairs, wondering if Carter had made it inside the house yet. When he reached the door to the butler's pantry, he paused again, to listen for footsteps. Hearing nothing, he eased the door open a crack and that's when a bloodcurdling scream echoed throughout the house.

Joelle!

He bolted out of the cellar and tore through the kitchen in the direction of the scream, almost tripping over Alaina's prone body in the hallway. He paused only long enough to ensure she was breathing then took off again. What if he was too late? What if, once again, he failed?

Although he didn't think it possible, he ramped his speed up another notch, not about to repeat the worst moment of his life. Especially not now, when it was more important that he succeed than any other time.

Because he couldn't imagine his life without Joelle in it.

He ran into the massive entry, pistol raised and scanning the area for any sign of Joelle. Voices sounded above him and he ran out from under the overhang. What he saw made his blood run cold. A man had Joelle's neck clutched in one hand and his pistol in the other, and even though his back was to Tyler, he rec-

ognized the frame he'd seen leaving the general store a couple of days before.

Joelle's face turned red as she pulled at his arm with both hands, unable to break free from his grasp. Her eyes rolled back in her head and Tyler had to force himself from running upstairs and beating the man to death with his bare hands.

Think smart, Duhon!

Lifting his pistol, Tyler tried to get a clear shot, but Dupree was too close to her. If he took a shot, the bullet might go through Dupree and into Joelle.

She gasped for air and her eyes flickered down and she caught sight of Tyler. He pointed down with his finger, hoping she'd understand what he wanted her to do. Dupree lifted the pistol, his finger positioned on the trigger, and Tyler sighted his gun on the back of the man's head, praying that Joelle acted quickly— before it was too late.

Suddenly, her legs buckled and she dropped to the ground. Without even thinking, Tyler took the shot, and it was deadly accurate.

The bullet passed straight through Dupree's head and hit the paneling on the wall in front of him, splintering the wood as it entered. At the same time, the front door flew open and the alarm went off as Carter ran inside.

Tyler ran up the stairs two at a time and rushed over to Joelle, who was crumpled on the floor. He glanced at Dupree as he passed, but it was clear the man was no longer a threat. He reached down to touch Joelle's face, worried that the strain had caused her to pass out or even worse, go into cardiac arrest, but as his fingers touched her cheek, she opened her eyes and smiled before leaping up into his arms.

Downstairs, Tyler heard Carter call for an ambulance

as he clutched Joelle close to him, saying a silent prayer of thanks that the woman who'd changed his life was still here with him. And if he had his way, she was going to be part of his life every day from this point forward.

"I thought I'd lost you," he whispered. "I couldn't have taken it."

"I know," Joelle said. "After what you'd been through before, I can't imagine how you felt, thinking you might not be able to save me."

"It wasn't failure that scared me." He pulled back a bit and looked down at her. "It was the thought of losing you. I don't pretend to have all the answers, or that us being involved will be without issues, but now that I've met you, I can't imagine my life without you."

Her eyes widened. "Are you sure?"

"It's the only thing in my life I *am* sure about."

She smiled and threw her arms around him again. He stroked her hair and felt her heart beating strong against his chest, and knew without a single doubt that he never wanted to let her go.

"How did you get inside?" she asked.

Tyler told her about the tunnel and finding Bert, who had been trying to find the diamonds.

Her eyes widened and she sucked in a breath. "I know where they are."

"What?"

"The diamonds." Joelle smiled, then started laughing. "They've been here all along."

"Where?"

"In a purple Crown Royal bag tucked underneath the seat of a school desk. They look like rocks—just like the rocks in the driveway."

"Then how do you know…"

"Because Mother gave them to me and told me never

to let Purcell see them. I'd bet everything I'll inherit that those diamonds have been tucked under the seat of that desk for over twenty-five years."

Tyler smiled, trying to wrap his mind around what Joelle said. "Wouldn't that be perfect?"

Joelle's smile faded. "It's not perfect until we find our mother, but it's going to happen. We're going to find out what happened to our mother and I'm going to move to Calais and start a life with you."

He gathered her in his arms again. "Sounds perfect to me," he whispered.

Chapter Twenty-One

Two days later

Joelle stopped at the entrance to the Eleanor Roosevelt Mental Treatment Facility and looked at Alaina and Danae. "Are you ready?" she asked.

They looked at each other, then back at her and nodded. Carter, Zach and Tyler stood behind them, a unified front supporting them. Tyler gave her a thumbs-up and she smiled.

"Let's do this, then," she said and pulled open the door.

Joelle walked up to the receptionist desk with Alaina and Danae. "Hi," she said. "We have an appointment with Mrs. Anderson. Well, the appointment is for Carter Trahan."

The receptionist checked her log and smiled. "Please step through the secured door when the buzzer sounds and I'll have Marie escort you to Mrs. Anderson's office."

The buzzer seemed incredibly loud in the relative quiet of the building, but Joelle pulled open the door and they all stepped through, where Marie greeted them and led them down several long, white hallways and into a room at the end of the hall.

A large woman with a big head of white hair met them at the front of an enormous room. Shelves, standing a good eight feet tall, ran in long rows from the front of the room to the back. File folders filled every shelf, and Joelle felt a wave of sadness run through her that so many people had needed such a place.

"Carter Trahan?" the woman asked.

Carter stepped forward and extended his hand. "I'm Carter. You must be Mrs. Anderson."

She smiled. "Please call me Emily. You weren't lying about bringing family with you, were you?"

"No, ma'am," he said and introduced everyone. "These three ladies think their mother might have been a patient here twenty-five years ago."

Emily frowned. "Then why don't you ask her?"

Carter explained briefly about Ophelia's supposed death and the dispersal of the sisters.

Emily's eye grew wider and wider and when Carter finished, she shook her head, giving the sisters a sympathetic look. "What a horrible story. I sure hope I can get you some answers. Grab some of those chairs and drag them over to my desk."

Three chairs were positioned against the wall. The men dragged them over in front of Emily's desk and Alaina, Danae and Joelle each took a seat as the men circled around the side of the desk.

"What was your mother's name?" Emily asked.

"Ophelia LeBeau," Alaina said.

Emily tapped on the computer, then scrolled through records, shaking her head. "No one by the name of Le-Beau has ever been admitted here."

Joelle's heart dropped. Surely they hadn't come all this way for nothing. "Are you certain?"

Emily nodded. "I've been entering the historical re-

cords myself. I didn't think I recognized the name, but I wanted to be sure."

Suddenly, a thought occurred to Joelle. "What if he didn't admit her with her real name? Someone might discover her that way."

"That would only be possible if he had the appropriate documents," Emily said. "Is that something he could have managed?"

Carter nodded. "There's no limit to what this man could manage."

"Okay," Emily said, "then let's take a look by time. Give me a year and month to start."

Alaina gave her the year and month they were told their mother died. Emily tapped on the keyboard again, then scrolled through records. Joelle was about to give the whole thing up as a rabbit trail when Emily put her finger on the screen.

"Only one woman around your mother's age was admitted at that time. Name is Mary Parker. That mean anything to any of you?"

Joelle looked over at Alaina and Danae, who both shook their head. "No," Joelle said, "but he would have used a name that couldn't be traced to her family or to himself, right? Why was she admitted?"

Emily blew out a breath. "Without knowing for sure she's your mother, I can't give out any information about her condition."

"But surely," Joelle said, "that doesn't matter after death."

Emily's eyes widened and she looked at each of them. "Mary Parker isn't dead."

Joelle sucked in a breath as Danae grabbed her hand and squeezed. "You're certain?" Joelle asked.

"Positive," Emily said. "She's still a resident here.

The staff always thought it odd that she never had a single family member visit her, but this might explain it all. I can arrange for you to see her…if you're prepared for that."

"Yes." All three of them spoke at once and Emily rose from her desk. "Now, I don't want you to get your hopes up. This woman may be someone completely different."

"We understand," Alaina said, "and we're ready to accept whatever comes of this, but we need to know for sure, either way."

Emily gave them a single nod and picked up the phone. She gave a brief explanation of the situation, then went silent. Joelle held her breath, hoping they weren't refused access. Finally, Emily hung up the phone and rose from her desk.

"I can take you up myself," she said and waved them out of the office.

They all followed Emily down the hall and crowded on the elevator. "Mary stopped speaking shortly after she got here. Shocked the heck out of everyone when she started trying to again a couple of months ago. I've said a few words to her myself. She has always been such a sweet lady, but so sad it hurts even looking at her. I have to admit, I hope you're her family. Maybe she can get better."

"You have no idea what's wrong with her?" Joelle asked.

Emily shrugged. "One of the nurse's aides said she thought she was paranoid schizophrenic, but maybe what everyone thought was paranoia was the truth, huh? Wouldn't that be something?"

She stopped at a large steel door and tapped a code into a security panel. Joelle heard a loud click and

Emily pushed the door open and waved them inside, then ensured the door closed and locked behind them. Joelle crossed her arms across her chest, a chill running through her at the thought of being locked in this sterile environment for twenty-five years.

"Since there's so many of you, her nurse thought it would be better to bring her into the activity room. It's empty right now, so you'll have plenty of privacy." She stopped in front of a door. "Are you ready?"

They all nodded, and Emily pushed the door open so that they could walk inside.

A nurse stood beside a chair, positioned near a plate-glass window overlooking a courtyard. The woman in the chair peered out the window, her long black-and-silver hair tied back in a ponytail.

Then she turned.

Alaina clutched Joelle's arm as Joelle gasped.

"I don't believe it," Danae whispered.

The woman focused on them and her eyes widened. She pushed herself up from the chair and walked toward them, the shock on her face turning to excitement with every step. They stood stock-still, none of them able to move.

Mother!

Life had taken her youth, but it couldn't take her delicate bone structure. Joelle would have recognized her face anywhere and at any age. As she stepped in front of them, her eyes shone and tears collected in her eyes.

"My girls," she whispered.

Those two words broke the spell and all three of them reached for her as they collapsed into tears. But this time, it was tears of joy.

Epilogue

Christmas Eve

Joelle ran down the kitchen hallway, pulling her heels on as she went. "They're here," she called out and looked up at the balcony. Tyler started down the stairs and she sucked in a breath at how gorgeous he looked in his black tuxedo.

He grinned at her as he ran down the stairs and lifted her up to twirl her around. "Have I told you yet how stunning you are in this dress?"

The dress was navy blue sequined and designed to fit every curve of her body, and Joelle knew she looked good in it. "Not in the last ten minutes," she said with a smile.

"Have I told you how I can't wait to get you out of it?"

She laughed. "Party first. Private celebration later."

He put her down and gave her a lingering kiss. "Promise?"

"It's going to be the highlight of my night."

"Really?" He lifted her hand to see the sparkling diamond he'd placed on her finger earlier. "I thought this was the highlight."

She looked down at the ring and sighed, unable to

help herself. "A girl's allowed more than one highlight on such a special occasion. Now, come on, before they start banging on the door." She grabbed his hand and pulled him to the front door.

She could already hear the voices outside as car doors slammed. Wave number one of the party guests had arrived. The first hour was for family—the people closest to the sisters and Ophelia—then after that, the entire town was invited to the celebration.

Joelle pulled open the door and beamed at everyone as they made their way toward the house. Carter and Alaina, looking every bit the golden couple they were. Zach and Danae, beautifully matched and so clearly in love. Amos, no longer on crutches but still refusing any help from his niece, who tried to assist him up the steps. Johnny, carrying a tray of food even though he'd been told only to bring himself.

The last couple made Joelle's heart swell with joy— William and Willamina.

Willamina was simply breathtaking in a long white sequined gown, and William was every bit his son's father in his black tuxedo. She had her hand on his arm and as they walked, he looked down at her, his adoration apparent in his smile.

"Look at my dad," Tyler whispered.

Joelle slipped her hand in Tyler's and gave it a squeeze. "I'm so glad you pushed him. They're made for each other."

Everyone filed up the steps, pausing only long enough to hug Joelle and exclaim over her ring before entering the house. Gasps filled the entry as they collected in the center of the large room, gazing around with obvious delight.

The house was returned to its previous splendor. A

thirty-foot tree sat at the back of the entry, its top almost reaching the vaulted ceiling. It glittered with white and silver ribbons and decorations. Thick garland made from real pine trees wove around the balconies and down the spiral staircase. Silver ribbon and white poinsettias that matched the tree adorned it.

When everything unfolded to the Calais residents, the entire town was stunned by the extent of Purcell's crimes and the number of Calais locals who had participated. They were equally surprised and thrilled that Ophelia was alive and back home where she belonged, but saddened that she'd lost so many years of her life locked away in a facility where she finally chose silence because no one would listen.

"It's beautiful," Alaina said. "Is everything ready?"

"Yes, it's been amazing how everyone in Calais pitched in and helped get the house ready. I can't believe all of this was accomplished in less than two months."

"Now that all the bad guys and ghosts are gone, people are happy to be here," Alaina said.

Danae looked around the beautiful room and smiled. "Next year, your first occupants will be moving in. I can't believe this former monstrosity is going to be a beautiful safe haven for abused women. It's such a wonderful thing you're doing, Joelle."

Joelle sniffed. "I couldn't have done it without you. After all, the house belonged to Mother and you've both invested some of your own trust funds in this."

"And I've never been happier to write a check in my life," Alaina said as Danae nodded in agreement.

Joelle reached out to grab her sisters' hands. "Let's go get Mother. She's been primping forever. It's time for her to get out here and see the people who care about her."

They headed to a newly remodeled bedroom at the back of the entry and Joelle knocked lightly on the door before poking her head inside. "Mom, it's us," she said and the three sisters slipped inside.

Ophelia stepped out of the bathroom and they all stared. She wore a long dress of satin and sequined teal. Joelle had called her genius hairstylist for an on-site consultation, and she'd trimmed Ophelia's long locks and eliminated the silver, restoring her hair to the lustrous black they remembered.

Her skin had developed a healthy glow from working outside, planting flowers alongside her daughters, but she'd kept hidden while the contractors and Calais locals were in the house, not yet steady enough to face everyone.

Ophelia didn't have an answer for how she'd been able to appear to each of them—only that she concentrated all of her will on making it happen and was sometimes able to see them, even speak. She'd also seen the other spirit—the one they thought was Purcell—and had driven him away. Since she'd returned to her home, no one had seen the bad spirit, and they all hoped that meant they were rid of Trenton Purcell once and for all.

"Mother, you're breathtaking," Alaina said.

Ophelia looked in the dresser mirror and pulled at a tendril of hair. "I don't know. This dress is cut so low and I'm not sure about my hair."

"Your hair is gorgeous," Danae said.

Joelle nodded. "And we have just the thing to take attention away from that low-cut dress."

Alaina pulled a velvet jewelry box from her purse and handed it to their mother. She gave them a questioning look.

"Just open it," Alaina said.

She lifted the lid, then her hand went up to cover her mouth. "How did you find it? He told me he sold it." She lifted the necklace out of the box—the necklace that matched the one in the painting.

"We didn't find the original," Alaina said. "But Joelle remembered where the uncut diamonds were."

Ophelia's eyes widened. "The purple bag. I can't believe I'd forgotten."

"Those stones brought you a lot of pain," Joelle said. "It's no wonder that you would compartmentalize them and lock that memory away."

"But with the stones discovered and the painting to guide us on design," Danae continued, "we were able to have a new necklace made—to replace the one that was taken from you."

"Let me fasten it," Alaina said, and stepped around behind their mother to fasten the necklace. She hooked the necklace in place, then stepped back around to stand beside her sisters.

The necklace glimmered at Ophelia's neck, but it came nowhere near to matching the brilliance of her smile.

* * * * *

THE SECRET OF CYPRIERE BAYOU

CAST OF CHARACTERS

Olivia Markham—She makes her living by renting haunted houses and writing about them, but when she rents laMalediction, she realizes it's the house from her dreams. She's determined to figure out her connection, but someone is just as determined to see that she doesn't.

John Landry—The New Orleans cop is on the hunt for his missing stepsister, and is desperate to find her before she becomes another missing-person casualty. Posing as a caretaker got him a position at laMalediction, his stepsister's last known destination, but he can't conduct an investigation with Olivia Markham looking over his shoulder.

Russ Wheeler—The attorney for the Borque estate should have informed Olivia that he'd hired a new caretaker, but he failed to mention it. Given the deterioration of the house and grounds, it looks like one was needed long before now.

Sheriff Blanchard—It is clear to Olivia that the small-town sheriff doesn't appreciate her appearance in his town and especially at laMalediction, but is he a superstitious fool or is he hiding something far more earthly?

Tom Breaux—The café owner gives Olivia directions to laMalediction despite the obvious disapproval of the sheriff, but doesn't seem happy to learn that not only has she located the house, but she intends to stay.

Aubrey Murphy—The old caretaker supposedly took leave due to a family emergency, but none of his family seems to know what the emergency is or where Aubrey is now.

To my critique partners, Cari Manderscheid and Cindy Taylor, for your constant cheerleading and support on every new venture I take with my writing career. To my friend Colleen Gleason, who always pushes me to action when I'm on the fence. To my friend, Tracey Stanley, who tells everyone who will listen about my books. To my daily chat buddy, Leslie Langtry, for always reminding me that we can't take ourselves too seriously. To my parents, Jimmie and Bobbie Morris, for never doubting I could accomplish anything I set my mind to. To Jimmie, Donna, and Katianne Morris, for your continued support in an unpredictable career path. To my agent, Kristin Nelson, for venturing into unknown territory and creating my relationship with Harlequin. To my editor, Allison Lyons, for your patience with me in learning the ropes and your enthusiasm for the work itself. It's always a pleasure to work with people who truly love their product. And to my cousin, Cathy Jane, who no longer has an excuse for not reading one of my books, as this one is short.

Chapter One

The sky rolled with a mass of gray clouds, and the air became thick with humidity. Olivia Markham glanced anxiously at the swirling sky as she pulled into Cypriere, Louisiana, all five weather-beaten buildings of it. Peering down each side of the street, she searched for signs of life. It would be the first she'd seen in well over two hours of driving deep into the bayous.

A wooden sign swung under the awning of an old brick building to her left. The painted lettering on the sign had long since faded, but Olivia could barely make out the word *café*. Surely someone inside would be able to give her directions. She pulled into an open parking space right in front of the café and hurried inside. Bells on the door jangled as she crossed the threshold and the eight or so patrons stopped what they were doing to stare at her.

She paused for a moment, but when any form of greeting wasn't forthcoming she launched into her own. "Hello," she said. "Apparently, I'm a little lost. Can anyone give me directions to laMalediction?"

The patrons dropped their gazes back to their tables without saying a word. A middle-aged waitress sloshed coffee on her hand and although the hot liquid must

have burned, the waitress froze, looking over at a man sitting at the counter.

A man with salt-and-pepper hair and a gold bar pinned on his shirt identifying him as Sheriff Blanchard turned to face her. "Ain't no one lived at laMalediction for over thirty years. What business you have out there?"

No business of yours. Olivia felt her back tighten with aggravation, in no mood to deal with another round of small-town mentality. "I've leased the house for the winter."

"What in the world would you do that for? Winter's wet and the road's cut off from town half the time. Nothing out there for a young lady to do."

"I'm a writer," Olivia said. "Horror novels, actually, and haunted houses are my specialty."

The sheriff inclined his head toward the plate-glass storefront. "You'll be wanting to stay in town until the rain stops. Bayou roads are no place for somebody unfamiliar with Cypriere, especially during a thunderstorm."

Olivia shook her head, the overwhelming urge to race away from these people overpowering any good sense she might have otherwise had. "I need to get settled before dark. I'll take my chances with the rain."

The sheriff narrowed his eyes at her, but before he could say another word the cook pulled a tablet out from under the counter and began to draw a crude map.

"You take the main road east," the cook said and pointed at a line on the map. "There ain't no street signs to follow, ain't no street either when it comes right down to it. It's more like a dirt path, and you're gonna have to find your way by landmarks. I've drawn them on the map and labeled them."

Olivia gave the cook a grateful smile. "Thank you. I'm sure I'll see you again. I'm not much of a cook, and I eventually tire of sandwiches."

The cook gave her a single nod and turned back to the grill, ignoring the sheriff's disapproving stare. Olivia took one step backward toward the door, feeling that she'd already overstayed her welcome even though she hadn't unpacked a single bag. She gave the frowning sheriff a wave, then turned around and left the café.

She glanced at the map, then backed her car up and headed east. What the heck was going on here? She figured laMalediction's bloody history would prevent the more easily spooked from speaking of it at all, but these people lived within miles of the structure. Surely they knew that it was only a house?

She glanced in her rearview mirror for a final look behind her. The sheriff was standing just outside the café, watching her intently as she drove out of town, but when she took a good look at his expression the annoyance she'd expected to see was nowhere in sight. Even though it was easily eighty degrees outside, she felt a shiver run through her.

The sheriff looked frightened.

"Damn it!" Olivia jammed her foot onto the brake as the road she'd been driving on disappeared into a wall of cypress trees. She must have missed a turn somewhere. Glancing up at the rolling black clouds, she bit her lip. That creepy sheriff was going to be right. Chances of her beating the storm to laMalediction were growing slimmer by the minute.

If it was the right way to begin with.

The thought ripped through her mind like one of

those bolts of lightning that was surely on its way. What if the cook had meant to get her stranded in the storm?

Stop it!

Imagining monsters when there were none was great for her stories, but she couldn't afford that kind of fantasizing in real life. She looked at the map once more and decided that she must have missed the twisted cypress trees that marked the last turnoff. Backing up slowly, she scanned the brush and finally located the trees almost hidden by a drape of moss and marsh grass. Mentally chastising herself for her earlier fear, she eased her car into the narrow opening. Only a thin strip of illumination from the fading sunlight passed through to the path.

Ten minutes later the light vanished completely and rain began to pour in giant, blinding sheets. Her visibility reduced to almost nothing; she eased her foot off the accelerator, slowing to a crawl. Seconds later her car dipped into a low spot on the path and came to a stop, the tires spinning in place. She grabbed her cell phone from the passenger seat. No signal.

Hitching a ride wasn't likely given the location, and she wasn't going to drive her car out of the hole it was stuck in. Walking was the only option. So did she brave a monsoon and try to locate a house hidden away in the bayou, or did she follow the path back to town, which would probably take hours?

Suddenly, lightning struck in front of her car, shaking the entire vehicle with its impact. The aftershocks of the blast echoed around her like flashes from a camera, illuminating an iron gate twenty yards in front of her. She felt her pulse quicken. Surely, the house was close. She kept a change of clothes, toiletries and her pistol in her backpack. That would do for the night. She

grabbed the backpack and a flashlight and stepped out into the storm.

The rain pelted her, stinging her face with its force. She lowered her head and rushed along the path as fast as her vision and the thick bayou mud allowed.

Would this house be the one?

She was holding one hand over her eyes to block the rain, straining to make out the jutting edges of the almost invisible structure in front of her when a burst of lightning struck right over the top of the house, lighting up the structure and the grounds surrounding it. She sucked in a breath so hard it made her chest hurt. Her heart pounded in her throat, blocking out the noise of the storm around her. She felt her fingernails dig into the palm of her hand as she clenched it.

She'd looked for it for eighteen years. And now, she'd found it.

OLIVIA RAN THE remainder of the way to the house, sliding to a stop on a covered porch. Her heart raced as she unlocked the massive front door. She felt inside the door for the light switch, but nothing changed when she pushed it up. Shining her flashlight into the pitch-black house, she saw a huge circular staircase in the center of a two-story entry with marble floors.

She pulled off her mud-caked boots and left them on the porch, then closed and locked the front door behind her. Without electricity, the smartest thing to do was find a bedroom and secure it for the night. In houses of this era the bedrooms were usually upstairs, so she grabbed her backpack and started up the spiral staircase to a long hallway.

The first two rooms were being used for storage, but she hit pay dirt on the third. A huge bedroom, complete

with king-size bed and adjoining bath. The bedding was dusty but would do for a night. She closed the bedroom door and turned the giant iron key in the lock on the inside, wishing she had the dead bolts from her luggage. Not that it mattered. A house this old would have secret passageways for servants, and she needed to locate them. Securing her sleeping quarters was her first task when entering old homes, and her need for security at laMalediction was stronger than any she'd ever had.

She started tapping the walls in the far corner of the room, working her way around and listening for a hollow sound or trying to detect flex in the paneling. After an hour of looking she gave up and slumped into a chair in front of an antique desk. When she got her luggage she'd have the tools necessary to do a thorough job. Right now she needed a hot bath and a good night's sleep.

She grabbed a T-shirt and shorts from her backpack, turned on the water in a huge, claw-foot tub and sighed with relief when it came out hot. She shrugged off her damp clothes and slipped into the steamy bathwater. *This is heaven.* Leaning forward, she placed her head under the faucet and began to rinse her short tresses.

And that's when she heard a creaking sound.

She bolted upright and banged her head on the faucet. "Who's there?" she called out.

Only silence greeted her.

She waited a couple of seconds and was ready to decide it was just the house settling when she felt a gentle current of cold air blow across her bare skin. Shivering, she rose quietly from the tub and reached for a thick towel that hung on the wall. She stepped silently onto the floor, cursing herself for leaving her weapon in her backpack, and crept to the bathroom entry.

Her flashlight was propped on a shelf above the sink and it cast a dim glow around her. Without so much as a breath indicating her presence, she leaned into the doorway and peered into the bedroom.

Empty.

She grabbed the flashlight and shined it into the bedroom for a better look. Still nothing. But as soon as she stepped through the doorway, she felt the remnants of cool air pass across her bare arms and knew it hadn't been her imagination. That draft had come from somewhere in the bedroom, and since both the windows and the door were locked tight only one explanation worked. There was another way into the master suite, and someone had used it.

She turned the flashlight on her backpack to see if anything looked disturbed, and that's when she heard a noise downstairs. Standing stock-still, she listened, hoping to hear the sound again, but there was only silence. Frustrated, she blew out the breath she'd been holding.

It's an old house. It makes noise.

But what she'd heard wasn't the normal creaking and settling of an old house. It was a whooshing sound. Like someone was moving something big—maybe the exit panel to the hidden passageway attached to her room.

Damned if someone was going to get away with spying on her. She hurried into the bathroom and pulled on her shorts and T-shirt, not even bothering to dry off, then grabbed her nine millimeter out of her backpack and slipped out of the bedroom and into the pitch-black hall. She paused a couple of seconds until her eyes adjusted somewhat to the dark, and then, lifting her gun next to her shoulder in a ready position, she crept down the padded center of the hallway.

At the end of the hallway, she crouched down and

peered between the wrought-iron banisters of the staircase. The entry was empty and she squinted into the black, trying to make out movement in the sitting room. Nothing.

Holding her breath, she strained to hear, hoping the sound she'd heard earlier would repeat. One second. Two seconds. Three. There it was again.

Now or never.

She took a deep breath and slowly exhaled, then, staying low, she eased down the stairs and slipped behind a life-size gladiator statue in the entry. She peered into the sitting room, and for a moment it looked as if a piece of the back wall shifted. And that's when she heard it—the shuffle of footsteps on ceramic tile.

An entryway that opened to the kitchen stood on the opposite end of the sitting area. She tightened her grip on her pistol and slipped around the corner and into the sitting room. Staying as close as possible to the wall, she made her way around the room and stopped at the edge of the kitchen entrance to listen again.

For a moment there was nothing, then she heard the footsteps, the sound so faint it barely registered. Her pulse was already racing and she felt her heart beating in her chest when she realized the footsteps were getting closer. She flattened herself against the wall and took aim at the entrance. Then the footsteps stopped.

Her heart beat so loudly she was certain it would give her away. She'd stopped breathing altogether. Did she stay put or confront the intruder? Surely, whoever was sneaking around wasn't expecting a woman with a gun. The element of surprise should be on her side. She closed her eyes and said a silent prayer. Then, before she could change her mind, she slipped around the corner and into the kitchen.

And that's when he grabbed her.

HE WAS FAST—FASTER than she would have believed someone could be and still not make any noise. Before she could even zero in on him, he'd disarmed her and had one hand over her mouth, holding in the scream she tried to let out. She felt her heart in her throat and for the first time in her life wondered if this was how it was all going to end, just like a scene out of one of her books.

Suddenly the lights blinked on and he spun her around to face him, one hand still gripping her shoulder.

"Who the hell are you?" he asked, his amber eyes blazing.

The man was probably mid-thirties, tall, and despite the hooded jacket he wore, Olivia could tell he was built for action. Olivia yanked her shoulder out from under his hand and took a step back, glancing at his hand that held her gun. "I'm the person with a key. Who the hell are you?" Olivia shot back, hoping her voice didn't sound as shaky as she felt.

"The caretaker. You're trespassing on private property."

"I'm not trespassing. I leased this house, and if you were really the caretaker, you would know that. Who hired you? Wheeler?"

The man's eyes narrowed at her. "You know Wheeler?"

"Look, I've already told you I have a lease. What I don't have is an answer from you. Now, do I have to call the police?"

He let out a single laugh. "Go ahead and try. The landline in the house hasn't been hooked up in years and cell phone service went out as soon as the storm hit."

"Rest assured, as soon as I can, I'll be calling someone about you." She held out her hand, forcing herself to keep it steady. "I'd like my gun, and I'd like for you to leave." She couldn't even breathe, waiting for him

to react. This was it. If he wanted to harm her, he had every advantage.

He studied her for a moment, then placed the gun in her hand. At first it surprised her that he'd returned her weapon without an argument, but then she remembered how he'd disarmed her with complete ease and in a pitch-black room. Her stomach clenched, and she realized that even with the gun in her hand she wasn't the least bit safe. She waited for him to leave, but he just stared at her as if he was sizing her up.

"You always walk around in the dark, half-dressed and carrying a gun?" he asked.

Damn it. Olivia suddenly realized she was standing in the bright light of the kitchen, soaking wet and wearing only a thin white T-shirt and cotton shorts. She crossed her arms and he smirked. "When I'm supposed to be alone," she said, "and I hear someone downstairs, then yeah, I walk around in the dark, half-dressed and carrying a gun."

"Well, you'll be all alone in about five seconds. I suggest you find someplace to park yourself until morning before you shoot someone." He whirled around and left through a back door, slamming it shut behind him.

Olivia stared after him, her heart still racing. What in the world? The only caretaker the attorney had mentioned was supposed to be eighty years old. There was no way the angry hulk of a man who'd just left was the person the attorney had described. She crossed the kitchen and locked the door behind him, then hurried upstairs.

She locked the bedroom door, pulled the antique desk over in front of it and set the chair on top of it for good measure. Stepping back to study her handiwork, she bit her lip, then glanced around the room. *Ugly green vase*

in corner. Perfect. She grabbed the tall, hideous vase from the corner and stuck it on top of the chair. Granted, with its weight, it didn't exactly add anything to securing the door but at least if someone tried to enter the bedroom that way, she'd hear them coming.

There was no way to easily dry her clothes so she toweled off the worst of the bathwater from her hair and body and slipped into bed, propped upright, gun in hand and every single light in the room blazing.

Chapter Two

John Landry let the kitchen door swing shut with a bang as he stepped out into the storm. What the hell was going on? The attorney had never mentioned someone leasing the house, and even if he'd known someone was taking up residence in the little mansion of horrors, the last person he could have imagined was the petite, mouthy, gun-toting spitfire he'd accosted. What kind of woman leased a derelict of a house, hidden away in a bayou, whose locally given name quite literally translated to "the Curse"?

The last thing he needed right now were complications, and women were always a complication. *This* woman could ruin everything.

The rain poured down and he pulled the hood of his jacket up over his head. He walked the length of the house, shining a flashlight behind the bushes that lined the exterior wall. Nothing. Finally, at the edge of the house, he saw them—a set of footprints in the mud just below a window in an empty downstairs room. He scanned the window and saw the wood chips at the bottom of the frame and the broken lock inside. Someone had pried it open, but there was no way to tell how recently.

He turned his attention back to the ground and fol-

lowed the footsteps to the edge of the woods that sur-
rounded the estate, where they disappeared in the brush.
Damn it! From his window in the caretaker's cottage
he'd seen a light downstairs in the main house maybe
fifteen minutes ago. It was small and erratic in move-
ment like a flashlight would be, and since the house was
supposed to be empty he'd gone to investigate. Then
he'd gotten sidetracked with that crazy woman play-
ing detective. Since she hadn't been carrying a flash-
light when he disarmed her, John knew he'd missed his
chance to catch the real trespasser.

Assuming the woman was telling the truth about the
lease and the key, she had no reason to sneak through
the woods and break into the house but someone had
a reason. A reason good enough to come out in this
storm. The question was, did it have anything to do
with his case?

He stepped out of the woods and headed across the
courtyard to the caretaker's cottage. The last thing he
needed was that woman hovering around, watching his
every move, especially when most of them had nothing
to do with repairs. That day he'd searched all the down-
stairs rooms of the main house and had stopped only
because the power went out. He'd planned on starting
up again as soon as power was restored, but with that
woman lurking inside with a firearm it looked like he'd
have to wait. John had no earthly idea why the woman
would want to lease a house like laMalediction, but first
thing in the morning he was going to find out.

Then he was going to figure out the fastest way to
get rid of her.

He gave one final glance at the main house as he en-
tered the cottage. The only light was upstairs, probably
in one of the bedrooms. He gave the grounds a final

glance, but apparently the trespasser was not interested in trying his luck again tonight. Or he'd gotten what he came for and escaped without a scratch.

John pulled off his dirty boots and left them next to the front door, then grabbed a beer from the refrigerator and slid into a chair at the tiny breakfast table that was serving as his work space. He picked up a plastic bag and studied the bright pink button inside. The button was new, and had no business being on the floor in the library of the main house. A room that by the amount of dust collecting on the shelves and tables hadn't been cleaned in a long time, quite possibly years. Unless the old caretaker was a fan of bright pink, someone else, most likely female, had recently been in that room.

Unfortunately, John had no way of knowing if the button belonged to his missing half sister. He'd already questioned his mother, who'd indicated that his sister owned quite a few garments in pink, but then, he guessed a lot of women did.

He slammed the bag back down on the table and took a gulp of beer. He was running out of time. John knew better than most that the longer people remained missing, the less likely they were to be found alive. And that was assuming you found them at all.

Finding Rachel dead wasn't an option. If he didn't bring his younger sister home alive and well, he knew with complete certainty that their mother, who was fighting a seemingly losing battle with cancer, would just give up.

He ran one hand through his wet hair and silently cursed the women in his life. Why couldn't Rachel have focused her master's thesis on something other than ancient southern architecture? At the very least, she could

have limited her research trips to only those houses that had been conveniently converted to bed-and-breakfasts instead of traipsing off to abandoned mansions in the middle of a swamp. There was far less chance of disappearing in a public place, but this forgotten estate, hidden away from the rest of the world, was just the sort of place to come face-to-face with trouble.

Of course, now that he'd seen laMalediction he could understand Rachel's fascination with the structure. The few press clippings she'd assembled in a folder marked "Research" had created more questions about the house than answers, and John knew his adventurous and highly inquisitive sister would not have been able to have left the "haunted" house out of her thesis work despite its remote location.

His mother was already in a panic, her health rapidly declining, and it had only been three days since Rachel had disappeared. She'd let him know in no uncertain terms that the only thing she would live for was the safe return of her baby. Like the additional pressure would magically give him answers he didn't have.

And now there was another woman in the mix, and from their brief encounter he'd guess she was just as obstinate and determined as his mother. The caretaker job had been an unexpected miracle, giving him legitimate access to the estate. Now that access would be under scrutiny that he couldn't afford.

It hadn't slipped his notice that the trespasser had appeared at the same time as the woman. That gun she carried was no toy, and despite the fact that he'd easily disarmed her, he could tell she'd had some training on how to properly use a weapon. He was fairly certain she wasn't the one who'd jimmied that window, but he had no way of knowing if she'd brought trouble with her.

No matter really.

Her presence in the house was trouble enough. Trouble he didn't need.

OLIVIA AWAKENED THE next morning with the sunlight shining directly in her face. Startled, she sat straight up in bed and realized she'd fallen asleep clutching her flashlight and Mace. Her pistol was still within easy reach on the nightstand. Squinting, she covered her eyes with one hand and blinked to adjust to the glare. The rain had stopped sometime in the middle of the night and she must have drifted off to sleep. Apparently her subconscious had decided the likelihood of a second intrusion was slim, or her mind was simply too exhausted to care any longer.

She looked over at the bedroom door. The key, desk, table, chair and ugly vase were all in place, but that didn't make her feel much better. Someone had come into the room last night when she was in the bath, and she'd bet everything she had that they hadn't used the bedroom door. Blocking the door last night had been a necessary thing to "fool" her frantic mind into some semblance of safety, but here in the stark light of day she knew that safety had been as fictional as the books she wrote.

Outside, an engine fired up and she climbed out of bed to have a look. That "caretaker" was on the front lawn, using a chain saw on a couple of large limbs that had fallen in the driveway. His straight dark hair was just a little too long to be considered tidy and his skin had a beautiful tanned glow, either from the sun or perhaps a Creole heritage. She tried not to admire the way he handled the piece of equipment on a limb the size of a horse, but it was impossible not to when he tackled

the tree limb as if he had a personal vendetta against the hunk of wood. *If he's not legitimate, he's pretending awfully well.*

She glanced at her watch and groaned. It wasn't even eight o'clock. She grabbed her cell phone from the nightstand and was pleased to see that service was restored. Scrolling through her contacts, she located the estate attorney and dialed. It was his personal cell and Olivia hoped she woke the man. It would serve him right after her being scared half to death the night before, and being left to dodge a potential chain saw murderer this morning.

"Hello," the attorney mumbled.

"Mr. Wheeler, this is Olivia Markham."

"Yes." The attorney sounded a bit more focused than before. "Ms. Markham, what can I do for you?"

"I'm sorry to call you so early," Olivia lied, "but I've run into a problem here at laMalediction."

"What sort of problem? Are you all right?"

"I'm fine, but I got a bit of a scare last night from a man who says you hired him as a caretaker. He obviously wasn't expecting me, either, and it's lucky I didn't put a bullet in him."

Okay, so there wasn't a chance for her to put a bullet in him or she would have taken it, but Wheeler didn't need to know that.

"I am so sorry, Ms. Markham." The attorney sounded completely flustered. "The old caretaker had a family emergency and had to leave unexpectedly. I've been trying to hire a younger, more capable man for quite a while, and Mr. Landry is the first suitable applicant I've had. The house needs extensive repairs before it can be sold."

"You never mentioned hiring a new caretaker and

you should have. And since Mr. Landry appeared as shocked as me, I can only assume you didn't bother to speak to him, either. Someone could have been seriously injured, Mr. Wheeler."

"I apologize. I meant to call both of you yesterday morning but got so busy I forgot. I tried in the evening and last night, but couldn't reach either of you. I assure you Mr. Landry's credentials are fine."

Olivia looked out the window, watching "Mr. Landry" stack the cut branches to the side of the driveway. "Good. Then you won't mind sending me a copy of his paperwork."

"I'm sorry, but Mr. Landry's paperwork is confidential. Without his consent, I can't really send you his information."

"Fine. Then I'll be by your office tomorrow to cancel the lease."

"Wait! Surely something can be worked out. I don't want you to cancel."

"And I don't want to cancel, but as you know, the house is very remote. I have every right to know exactly who I'm sharing space with. If you're not willing to provide that information, then I won't feel comfortable staying."

"I understand," the attorney said, but Olivia could tell by his tone that he wasn't the least bit happy with the situation. "I will contact Mr. Landry today and explain the situation. I'm sure he'll give me approval to forward his paperwork to you for your review. If not, then I'll relieve him of his responsibilities and find another person for the position. Will that suffice?"

"For now, but I want that paperwork before the day is over. Email all the documents to me. Does Mr. Landry have a first name?"

"John. As soon as I get to my office, I'll contact Mr. Landry and get his permission to forward the documents. Give me a couple of hours."

"Thank you. I'll be looking for it." She flipped the phone shut and tossed it back on the nightstand. The attorney had annoyed her with his forgetfulness and seeming unwillingness to understand the situation he'd placed her in. Did he really think it was acceptable for her to be shut away in the middle of nowhere with a stranger? If so, he'd obviously lost all common sense.

She stretched, touching the floor with her hands, then rose back up, thinking about her agenda for the morning. First, she was going to brush her teeth, then she was going to put on her mud-caked boots, stroll outside in her makeshift pajamas and ask John Landry to show her some ID. Then she was going to convince him to help get her car out of the mud.

Piece of cake.

Ten minutes later she stepped outside and walked to the middle of the huge circular drive. She slowly turned to get a good look at it in the daylight. The bizarre angles of the roof, the two round attic windows positioned on each side of the chimney, the stained-glass window that created prisms of light in the entry—all of them exactly as she remembered. She took a deep breath and blew it out slowly, her heart pounding in her chest.

She hadn't been mistaken last night. Her view of the house hadn't lasted more than a second before the flash from the lightning had faded, but that one second had been enough. This was definitely *the* house. She crossed her arms over her chest as a chill swept over her, despite the heat and humidity of the early morning. For as long as she could remember, she'd dreamed of this house. Frightening dreams that she awakened from in

a cold sweat, but the only thing she ever remembered was the house.

The house she was certain she had never, *ever* set foot in before last night.

Chapter Three

John heard the front door of the main house close and looked up from his work as the woman walked to the middle of the drive then turned and faced the house. She was wearing the same clothes as last night, but then once he'd realized there was no car in the drive and saw her mud-covered boots next to the front door, he'd gotten a clear picture of what must have happened. She'd probably grabbed the minimum amount of necessities and hiked from wherever her car had gotten stuck. He could only hope that the lack of reliable roadways, utilities and phone service would send her running straight back to whatever big city she'd matriculated from.

Though he knew less than nothing about ladies' shoes, he recognized her boots as an expensive designer brand that his half sister had been drooling over the last time he'd met her in the French Quarter for lunch. Fancy, soft leather. Not even a steel toe. Women who spent eight hundred dollars on a pair of shoes couldn't possibly find much of interest in a dusty old house in a town with only a café and a gas station serving as the local commerce. At least that's what he was banking on.

He picked up several pieces of the branch he'd been working on and carried them to the pile he'd started at the far end of the circular drive. With every step he

took, a curse came to mind. He needed to be in that house, looking for something, anything to help him find his sister. That rotten branch could have waited another fifty years by the looks of the rest of the estate, but here he was slaving over debris blocking a drive that no one had used in years and it was all that woman's fault. He flung the wood onto the pile and spun around. It was time for action. He didn't have time to lose.

She stood at the edge of the circular drive nearest the house, with her back to him. He paused for a moment, wondering what in the world she was doing, staring up at the roof of the house, following the lines from one end to another, but then he set his jaw and strode up behind her.

"Not much to look at in the daylight, is it?" he asked, wondering why she still hadn't turned around when she should have heard his footsteps.

She jumped at the sound of his voice, but her gaze remained focused on the house. "No, I guess it isn't," she said, although she didn't sound convinced. Finally, she turned to face him, a pleasant, but determined look on her face.

Uh-oh. He'd seen that look before. His mother and sister wore it very well, especially when they wanted something. Well, he didn't care what Fancy Shoes wanted. He wasn't agreeing to anything.

"I spoke to Mr. Wheeler this morning," she began, "and he assured me he hired a new caretaker. He'll be calling you as soon as he gets into the office to get your permission to forward your employment paperwork to me. If you don't mind, I'd like to see some identification now."

"And if I *do* mind?"

"Then he also assured me that if I was uncomfortable, he would ask you to leave."

John's jaw clenched so hard it ached. She held all the cards. He couldn't afford to lose the job, and he definitely couldn't afford Ross Wheeler digging deeper into his background to placate some crazy woman. The New Orleans police had already asked the attorney for permission to search the estate, but unless they produced a warrant, Ross Wheeler wasn't going to allow a bunch of law enforcement officials to "tromp through a house of valuable and delicate antiques."

The Cypriere locals claimed they'd never set eyes on his sister when questioned by the New Orleans police, and without any proof whatsoever that Rachel had ever been to laMalediction, there was no chance of getting the warrant Wheeler required. If Wheeler found out John had lied about his real purpose for wanting the job, he'd have every right to press charges against John and the New Orleans police department. And since the department hadn't exactly sanctioned what he was doing, there would be fallout all the way around.

"I assume my license will do," he said as he reached into the back pocket of his jeans and pulled out his wallet. He pulled his license from inside and handed it to her, biting his tongue as she looked at the license, then handed it back to him.

"Thank you, Mr. Landry," she said and tentatively stuck her hand out. "I'm Olivia Markham. I'm sorry we got off on the wrong foot, but a single woman can't be too careful these days."

John started to ignore her hand, but her words resonated through his head. *A single woman can't be too careful these days.* If only Rachel had paid attention when he said the exact same thing to her. And here he

was angry at a woman for doing just what he would have advised. He shook her hand, momentarily surprised at the firmness of her grip.

"I understand," he said. "I would apologize for scaring you last night, but since that's exactly what I was trying to do at the time, I guess it wouldn't exactly make sense. Wheeler should have contacted both of us. Last night could have been ugly."

Olivia looked relieved. "Yes, it could have, and I gave him a big piece of my mind this morning. In fact, I got him out of bed in order to do so, and I have to admit that I got a small amount of satisfaction out of it. I know Mr. Wheeler will be calling you later, but I'd be happy to show you a copy of my lease."

"That won't be necessary, Ms. Markham. You don't exactly fit the profile of a swindler or thief. And since the road to the estate is hardly a highway, I can only assume you actually have business here or you would never have found the place." With any luck, she'd tell him what that business was and he could figure out a way to use it to his advantage.

She waved a hand at the debris on the drive. "I know you're busy with the mess from the storm, but I really need a favor. My car got stuck last night in the rain, and I'm afraid it's completely blocking the path to the estate. Can you help me get it out?"

John's thoughts swirled around, trying to zero in on the decision that might push her into leaving. He couldn't outright refuse, as then she'd have ammunition for Wheeler to dismiss him but then he also needed to discourage her from staying. "I think there's a mechanic in town with a tow truck. It would probably be better if you called him in case there's also something wrong with the car." Surely Olivia "Fancy Shoes" Markham

wouldn't isolate herself at the estate with no way to leave, gun or no.

Olivia frowned. "I hope nothing is wrong. The rental company isn't likely to drive all the way out here to give me a replacement. Look, I know towing my car isn't what you were hired to do, but I couldn't help but notice a truck parked at that little house across the driveway so I thought maybe you could help. I just want to get my clothes and equipment into the house, and then I promise I'll be out of your hair."

John felt himself relenting and silently cursed his mother for training him to assist helpless females. Surely it was meant to be a matter of manners and not a burden, but it didn't feel that way at the moment. "If that's what you think is best. I think I saw a chain in the storage shed. I'll be back in a minute."

He carried the saw to the storage shed and dug out a chain he'd seen the day before. There was still the glimmer of hope that the car wouldn't run. He could tell by Olivia's expression that she hadn't thought of that possibility until he'd mentioned it. It was also clear she wasn't happy with the thought. Best case, the car would have to be towed back to New Orleans and she'd stay there a few days waiting on a replacement. Those few days might just buy him the time he needed to finish searching the house.

Worst case, the car might make it to the house but stop working afterwards. That was something he was fairly certain he could arrange.

OLIVIA WATCHED JOHN walk away, completely confused by the man. He was abrupt and she got the impression he wanted to be rude most of the conversation but it seemed like something was holding him back from say-

ing what he really wanted to say. Since Olivia was used to dealing with either New Yorkers, who tended to be very direct, or with B and B owners, who tended to be overly accommodating, John Landry was definitely a departure from the norm.

Her thoughts were interrupted by her cell phone ringing. She reached into her shorts' pocket and pulled it out. Speaking of New Yorkers, it was her editor. Great. She wasn't exactly on schedule for this book, and wasn't looking forward to admitting it. "Hello, Irene," she said, trying to sound cheerful.

"I never heard from you yesterday and got worried. Is everything all right?"

"Oh, no. I was supposed to call." Olivia smacked her forehead with her palm. "I am so sorry. I didn't mean to worry you."

"That's okay. It's just unlike you to forget to call, so I figured I'd better check in. So I gather you made it?"

"Sort of. There was a huge storm last night as I was driving in. The house is basically buried back in the bayou with only an overgrown dirt path to get to it. The car got stuck a ways from the house, and I had to make a run for it. There was absolutely no cell phone service. There was no electricity either. In fact, without my luggage there was a whole lot of nothing."

"I don't know why you insisted on that house. It's the worst of the lot as far as convenience, location, communication and just about everything else. Are you sure you want to do this? There's that lovely house in Boston that's been converted to a very nice B and B. It has a spa...."

Olivia took a second to imagine a hot shower and a mattress less than fifty years old. "Don't tempt me. I know this wasn't the location you wanted, Irene, but

I think the story is here. My mind is already whirling with possibilities, and I never got that feeling in the other house."

"I suppose," Irene said, but Olivia could hear the disapproval in her words. "Well, I hope this problem with your car hasn't set you behind. Howard's called twice this morning wanting a status report, and he's frothing at the mouth like a demon child."

Damn. Howard was the vice president, and he disdained his company's recent foray into what he called "mass market trash." The fact that Olivia and the other authors of that "mass market trash" were the only thing keeping the publisher afloat in a tenuous market seemed to make him even angrier. If Howard had his way, the publisher would only print thick coffee-table books with bizarre photos of fruit and dead flowers. Or the obscure literary journal that would sell five or six copies, purchased by the author's family to see if they were mentioned.

Olivia bit her lip, then finally blurted out what she needed to say. "If I run into problems with the car, I might have to backtrack to New Orleans for a day or two. I know I'm already behind my normal schedule for finishing a rough draft because of the time it took to work out the lease arrangements here, but if there is a delay I don't see it being more than two days, max." She clamped her mouth shut, realizing she was rambling.

For a couple of seconds there was dead silence on the other end of the line, and Olivia steeled herself for the disapproval that was surely to come.

"I don't have to remind you that marketing has already spent a literal ton of money on this book," Irene said. "The book that you seem to find excuse after excuse to delay."

"I know this is an important release, and I promise you that I'll make up the time as soon as I've gotten everything under control here."

"Is there something else wrong? You don't sound like yourself, Olivia. You sound like you're on the ragged edge of sanity."

"Everything will be fine. I think I'm getting a little jumpy and starting to panic. I guess I'm overreacting."

"Really? That's interesting considering you're the most organized, controlled person I know, and that's saying a lot. What's got you spooked? The storm? I know it can't be the house itself. It's not like you haven't done this a time or two before."

Olivia looked up at the house and shook her head. "I don't know, exactly. I mean, this is definitely the most remote location I've ever been to, and the house hasn't been occupied in over thirty years, so that gives it a much different 'feel' than the others. And given that I arrived in the midst of a monsoon, and had no power... then there was a run-in with the caretaker."

"What run-in?"

Olivia described the scene in the kitchen from the night before. "I called the estate attorney first thing this morning and everything checked out," she finished, "but it scared the life out of me."

"I should say so. Well, if you won't consider a more civilized location for this book, will you at least consider relocating to a hotel in New Orleans until I can arrange you security of some sort? I can't afford for some angry caretaker to distract you from your work. There's a firm in New Orleans that I've used before. I could probably get someone assigned to you within a week. You could work from photos until then."

"A week at a hotel in New Orleans. I have to admit,

it's very tempting, but I really think the story is here. I'll call you back if I change my mind."

"Okay," Irene said, but didn't sound convinced. "Promise me if you run into any problems that will delay this book, you will let me know immediately. Olivia?"

Olivia looked over at the storage shed as John walked out carrying a long length of chain, the grim look on his face clear as day, even from a distance. She was apparently three for three in making people's day this morning. "I promise. Look, I've got to go. I'll let you know in a couple of hours what I'm going to do."

She flipped her phone closed and dropped it back in her pocket. If Olivia was a betting woman, she'd bet everything she had that she was the source of John Landry's discontent. But if she was such a trial, why bother with her at all? He certainly could have made up any sort of excuse for not wanting to tow her car with his truck.

Granted, she could cost him his job if she wanted to be a real bitch about it, but was a handyman job in the middle of nowhere all that great a gig? With all the hurricane reconstruction going on in New Orleans, the last place she'd expect to find a young, able-bodied man would be hidden away in Cypriere.

In fact, the more she thought about it, the more John Landry didn't add up at all.

THE MAN WATCHED her from his hiding place behind the overgrown bushes that surrounded one piece of the drive. While he would have recognized Olivia Markham from her photo in the back cover of her books, the picture really didn't do her justice at all. She had that fine facial bone structure that seemed to grace only a few

each generation, and a toned but curvy build. The entire package was reminiscent of the old portraits of upper-class women, which was appropriate if one considered the circumstances.

Her conversation with the caretaker concerned him some. It was obvious that the caretaker wished Olivia would leave, but given everything he knew about things to come, that just didn't make sense. Thirty years he'd been waiting for things to fall into place, for things to align as they were supposed to when the time was near. Surely, the caretaker wouldn't have come unless he had a part to play.

The person Olivia had talked to on the phone concerned him more. For whatever reason, he'd gathered from their conversation that the person Olivia had been speaking to had suggested she leave the house and go to New Orleans for a week. And it had sounded like Olivia was considering it. No matter what, he had to make sure that didn't happen. He'd been watching the moon, and was certain—the day and hour for fulfilling the prophecy was fast approaching.

The first woman who'd come to the house hadn't given him the answers he was looking for. He'd thought she was the one. She had eyes like the photo, but maybe he had been wrong. Olivia didn't have eyes like the photo, but otherwise, the resemblance was clear. Surely, Olivia was the one. It had been decades since a woman had even set foot at laMalediction. Now there had been two in one week. One of them had to be *the* one.

Regardless, neither of them was leaving laMalediction until the prophecy was fulfilled.

Chapter Four

John glanced in his rearview mirror at Olivia's car. Despite being stuck in a good foot of mud, it had started right up and was managing the drive to laMalediction. It figured. He'd hoped an out-of-commission vehicle would send her running to the city for a replacement, at least for a couple of days, but no such luck. Now he needed a plan to work around Olivia Markham without her alerting the attorney that something was suspicious.

He parked in front of the mansion and waited until Olivia pulled up beside him. She was smiling when she got out of the car. "I'm so relieved it's running," she said and reached back into the car to pop the trunk.

John couldn't have disagreed more, so he just nodded and looked over at the boxes in her trunk. Whatever Olivia Markham was doing at laMalediction, it looked like she'd packed enough for a long stay. "There's no food or supplies at the main house. I picked up bread and lunch meat for myself, but I wasn't expecting company."

Olivia waved one hand at the boxes. "I brought supplies," she said. "Just some bagels, peanut butter, chips and drinking water. I've gotten in the habit of traveling

with a minimal amount of food. I figure in another day or two I should be able to drive back into town, right?"

"Probably." He held in a sigh. Apparently, it was going to take more than bad weather, a reported haunted house, flaky electricity, no cell phone connection and a lack of groceries to get rid of her.

"Do you need some help moving that stuff inside?" Maybe he could figure out why she was here and that would give him an angle.

"Seriously? That would be great." Olivia pulled the first box out and shifted it to balance. "The boxes are all electronics, so please be careful."

Electronics? John grabbed a large box from the trunk and followed her into the house. Seemed a strange hobby at a house that lost power every time it rained.

Olivia stopped in the entryway. "I don't suppose you know of a library or study in the house? A place with a good desk or table for working?"

John nodded. The library was where he'd found the pink button. "There's a library straight back past the stairwell, then turn left down the hall."

"Great." Olivia headed toward the hallway. "I didn't know if you'd taken stock of the house yet or were only concentrating on the outside maintenance."

John followed behind her, his mind forming an idea that just might get him around Olivia until he could get rid of her. "Actually, I'm supposed to be working on the main house, but I didn't want to disturb you this morning, so I worked in the drive. I'm an early riser."

Olivia stepped into the library and placed her box on a long, dusty table in the center of a room with floor-to-ceiling bookcases on every wall. "I love this," she said, looking around the room. "All it needs is a good cleaning."

John placed his box on the table. "I'm not going to disturb your work if I go about my business upstairs, am I?"

"I doubt it. What are you doing, exactly?"

"Right now," he said, as he formulated the lie, "I'm just assessing everything and making a list of necessary repairs so that Wheeler can order the supplies I need. I do a lot of banging wood and moving stuff, though."

Olivia waved a hand in dismissal. "I've trained myself to write in almost any circumstance. I acclimate to the sounds of a new house quickly, so your work shouldn't bother me at all."

John stared at her for a moment, not certain what to say. A writer? He would have understood if she was an antiques dealer looking to catalogue the furniture or a real estate agent looking to get a contract on the house, but why in the world would someone choose laMalediction as a place to write a book? "You're writing a book?"

Olivia nodded. "I know. Most people find it strange, but this is my niche. I stay in a reputed haunted house and write a ghost story about it. My next book is due soon and it will be set at laMalediction."

"Haunted houses? Do you believe in that sort of thing?"

Olivia pursed her lips. "I think a fair statement would be that I don't limit the universe to what I understand. I've seen things I can't explain, but that doesn't mean there isn't an explanation." She smiled. "The good news is I don't spook easily, so you won't have to worry about catering to a damsel in distress."

John nodded, feeling his options lessening by the second. "I'll go grab another box," he said and left the library.

I don't spook easily.
She said that like it was a good thing.

Olivia dropped the filthy sponge in a bucket of dirty water. Three hours of scrubbing and the room was finally fit for habitation. She sank down on the floor and leaned back against one of the now-sparkling maple bookcases. It really was a beautiful room. In fact, everything she'd seen of the house so far was gorgeous. It was a shame that no one lived there enjoying it, although she guessed most people wouldn't enjoy being sequestered out in the bayou with only a small town of strange people and a swamp of all kinds of creatures as company.

A crash above her caused her to jump and she slowly pulled herself up from the floor. John Landry had been making good on his noise-making promise. He'd been banging and knocking upstairs as long as she'd been cleaning downstairs. She sometimes wondered if he was creating more work.

She grabbed the bucket, headed to the kitchen and dumped the dirty water in the sink. She rinsed the bucket and placed it upside down in the sink to dry, then pulled a bottle of water from the refrigerator and rubbed it across her forehead before taking a huge swig of it. The humidity was something she'd expected to encounter but it was worse than what she'd imagined, especially with no air-conditioning.

She grabbed a bag of potato chips from the kitchen counter and headed back to the library. Unpacking and setting up her laptop and printer was next on her list, then she'd be ready to work. No more excuses. She smiled when she thought about all the ideas that were

already flowing through her mind for the book, and then stopped short when she stepped into the library.

Something is wrong.

She scanned the empty room. Nothing seemed out of place, but yet, she knew it wasn't like she'd left it. All five of her boxes were still stacked at one end of the long table and at the other end of the table was a lamp. She felt her breath catch in her throat. A lamp that used to sit on a tiny table on the far wall.

Taking a step closer to the table, she checked her boxes more closely. They were still sealed and didn't appear to have been shuffled around at all. A loud thump upstairs caused her to jump. Her water bottle slipped out of her hands and onto the floor.

Get a grip. It's just John, you know, the man you told you didn't spook easily.

Could John have moved the lamp just to mess with her? She thought about her trip to the kitchen, trying to recall if she could still hear him banging around when she'd been cleaning the bucket but she'd grown so used to the noise that she simply didn't know. Surely, that was it. He was playing a joke on her. Trying to prove she wasn't as tough as she thought she was. She crossed her arms across her chest, suddenly chilly in the previously stifling room.

Well, it wasn't a very funny joke, and she wasn't going to stand for it.

She picked up her water and set it on the table with a thump, then strode down the hall and up the stairwell, ready for battle. She found John in a bedroom at the back of the house, probably positioned over the library downstairs, and he was covered all over with something white.

One glance at the gaping hole in the ceiling and the

mess surrounding him on the floor gave her a clear idea of where the white substance came from. "What happened?" she asked.

He was standing on a stepladder with his head poked up in the hole in the ceiling. Leaning down a bit, he looked out at her. "Ceiling fell in is what happened. Didn't you hear all that noise earlier?"

She remembered the loud crash she'd heard when she'd just finished cleaning. "That was the ceiling? Wow. I guess you were standing under it."

"Unfortunately. I thought the light fixture was loose but it was the entire ceiling that was sagging. I barely touched it and the whole thing came crashing down on me." He stepped down the ladder and retrieved a water bottle from the dresser, leaving white tracks everywhere he stepped.

Olivia stared at the white shoe prints then back into the hall. It was dusty and dirty, but not a single white ring in sight.

"Did you need something?" he asked.

"No. I just thought I ought to check and make sure everything was okay…you know, with the noise."

John narrowed his eyes at her. "So you thought I might be injured but waited a good five minutes to come up and check?"

"Yeah," Olivia said as she backed out of the room. "Sorry, you're right. I should have checked sooner, but I was pouring out a bucket of dirty water." She pointed down at his feet. "You might want to take your shoes off before you walk around much more. Not that the place is clean or anything."

John glanced down at his feet and frowned. "You're right. No sense making it worse." He looked back up

at the ceiling and sighed. "This is going to be a real mess to fix."

"Well, I'll leave you to it," Olivia said and fled down the hall.

She checked the front door, but the dead bolt was still securely in place. A quick check of the back door in the kitchen revealed the same thing. He could have taken his boots off before coming downstairs. That would make perfectly good sense, especially if he didn't want her to hear his footsteps on the marble flooring in the entry. But Olivia would swear by his expression that he hadn't even noticed the state of his boots until she'd pointed it out.

Unless he was a very good actor.

Olivia hurried back to the library, determined to hook up her computer, contact Wheeler and make sure she had all the information she could get on John Landry. She stopped short in the doorway.

The lamp was back in place.

JOHN WATCHED OLIVIA flee the room and shook his head. For someone who claimed she didn't spook easily, the woman looked like she'd seen a ghost. She'd obviously come upstairs for a reason, but whatever that reason was, she'd changed her mind about it. He didn't believe for one minute it was the crash that had brought her scurrying up the stairs. If she had been that worried about it, a bucket of dirty water would have been the last thing to detain her.

He'd thought about pushing the issue but finally decided that if something was bothering Olivia, that would likely only work in his favor. Staring back up at the ceiling, he sighed. He'd had no intention of creating more work for whoever replaced him, but that's exactly what

he'd managed to do. He dug through the pile of Sheet-rock and pulled out the light fixture that had attracted his attention in the first place.

It was coated with Sheetrock dust and any chance of gaining a fingerprint was probably long gone, but he wanted to make sure he hadn't been imagining things. He wiped the dust off the light fixture's ceiling plate with the bottom of his shirt. Just as he'd thought—scratches lined the bottom of the ceiling plate close to the screws that held the fixture in the ceiling.

There was no way to tell if the scratches were new, but John would bet everything they were. The ceiling plate had been wiped clean. That's what had drawn his attention to the fixture in the first place—a shiny plate in a room of otherwise dusty items. He'd brought in the ladder hoping to get a closer look, but when he'd placed a hand on the ceiling to steady himself, the whole thing had come crashing down.

He looked at the light fixture. Maybe the old care-taker had been aware of the ceiling problem and started taking the fixture down to make the repair. He placed the light fixture on the floor and blew out a breath. He was wasting time. It didn't matter what the old care-taker had intended, or if every upstairs ceiling dropped down on him.

He had to find his sister.

Despite Olivia staying out of his way, this afternoon had been a total waste. He'd found nothing new. No indication that his sister had been on the second floor. And maybe she hadn't been. If she'd even made it to la-Malediction, maybe she'd run into trouble before she'd ever gotten the chance to do much poking around.

He ran one hand through his hair, scattering Sheet-rock dust around him. What if he'd made a mistake

about her destination? What if she'd scheduled her visit to laMalediction on her calendar and changed her mind? If his sister had never been to this house, he was losing valuable time here. If only he could find evidence, anything that told him for certain that she'd been here. The pink button was a sketchy clue, at best.

He pulled his cell phone from his pocket. No messages, but at least it had decent signal strength. He pressed the number for the New Orleans police department and asked for the captain.

"Landry?" Captain Reeves answered the phone. "Where the hell are you? Harrison's been by your apartment twice and says your phone's turned off."

"I went to visit an aunt my mom used to check on. She lives out a ways in the bayou. Cell phone signal's sketchy."

"An aunt, huh? So your sister's missing and your mom's in the hospital, and you want me to buy that you took vacation time to visit some old lady?"

"Yes, sir," John replied, keeping his voice steady. If the captain found out he was at laMalediction after Wheeler had forbidden the police to enter the property, he'd have John's badge. "Is there any news?"

The captain was silent for a moment and John was afraid the man was going to call him on his lie. The captain was no one's fool and knew John about as well as anyone did. Well enough to know that John wouldn't bail on the investigation without a really good reason— like a lead that the police didn't have the authority to pursue.

"Not much. Harrison was just here and said they found a store clerk about twenty miles outside of New Orleans on I-10 who remembers your sister filling up there five days ago."

John felt his pulse quicken. He'd driven past that filling station on the way to laMalediction. Rachel could have been pursuing another house in the same direction, but there was no mention of another house on her calendar until weeks later. At least it was something. "Is the filling station guy certain it was Rachel?"

"Yeah. I got the impression he liked what he saw. Described her and her car pretty well and seemed certain when Harrison showed him the picture."

"But no indication of where she was going?"

The captain hesitated. "He says she asked about Cypriere."

"Damn! I knew it. Now are you going to get a warrant?"

"I hung up with the district attorney right before you called. It's thin, probably not enough for a warrant, but he's going to ask one of the judges for a favor given this is a cop's family. The judge has a cousin who went missing twenty years ago and was never found. The D.A. thinks he'll be sympathetic."

"How soon can we get access?" If he didn't have to hide, he could flood the house and grounds with men and equipment. No sneaking around and making excuses. No more hiding behind a stepladder or a chain saw.

"The judge he thinks will give the warrant is out of town for two days."

"You've got to be kidding me! Tell him to get another judge."

"There isn't another judge who's willing to put his neck out. The D.A.'s already asked around on this and been told no. There's entirely too many things that could have happened to Rachel between that filling station and wherever she was headed. Unless someone can put

her in Cypriere, then none of the other judges are willing to risk it."

"I don't have to tell you how much time has passed."

"No, you don't. I don't like it any more than you do, but I have to tell you, John, that if you do anything to risk this investigation, it will not be good for your career. Do not go near that property until we have a warrant. Are we clear?"

"Crystal."

"I mean it, Landry. Do not set foot in Cypriere."

"No problem." John closed the phone. He hadn't really lied. He had no intention of setting foot in Cypriere, the town. If his sister was going to be found, he had a feeling it would be at laMalediction.

He tucked the phone into his pocket and headed downstairs. There had been no sign of Rachel on the second floor, so he'd save the attic until last. The basement was his next destination and he'd seen an access door in the kitchen. He hurried into the kitchen and almost collided with Olivia.

A camera slipped in her hands, and she clutched it to keep from dropping it. He grabbed her shoulders to steady both of them. "Sorry. I keep forgetting there's someone else here." He looked down at the camera and blinked. "Nice camera."

Olivia frowned. "Yeah, it is. I found it in the cabinet when I was putting up my supplies. I thought maybe it was yours. I was coming to ask."

John's pulse began to race. He'd bought that exact model for his sister for Christmas. "No, but maybe the old caretaker kept it here to take pictures for Wheeler."

Olivia shrugged and handed him the camera. "Maybe so. Guess you'll need it then. I'd start with that ceiling

upstairs if I were you. It didn't come down by itself. If there's a leak somewhere it can get way worse for you."

John took the camera and turned it on, pleased that the batteries were good. "You're absolutely right. I think I'll do that now." He left the kitchen, studying the display on the camera. Twenty-two pictures stored.

Maybe one of them would give him a clue to finding Rachel.

Chapter Five

Olivia trudged up the stairs, holding a printout on John Landry that she'd received from Wheeler. She planned to read it again while soaking in a hot bath, but her initial review had shown nothing even remotely questionable. It had taken her an hour to set up her equipment and another hour to finally acquire a decent enough satellite connection to download the documents, but at least that part of the necessary work was done. With any luck, the bath would revive her and she might get a second wind and do a little work that night.

She entered the bedroom and went to retrieve her change of clothes from her suitcase on the bed and that's when she saw it—a small, framed, black-and-white photo lying on top of her luggage. She whirled around and looked into the bathroom, then checked in the hall but saw nothing. Maybe John had left it there when he was doing his repair inspection. Maybe he'd moved it so it wouldn't be damaged and forgot to replace it.

Except for the fact that there had not been a single photo in the room the night before, it was a perfectly logical theory. She started to set the photo on the nightstand to deal with it later, but then took a good look at the picture. It was a woman in a fancy dress and had to have been taken a long, long time ago, sometime well

before the turn of the century. But the preserved nature of the photo was not what made her gasp.

The woman looked just like her.

Olivia clutched the photo and sucked in a breath, both frightened and excited at the same time. She'd come here looking for answers. Maybe she was finally going to get them. She felt her stomach roll. Who was helping her? That picture hadn't appeared out of nowhere, and it was no coincidence that it had been left in her room.

John was the logical choice. He'd been upstairs working all day. Maybe he'd seen the photo and thought she would find the resemblance interesting. That must be it. A completely logical explanation, for a change.

Maybe.

But then, if they were the only people in the house, who had moved the lamp or, for that matter, entered her bedroom the night before while she was bathing?

She stepped into the hallway and called out. "John. Are you still working up here?" No answer was forthcoming, nor could she make out any noise at all. In fact, now that she thought about it she realized she hadn't heard a peep since he'd accosted her in the kitchen and left with the camera.

She slipped the papers on John into a drawer in the nightstand, grabbed the photo and headed back down to the library. While dusting, she'd noticed several photo albums on the bookcases. If they were labeled, she might be able to identify the woman in the photo. She grabbed several of the heavy albums off the bookcases and laid them on the table.

The first one contained color photos and was clearly far too recent. The second book was close to the right era, but the woman was not in any of the photos. In the

third book, she hit pay dirt. An eight-by-ten photo of a woman and a man standing in front of laMalediction. The woman was wearing a different dress, but there was no mistaking the facial features and the hair. This was the woman from the photo.

Franklin and Marilyn Borque, 1861.

Olivia felt a chill pass over her. No, it couldn't possibly be.

"Must be interesting." John's voice sounded behind her and she jumped.

"Oh, my God," Olivia said, her heart racing. "I didn't even hear you come in."

He raised his eyebrows. "I wasn't exactly sneaking."

"No, I'm not saying that. I guess it *was* interesting." She looked up at the man standing in the doorway and bit her lip. Did she come out and ask him if he was messing with her or keep her cards hidden? What if he said it wasn't him? Would she know if he was lying? So far, John Landry seemed a bit of an enigma.

"Look at this," she said and lifted up the photo album before she could change her mind.

John looked at the photo, then her, then back at the photo. "Wow. No wonder you didn't hear me. You look just like her."

Olivia blew out a breath she didn't even realize she'd been holding. "So you see it, too?"

"Hard to miss. Just a little different in the eyes, but really close. Is she a relative?"

Olivia shook her head. "Not that I'm aware of, but then I don't know anything about my family."

John frowned. "But you just happened to lease this house, and just happened to find a picture that looks like you in the library?"

"Actually, that's something I wanted to ask you

about." She picked the smaller photo up off the table and handed it to John. "That picture was on my bed when I went upstairs earlier."

John's head snapped up from the photo and his eyes narrowed on her. "How did it get there?"

"I thought maybe you could tell me."

John stared at her in surprise. "Me?"

"Well, you were upstairs all day. I thought maybe you saw the resemblance and left the photo for me, but I guess not."

John shook his head. "I've never seen this before now, and I've been through every room in this house on the first and second floor."

Olivia studied his expression as he looked back down at the photo then again at Olivia, but he appeared as confused as she was.

"So how did it get there?" she asked.

"I don't know, but I don't like it, and I don't believe it's a coincidence that the photo looks like you. It's easy to fake photos these days, but then the real question would be, who's trying to scare you?"

"No one."

John raised one eyebrow.

"I swear." Olivia raised one hand as if taking an oath. "I don't have a problem with anyone, and very few people even knew I was coming here. Besides, there's a whole photo album here with the same woman. Do you think someone faked all of it?"

John frowned. "Look, I know you write books about monsters and stuff, but I don't believe in any of that. What I *do* know is that a ghost didn't put that picture on your bed."

"I know. I don't believe it was a ghost, either."

"No one would go to such lengths unless it was per-

sonal. Are you sure you haven't hacked anyone off lately? An angry reader, maybe?"

Olivia shook her head. "I don't see how. I don't write under my real name and my publisher is very careful about keeping my real identity a secret."

"I don't suppose your publisher would stoop to scaring you for a better novel, would they?"

"Heavens, no. Something like this makes it harder to concentrate on writing, not easier."

"Well, despite the veil of secrecy you claim you're under, anyone can be gotten to if a person wants to bad enough." He paused for a moment. "I don't think you ought to stay here. Maybe you should go to New Orleans for a couple of days. Give me a chance to poke around and see what I can find."

Olivia knew that what John said made sense, but she just couldn't bring herself to agree. Olivia didn't believe for a minute the photo was a fake. No one would go to the trouble of creating an entire album just to scare her. Even her editor didn't know about her past. How could anyone else?

This might be her last chance to learn something about her family, to figure out why she kept dreaming about the house. If she left now, she might not have the opportunity again. Whoever had left her the picture was probably trying to scare her, but it had done just the opposite—it had made her determined to stay and check into its authenticity.

"No," she said finally. "I don't respond to scare tactics."

"Olivia, I can't guarantee your safety. The doors to the house have been locked, and if someone was strolling around upstairs, one of us should have heard or seen them."

"Why didn't you see them?" Olivia shot back. "You were working upstairs."

"Not late this afternoon. I finished upstairs and moved down to the basement. If someone came in through a window or even the front door, I wouldn't have heard them."

Olivia blew out a breath. "Then I suggest both of us start poking around. I don't like the idea that someone besides the two of us has access to this house. They have to be getting in somehow and the dead bolts are in place on both doors."

John hesitated for a second and Olivia could tell he clearly wanted her out of the way, not in the middle, but running didn't fit into her agenda.

"Fine," he said finally. "Where do you want to start?"

"Outside? I mean, that's logical, right? He didn't drop in from the sky."

"He certainly didn't park in the drive and stroll inside," John agreed. "We can walk the perimeter of the house. The ground's soft from the rain. There ought to be footprints." He gave Olivia a nod and headed for the front door. Olivia pulled on her tennis shoes and followed him outside.

Thirty minutes later, Olivia tugged off her muddy tennis shoes and set them on the front porch. They'd circled the house twice, searching every square inch of the ground within twenty feet of the house, but they'd found nothing. On the second pass, John never spoke a single word as they searched the grounds around the house, frowning the entire time.

He pulled off his dirty shoes and tossed them next to hers, but he stared across the courtyard, his brow

furrowed in concentration. "What are you thinking?" Olivia asked.

He didn't answer her immediately, and after several seconds passed, Olivia wondered whether he was going to answer her at all. Suddenly he turned to face her, his eyes locking on to hers. "You're certain the picture wasn't there before?"

"Absolutely." Olivia frowned, wondering where he was going with his line of questioning, then suddenly it hit her and she sucked in a breath. "He was already in the house. That's what you're not saying. That he's been in the house all this time… Oh, my God. If there're no footprints then he hasn't left either."

"Maybe not. He could have left out the front door when we were around back."

"But he may still be in there."

"Yeah."

Olivia took a deep breath and blew it out. "Then I guess we better get to looking."

"And start where? There's probably a million places to hide."

"My room."

John frowned. "Why there?"

"Because that first night during the storm someone came into the room while I was bathing." She explained the draft and her theory of secret passageways.

"And then you came downstairs dripping wet, half-dressed and toting a gun. Makes a lot more sense now." He shook his head and gave her a begrudging look of admiration. "You've got backbone. I'll give you that."

"I told you—I don't spook easily. And I don't like people messing with me."

John nodded. "I'll bet you're right about a secret passageway. Let me grab my tools from the basement, and

we'll start now. I don't want you sleeping in there if we can't secure the room."

Olivia watched as he walked away, wondering about the enigma that was John Landry. He was the stereotypical strong, silent type, but then things got muddy. She could tell he preferred to be left alone, but yet if he felt her security was threatened he jumped immediately into action. Olivia had no doubt that if called for, he'd fight with deadly force. He had a dangerous edge to him, something just beneath the surface that told her this man wouldn't necessarily play by the rules if it didn't make sense.

I can't guarantee your safety.

John's words flashed through her mind. She knew what he said was true. If someone wanted to get to her they eventually would, but for whatever reason she felt better about her chances here with John than anywhere else without him.

JOHN TAPPED ON a wall in Olivia's bedroom and listened for a hollow sound, an indication that there was space behind the wall. Olivia's story troubled him on many different levels. He still thought she was hiding something, but he believed her when she said she had no idea who could be behind the intrusions. It was clear to John that someone was playing a game with her, but why? And even though he thought she was still keeping secrets, John didn't think Olivia had an answer to that question, either.

Her proclamation of secret passageways for servant usage was both surprising and frustrating. It was something he hadn't taken into consideration, but would explain why someone had been able to move through the mansion without being seen. Whoever was play-

ing tricks with the photographs knew the mansion intimately, and that led to a whole other set of questions. Was the intruder someone from Cypriere, or was Olivia's identity not as hidden as she thought it was?

"You find anything?" Olivia's voice sounded behind him.

He rose from the floor to face her and shook his head. "No. All the walls appear solid. What about you?"

Olivia shook her head and gave the room a quick glance. "I didn't imagine that breeze, and there's no other source that could have created it. The windows are sealed remarkably tight given the state the house is in and there's no gap in the door, either."

"I agree."

She gave him a half smile. "With what part?"

"All of it. I don't think you imagined anything, and I think the most logical explanation is that someone entered the room."

Olivia blew out a breath. "I was afraid you'd think I was crazy."

"I never said I didn't think you were crazy. The way you go about making a living is definitely borderline crazy."

Olivia laughed and John smiled back before he even realized it. Despite being in the way, Olivia Markham was a hard woman not to like. She was tough, logical, independent and definitely not hard on the eyes, especially for a man who preferred an athletic frame and natural good looks to women made up so perfectly they looked as if they'd been varnished.

And she still needs you.

The thought tipped through his mind like a knife and he clenched his jaw. He had no argument for the truth. Despite Olivia's capabilities, she still had a situation on

her hands that she couldn't handle alone, which meant that now he had three women who needed something from him. And that was something he'd been trying to avoid.

A bolt of lightning flashed outside the bedroom window and the thunder that followed made the old glass panes shake. "Wow," Olivia said. "Looks like we're in for another doozy."

Her words jolted him from his thoughts and he nodded, willing his mind to return to the business at hand—finding the secret passageway. "Weather report says it should be a short storm, but powerful."

"You zoned out there for a minute," Olivia said. "Is anything wrong?"

"No. Just thinking." He pointed to the wardrobe. "The only section of wall we haven't tested is behind that."

Olivia nodded. "I thought the first night that maybe the previous occupants shoved it there to block the passageway for privacy, but if it's blocking the passageway, then how could someone have gotten into the room?"

John crossed the room to the wardrobe and opened the doors wide. The wardrobe had drawers and shelves on one side and a hanging area for clothes on the other side. "A man could easily fit in here," John said, pointing to the side of the wardrobe with the rod. "Maybe he was already in the room and hid in the wardrobe when you came in."

Olivia shook her head. "I opened the wardrobe on the off chance there were clean linens. Besides, even if someone was hiding there, they had to get out. The windows and door were both locked from the inside."

John stared at the wardrobe and frowned. "Maybe the *wardrobe* is the passageway."

"Like a C. S. Lewis book?" Olivia said.

John stepped into the wardrobe and ran his fingers over the back panel, starting at the top. "I don't think it's a doorway to another world, but someone might have modified this wardrobe to cover the original opening."

He squatted and continued to search the panel at the bottom. In the right corner, he felt the panel give a bit. He pressed the almost unnoticeable indention and the back of the wardrobe slid silently open, exposing a narrow passageway. He heard Olivia gasp behind him as he stared at the passageway in disbelief.

He'd known Olivia's idea was the only one that made sense, and he didn't believe she'd imagined the breeze in her room that first night. But thinking something could be real and seeing it in front of him were two different things—and opened an entire realm of possibilities that he hadn't considered before.

Possibilities that might lead him to his sister.

He poked his head into the passageway but couldn't see anything in the pitch-black tunnel. The wardrobe barely allowed light across the threshold of the entry but the passageway ran the length of the room, allowing no illumination beyond the first foot of the opening.

"Hold on a sec," Olivia said, and he heard her rustling in the room behind him.

He turned to see what she was doing, and she stepped into the wardrobe doorway and handed him a spotlight. He raised his eyebrows at her and she shrugged.

"Do you really have to ask?"

He turned on the spotlight and stuck it in the passageway. The woman had a point. If staying in large houses of horrors was a normal part of her job, she probably carried a more unusual set of business supplies than the average writer. He'd already been impressed

with her tool set she'd brought to check the walls, complete with stethoscope. There was something to be said for a woman whose luggage included more tools and equipment than clothes.

He shone the light to the right of the opening, but there was only a wall. On the left the passageway extended about ten feet, then appeared to end. The entire passageway was maybe two feet wide and the ceiling was barely higher than his head. Servants back then must have been short and skinny.

"Well?" Olivia asked, poking her head into the tunnel.

"I can't tell if it turns at the end. I'm going to take a look."

"Be careful. The floorboards could be rotten or weak."

John shone the light down on the wooden pathway. Fresh, new lumber shone back at him. "Looks like someone kept this part of the house repaired." He took a couple of steps down the passageway.

"What the hell?" Olivia asked.

He glanced back as Olivia shone a flashlight on the repaired floor.

"Why in the world would someone make repairs here?"

John continued down the passage, checking each section of the wall for a possible sliding panel to an off-shooting tunnel. "I think if we had the answer to that question, we'd know who was sneaking around here and why."

"Do you see anything?"

"Not so far." He covered the last couple of feet in the passageway and frowned when he realized the wall simply stopped, rather than turning as he'd hoped. He

knocked and pressed on the end wall, hoping to find some way to make it shift or open but it didn't budge. "I don't understand. It's a dead end." He looked back at Olivia. "You seem to know some about the architecture of these homes. Do you want to take a look?"

Olivia bit her lip and stared at him.

"Is something wrong?" he asked.

"No, yes… It's just that I'm a little claustrophobic."

"You're kidding me. With your job?"

"I don't write in closets," Olivia shot back. "Give me a second." She took a single step into the tunnel, took a deep breath, then slowly blew it out. She inched down the tunnel toward him and after what seemed like forever, finally stood behind him.

She placed one hand on his shoulder and peered around him at the solid wood wall. "There's got to be a way around it. Whoever replaced that flooring did it for a reason. Did you feel the edges for a release?" She pointed up at the corner of the passage end. "What's that?"

He looked at the corner. "I don't see anything."

"There's something shiny up there. On the framing at the top corner."

John shone his light up in the corner. "I don't see anything."

"My flashlight caught it for a moment. Turn your light off and let me see if I can get it again."

John turned off the spotlight and eighty percent of the illumination left the tunnel. He heard Olivia suck in a breath, then she shined her flashlight at the corner, slowly moving the light across the studs. Suddenly, she stopped.

"There," she said. "Where the bracing comes down at an angle in the top corner. Do you see?"

John looked up and saw a glint of something where the two studs met. He reached into the corner and felt lightly with his fingertips, just in case it was something sharp. But whatever was shining was small and smooth and connected to some sort of fuzzy material. "It's metal."

"Could it be a release?"

"No. It's not attached to the wall and there is some sort of material attached to it. Hold on." He balanced the object between his fingers, careful to get a good grip, and carefully removed it from the corner.

"What is it?" Olivia asked, her ragged breathing giving away how hard it was for her to stand there.

John looked down at the object in his palm. "Some sort of bag with a shiny clasp on top. I'm not sure."

"Let's go back into the room and take a look."

John managed to turn around in the narrow space and followed Olivia out of the tunnel and back into the master suite. He opened his hand to show her the object as soon as he stepped out of the tunnel. Olivia's eyes widened as she stared at the black velvet pouch with a metal clasp. John opened the clasp and turned the pouch upside down, dumping a tiny bit of gold jewelry onto his palm.

Olivia took one look at the object and gasped. A bolt of lightning broke across the sky and the lights went out, pitching the room into complete darkness. As he struggled to find the switch on the spotlight Olivia staggered backward, and he dropped the light and caught her with one arm before she fell. He could feel her heart pounding against his chest as he clutched her warm body against his. The honey-sweet smell of her hair flooded his nostrils and his body began to respond in entirely inappropriate ways, now or ever.

He released her slowly, making certain she wasn't going to collapse, and retrieved the spotlight from the floor. He pressed the switch and the room flooded with light. Olivia slumped onto the end of the bed, clutching her flashlight and staring at his hand as if the object was going to leap up from his palm and attack her.

John took in her flushed face, ragged breath and shocked expression. He narrowed his eyes at her. "I think it's time you and I have a talk about exactly why you're here."

Chapter Six

Olivia sipped on her cup of tea and looked across the kitchen table at John. A lantern on the table cast a dim glow in the room, causing shadows to dance on the walls like the night creatures in some of her stories. She struggled to get control of herself, but her hands shook as she placed the cup back on the table.

"Thanks for the tea," she said. "I'm sorry I freaked out on you. You've been really patient, but I know I owe you an explanation." She opened a small plastic container she'd brought with her from the bedroom. A container that she never traveled without.

"Everything I know about my past is in this box," she said.

"I don't understand."

"I was raised in an orphanage. All the nuns could tell me was a woman left me there one night in the middle of a thunderstorm. I was only a year old. The woman said she couldn't be responsible for what would happen to me and begged them to take me."

"Did they call the police?"

"Yes. The police issued a statement to the public asking for people to report anyone who used to have a baby but didn't any longer and gave a limited description of the woman. It was dark and she wore a hooded jacket,

so the nuns couldn't provide the police with much to go on."

"But no one ever came forward."

"No. They finally assumed the woman wasn't from the area, which is why no one had identified her. Since I was safe with the nuns, no one felt the need to escalate it to a national level, so I stayed at the orphanage with the nuns."

"They didn't try to get you adopted? I would think someone would be interested in a baby so young."

Olivia stared down at her tea, knowing she needed to tell John everything, but she doubted he'd believe her. No one else did. "I was placed a couple of times, but both ended badly so the nuns didn't try again."

"Ended badly?"

"The nuns said I would scream like I was being murdered and wake everyone up from a dead sleep. Nothing they did would soothe me. It took hours for me to calm down. The nuns had me checked repeatedly by doctors, but they couldn't find anything wrong."

"But obviously it stopped."

"No. I just stopped screaming."

John's eyes widened. "What causes it?"

"A dream. I've had it as long as I can remember. Sometimes once a month, sometimes every night, but it's always the same."

"Can you tell me about it?"

Olivia blew out a breath. "I don't want to, but I think I have to. I need someone to tell me I'm not crazy or paranoid."

John nodded, but Olivia noticed he didn't make any promises.

Olivia took a deep breath and began. "It starts off like I'm flying over a wooded area. I swoop down into

a clearing and approach an enormous house. I fly inside an upstairs window and then the dream shifts. I'm in a bed sleeping. It's a large room and the bed is ornate with tall pillars on each corner and gauze draped around it. A man walks into the bedroom and stands next to the bed, staring down at me. Even though I'm asleep in my dream, I can see him standing there almost as if I'm also floating above the bed."

Olivia took another drink of her tea and focused on staying calm. "As I open my eyes, he raises a dagger above me and plunges it into my heart. I can see his eyes as clearly as I see yours now. They're completely dead, and I know he doesn't feel an ounce of remorse for what he's done. I gasp for air, but I can feel my lungs collapsing, my heart beating so loudly that it drowns out all the nighttime noise. I clutch my chest and scream, trying to drown out the sound of my fading heartbeat. Then I wake up."

"Do you recognize the man?"

"No. In my dream, I know that I know him, but when I'm awake, I can't remember his face. Only his eyes."

John hesitated for a moment and Olivia could tell he was struggling for the right thing to say. "I'm sorry you have to deal with that, and it sounds truly horrifying, but I don't understand what it has to do with your being here."

Olivia pulled a small jewelry case out of the container and opened it. She held the case across the table for John to see. "This is the other half of the locket you took from the tunnel. I was clutching it when the nuns took me."

John stared at the two broken pieces, and Olivia could tell he desperately wanted another explanation, an easy, risk-free answer. "I'm sure there was more than

one locket made. I admit, it's a startling coincidence, but I think you might be reaching."

Olivia shook her head. "That locket was not mass produced. I took my half for appraisal. The jeweler said it was handcrafted and about one hundred and fifty years old. I'd bet anything that if we take both pieces to a jeweler, he'll say they're a match."

"So maybe someone followed you here. Someone who's always had the other half and for some reason is choosing now to try to freak you out. This situation still has all the makings of a stalker."

"Maybe, but I don't think so."

"Why not?"

"Because this is the house from my dreams."

John's eyes widened.

"And that woman in the photo—the one that looks like me," Olivia continued, "was murdered by her husband."

JOHN GLANCED OVER at the couch in the caretaker's cottage, but even with the dim light of the lantern he could see Olivia was out cold, probably from sheer exhaustion. Wavy locks, the color of caramel, fell across her forehead and rested on her perfectly defined cheekbones. Even in her sleep Olivia's face had that timeless beauty to it, just like Marilyn Borque. She hadn't even argued when John had suggested she stay at his place that night, which meant she'd either seen the logic behind leaving a place where no room was necessarily secure, or she'd simply been scared to death. Maybe both.

Not that he blamed her.

The entire situation was more bizarre than what he was used to, and Olivia had every right to be scared and upset. The situation disturbed him on so many levels,

he was having trouble wrapping his mind around them all. He stared out the kitchen window at the sheets of rain and sighed. The last thing he needed was to take anything else on right now, but it didn't look like he had a choice. Like it or not, Olivia might be the key to unlocking the secrets of the house and finding his sister.

John didn't buy into some past-life dream transference, and he could tell Olivia was skeptical as well, but the reality was that some very strange things had happened and at the moment neither of them had a logical explanation. The only thing he was certain about was that someone, a living breathing someone, was laying a trap for Olivia with the photos and the jewelry. Someone who wanted to remain hidden in the shadows but someone with an agenda.

What John needed was more information—about the house and Olivia, but after she'd delivered that last statement about the murdered woman it was clear her defenses and emotions were crumbling fast. He needed information, but he needed her thinking clearly when she gave it. So instead, he'd offered her a glass of wine and a safe place on his couch and planned to question her again first thing in the morning. They couldn't afford to waste much time.

John had two theories based on what Olivia had told him, but neither were much more credible than a vision in a dream. The first theory was that Olivia had been to the house as an infant. The second theory was that her biological mother or someone close to her, maybe a foster parent, had been murdered and Olivia had seen it. Even though she'd been a baby, maybe something had been impressed on her memory. Something that came back to her in her dreams.

He blew out a breath and shook his head. If that didn't sound like an *X-Files* episode, he didn't know what did.

Regardless, all signs pointed to something big whirling around Olivia Markham—something even Olivia didn't have a grasp on. John wondered exactly what his sister had had the misfortune to step in the middle of. Whatever it was, the intruder probably hadn't counted on an extra person in the mix, and assuming his sister had come across this person, what had he done to her? John could only hope that whatever the intruder's ultimate plan may be that it didn't include murder.

He'd hoped the camera Olivia had found would give him proof that his sister had been at laMalediction, but he'd only found pictures of the exterior of the house and a couple of shots of the entryway. They were definitely things his sister would have taken pictures of for her thesis, but it couldn't be considered concrete proof. Frustrated, he rose from the table and pulled a beer from the refrigerator.

He should be inspecting the attic or trying to figure out where that tunnel was supposed to lead, but he didn't want to leave Olivia alone. The photo on Olivia's bed was proof the intruder was escalating, and as soon as John got a chance he needed to dust the photo and the tunnel switches for prints. Leaving that photo was brazen, even with the tunnels, in the middle of the day and with both of them right there in the house.

Then there was the flip side—if the intruder had his sister, the best way to get to him was through Olivia. He felt a moment of guilt that he was using her, but he pushed it aside. He might be using her, but in doing so he was also protecting her.

At least that's what he was telling himself.

OLIVIA FLEW OVER the swamp surrounding laMalediction. She knew she was dreaming, but no matter how hard she tried she couldn't force herself awake. It was the same as before, the storm, the outline of the house, and she clenched her eyes, trying to block out what she knew she'd see, but everything remained in full view. This time she hovered in front of the house and Olivia saw Franklin Borque pass in front of the window in the formal living room.

She dipped down and the view changed, almost as if she were peering into the house from the outside wall. Franklin Borque was in the kitchen, opening one of the cabinet drawers. He was wearing dinner clothes, but Olivia somehow knew it was the middle of the night. He pulled something from the drawer, but his body blocked the object from Olivia's vision.

When he turned, the blade of the knife flashed in the light of the lone candle on the kitchen table, and Olivia sucked in a breath. He looked down at the blade, turning the knife over and over in his palm. He smiled as he looked at it, his eyes flashing wildly with excitement and anticipation. He drew the blade of the knife across his open palm and blood spilled from the cut. He brought his palm up to his face and licked it, smearing blood across his jaw.

Olivia knew for certain that he was mad.

He walked up the stairs, blood dripping from his cut hand, the knife clenched in the other. The door to the master bedroom was closed and he didn't even attempt to open it. Instead he continued past it several feet, then pressed his hand on the wall, leaving a bloody handprint on the white plaster surface. A section of the wall slid back and Olivia realized he was entering the passage that led to the master bedroom from the hallway.

The dream shifted immediately to the inside of the master bedroom and Olivia expected to be in the bed, but this time the dream changed and she hovered above the bed watching the scene play out below. Marilyn Borque lay sleeping in the bed, completely unaware of the danger in the hallway. The wall where the wardrobe now stood was bare and Olivia watched as the panel slid back and Franklin Borque entered the room.

Olivia screamed at Marilyn, trying to wake her from her deep sleep, but no sound came out. Her throat burned as she struggled to make a noise, and she felt her lungs would explode as Franklin stood above Marilyn and thrust the knife deep into her heart.

The sound of tearing flesh freed her throttled voice and her screams finally broke free. She bolted upright in a panic at her unfamiliar surroundings. Where the hell was she? Her vision blurred, and a second later someone grabbed her shoulders and shook them.

"Olivia, wake up!"

She gasped for air, clutching the fabric of the sofa, and finally remembered she was in the caretaker's cottage. Her vision began to clear and she saw John standing over her, felt his hands on her shoulders, his voice trying to bring her out of the nightmare. She took a deep breath and blew it out slowly, then lay back on the couch, trying to slow her racing heart.

John crouched beside her. "Was it the dream?"

Olivia nodded, not yet able to speak.

He placed his hand on her arm. "From your description last night I knew it had to be horrifying, but I have to tell you, you scared the hell out of me. Your scream was so primal, the fear so evident. And when I found you…your eyes were wide open, but it's like you couldn't see me. Like you were trapped in there."

"I was. That's the worst part. I know I'm dreaming but I can't wake myself up."

"Was this one the same as before?"

Olivia shook her head and told him about seeing Franklin Borque in the kitchen. "He was mad, and I mean in a clinical sense. I could tell by his expression."

"You're not going to get any argument from me. Anyone who cuts open their own palm before murdering their wife clearly has issues." John frowned and stared at the wall behind her for a couple of seconds. "The dream has always been the same until now, right?"

"Always."

"So why do you think it changed now?"

Olivia rose to a sitting position and tucked her knees in front of her, encircling them with her arms. "Maybe being at the house? The house, the storm, even some of the furniture is the same."

John nodded. "Maybe so. Given your past, the horrific history of the house's residents and your imagination, it's not any wonder that your subconscious would whirl out of control with the stimulus it's received."

"But it seemed real. I know you find this hard to believe, and I'm not saying you aren't right in your assessment, but I think what I saw may be the truth."

"Are there any official records?"

"Yeah, but they're sketchy. Mostly, the police had only the servants' word to go on because Franklin died the same night."

"Of what?"

Olivia shook her head. "I don't know. I couldn't find anything on it, except that one of the servants walked for two days to get the police. Cypriere was no more than a village at the time. The police arrived to find

Marilyn Borque stabbed to death and Franklin dead in the middle of the courtyard."

John frowned. "He died in the courtyard and the servants left him there for days?"

"People are superstitious in these parts. You know that. No one wanted to touch the body of 'the devil.'"

"And the police never determined cause of death?"

"Not that I could find. After the initial discovery the entire story just fell off the map as far as paperwork goes. It's like everyone wanted it to go away." Olivia took a deep breath and blew it out. "With everything I know about the murder, it could have happened exactly like my dream. Nothing in my dream contradicts the actual reports."

"Very slim reports," John pointed out. "I…I'm sorry, but I can't go there. It's too far beyond what I believe. People who've been in horrendous situations often have issues with dreams. Like soldiers with post-traumatic stress disorder."

"But I've never seen a murder or anything else that traumatic. I think I would remember if I had. And how do you explain my seeing the house in my dreams before I'd ever been here? I don't pretend to have the answers, but I don't think you do either. I think somewhere between our two differing opinions lies the truth."

"Maybe, but all we have to work with now is reality." He rose from the floor. "It's almost dawn. I figure you have no intention of going back to sleep, so I'll make some coffee."

He stepped into the kitchen and started spooning coffee grounds into the coffeemaker. Olivia rose from the couch and headed for the bathroom. Maybe a dash of cold water on her face would help clear the fog from her mind. She was fully awake but her mind still felt

cloudy, as if she were stuck in limbo between reality and her dream.

She closed the bathroom door and stared at herself in the mirror. The one thing she was certain of was that the dreams were no coincidence. Despite her talent for inventing spooky stories, she somehow knew that this story wasn't a fabrication of her overactive imagination. Olivia was certain that somehow, she'd witnessed a murder that had happened over a century ago.

Ten minutes later, Olivia took a huge sip of coffee and avoided looking across the table at John. In the dim light of day, she felt foolish for her panic the night before and was mortified that not only had she slept on the couch of a man who was practically a stranger, but also she'd awakened him by screaming like a frightened child. Olivia had always avoided sharing personal information with others, especially men, but there was something about John that made her want to trust him. Which went against something else she'd always avoided—men.

"I've been thinking about the tunnel," John said.

"Yeah. What about it?"

"Well, obviously someone planned to use it or they wouldn't have made repairs."

Olivia nodded, even though the only reason someone would have for needing the tunnels was her occupancy of the house. "It's because of me, right? I mean, the house has been empty all these years, so no one would need a way to sneak around if I wasn't there."

"Based on everything that's happened, I have to assume the intruder is here because of you. I may be wrong, but…"

"It would be a huge coincidence." Olivia shook her head. "I don't do huge coincidences, not even in my

books. I know they happen, but not near as often as people might think. Usually there's someone with a motive."

John narrowed his eyes at her. "That sounds like something a cop would say."

Olivia shrugged. "I have to understand a lot of personality types to write good books, including the bad guys, and I spend a fair amount of time consulting with law enforcement as well as with behavioral analysts. Everyone's got a motive, John. Some of them are good, decent and altruistic, but there's always a reason behind what people do."

"Well, I'd prefer not to wait until the big showdown to figure out what this guy's motive is, so we need to come up with a plan."

"Okay, but where do we start? I don't think whoever put the picture in my room entered through the main hallway, like my dream. The walls there don't have plaster now, but wallpaper, which would show a seam. Besides which, if he was going to stroll through the house and up the stairs, why use a panel in the hallway when the door to the bedroom wasn't locked?"

"I agree," John said. "There's nothing in the hall to indicate a panel still exists, assuming it ever did. Besides, the tunnel doesn't run the length of the bedroom wall. It stops short of the hallway by a good five feet."

Olivia sighed. "I need to go through those albums in the library and see if I can get more information on the Borques. You need to find the trip switch in the tunnel and figure out where all the entry points are, otherwise I'm sleeping in the kitchen pantry to be safe.

"And then there's the fact that both of us have real jobs to do, and I don't think we're making much progress." Olivia didn't even want to think about how far

behind schedule she was on the book and no way was she notifying her editor.

"The maintenance can wait," John said. "I think your safety trumps repairs."

Olivia pursed her lips and thought for a moment. "What do you know about the previous caretaker?"

"Not much, really. Wheeler said he had a family emergency and had to take off for a while, but apparently Wheeler had been trying to hire more capable help before that."

"So he was already gone when you got here?"

"Yeah. Wheeler told me to use his cottage until he got back, but said he didn't know when that would be."

"I wonder if someone repaired the floor in that tunnel before he left and if so, how did they manage without him noticing?"

John frowned. "I know he's old, and Wheeler said he was hard of hearing, but you're right. Someone would still have to haul lumber in here and cart it upstairs before they even began cutting and nailing. Hard to believe he could miss all that."

Olivia nodded. "I think we need to locate the old caretaker and ask him a few questions. It doesn't sound like Wheeler knows much of anything."

"No, it doesn't, but I can still call and ask."

"And say what?"

"I'll make something up. Pass me my cell phone."

"It's barely daylight."

"That didn't stop you from calling him yesterday. From where I sit, Wheeler has a fair amount to answer for. If he has to do it with the chickens, that's not my problem."

Olivia pushed John's cell phone across the table and he punched in Wheeler's number. Olivia hoped the at-

torney knew more than they thought he did. The old caretaker might be able to clear everything up.

"Wheeler, this is John Landry at laMalediction."

Olivia perked up and waited for John to question Wheeler.

"No, everything's as expected given the lack of maintenance over the years, but I'm having some trouble locating breakers for some of the wiring in the main house. I wondered if you had a way I could contact the old caretaker for a quick chat about that and a couple of other things. It would save me a ton of time."

Olivia gave John a thumbs-up. At least his story was a plausible one.

John listened for a couple of seconds, then frowned. "So you have no idea how to reach him? Do you even know where he was going?" John looked over at Olivia and shook his head. "Well, I guess I'll make do without him. But if you happen to hear from him, would you please ask him to give me a call on my cell?"

John closed the phone. "Dead end. Wheeler says Aubrey, the old caretaker, didn't say where he was going, doesn't own a cell phone and he has nothing in his files on the man other than his name and social security number."

"Aubrey's probably been working at laMalediction longer than Wheeler has been alive. No reason for him to dig into the man's business, I guess. So what now?"

"We could always take a trip to town and ask around."

Olivia frowned, not relishing a visit to the town that officially gave her the creeps. "Do you think they'll talk to us? I stopped at the café for directions on my way in and you would have thought I'd asked them to sacrifice their firstborn."

"They probably just don't like outsiders."

"I'm sure they don't, but it was more than that."

"What was it, then?"

Olivia's mind played back her visit to the café. "They were skittish…uneasy." She looked John directly in the eyes. "It was like they were all afraid."

HE LOOKED DOWN at the caretaker's cottage from a tiny window in the attic tower. He'd left the photo hoping to hurry the woman along to her discovery…her destiny, but something had gone wrong. They'd found the tunnel entrance in her bedroom and that complicated everything, but he hadn't expected her to flee the house and hole up with the caretaker. Even the discovery of the tunnel shouldn't have caused that much panic.

Something else had happened. Something he didn't know about and hadn't planned for. And that bothered him more than anything else.

The front door of the caretaker's cottage swung open and he watched expectantly as both of them stepped outside. She would come back into the house. She had to. It was written.

But instead of crossing the circular drive, they got into the caretaker's truck. He clenched his hands as they drove away from the estate. They didn't carry any luggage so they were likely only going to town, but this wouldn't do at all. There was no time to waste. The full moon was approaching. Three more days and Olivia Markham would fulfill the prophecy.

His life would be set. Hers would be cut short.

Chapter Seven

Huge droplets of rain began to fall from the gray sky as Olivia stepped out of John's truck and hurried across the street. Three men sitting in the corner of the otherwise empty café looked up as Olivia stepped inside, but all it took was a single glance for them to lower their eyes and lean forward to whisper across the table. John had suggested the cook might be more comfortable if she was alone, as the man had helped her before, so he'd gone to the gas station to pick up some supplies.

Olivia slid onto a stool at the counter and waited for the cook to plate some eggs and toast and deliver it to one of the men in the corner. The man spoke to the cook and the cook glanced at her before shaking his head and saying something to the man that made the entire table frown.

The cook headed back to the counter and gave her a nod. "I guess you made it all right?"

"Yes, thank you so much for the directions. I missed the twisted trees on the first pass, but your map was great."

"No problem. Coffee?"

"Please, and the breakfast special. I've been living on protein bars and peanut-butter sandwiches."

The cook broke a couple of eggs on the grill and slid

bread into the toaster. "So you haven't changed your mind about staying there?" he asked, but he kept his gaze directed away from her.

"Not until I'm finished with my book."

The cook placed a full cup of coffee in front of her, and Olivia took a second to breathe in the strong aroma. Rather than immediately moving away, the cook stood there and studied her.

"Doesn't it make you nervous?" he asked.

"No," Olivia lied, and realized that was the first time her answer to that particular question was a lie. "I'm used to it by now. I live in a different house for every book."

"Probably ain't seen anything like laMalediction, though. Place is cursed."

Olivia nodded. "It's that sort of rumor that makes it a great place for a story."

The cook's eyes darted to the men in the corner, then back at Olivia, and he shook his head. "The things that happen at laMalediction ain't no story in a book. Place ain't safe, if you ask me."

Olivia mentally cheered. The cook had given her exactly the opening she'd been looking for. "It *is* very run-down. I'm careful when I use the stairwell or walk in the upstairs rooms to check the flooring first. The lights don't work in a large section of the house. I figure there's a breaker tripped, but I haven't been able to locate the box."

The cook narrowed his eyes at her. "Aubrey's lived there his whole life. How come he won't fix it?"

"Is Aubrey the old caretaker?"

"If you mean old as in age, yeah, he's ancient."

"No, I meant he's not there now. The estate attorney said he had a family emergency and sent a new guy to

cover for a while. But he's been so busy with damage from the storm that he doesn't have time to mess with the lights. He figures I should make do with the other parts of the house until he can get to it."

"Family emergency?" The cook frowned. "I don't recall hearing anything about that." He turned back to the grill to plate her food.

"Maybe it came up at the last minute," Olivia suggested. "I wish I knew where to find him. A simple phone call would probably save me an afternoon of hunting around in the basement. Part of the section without lights is the library and I want to dig through the books and family albums for research." Olivia gave herself a mental pat on the back for the lies that rolled off her tongue.

The cook turned and slid the plate in front of her. He rubbed his jaw with one hand, his brow wrinkled in concentration. "Best I know, Aubrey's family is all in Johnson's Bayou, a little town a couple of hours west of here. I don't know any of them, but the family name is Murphy."

Olivia smiled. "Thanks! I'll try looking them up."

The cook frowned. "Thing is, though, I could swear I saw Aubrey's truck driving through town last night."

Olivia stared. "What time?"

"Late, after the storm started. I was still up here hassling with a broken gas line on this grill. Guess I could have been mistaken. It was still storming and there ain't no streetlights to speak of."

Olivia shrugged, trying not to let on how much the cook's words interested her. "Well, he sure hasn't been to the house. But I'll see if I can get in touch with him today and get those lights working. I really appreciate the help."

The cook nodded and glanced at the men at the corner table. Olivia could barely see them from where she sat, but she could tell they'd stopped talking as soon as she'd started and were likely hanging on every word. That didn't seem to please the cook at all.

"My name's Olivia, by the way," she said and extended her hand across the counter. The cook hesitantly shook it. "I was in such a hurry to beat the storm the other day that I don't even think I introduced myself."

"I'm Tom Breaux. I own this café."

"It's nice to meet you, Tom." Olivia glanced at the men in the corner, leaned across the counter, and lowered her voice. "Can I ask you a question?"

"Yeah," Tom said, nervously. "I guess so."

"Why does my staying at laMalediction seem to bother people?"

Tom's eyes widened. "Surely, you know about the house. I mean, that smooth-talking attorney didn't con you into thinking it was safe there, did he?"

"I know the house's history, if that's what you mean."

"Then you know that people who go there rarely come out unless it's with the coroner. Aubrey's the only person that's been to laMalediction in my lifetime that ever came back out."

Olivia's heart skipped a beat and she forced herself to sound normal. "Are you saying other people have died there besides the original owners?"

Tom nodded. "Couple of surveyors a few years ago was poking around, said they had to measure the bayou or something foolish. I figure they was really trying to see if the land held oil, then they'd try to pick it up for a song."

"What happened to them?"

"The sheriff tried to keep it all hushed, so as not

to scare people, but I heard the rumors all the same. Those two men shot each other. Ain't no one got a reason why. But my friend Billy works for the doctor two towns over and he drove the bodies to the morgue. He unzipped the body bags and took a peek."

Olivia stared at Tom, not even blinking. "What did he see?"

Tom glanced at the men in the corner and leaned further across the counter, his voice a whisper. "He said their faces looked like they'd been scared to death."

Olivia fought the urge to cross her arms across her chest. "Wow. You're right. That is a scary story. Are they the only ones you know about?"

Tom nodded. "The only ones they had bodies for, but every couple of years or so, someone comes into town wanting to poke around the house. I see 'em come into town, but I never see 'em leave."

"Maybe they leave when you're at home or busy."

"Maybe. Or maybe they're still at that house. Maybe the reason the lights don't work is they're trying to speak to you. Trying to warn you, even."

Olivia studied the man's face, but she saw no slyness in his expression. Whatever was going on at laMalediction, it was clear by the expression on Tom's face that he believed it was malevolent. "I'm careful because I know it's in bad need of repair," Olivia said, "but it's just a house. There's nothing evil about it."

She saw him clench his jaw, and he leaned toward her, staring her straight in the eyes. "No, ma'am, that's where you're wrong. I'm not given to fanciful things, but the truth is, there's more things in these bayous that can't be explained than can. I know deep in my bones that pile of stone and wood is not *just* a house. Some-

where between 'nothing' and those stories you write is the truth."

Olivia felt the hair rise on the back of her neck as Tom turned and began scraping the grill. What did it take to make a grown, strong, able-bodied, seemingly sane man that intense over a structure of stone and wood? Maybe if Tom had been sequestered here his entire life she'd get it, but she recognized the military tattoos on his arms. Tom was no backwoods hick who'd never crossed the parish line.

But he still believed in monsters.

JOHN STEPPED INTO the doorway of the library and paused when he saw Olivia looking out the window, talking on her phone. She turned to face the doorway and waved him inside, frowning as she thanked whoever was on the phone and disconnected. "Any luck?" he asked.

Olivia shook her head. "None of Aubrey's relatives have seen him in years, much less in the past couple of days."

"Any other relatives we don't know about?"

"According to his niece, the family in Johnson's Bayou is all Aubrey has left."

"Girlfriend?" John suggested, but he knew it was a stretch. Hard for a man who'd been sequestered at la-Malediction for eighty years to find a girlfriend.

"No chance. His niece said women irritated him and made him paranoid. Apparently, he thinks we all have ulterior motives."

"Don't you?"

"Motives, yes. Ulterior, depends on the woman." She dropped into a leather chair and looked up at John. "This missing caretaker thing…it's that coincidence dance all over again." She sighed. "I don't buy it."

John shook his head and slid into the chair across the table from her. "I don't, either. There's simply too many things at play and none of them add up."

Olivia bit her lower lip then asked, "What do you think happened to him?"

"I have two guesses. Either he had a run-in with our intruder…"

"Or?"

"Or he *is* our intruder."

Olivia's eyes widened. "You really think so?"

"Yeah. Considering he told Wheeler he had to leave for a family emergency but none of his family is aware of an emergency, it looks like he lied. He wanted people to believe he'd left laMalediction."

"That makes sense, and would explain why Tom Breaux saw his truck last night. Even if he was old and slow, he'd still know every square inch of the house including the secret passages."

John nodded. "And he wouldn't have to hide the passage repairs from himself."

"But how is he getting back and forth from wherever he's hiding?"

"Maybe he never left the house," John suggested.

"Then why did Tom Breaux see his truck?"

"Maybe he was mistaken."

Olivia frowned. "Maybe. But let's just assume Tom Breaux wasn't mistaken and it was Aubrey's truck. That means he's driving to and from somewhere, and he's certainly not driving up the main road and parking in the front drive."

"No, he's not, but God only knows how many trails run through these woods. And if anyone would know an alternate route to laMalediction, it would be Aubrey."

John pointed to Olivia's laptop. "You got internet on that thing?"

Olivia held up her satellite phone attached by a cord to the laptop. "Yes."

"Then pull up Google maps and see if we can get a satellite view of the area. If the alternate route isn't covered completely by the trees we might be able to see it."

Olivia smiled, pulled up Google maps and typed in the town of Cypriere. "I don't know why I didn't think of this. I pulled up Google maps of the house before coming here and didn't even think about it. And I'm supposed to be good at research."

John pulled a chair over next to her and watched the screen as an aerial view of Cypriere developed. Olivia could feel the heat coming off of his body, but instead of making her nervous it made her feel safe until she thought about it in that vein and then *that* made her nervous. Depending on other people wasn't a weakness Olivia had ever had, and was one she couldn't afford to develop. Depending on hot, strong men all alone in the middle of nowhere was just asking for trouble.

She lifted her arm up a tiny bit, just so his forearm was no longer touching her, and clicked the mouse to select a satellite view. She zoomed in on the area a couple of times, then pointed to a hazy set of buildings. "There's the town. This house is east and maybe a little south, right?"

John leaned in further to study the screen and his forearm touched hers again. "That sounds right."

Olivia clicked the mouse a couple more times, shifting the satellite image southeast until they saw a large clearing in the forest. "That's it," Olivia said, pointing to the roof of the main house.

John stared at the screen and frowned.

"What's wrong?" Olivia asked.

"You said you looked this up before coming here, but you didn't know it was the house in your dreams before arriving."

"I know. I think it's because in my dream I'm flying toward the front of the house and into the window. Just seeing the top of the roof wasn't enough to trigger anything with me. But from the front of the house, you can see all the gables and the stained glass."

John nodded. "A matter of perspective." He pointed to a winding line on the west side of the estate. "That's the main road and even that doesn't show. The cypress trees really have it covered, and it's hazy. It must have been raining when the satellite took the shot."

"There's a shocker." Olivia inspected the tiny line that appeared intermittently on the screen, then scanned the woods surrounding the home hoping to spot something similar. "What's that north of the house, in the woods behind the caretaker's cottage?" Olivia pointed to a minuscule break in the trees some distance behind the cottage.

John studied the screen and pointed above her finger. "Yeah. Look at this break a little farther north. It could be a road buried back there. Move the satellite view farther north."

Olivia clicked the mouse and the screen shifted to expose a larger area of woods and marshland north of the estate. "There." She pointed to a thin, curving line. "It looks like it runs to a river."

"Bayou," John corrected. "It isn't big enough to be a river, but southern Louisiana is full of bayous and channels. Zoom in on the bayou north of where we saw the path."

Olivia zoomed in as far as the satellite photo allowed. "It's roofs. Do people live there?"

"Probably. And some that have houses elsewhere keep another place on bayous to fish. They call them camps, but a lot of them are little more than shacks that would crumple in a high wind."

Olivia scanned the photo surrounding the camps. "I don't see any roads to the camps. Just the barest traces of a trail from laMalediction."

"They probably get there by boat."

Olivia sat back in her chair. "Great. So we can be attacked by land or water, and since everyone in this town probably owns a boat, then we haven't exactly narrowed things down."

"Not exactly. But whoever owns those camps would be our best bet for someone who knows about a path to laMalediction."

Olivia nodded. "So what do you want to do?"

"You got any hiking boots and a raincoat in one of those boxes?"

Olivia smiled. "As a matter of fact, I do."

Chapter Eight

It took almost an hour of stomping through the dense brush behind the caretaker's cottage before they located something that could barely serve as a pathway for a vehicle. It was about a hundred yards behind the caretaker's cottage and there was no way someone in the main house could see anyone approaching from that direction.

John glanced at his watch. "Even though the rain stopped, it's still really overcast. We've got a couple of hours before we start losing light, maybe less because of the trees."

Olivia pushed the hood of her rain jacket back and wiped sweat from her forehead. "Assuming this takes us to those camps, how far do you think it is?"

"A couple of miles maybe. It's hard to tell from the satellite map, especially if the path winds a lot."

Olivia nodded. "Then I guess we best get moving."

John gave her the once-over, and Olivia hoped the exhaustion she was beginning to feel didn't show. "You sure you're up to this? Even though it's fall, the humidity here gets to people who aren't used to it."

"It will be humid again tomorrow and I want to know what's going on."

"Then let's make tracks. I don't want to get caught

out here after dark." He turned and started down the path, disappearing as he rounded a corner in the brush.

Olivia set out beside him, trying not to think about the things John had left unsaid. The dense brush and gray sky had already choked half of the light out of the swamp. The glow of the moon wouldn't even scratch the surface. *I don't want to get caught out here after dark*. But it wasn't the dark that they had to be afraid of. It was the creatures that hunted in the dark and this marsh was probably full of them.

Not to mention whoever was trying to scare her. Olivia was pretty sure she didn't want to run into him in the dark, either, even with her pistol tucked in the waistband of her jeans.

Olivia walked silently beside John, carefully observing the terrain before she took a step. The last thing she needed was a sprained ankle when the nearest doctor was probably light-years away.

It took forty-five minutes to reach an abrupt end to the path, a giant wall of brush. John pointed to a muddy area just behind the brush. It looked like branches had been dragged through the mud. "Someone thinks he's being clever."

"He *is* clever. Who knows how long they've gotten away with using this path."

"Let's find a way around this mess. I want to leave it intact and try not to step in the open muddy area. I don't want to leave footprints for him to discover."

Olivia nodded and followed John around the side of the brush, careful to place her feet on dense undergrowth. They picked up the path on the other side of the brush and followed it another five minutes when suddenly John crouched behind a bush, pulling Olivia down with him. He placed one finger over his lips and

pointed. Olivia peered through the brush and realized they were directly behind the camps from the satellite photo, and someone was approaching in a boat.

Olivia peered through the branches and tried to make out the man as the boat pulled up to the pier, but he had a cap pulled low and he was looking down as he docked the boat. He tied the boat to a pylon, then grabbed a box from the boat and placed it on the pier. When he rose all the way up with the box, Olivia placed her hand on John's arm and squeezed.

"That's the cook," she whispered. "Tom Breaux."

"You're sure?"

"Positive." Olivia looked back toward the pier and watched as Tom placed two more boxes on the pier. "I can't make out the writing on the side of the boxes."

"Too far away," John agreed.

They watched as Tom stepped onto the pier and picked up one of the boxes. He headed toward the middle of the three camps and set the box on the steps next to the back door, then repeated the process for the other two boxes. After setting the last box on the top of the pile, he knocked on the back door and it opened. Olivia narrowed her eyes, trying to make out the figure inside the camp but it was dark and she didn't have a clear view.

The door to the camp opened and Tom carried the boxes insides, one by one. Ten minutes later, he stepped outside and started back toward the dock. In the branches of the tree above their hiding place, a hawk cried out and took off, breaking a branch off the tree with his launch.

Tom stopped short at the sound of the breaking branch and looked directly at their hiding place. Olivia released the branches and ducked farther down

behind the bush, almost colliding heads with John as he ducked, as well. Even though she knew he couldn't hear her breathing from that distance, she sucked in a breath and held it, praying that Tom wouldn't decide to take a closer look.

The seconds ticked away like hours and Olivia focused on an ant crawling across the top of her hand. She felt John shift beside her and he tapped her on the shoulder. "He's leaving," John said.

Olivia straightened back up to a crouch, releasing the breath she'd been holding out with a whoosh. She peered through the bush just in time to see Tom start the boat and back away from the dock. She turned to face John and was suddenly aware of the proximity of their bodies. "What do you think?" she asked as she tried to shift backward and increase the inches between them.

John stared at her for a moment then looked back at the bayou. He rose from the hiding spot and shook his head. "I don't know. Could be it's his place. Could be he was delivering to someone. I didn't get a look at whoever opened the door."

Olivia rose to stand beside him. "I didn't either. It could be a man or woman or Bigfoot for all I could see." She scanned the area surrounding the camps. "I don't see any vehicles here, though."

"No, but someone could easily navigate the path with an ATV. One would fit in that storage shed over there with no problem."

"Do you think we should try to look inside?"

John scanned the camps, and Olivia could tell his mind was processing the pros and cons. "No, it's too risky," he finally said. "And wouldn't prove anything except that someone has access to laMalediction, which

we already know. It wouldn't tell us if that person is Tom or Aubrey or someone else completely."

Olivia nodded. "I don't see another road."

"Yeah, I noticed that. You can probably only get to these camps by boat."

Olivia shoved her hands in her pockets and looked up at John. "I don't like it. Tom basically warned me away from the house, insinuating that it made people die or disappear, and he's the one who claimed he'd seen Aubrey's truck driving through town, but he's got a pathway to laMalediction in his backyard."

"If the camp is his."

"Yet another coincidence?"

John frowned.

Olivia opened her mouth to continue, but John clamped his hand over it. Instinctively, she started to struggle, but then realized he was looking back toward the camps.

"It's Tom again," John whispered. "He's docked his boat and is coming this way…with a shotgun." He grabbed her hand and pulled her off the path and into the dense foliage of the swamp as he began to run.

Olivia lurched forward at his tug and then broke out into a run behind him. Branches slapped against her face, slinging rainwater into her eyes and causing her vision to blur. Her thighs burned with the effort of running through the dense brush wearing the heavy hiking boots. John was about ten feet ahead of her, but he glanced back every couple of seconds to make sure she was still behind him. Olivia could hear Tom tearing through the brush behind her, so she knew he was in pursuit, and from the noise level, it sounded like he was getting closer by the minute.

For a split second, she worried they were running the

wrong way. The cypress trees seemed to close in, confusing her sense of direction. What if they'd veered too far off the path and got lost in the swamp? She was just about to pull her pistol from her waistband and prepare for the worst, when they broke out of the swamp and into the lawn just to the east of the storage shed near the caretaker's cottage.

John made a dash for the shed and slipped inside, leaving the door open. Olivia reached to close it, but John put his hand out to stop her. "It's better if he thinks we're working. That it wasn't us he was chasing."

John handed her a set of safety glasses and a pair of welding gloves, then grabbed the chain saw and headed out of the shack. "Take a couple of deep breaths and act normal," he whispered.

"I appreciate your help with this," John said in his regular voice as they left the storage shed. "I hope I didn't interrupt your work."

"No." Olivia waved a hand in dismissal, trying her best to appear nonchalant. She couldn't see Tom anywhere, but she would swear she could feel him watching. "I needed a break and sometimes physical activity is the best way to loosen the creative mind."

"Really?" John smiled. "Then prepare to have your mind well loosened. I'd like to get the rest of that tree cleared out of the drive before it gets dark. The rain got me a little behind." He stopped in front of the tree and pointed to her welding gloves, which she slipped on. "Grab the other side of this branch."

Olivia stooped down to wrap her arms around the thick branch. John bent over at the other end of the branch, his head just inches from her. "He's in the brush just behind the storage shed," he whispered without raising his head to look at her.

Olivia took a deep breath and fought the urge to look over at the storage shed.

"Ready?" John asked out loud.

Olivia nodded and they lifted the branch and carried it over to the pile John had started just outside the driveway. On the way back to the downed tree, John said in a low voice, "He's gone."

"Are you sure?"

"No, but he's not standing where he was before."

"So what's the plan? If Tom's our intruder then he could easily slip into the main house and watch us the rest of the day, and we can't stay out here all afternoon just to throw him off track."

John motioned to the end of another thick branch. "Lift your end, then drop it," he said in a low voice. "Grab your wrist like you hurt it."

Olivia nodded and lifted her end of the branch. She took one step backward and lost her grip. She pretended to stumble, then let out a cry and grabbed her wrist with her other hand. John immediately dropped his end of the log and rushed over to her. He told her to hold out her wrist and he slipped off the welding glove, pretending to inspect her wrist.

"Good job," he whispered, then in his regular voice said, "You need to clean this and then I'll help you wrap it." He motioned toward the cottage. It had only one entrance and that had been in John's sight the entire time. "I've got supplies in the cottage. Go ahead and get it cleaned. I'll put the tools up and be right in."

John picked up the chain saw and her gloves and headed for the storage shed. Olivia left the drive, trying to walk at a normal pace even though her body was practically crying to break out into a run. It seemed like forever, but she finally slipped into the caretaker's cot-

tage and closed the door behind her. She leaned back against the door and slowly slid to the floor, her heart still pounding.

JOHN PLACED THE chain saw and gloves back on a shelf in the storage shed and pulled the door closed behind him. He'd scanned the brush as he walked toward the caretaker's cottage, trying to make out any movement or color that didn't belong, but everything was silent. The optimist in him wanted to believe they'd fooled the cook with their little stunt, but if Tom Breaux was the intruder, the realist in him didn't think it worked.

If anything, their act might have made things worse because they'd alerted the man that they were on to him and trying to play games. Lack of respect was an insult to people who were a little off mentally, and John didn't think for a moment that someone sneaking through tunnels to leave creepy old photos on the bed of strange women was the least bit sane.

Which made him worry about his half sister even more. If she'd come to laMalediction like her calendar indicated, then it was very likely she'd stepped right into the middle of something very strange. And from the looks of it, dangerous. Whatever was going on, he needed to figure it out fast, before things got worse. He'd managed to dust the tunnel for prints that morning while Olivia was working in the library, but the only prints were his own. He had no doubt the photo would be the same, and couldn't help but remember that Tom Breaux had been wearing gloves when he unloaded those boxes and chased them through the swamp.

John blew out a breath. He was getting in deep with Olivia and the mystery surrounding the estate. He kept telling himself that his sister was somehow mixed up

in all of this—that solving Olivia's problem would ultimately lead him to his half sister, but was he just fooling himself? He couldn't deny that Olivia brought out feelings in him that he usually kept repressed. His mother and sister were enough responsibility for one man, and John had no intention of adding to the mix. But he couldn't deny that he found her interesting, both mentally and physically. She would be a hard woman to ignore even under normal circumstances.

He stepped into the caretaker's cottage and closed the door behind him. Olivia was in the living room, peering between the slats of the blinds. "You see anything?" he asked.

"Nothing." She turned to face him. "What about you? Did you see him when you were putting the tools away?"

"No," he said.

"So do you think it worked?"

John blew out a breath, not wanting to share all of his thoughts on the matter, especially as they'd probably only scare her more. "I don't know. I'd like to think so, but we fled fast. I don't know if we left footprints."

"Oh, no." Olivia covered her mouth with her hand. "I didn't even think about leaving footprints. It has to be him, right? I mean, why else would he chase us?"

John shook his head. "For a million other reasons I can think of, just off the top of my head. A lot of illegal activity goes on in these swamps. Drug deals, arms trading and a host of other activities. If Tom was mixed up in something illegal delivering those boxes, and he thought something was out of order, he would check it out."

"He was running after us with a shotgun," Olivia pointed out.

"That's one way of checking things out on the bayou."

Olivia threw her hands in the air. "What now? If we assume it's the caretaker, he's got the advantage of home turf. If we assume it's the cook, he's got a way in and a loaded gun, and a bunch of creepy stories to scare everyone else away. We're at a disadvantage either way. They've both had years to learn everything about this swamp and the house. How can we possibly combat that?"

"One of the first things we can do is figure out where the tunnels run in the house. We can't keep him from approaching laMalediction through the swamp, but we need to cut off his method of movement through the house."

"I didn't even ask you if you had any luck with the bedroom tunnel this afternoon."

John shook his head, knowing his frustration was showing. "No. For the life of me, I can't figure out how to go beyond that wall at the end. There has to be another opening, but everything seems solid—sounds that way, too."

"There's no reason to build a tunnel to nowhere and even less of a reason to repair it. There has to be an opening somewhere."

"I don't suppose… No, never mind." The last thing he needed was Olivia taking more risks.

Olivia bit her lower lip. "You want me to take a look at the tunnel."

"Forget it. I don't want you to do anything that makes you uncomfortable. I'll figure it out. It's just a matter of time." Time he didn't really have.

Olivia shook her head. "Don't waste time coddling me. If you need me to look at the tunnel, I will. Since

whatever is going on seems to center around me, the least I can do is help solve my own problems."

John felt a wave of relief, then admiration pass over him. Despite a dramatic night of personal revelations and an all-too-recent brush with death, Olivia was still willing to take chances. "I rigged your spotlight at the top of the tunnel entrance this morning so I could work without having to hold a light. It's pretty bright in there if that makes a difference."

"Yes, it does. In the dark things seem closer. It makes the claustrophobia worse."

"Okay. When do you want to do this?"

"No time like the present."

A wave of relief washed over John that Olivia wasn't going to delay entering the tunnel. With her knowledge of old homes, she might be the key to unlocking whatever secret the tunnel held and ultimately the secret to what might have happened to his half sister.

They exited the caretaker's cottage and crossed the courtyard to the main house. John scanned the brush as they walked, but didn't see anything that indicated they were being watched. In the main house, he headed upstairs to the master suite, Olivia trailing behind.

He turned on the spotlight and illuminated the tunnel, then handed Olivia a smaller flashlight. It wasn't really needed with the spotlight, but he figured holding the light in her hands would help keep Olivia from panicking in the closed space. Olivia stepped into the wardrobe and poked her head inside the tunnel, then leaned back, took a deep breath and stepped into the tunnel.

"I'm going to talk while I look, okay?" Olivia asked. "Talking helps keep my anxiety down."

John stepped into the wardrobe and peered into the

tunnel. "Whatever you need to do. Why don't you tell me about the history of these tunnels."

Olivia stood just inside the tunnel and shined her flashlight on the back wall, then began pressing the surface with her fingers. "In the old days, the wealthy believed servants shouldn't be seen, so they built these passageways so the servants could move throughout the house performing their regular duties without disrupting houseguests or the master and mistress of the house."

"Sounds sorta rude, and vain."

Olivia let out a short laugh, but John could tell it was forced. "It was rude, and vain, but they lived in a different time and were expected to live as other wealthy people dictated. It probably saved the servants a lot of grief, if you think about it. You can hardly be accused of scuffing a marble floor you don't walk on or ruining a rug by spilling drinks, when the only way you traverse the house is out of sight."

"Maybe, but I'm sure they got blamed for everything anyway."

"Cynic." Olivia took a couple of steps more down the tunnel and started her analysis of the next piece of wall. "But you're probably right."

She stopped working on the wall for a moment and looked back at John, frowning.

"What's wrong?"

"I was just thinking that I'm wasting my time with these sides. There's no reason to design a tunnel this long unless the other doorway is at the end. I mean, there may be another offshoot, but why extend something to nowhere?"

"That makes sense, but I checked every square inch

of the walls at the end of that tunnel. They're solid. I would swear to it. No hollow sound at all."

Olivia stared at him for a moment. "Maybe it's not the walls." She walked to the back of the tunnel and shined her flashlight on the ceiling.

"Do you want me to help?" John asked.

"No. You would block the light, and it would make the tunnel feel smaller."

"Are you calling me fat?" John asked, trying to take Olivia's focus away from the narrow space she occupied.

She laughed this time for real. "Hardly. If you have an ounce of fat on you, it's probably in your head."

John smiled, pleased to know that she'd noticed him that way. "There are a lot of people who would probably agree with that assessment."

Olivia shot him a grin as she felt across the ceiling with her fingers. She paused when her fingers reached the corner. "This feels different. It has some give."

"Be careful."

"What's the worst that can happen—another panel slides open?" She pressed her fingers into the ceiling and John heard a single click, then the floor beneath her dropped.

Chapter Nine

He ran into the tunnel, but before he could reach her she was gone and the floor had closed. "Olivia!" he yelled, but there was no reply. Panicked, he stood back from the end of the tunnel and reached forward, pressing the ceiling where Olivia had been working. He located the trip switch and pressed it.

The floor in front of him slid back, and he looked into the hole. "Olivia!"

"John!" she yelled back.

John felt relief wash over him, even though they weren't out of the woods. "Are you all right?"

"I think so. The lift sorta dropped at the very end, and I twisted my ankle when I fell off, but I'm okay."

"Do you have your flashlight? You need to get back on the lift and figure out a way to get it up."

"I dropped it but I think I felt it with my foot. Hold on."

John heard shuffling and then Olivia's voice came back, sounding more strained. "It's broken."

"Don't panic," John said and rushed to the tunnel entry and yanked down the spotlight. He hurried back to the opening and shined the spotlight down the hole, then drew in a breath when he realized exactly how far down Olivia was. It was at least a thirty-foot drop. "Don't look

up," he instructed her, "or you'll blind yourself. But see if you can find a release to send the lift back up."

He watched as she stepped onto the lift and could tell she was favoring her left ankle. She felt the walls around and then she stopped. "I think there's a problem," she said, her voice shaky.

"What is it?"

"It's a broken cable. That's why the lift seemed to crash at the end."

John blew out a breath and tried to think. "Can you see another way out? The lift has to go somewhere."

"The light doesn't go much beyond the lift. I could try feeling my way."

"No. We have no way of knowing what's down there. You could end up injured."

"How far down am I? It felt like a long drop."

John hesitated for a second, not wanting Olivia to know just how closed in she was.

"John?"

"About thirty feet."

"Oh."

That single word said it all. John knew he had to get her out of there, and fast. He'd heard horror stories of claustrophobics who had died of a heart attack when they were closed in. And there was also the chance that Olivia wasn't down there alone. "Olivia, I need to set the light down for a couple of seconds. I promise it won't be long, but I need you to be still, okay?"

"Okay."

John hurried to the tunnel opening and removed the strap he'd used to secure the spotlight to the ceiling. He rushed back to the opening and shined the spotlight into the hole. "I'm back. I'm going to secure the spotlight

to the ceiling above the opening so that I don't have to hold it. Give me another couple of seconds, okay?"

"Yeah."

John shoved the strap through a ceiling beam, concerned with the one-word answers and the weak sound in Olivia's voice. He secured the strap through the handle of the spotlight and tied it into place. "Okay, the light is secure. Are you all right?"

"I'm okay."

"I need you to take deep breaths. I'm going to get you out of there."

"How?"

John felt his heart clench at the scared but hopeful sound in her voice. "There's a long rope in the storage shed. I'm going to get it and lower you a light. That way you can find another exit. You have to be somewhere in the basement. Once you have a light, I'll go down to the basement and see if I can help from there."

John waited a couple of seconds, but there was no answer. "Olivia? Did you hear me?"

"Promise me you'll come back."

"I promise. Nothing in the world can keep me away, okay? I should only be gone about five minutes. I'll be right back." John rushed out of the tunnel and ran down the stairs and out of the house. Stupid, stupid, stupid. He'd put her in that hole. Risked her life to find his sister, and as much as he wanted to find his sister, what he'd done wasn't fair or right. But he was going to fix that, now.

And hope she didn't have a nervous breakdown before he made things right.

OLIVIA SAT ON the lift, her knees pressed against her chest with her arms surrounding them. She struggled

to control her breathing, to keep from panicking. This was her nightmare—stuck in a small space with no way out. Thank God for the floodlight, otherwise she'd probably lose her mind. She lifted the leg of her jeans a bit and looked at her ankle. She could already see the swelling. It didn't feel broken, but if she was being honest, she didn't really feel it at all over her beating heart.

It's only a couple more minutes.

Surely, John had been gone for a few minutes already. He would be back anytime now. Soon. With a rope and a plan. She checked her watch and was horrified to realize barely a minute had passed. She tapped the face of the watch, wondering if it had stopped working but in her heart she knew it hadn't.

She stared ahead of her, straining to make out something, anything, but not a ray of light illuminated her surroundings. She could be sitting in a closet or a performance hall for all she knew. If only she hadn't dropped her flashlight on the way down. She couldn't help but wonder if the intruder was somewhere in the house. If so, she was a sitting duck.

She took a deep breath and slowly blew it out. Pulling at a frayed spot on her jeans, she wondered if she should sing or count backward from a thousand, something for a distraction. Then she heard a noise above her.

"John?" she called out, overwhelmed with relief. Her watch had been wrong. John was back and he was going to get her out of here. She waited a couple of seconds, but he never answered. She felt her heart drop, realizing she must have imagined the noise.

Until she heard it again.

"John! John, if that's you, please answer!" She held her breath, trying to make out the noise, and was certain she heard rustling above her.

Then everything went black.

She screamed and clenched her hands so hard she felt her fingernails dig into her palms. Sweat broke out immediately on her forehead and her palms and she swayed dizzily, unable to center herself in the pitch-black. What if it had all been a trick? What if John's intention from the beginning was to trap her in the basement and leave her there?

Sure, he couldn't be responsible for all the things that had happened, but how did she know he wasn't working with someone else? For all she knew, the intruder and John could be in on everything together.

Stop it!

Olivia tried to gain control of her racing mind and focus on the truth. Unless he was the best actor in the world, the panic in his voice after she fell on the lift was real. John was the good guy, but he was obviously not alone in the house, and the intruder knew exactly where she was.

Trapped.

If the drop was thirty feet, that meant she was in the basement. The lift must have been a laundry chute, which meant the tunnel probably led to the laundry area in the basement. Olivia took a deep breath and rose to her hands and knees. Damned if she was going to sit and wait for him to come get her. She was going out fighting, even if she had to do it crawling.

She inched forward, feeling the floor beneath her before placing her body weight on it. The stone floor of the tunnel was cold and clammy beneath her hands, making her want to yank her hands back, but she had to be careful. The last thing she wanted was another surprise drop. She reached out to her sides and felt brick walls about four feet apart. Like a hallway, she told her-

self, trying to put the word *tunnel* and all its connotations out of her mind.

She passed her hand lightly over the floor in front of her to make sure no sharp objects could pierce her; then she pressed harder, ensuring the floor was solid; and finally, she felt the walls on both sides of her to make sure there was no door or that the hallway didn't shoot off in another direction. Not that she had any idea what to do if that happened.

She grew dizzy again and realized she was holding her breath. She let out the old air and drew in a deep breath, the stale air causing her to cough. Her heart beat like a metronome on high speed as she inched through the darkness. One beat, two beats, three beats. She found herself counting and moving to the rhythm.

And then she hit a brick wall, literally.

She felt the wall in front of her then felt to the sides again. It was a dead end. Both sides were completely encased in brick. Like a tomb.

She shook her head and struggled to redirect her mind. A dead end made no sense. Someone had used the tunnel so there had to be an opening. It was just a matter of finding the trip switch. A brick wall could move, right? She'd seen it in the movies, and of course, everyone knew that if you saw it in the movies it must be true.

She let out a sharp laugh. If she could still manage sarcasm, she must not be as bad off as she thought. Rising from the floor, she tried to place the majority of her body weight on her good ankle. She felt the walls as she rose, trying to locate the trigger that would provide an exit. The brick was smooth and cold with patches of fuzzy growth that Olivia didn't even want to think about. The place was probably teeming with spiders. She absolutely hated spiders.

Concentrate.

She ran her hands across the wall, pressing, feeling, looking for the way out. Her heartbeat seemed to increase with every pass of her hands across the brick, and she felt the panic stirring in her stomach, the anxiety moving up her body like a slow burn. When she reached the top of the wall she sucked in a breath, trying to regain control.

It was too late.

Her heart pounded like it would leap out of her chest. Each beat sent a rush of blood to her head and she leaned against the wall, trying to steady herself. This couldn't be happening. Not like this. No one should have to die in their own personal nightmare.

Then anger, despair and fear overwhelmed her and she began to pound on the brick wall, screaming the entire time.

Chapter Ten

John tore open the door to the storage shed and grabbed a coil of rope from a shelf on the back wall, then ran back to the main house, hoping to God that the length of rope was long enough to reach Olivia. And that Olivia hadn't panicked. He took the stairs two at a time, each step pounding out an echo through the house. He ran into the wardrobe and stopped short in the pitch-black.

What had happened to the floodlight?

He stepped back into the bedroom and lit the lantern on the nightstand, then dashed into the tunnel, his heart pounding so hard it made his temples throb. He lifted the lantern at the end of the tunnel, but the floodlight was nowhere to be seen. He lowered the lantern and saw the false floor was back in place, closing Olivia off completely.

Panicked, he pressed the trip switch on the ceiling and the floor panel slid silently back. He held the lantern into the opening, cursing when the light exposed only a couple of feet into the inky black. "Olivia! Olivia, can you hear me?"

But no one answered. "Olivia!" He strained to make out a noise, anything that might indicate she was still there and still breathing but the silence was deafening. He took a deep breath and tried to think. The bottom

of the lift had to be in the basement. He needed to look in the basement.

He left the tunnel and studied the wall in the bedroom, estimating the length from the front wall of the house to the lift in the tunnel was about twenty feet. Based on his assessment of the second-floor rooms the day before, he figured the tunnel was thirty to forty feet from the west wall of the house. He pulled his pistol from his ankle holster and checked it, then slipped it into the back of his jeans. That floodlight hadn't removed itself, and if he ran into whoever was playing games they were going to get a long look at the short end of a gun.

He rushed down the stairs and into the kitchen where the entry for the basement was located. At the bottom of the basement stairs, he flipped the light switch to illuminate the cavernous space. It only took a second to get his bearings, then he hurried across the basement to a laundry area. The area was separated from the rest of the basement with a partial wall and the lights were out in the entire section. John had noticed it when working in the basement the day before, but hadn't thought much of it. Now he wished he had.

He held the lantern close to the wall, scanning every inch of it with his eyes and free hand. This had to be it. His calculation of where the chute dropped was correct. But he found nothing to indicate an opening. Damn it. The desire to punch his fist straight through the brick wall was overwhelming and he struggled to get his raging emotions under control.

He had to think. He had to think quickly and accurately.

Looking back at the basement stairs, he assessed the distance once more but couldn't find anything off

from his original assessment. It was here. It had to be. Desperation overwhelming him, he lifted a loose brick from the ground and was just about to smash it into the wall when he heard something. He froze, certain he was imagining things, but it was still there. It was faint, but he could hear a woman screaming.

Olivia!

He stepped out of the laundry area and followed the brick wall down the middle of the basement. The screaming was still faint, but he could tell he was closing in on her location. He held the lantern close to the wall, scanning the surface as he walked and then he drew up short. *There.* The screams were behind this section of the wall.

He set the lantern on the ground and ran his hands across the wall. Her screaming made his heart clutch, but at the same time gave him some relief that she was still alive and he knew where to find her. He could only hope she wouldn't be mentally damaged beyond repair.

He passed his hands over the brick wall a second time, then he felt it. A brick that gave ever so slightly. He pressed it and the entire wall slid silently back, spilling Olivia out of the darkness and into his arms.

OLIVIA CLOSED HER eyes, blocking off the glare of the lantern, and clutched John, unwilling to let go. She struggled to catch her breath, but her anxiety had taken over, making breathing hard. John stroked her hair and hugged her close to him.

"You're safe now," he whispered. "I am so sorry."

"The light went out. I thought it was all a trick. That you'd tricked me into the tunnel to leave me there."

"God, no. Olivia, I would never hurt you! You have to believe me. But when I find who did…"

Olivia loosened her hold on him enough to look up. "I heard someone in the tunnel above me. He was there, John."

"I know. He took the light and closed the trapdoor in the tunnel." John looked down at her, the lingering panic and overwhelming relief clear in his expression. "Are you all right? Your ankle?"

"I twisted it a bit, but I think it's fine. I'm fine. I called out, but no one answered. Then everything went black. I started crawling, feeling my way down the tunnel until I came to the end. I tried to find a release but couldn't. I couldn't find it. Then I panicked. I thought it was all over."

John shook his head. "You are one tough cookie. Tougher than most of the men I know, and that's saying a lot."

Olivia dropped her gaze to John's chest. "I was on the verge of a heart attack. I'm not tough."

John put one finger under her chin and lifted her face up, looking her straight in the eyes. "You were confronted with your worst fear in a house that's been in your nightmares for as long as you can remember, and you were still collected enough to find your way down the tunnel to the exit. You're incredible, Olivia."

He stared at her for a moment, the indecision on his face clear as day, and that's when Olivia realized he was going to kiss her. Her heart leaped into her throat as he lowered his lips to her, kissing her softly, his lips barely brushing her own. Her skin tingled everywhere their bodies touched. She leaned into him, the heat radiating from him making her feel warm and secure. The kiss deepened and her skin, previously cold from fear, began to tingle and warm from desire.

Suddenly, he broke away and took a step back. "I'm sorry. I didn't mean to…"

He stared at her, his expression filled with both surprise and fear. "We should get out of here and see to your ankle," he said. "And I think it's time we call the sheriff."

Olivia watched as he crossed the basement and started up the stairs. Her body was screaming for him to come back and finish what he'd started, but her mind knew it wasn't a good idea. How very interesting. If she was a betting woman, she'd bet anything that John was more afraid of that one little kiss than she'd been locked in that tunnel.

OLIVIA SAT SIDEWAYS at the kitchen table across from the sheriff, her foot propped up on another chair. Once they'd decided it wasn't broken, John had carefully wrapped her ankle after calling the sheriff. He'd half-heartedly tried to talk her into seeing a doctor, but both of them knew the nearest doctor with any sort of equipment was probably hours away and not worth the trip for what was probably a sprain.

John paced the kitchen in front of the table, clearly unhappy with the sheriff's stance on the situation at laMalediction. Sheriff Blanchard jotted down a couple of things on a notepad and looked across the table at her. "I understand how frightening that must have been, Ms. Markham, but you need to be more careful. Investigating secret tunnels like you're Nancy Drew in a house that hasn't had good upkeep in decades is just inviting trouble."

Olivia bristled at the condescending tone and held one hand up to stop John, who was either about to speak or clock the man. "While I appreciate that my trip down

the laundry chute wouldn't have happened if I hadn't been doing research for my book, unless 'Trouble' lives nearby and wanted a spotlight, I don't think my snooping is the problem here."

Sheriff Blanchard looked up at John, who was glaring down at him. "You sure you left the spotlight? I could see where in a panic, you mighta took it with you and forgot."

Olivia saw John's jaw twitch. "I did *not* take the light with me," John said. "Even panic doesn't mean one becomes an imbecile."

"Now, there's no cause to get riled," Sheriff Blanchard said. "I'm sure there's a logical explanation for it all."

"So am I," Olivia agreed. "And I'd like you to see to locking up that logical explanation. This is not the first time I've found evidence that someone was in this house besides me or John. I'm not crazy, Sheriff, and I want your word that you will look into this."

Sheriff Blanchard glanced up at John, then back at her, his expression a mixture of resignation and aggravation. "I'll ask around, of course, but it was probably kids. They'll sell that spotlight to a pawnshop up on the highway."

Olivia laughed. "Let me get this straight. This house is probably full of expensive antiques, and everyone in this town believes that if you set foot here, you'll die, but you think kids broke in here to steal my spotlight?"

Sheriff Blanchard frowned, clearly not used to logic being used against him. "Well, now, I'm not saying that's why they broke in, but if they was already in the house and realized you was trapped in that laundry chute, then they mighta taken advantage of the situation and took the light both to make some money and scare you at the same time."

"And they would want to scare me, why, exactly? I was under the impression that the locals stayed away from this place altogether."

Sheriff Blanchard rose, apparently done with the conversation. "Most of the old-timers do, but kids ain't got no respect for tradition or lore."

"Or other people's property, apparently," John said.

Sheriff Blanchard narrowed his eyes. "There's no cause to start calling folk out. I'll give the kids a talkin' to if I find out who it was, but as there wasn't any real harm done, I can't do much else."

"I beg to differ," Olivia said. "I could have been seriously injured trying to get out of the tunnel and that spotlight cost over a hundred dollars, so I'll be expecting payment if you catch the kids that took it."

"I'll do what I can, Ms. Markham."

"Oh, and, sheriff," Olivia said and he paused at the door to look back at her. "You might also want to pass on to the kids that trespassing is a crime. I'm licensed to carry a gun and I know how to use it. I'm also well versed on my rights concerning breaking and entering in this state. I would hate for anything untoward to happen to some kids over a 'harmless' prank."

Spots of red rose up Sheriff Blanchard's neck and Olivia could see his jaw clench. He gave her a single nod and left.

"Pissed him off," John said.

"I intended to."

John looked down at her and frowned. "I'd bet everything it wasn't kids that took that spotlight."

Olivia sighed. "Me, too."

"Then why the parting shot about the gun?"

"Because I think Sheriff Blanchard knows who did

it, or has a good idea, and I wanted him to warn whoever it is he suspects."

"If it's the same guy that left that picture, do you really think he'll stay away?"

"No. But when I shoot him, my butt will be covered."

John smiled. "I like your style. Just remember to make sure I'm clear before you fire."

"Based on the way you disarmed me my first night here, I doubt you're in much danger." She frowned. "Where did you learn that, anyway?"

John shrugged and looked away. "I just got lucky."

"No. It wasn't luck. I was as quiet as can be but you still knew exactly when I stepped into that doorway, even in the pitch-black."

"I grew up hunting. If you're going to hunt in the bayous and the swamps, you learn to be very quiet and listen really hard. Otherwise, that day of hunting may be your last on earth."

Olivia's mind flashed back to their dash through the swamp that morning. "I hadn't really thought of it that way. I guess you could hear me walking."

John nodded. "And breathing and when your body rubbed down the side of the wall. It was faint, but there." He looked out the kitchen window and blew out a breath. "I hate to mention this, but I see lightning in the distance. I think we're in for another big storm."

"Great. Another night with no power, trapped in a haunted house with an uninvited guest. If I had blond hair and big boobs, I'd be a living a cliché."

John laughed, then stared out the window and frowned. He was silent for a while, then looked back at Olivia, his expression serious. "I know we've already been over this, but maybe it's time you consider leaving. You could have been seriously hurt today, and there

was nothing I could have done to prevent it. We're behind the eight ball here."

Olivia nodded. "Like rats being forced through a maze. That's what it feels like."

"Someone was prepared for your arrival, Olivia. Someone who knows more about your past than you do, if those stunts with the photo and the locket are any indication. You can't get the best of an enemy when they're invisible."

"But how could he have been expecting me? Only my publisher and Wheeler know I rented this place."

"My guess is it leaked from Wheeler's office, probably a secretary or receptionist looking to make a quick buck. You have to understand, it's big news in these small towns—a famous author in a haunted house. Hell, I'm surprised it wasn't plastered across the front page of the *Times Picayune*."

Olivia sighed. "I guess so, but that still doesn't explain why someone would go out of their way to try to scare me. And no one could have known about my dreams. I've never told anyone until you. I mean, I think the nuns suspected, but they never knew exactly what was happening to me."

John shook his head. "I don't know what to tell you. If it's all a big prank, then it's a huge coincidence that someone chose this house to try to scare you."

"And if it's not a prank?"

"Then we have to assume that someone has been waiting for you to come here. Someone who already knows about your connection to this house." He took a step closer to her and dropped one hand on her shoulder. "I don't want you to get hurt—any more than you already have been."

Olivia felt her chest tighten as she looked up at him.

He was trying so hard to look stern and tough, but it was impossible to miss the care and worry in both his expression and tone. This man, a veritable stranger, had touched her in a way no other man ever had, and that both excited and scared her. Based on his retreat after kissing her, Olivia knew that John was just as confused by his feelings as she was.

Was she being fair to him? Staying at the house put pressure on him to take care of her, but regardless of feelings she wasn't his responsibility. Not to mention her remaining at the house might be putting him in danger.

"You're right," Olivia said finally, guilt getting the better of her. "But I can't do anything until tomorrow at the earliest. I need to tear down and pack all my equipment."

John gave her shoulder a squeeze. "You shouldn't leave in the dark, anyway, and certainly not in a rainstorm. You want to be well clear of Cypriere in the daylight, on a clear day, that is."

"Yeah. I figured that one out the hard way."

"You'll stay in the caretaker's cottage tonight," John said. "It's easier to secure and I doubt there's a secret passage in all eight hundred square feet of it."

Olivia felt her heart leap at the thought of being in such close quarters all night with John. She'd been there the night before, but exhaustion had taken over, leaving no options but collapsing on his couch. But being locked up with him in a storm, probably with no lights, already aware that both their feelings were running high, made her edgy.

Leaving was definitely the right thing to do, before they did something both of them would regret. "Well, we still have power now. I'm not the fastest investigator in the world, with my limp, but I want to help while

I'm still here and while we still have lights. Where do you want to start?"

John stared down at her, his indecision clear. "I don't think it's a good idea for you to go poking around anymore."

"Probably not, but since you want to go poking around and you're not going to leave me here like a sitting duck I'm suggesting a compromise."

"Okay. The logical place to start is the basement. I want to reopen the tunnel you were trapped in and see if there are offshoots somewhere else. The dimensions of the basement are considerably smaller than that of the house."

"Really? Then there could be an entire maze of tunnels and rooms down there, hidden by stone walls."

"I know. That's what I'm afraid of."

Olivia shifted her propped leg onto the floor and turned in her chair to rise. John held on to her shoulder while she rose from the chair, steadying her as she stood. "You okay?"

Olivia placed her injured foot flat on the floor and shifted some of her body weight onto it, surprised when she felt only a small tingle of pain. "It's not bad. Much better than I thought it would be, actually." She walked across the kitchen to the basement door, careful to keep as much pressure off her injured foot as possible. John trailed closely behind her, apparently ready to intervene if she lost her balance.

"Good. It's probably only a light sprain, but you need to be careful not to do more damage. I'll help you down the stairs. I want you to put as much of your weight as possible on me, okay?"

John opened the basement door and slipped his arm around Olivia's shoulders, pulling her tightly to him.

Olivia felt the hard, muscular lines of his body press into her side and a flush started at her chest and crept up her neck.

Leaving was definitely the best thing to do—for both of them.

FROM HIS HIDING spot above them, the intruder listened to their conversation. He clenched his hands when the man suggested the woman leave. Surely, she wouldn't agree with all that he'd tempted her with. But she had agreed, and that just wouldn't do.

It was the caretaker's fault. He'd thought the caretaker had appeared at the property in order to help fulfill the prophecy. Why else would he appear out of nowhere after all these years? The spirits often sent others to aid, but maybe he'd been wrong. He was certain the woman wouldn't think of leaving if the caretaker didn't keep insisting. The caretaker had to go.

No matter what, Olivia could not be allowed to leave.

Chapter Eleven

Olivia shrugged off her dirty clothes and stepped into the steamy shower in the tiny bathroom of the caretaker's cottage. She sighed with pleasure as the hot water ran over her head and trailed down her body. She'd tromped through a swamp in the rain, been chased by a man with a gun, fallen two stories, twisted her ankle and been locked in a dark tunnel in a haunted house. It had definitely been a full day.

And then there was the kiss.

She poured shampoo into her hands and lathered up her hair, trying not to dwell on the kiss, especially while she was naked and wet. That was a recipe for disaster. She was leaving tomorrow. Thoughts of John Landry in the naked and wet position had no business in her mind.

She let out a sigh and stuck her head under the spray to rinse the shampoo. Who was she trying to fool? Ever since that kiss, she'd been more aware than before of how John affected her. Even the brush of his arm brought her body alive in a way that she'd never felt before. It was a good thing she was leaving. Her feelings for John worried her almost as much as the hidden agenda of the mysterious intruder. Almost.

Even though she would have loved to have stood beneath the steamy water for an hour or two, she finished

up her shower and grabbed a towel from the rack in the corner. John would need a shower, too, and there was only so much hot water in a tank.

As much as she hated it, she needed to email her editor and let her know she'd be packing up and moving once again. While the spa visit in New Orleans that her editor had recommended was tempting, Olivia knew it would be better for everyone if she got far away from Louisiana and whoever was having fun at her expense.

She wasn't even going to consider the possibility that the intruder would follow her.

JOHN PULLED HIS cell phone from his pocket and glanced at the bathroom door. He waited to hear the shower start up, then pressed in the number for a friend in the precinct. The basement search had been a dead end. The laundry chute tunnel didn't have another access or take another direction that they could find, and they'd been unable to locate another tunnel entrance before John had decided they had to give up for the night. Olivia was clearly exhausted and stressed and his own thinking was sketchy. He needed to regroup and come up with a plan.

"Fredericks," his friend answered.

"Brian, it's John. I need a favor."

"What the hell are you up to? The captain's been all over me like I know something."

Damn. "What have you told him?"

"Nothing. I don't know anything, and it sounds like that's a good thing."

"Well, you're about to know something. You know I wouldn't ask if it wasn't important."

Brian sighed. "The only thing that bothers me is that

you didn't come to me earlier. You know I'll help you any way I can."

Gratitude and guilt washed over John like a tidal wave. He didn't deserve a friend like Brian. "It's not that I don't trust you. I didn't want you risking anything for me. You've already had enough trouble with the captain."

"Man, this is Rachel we're talking about, and your mom. You guys are like family."

"You're right. I shouldn't have left you out."

"I understand. What can I do to help, now?"

"I need you to do some digging on a sheriff in Cypriere, name of Blanchard, and a café owner, Tom Breaux."

"Okay. You think they got something to do with Rachel?"

John gave his friend a brief rundown on the happenings at laMalediction and the earlier conversation with the sheriff. "I think he's lying, but I don't know about what."

"And the cook with the gun?"

"I don't know. Could be he's running something illegal through the bayous and it has nothing to do with this place. Could be he saw something and doesn't like people creeping around. Could be nothing."

"But might be something. I get you. I'll see what I can find out. Do you need me to come out there?"

"No. I need you back in New Orleans where you can check on things."

"Okay, man. I saw your mom after work today."

John felt his lower back tense. "How is she?"

"Upset, worried, exhausted. She said she hasn't heard from you since yesterday."

"Yeah, well, I've been a little busy. I'll call her later tonight unless I lose phone signal."

"Do that. Hey, what about that woman who's renting the place? Seems sorta strange a woman wanting to stay at some creepy old house in the middle of nowhere. You want me to run down some information on her, too?"

John glanced at the bathroom door again, trying to block the mental image of Olivia in the shower from his mind. "No. She has nothing to do with Rachel."

"She's messed up in something, though?"

"It looks like it."

"But she's not saying what."

"I don't think she knows," John said. "She's scared, and I get the impression that's not her norm."

"Maybe she knows more than she's letting on."

John bristled a little at Brian's words, but he knew his friend wasn't saying anything that he wouldn't have said had the situation been reversed. They were cops. They had to think that way. "She says she doesn't know and I believe her."

"What does she look like, this writer?"

"What's that got to do with anything?"

Brian chuckled. "Thought so. If she was an old hag, you would have described her straight out. Be careful, John. I know you've got good instincts, but you really don't know that woman, and your emotions are already running high with Rachel missing. Even if that writer doesn't know what she's mixed up in, that house of cards could come crashing down on you, too."

John stared out the window at the rain coming down in sheets. "I know. Call me when you get something, okay?" John closed his phone and tossed it onto the tiny table in the kitchen. He knew he should call his mother but he dreaded the conversation, knowing he couldn't lie to her even though he didn't want to tell her the truth.

He reached into his pocket and pulled out a silver

charm bracelet—a bracelet he'd given Rachel for her birthday the year before. He'd discovered it when he and Olivia had searched the basement. It had been underneath an old table, just at the edge. A link was broken, which could mean nothing, but it could also mean that she'd hit her arm on the table or someone had manhandled her enough to break the bracelet. No matter the scenarios he could create, none of them were good. The bracelet proved Rachel had been in the house. Where was she now?

He needed to get back over to the main house and find out before the trail got any colder, but he needed to do it without Olivia. He blew out a breath. Looking for Rachel meant leaving Olivia unprotected, pure and simple. He'd already seen the results of that once. Could he risk it again?

"What's wrong?" Olivia's voice sounded behind him.

He turned to face her, surprised he hadn't even heard her come out of the bathroom. She had on gray athletic shorts, a NY Yankees T-shirt and was towel-drying her hair, and damned if she still didn't look great. Brian was right. He was in trouble.

"The Yankees, huh?"

Olivia smiled. "It was a gift from my editor."

"That explains a lot."

"Really? Like what?"

"Like why someone locked you in a hole. He probably went through your luggage first."

Olivia laughed. "Ah, that whole Mason-Dixon thing. I didn't even think about it. I guess I figured an eighty-year-old caretaker and a house full of ghosts wouldn't care."

"Well, technically, Louisiana is more into football."

"Technically, so am I."

"Please don't tell me you like the Giants."

"Actually, I always kinda liked the Dolphins. I like the ocean."

"Now, there's a unique method of choosing a favorite team." He glanced back out the window at the main house. Did he run the risk or not? Now was the time. "I want to ask you something, but you have to say no if you're not comfortable."

Olivia gave him a wary look. "Okay?"

"I've been thinking about the intruder and how he gets around. I'd like to set up a trap in the basement."

"What kind of trap?"

"Nothing permanent, but tracking that Sheetrock all over the upstairs of the house yesterday gave me an idea. I could put some of the drywall dust from that ceiling collapse at the opening of the tunnel you were trapped in and at the bottom of the basement stairs. With any luck, the intruder will walk through it without noticing and give us an idea where another tunnel opening is hidden."

Olivia nodded. "It's a good idea, really. The lighting in the basement is so dim, no one would notice unless they look down. I mean, it's worth a shot anyway."

John blew out a breath of relief. "I'd need to do it now, before the storm gets worse. It's just starting up now."

"Sure. What's the problem?"

"I'm worried about you staying here alone."

Olivia waved a hand in dismissal. "I'm fine. There's only one door into this place, I'm pretty sure, and I can see every room from the kitchen table. I'll be right there working with a clear view of the front of the main house."

John studied her. The expression on her face was

normal, but she pulled at the bottom of her T-shirt with one hand. She wasn't as comfortable with the situation as she wanted him to believe. He placed his hand on her arm, his fingers clasped gently around her soft skin. "Are you sure? Because I can do it tomorrow…"

"No. Then you lose the whole night, and he might come back tonight."

"Okay," John said and dropped his hand. He grabbed his jacket off the back of a kitchen chair and pulled it on while walking to the door. Olivia followed him to the doorway and put her hand on his shoulder before he slipped out.

"Be careful," she said.

John gave her a single nod and stepped out into the rain.

OLIVIA WATCHED AS John crossed the courtyard and slipped into the main house. She crossed her arms in front of her chest as a shiver passed over her. Her damp hair must be giving her a chill. She sighed as she stepped away from the window and back into the bathroom. Even she didn't believe that weak excuse, but at least she'd managed to fool John. Maybe. He hadn't exactly looked convinced when he left, but Olivia wanted him to go. If they could catch the intruder before she left, she might finally get the answers she'd been looking for all these years.

A quick glance around the tiny bathroom didn't reveal a hair dryer, but she wasn't surprised. John didn't exactly strike her as the primping sort of man. She grabbed a dry towel from a rack in the corner and wrapped it around her damp hair with a twist, then walked back into the kitchen. Her laptop was stuffed in her backpack along with the few other supplies she'd

brought with her from the main house, so she pulled it out and set it on the kitchen table.

Staring out the window, she watched the drizzle that had been falling for an hour turn into heavy drops with wind gusts, seeming to blow in sheets across the courtyard. LaMalediction looked just like it did in her nightmare as she seemed to fly in from a distance. The jagged lines of the roof, the storm...the overwhelming feeling that something bad was about to happen.

Her nine millimeter was in the side pocket of her backpack and she pulled it out. She already knew the clip was full but checked it again. Instead of slipping it back into her backpack, she sat it next to her laptop and slid into the chair at the end of the table. The one that offered a clear view of laMalediction.

She opened her laptop and pulled up the rough draft of her book, what little she had managed to write in between being stalked and trapped in small, dark places. Never in her career had a house made her so uneasy. Never had she spent so much time on edge, fear hovering just beneath the surface. Every emotion, whether it was fear or anger or attraction, seemed to be magnified times ten. By all rights, she ought to be typing her best work ever, but instead she was wrapped up in a maze of secrets.

Sighing, she tried to focus on the document on her screen but images of John kept replaying through her mind. The relief on his face when she fell out of the tunnel and into his arms. The hesitation before he'd left her alone in the caretaker's cottage.

The fear in his eyes after he kissed her.

And ultimately, that was the clincher. John would investigate with her and protect her, but beyond that he'd drawn a line regardless of the obvious chemistry be-

tween them. Olivia didn't know whether to be relieved or disappointed.

Her body definitely wanted him and she could hardly blame it, but her mind knew that even if she told herself it was just hot sex, she already felt more for John than was comfortable. While sex could sometimes be a welcome relief, Olivia instinctively knew that in this case it would just complicate everything, and more complication was something she definitely didn't need.

She forced herself to look at her rough draft, read the last paragraph she'd written and groaned. The independent, hardheaded heroine had just been rescued by the dark, mysterious hero.

Great.

JOHN SPREAD A thin layer of Sheetrock dust at the bottom of the basement stairs, making sure he kept it in the area of the floor where the bottom step cast a shadow. With any luck the intruder wouldn't shine a light directly on the surface. Worst case, if he noticed, maybe he'd assume someone had spilled the detergent. John couldn't afford for the intruder to know they were trying to track him, especially when he had high hopes that the tracks would lead him to his sister.

He felt a momentary tug of guilt for continuing to mislead Olivia. He'd left her alone tonight claiming he was doing this for her, but his sister was the primary reason he'd wanted to set a trap. If it had only been for Olivia he would have just caught the man and turned him over to the authorities, but he couldn't afford to do that given the situation with his sister. Too many crazies refused to tell where they'd stashed their victims and lots of times the time lost finding them was the difference between life and death.

And all that meant, in a way, was that he was using Olivia as bait.

He gave the basement one final glance, then headed up the stairs to the kitchen. As he closed the basement door behind him, he heard the click of a door closing at the front of the house. He froze for a couple of seconds and listened, but heard nothing. Surely if Olivia had decided to leave the caretaker's cottage to find him she wouldn't be so quiet about it.

He turned off the kitchen light and waited until his eyes adjusted to the dark. He'd left the light on in the front entry and it cast a dim glow through the sitting room and into the kitchen entry. He moved silently across the kitchen and peered around the entryway. The sitting room and front entry were empty, and the front door was closed, but John knew he hadn't imagined the sound.

He slipped through the sitting room and into the front entry, then peered out one of the narrow windows that framed the front door. The stained glass made it hard to decipher if anything was moving outside, and the blinding storm combined with meager outside lighting didn't help. He could barely make out the glow from the kitchen window in the caretaker's cottage.

Dual desires warred within him. He should go back to the cottage and make sure Olivia was protected, but he couldn't help feeling that he was missing an opportunity to investigate if the intruder was in the house right now. Finally he decided a quick scan of the downstairs wouldn't take that much time and he backed away from the window. That's when he noticed that the front door was unlocked.

He reached up and twisted the dead bolt, just to be certain, but he already knew before it clicked into place.

The noise he'd heard wasn't someone coming into the house. It was someone leaving. He drew his pistol from the waistband of his jeans, opened the door a crack and scanned the circular drive. Stupid! He'd played right into the intruder's hands, leaving Olivia alone in the caretaker's cottage.

He eased out the door and stepped behind one of the huge columns that lined the front porch. The single light next to the front door barely cast light beyond the porch, and he strained to scan the circular drive in the storm, barely able to even make out the cars parked in the drive. Pulling the hood of his jacket over his head, he decided to make a run for it.

The instant he stepped out from behind the column, he heard gunshots. He ducked down and whirled around behind the column again just as a bullet hit the column right above his head, scattering plaster with the blast. He didn't even have to assess the situation to know that he was screwed. The intruder had a clear shot at him and he had nowhere to run. Olivia's car was fifteen feet away in the circular drive and the front door, while only five feet from where he stood, was locked and had a light shining right above it.

At least one of the intruder's advantages had to go. Then maybe he could make it to Olivia's car. He edged around the column toward the house and pointed his pistol at the entry light next to the front door. He paused for a moment, knowing that as soon as he made the shot he had to be ready to run. Taking aim, he squeezed the trigger and took out the light in one shot.

The porch went immediately black, and he ran across the circular drive toward Olivia's car. He could hear gunfire, but couldn't tell the bullets' path because of the rain and thunder. He was almost to the car when a

burst of lightning lit up the driveway. A second later he heard a shot fire and felt a sharp pain, then a burn in his thigh. He dove behind Olivia's car, cursing the storm for exposing him at the absolute worst moment.

He glanced at the caretaker's cottage, but the twenty feet may as well have been a mile now that the intruder knew where he was. The situation had gone from worse to impossible.

Chapter Twelve

Olivia grabbed her pistol and dove out of her chair at the first sound of gunfire, then cursed herself for sitting right in front of the window. She crawled over to the wall and peered into the courtyard. The light from the front porch barely extended a couple of feet from the caretaker's cottage and the rain came down in sheets, never seeming to lessen.

She pulled the unraveled towel from the top of her head and tried to think. Could it have been thunder that she heard? But she knew better. She'd been to the shooting range so often that the sound of gunfire was ingrained in her mind.

Think, Olivia. What the hell is happening?

If someone had been trying to shoot her they should have succeeded, but they hadn't even hit the picture window she sat in front of. That could only mean that they were shooting at John. She stared into the blackness trying to make out movement, when the light at the main house went out and the gunfire began again. She could barely make out a figure run from the porch and dive behind her car.

John.

She ran for the front door and threw it open, then turned off the porch light to mask her movement and

slipped outside behind an old tractor, several feet from the entry. Another shot sounded across the courtyard and the driver's window on her car shattered. She peered over the tractor wheel, trying to determine where the shots were coming from. Based on the angle, it had to be from the far side of the courtyard, but where?

"John!" she yelled.

"Olivia?" John's voice sounded from behind her car.

Thank God. "I'm going to open fire. Run for it!" She laid her arms across the tractor wheel and squeezed off two rounds toward the far end of the courtyard nearest the main house, then directed her aim ten feet over from there and squeezed off another two rounds. She couldn't hear anything but the gunfire and the storm, and hoped that John was able to run. Aiming her pistol a little farther down, she squeezed off another round before she felt a hand on her shoulder pull her down just as a bullet grazed off the fender of the tractor with a zing.

"Get inside," John yelled above the storm and she lowered her weapon and ran back into the caretaker's cottage, John close behind. He slammed the door behind them, threw the dead bolt and pulled her into the bedroom at the back of the cottage. Only after he'd drawn the drapes did he slide onto the floor, his back against the bed, weapon still drawn, with a clear view of the front door.

Olivia slid down beside him, trying to assess his injuries by the dim glow of the bedroom lamp. He was soaked to the skin, which made things more difficult, but she sucked in a breath when she saw a dark circle at the thigh of his jeans. "John, you're hit," she said. "We have to get you help."

"It's just a scratch. The bullet grazed me."

"What the hell is going on here, John? It makes no sense."

"Maybe the sheriff asked some questions and let whoever locked you in that tunnel know you were armed."

"Then why didn't they shoot me? I was sitting at the kitchen table, the light on, in full view of anyone."

John stared at her for a couple of seconds. "I don't know."

Olivia blew out a breath. "Because he wasn't trying to shoot me, and you know it. You're just not saying it. If he wanted me dead, I would be right now, but instead, he came after you. Why?"

John ran one hand through his wet hair and Olivia could tell he was stalling. He had an idea, but he didn't want to share it with her.

"You know something," Olivia said.

John shook his head. "I don't know anything for sure."

"But you have an idea?"

"Yeah, I have an idea that whatever he wants from you, it requires you being alive. Based on the picture you discovered, I have to think it's personal, too, and that's the part that bothers me the most. A simple thief I could handle."

"But why go after you?"

"Maybe because he wants you alone."

Olivia felt a chill run through her at John's words. She'd known, deep down, that she was at the core of everything going on at laMalediction, but still couldn't wrap her mind around being the center of something she knew nothing about. It was unfathomable, but it *was*.

John rose from the floor. "I don't think he's going

to try anything with you in the house. He obviously needs you alive."

Olivia bit her lower lip and watched him head into the bathroom. She was putting him at risk. Just her presence at laMalediction was risking his life. There truly was no option any longer. She had to leave. Despite the overwhelming feeling that she was close to solving the mysteries of her past, she couldn't risk someone else's life to do it.

She rose from the floor to go see if he needed help dressing the wound. Tomorrow she'd leave the house and never return. She could disappear if she had to and her publisher would be perfectly willing to help, even if it meant getting her out of the country. At least long enough to find out what was going on.

John stood in the bathroom in front of the sink, inspecting the wound on his thigh through the torn patch on his jeans. "How bad is it?" Olivia asked.

"Not bad. I just need to dry it off and cover it. Even wet, it's barely bleeding."

"Why don't you take off your jeans and let me cover it?"

"I can get it."

"It's toward the back. I'll be able to reach it easier than you." She looked up at him. "What? You think I've never seen a man in his underwear before?"

"How many men have you seen in their underwear with a gunshot wound?"

Olivia shrugged. "Okay, you got me there. This is definitely a first, and hopefully a last—the gunshot wound part, anyway. I'd sorta like to see a man in his underwear again before I die."

"Then I guess I'll accommodate you," John said and unfastened his jeans. Olivia reached for a clean towel

on the rack behind him and watched as he carefully tugged the damp denim over his thigh and stepped out of the jeans. He pulled off his soaked T-shirt next and tossed it on the floor next to his jeans.

Olivia handed him the towel and tried not to notice the way the muscles in his abdomen rippled as he stretched to dry his back. He ran the towel down one long, muscular leg then the other, stopping short at the gunshot wound, which he patted gently.

"What do you think?" he asked.

Olivia's gaze flashed immediately from places it had no business being to his face. "I think you're perfect," was right on the tip of her tongue before she realized he was referring to the bullet wound. "Oh, uh, well, let's see." She bent over to inspect the wound, hoping he couldn't see the blush she felt creeping up her face.

She took a close look at the wound and reached for the cotton balls and peroxide he'd placed on the counter next to the sink. "It looks okay. Shallow, like you said. I'll clean it and bandage it so it doesn't rub against your jeans. Do you have any ointment?"

"There wasn't any in the cabinet that I could find."

"Wait here. I have some in my backpack." Olivia hurried into living room, then remembered her backpack was on the kitchen table—right in front of the picture window. She took a deep breath and dashed into the kitchen, snatched her bag from the table and rushed back into the bathroom. She took a deep breath as she placed the backpack on the counter next to the sink.

"You all right?" John asked.

"Yeah. My backpack was on the table in the kitchen, so I rushed."

John frowned. "You should have let me get it."

Olivia shook her head and pulled a tube of antibiotic

cream out of her backpack. "How does that make sense
if it's you he's after?" She fixed up a cotton ball with
peroxide and dabbed it on the wound. "Does that hurt?"

"No."

Olivia held in a smile and kept cleaning the wound.
Likely his leg could be completely severed and he'd
swear it didn't hurt. John was definitely a man's man.
"It's not deep," she said once she'd wiped away the
blood. "I doubt it will even scar." *You'll still be perfect.*

She sighed and began to spread the cream on the
wound, then covered it with a medium bandage to pre-
vent chafing. When she rose, he turned to face her di-
rectly, their bodies as close as they could be without
touching. She sucked in a breath as she felt the heat from
his body on her own. She looked up at him, expecting
to see aggravation or impatience, but instead his amber
eyes were fixed on her, the attraction undeniable.

She expected hesitation and retreat, but instead, he
lowered his head and placed his lips on hers. Gone was
the tenderness from earlier. Instead this kiss was urgent,
hungry, and Olivia responded with the same energy,
pressing her clothed body against his almost bare one.
He stiffened slightly and Olivia thought for a moment
he'd pull away again like he did before, but this time
he gathered her in his arms and pulled her in closer.

Olivia wrapped her arms around him and ran her
hands down his back and across his rear end, like she'd
been dying to do earlier. His body was hard and mus-
cular, and she felt the heat in her rise as she imagined
this man over her. *In* her.

He pressed his hips into her and she felt the long,
hard length of him, only two thin layers of cotton sep-
arating them. She moaned and he lifted her from the
floor and carried her into the bedroom. They stood at

the end of the bed and he pulled her T-shirt over her head, exposing her bare breasts. He kissed her again, his hands caressing her breasts, his fingers circling around her nipples until she thought she would scream.

He pushed her cotton shorts over her hips and they slid to the floor. She dug her fingers into his back as he trailed kisses down her throat and took one engorged nipple into his mouth. His hand slid down her stomach and between her legs, his fingers stroking her where she ached for him the most. She pushed his briefs down and took the length of him in her hand and he shuddered. She stroked him with the same rhythm he used on her, back and forth, her hands moving across the smooth, hard skin.

She felt the climax build within her and cried out as wave after wave of pleasure rocked her body. He raised his head from her breast and smiled at her, then lifted her up once again and placed her on the bed.

"Protection?" she asked. "If you don't have any, I do. Front pocket of my backpack."

He raised his eyebrows at her. "More supplies?"

"I like to be prepared for anything." Olivia grinned. "They've been there awhile, though. I hope they haven't expired. That would be sad on so many levels."

John laughed and rose from the bed. "I'll check."

Olivia took a deep breath as he left the room, trying to absorb that she was about to sleep with a veritable stranger. Her mind flashed back to the way he felt in her hand and her already pleasured body throbbed for more. Hopefully those condoms were still good.

John walked back into the room, condom in hand. "You made it just under the wire." He lay down beside her and rolled the condom. He shifted over her and she parted her legs, allowing him to sink between them.

When he entered her, she gasped and clutched his back, pulling him deeper inside her.

He set a smooth pace, their bodies and breathing in sync, and Olivia felt the pressure building in her again. His body stiffened and she felt her pulse quicken, anticipating the release that was about to come. With a final thrust, he sent them both over the edge.

JOHN WAITED UNTIL the climax subsided and kissed Olivia gently before sliding to the side, his arm still draped across her. His body was charged and sated all at the same time, reveling in a satisfaction he'd never felt before. This woman, Olivia, was different from the others before her, and John had no idea what to make of that. Especially now, with everything going on.

When his breathing became more normal, he pushed himself up on one elbow and looked down at her. She was beautiful—her hair tousled, her lips pink from kissing. Her eyes were closed and she wore nothing but a satisfied smile. John felt fortunate that he'd been the man to put that smile on her face, especially since she'd be leaving the next morning.

That bothered him, more than he wanted to admit, but it was the only way to keep Olivia safe and free him to look for his sister completely unencumbered by lies and misdirection. "So you really meant that whole 'preparedness' thing," he said.

Olivia looked up at him and smiled. "I never know when I might get lucky."

"The box hadn't even been opened."

Olivia waved a hand in dismissal. "Don't remind me. It's sad."

John laughed. "I guess it's hard to meet people with what you do."

"That, and then there's the fright factor. What I do tends to scare people away. They don't want to visit haunted houses and I don't stay in one place very long." Olivia raised one hand to stroke his face. "You know, I really hate wasting things. I bet we could use that whole box if we worked at it."

"In one night? I'm flattered, but even I have to admit I'm no superhero. Maybe when I was fifteen…"

Olivia's expression changed from playful to serious. "I don't have to leave. I mean, I know that's what we talked about, but I wonder if it's the best idea. I'm a good researcher, and I know a lot more about these houses than you. I could be a big help."

John's pulse quickened. This was a complication he didn't need. With Olivia safely out of the way he could concentrate all his effort on finding his sister. If she remained, he knew his loyalties would be divided. He looked at her—the earnest expression with just a touch of excitement behind it. But was it for the thrill of the hunt or because of him?

Either way, he couldn't afford the liability. Making love to Olivia had been a huge mistake. It had shifted the playing field and created a situation he hadn't planned on dealing with. He had to convince her to leave, but he knew logical argument wasn't going to be enough. Olivia already knew the logic behind why she should leave. No, the only way she would budge now was if it was personal.

He rose from the bed and paced the length of the room. Olivia sat up on the bed and looked at him. "What's wrong?" she asked. "I thought you'd be happy to have my help."

John ran one hand through his hair. *Now or never, Landry.* "There's something you need to know about me."

"Okay."

"I'm not the person you think I am." He grabbed his wallet from the dresser and pulled out his badge. "I'm a cop—New Orleans Police Department."

Olivia stared at the badge, her confusion apparent, then looked back at John. "I don't understand. Are you investigating me?"

"No. I'm trying to find a missing girl. We think she intended to visit laMalediction, but without proof that she was in Cypriere, Wheeler won't allow the police to search the property and we don't have the evidence to get a warrant to compel him to do so."

"You lied to Wheeler to get access to the estate?" Olivia frowned.

"It was the only way, and we're running out of time. The longer someone remains missing, the less likely they're ever found."

"And you lied to me," Olivia continued, "but what I don't understand is why."

John looked down at her, already hating himself for what he was about to say. "For all I know, you might have ratted me out. I couldn't afford to risk my job and the victim over someone I didn't know."

"Why would you risk your job for this girl?" Olivia jumped up from the bed, her hand over her mouth. "It's personal, isn't it? Oh, my God. It's your girlfriend. I just slept with some missing girl's boyfriend."

She closed her eyes and swayed, and for a moment John was afraid she was going to pass out. He rose from the bed and grabbed her shoulders with both hands to steady her. "It's not my girlfriend. It's my half sister."

Olivia opened her eyes and looked at him, the disbelief still resident. "Then once you got to know me, why didn't you tell me? Surely, you know me better than to

think I would get you fired and leave some poor woman trapped in this heap."

"I…I was afraid if I told you how dangerous I thought this place was, you'd leave."

Olivia stared at him for a moment, then her eyes widened and she pushed him away from her. "You *used* me. You knew someone was stalking me, and you hoped I would lead you to your sister. I guess having sex with me was the icing on the cake, right? Did you think I would be so wrapped up in you that I wouldn't care about all your lies?"

"Olivia—"

"You expected me to argue with you when you told me to leave this evening, didn't you? I must have ruined all your plans when I agreed to go, so you upped the stakes by having sex with me." She grabbed a spare blanket from the end of the bed and wrapped it around her. "Your days of using me are over. First thing tomorrow, I'm out of here. But don't worry—I won't tell Wheeler your little secret. *I* have higher standards than that."

Pushing past him, she left the bedroom, slamming the door shut behind her. John sank onto the bed with a sigh. He'd done what he needed to do. Olivia would be safe away from laMalediction and that was all that mattered.

Then why did he feel like such a heel?

Chapter Thirteen

The sound of the front door opening woke Olivia and she bolted upright on the couch just in time to see John slip out. She started to call out, remind him that a madman with a gun was on the loose somewhere out there, but she figured he probably hadn't forgotten and being a trained law enforcement officer, probably didn't want her advice. Although her watch indicated it was a little after seven o'clock, the cottage was gray and dim and Olivia could hear the storm still raging outside.

The power had gone out right after she'd settled in on the couch, and based on the sounds of the storm she had little hope that it was back on now. She rose from the couch and took a peek out the living room window. Rain poured from the sky and lightning flashed almost in sync with the rumbling thunder, letting her know the storm was right on top of them. She flipped the light switch to the living room, but nothing happened.

Great.

She shuffled into the kitchen and put a pot of coffee to brew on the camping burner, then stared out the picture window as John entered the main house. Probably off looking for his missing sister and hoping she wasn't going to blow the whistle to Wheeler about his

little undercover charade. Her jaw involuntarily flexed as she thought about his revelation the night before.

She'd accused him of using her and he hadn't denied it. Now that she'd had the night to cool down a bit, she realized that wasn't necessarily true. John had recommended she leave at the beginning of all the madness. Sure, he'd taken advantage of her knowledge and the intruder's focus on her to try to gain insight into the house and into the man who may have taken his sister, but she was the one who'd insisted on staying, so why shouldn't he benefit from what she knew?

She poured a cup of coffee and let out a sigh. As much as she'd like to be angry at him for lying about who he really was and why he was at laMalediction, she couldn't blame him for it, either. No matter the heat between them, she was still essentially a stranger and John was breaking a lot of rules and a couple of laws with his undercover mission.

He shouldn't have made love to her without telling her the truth. That was the part she found hardest to get past. She'd thought there was something between them more than just the heat of the moment, but apparently it was all one-sided. Anyone who could have sex with someone, hiding such important things from them, couldn't possibly care about anything but their own agenda.

Not that it mattered anyway, since a man didn't fit into her life…any man. Maybe it was her heightened emotions being at laMalediction and the intensity of the dreams that had momentarily weakened her into thinking about a normal life. Thinking that someone could care about her enough to be honest and not abandon her. John had abandoned her before they'd ever got started, and it was a cold pill to swallow. Not that he

wasn't invested, because that was certainly his right, but that she'd believed for just a moment that *she* could be.

She stepped up to the picture window in the kitchen and groaned. She'd completely forgotten that the window on her car had been shot out the night before. A foot of water was probably standing inside. The insurance company was going to be very unhappy, especially as she made it a rule to always purchase the rental company's insurance policy.

Well, foot of water or no, she was still leaving. If she couldn't drive herself, she'd call Sheriff Blanchard to come get her in his four-wheel-drive pickup. He'd probably be happy to escort her out of town.

Her laptop was still open at the kitchen table, forgotten from the night before. She jiggled the mouse to wake it up and clicked on her email account. The icon whirled for a moment, then returned an error message. No signal. Shocking. She picked up her cell from the table, but it was faring no better in the storm—zero bars. A tiny trickle of fear ran through her. What if she couldn't leave?

The rental car had gotten stuck on her way to laMalediction in just such a storm, and the road was still muddy when she and John had gone into town yesterday. It was probably a river by now, or a bayou…whatever they called them. And without a way to call for the sheriff, that was a dead end, too. She closed the laptop and shoved it in her backpack, then tucked the mouse in beside it. Worse case, she'd ask John to take her to Cypriere and she'd call a taxi to take her to New Orleans. She could always deduct the million dollars or so the taxi would likely charge as a business expense.

No matter what, she wasn't staying at laMalediction one more night.

She made a quick trip through the bedroom and picked up her discarded clothes, trying not to think about the night before…how she'd felt so alive, then so destroyed all in a matter of hours. Wasted emotion, and on what—a fling with a stranger that, at best, was over when she finished her book? So it had ended a little early, and a little abruptly, but the outcome was still the same—she would leave Louisiana. He would not.

Her few belongings stowed in her backpack, she sat on the couch and pulled on her tennis shoes, preparing for the fifty-yard dash to the main house. It would take her a couple of hours to pack the rest of her equipment and belongings, then there would be nothing keeping her here.

The front door of the cottage opened and her heart clenched when she saw John walk inside. His expression was troubled, but not like it had been the night before. This was different. "What's wrong?" she asked.

He pulled off his wet jacket and hung it on a hook by the front door, seeming to avoid looking at her. "There's a tree down just before the main gate. It's completely blocking the exit to the estate."

"But we can move it, right? I mean, you have that chain saw, and I'll help."

John shook his head. "It would take weeks to cut a tree that large, and I don't even have enough gas to last that long, even if I wanted to try. It's not going anywhere without a tractor to pull it out of the way."

Olivia bit her lip. "My cell phone doesn't have a signal."

"Neither does mine." John shuffled his feet a bit and ran one hand through his hair. "Look, I don't know how to tell you this, so I'm just going to come out and say it."

Olivia took in the unhappy, almost pained look on

his face, and knew she didn't want to hear whatever excuse he was about to deliver from the night before. It wouldn't change a thing. "You don't have to—"

"That tree was cut. Intentionally. Someone took a chain saw to the base of it so that it would fall right across the front of the gate."

Olivia gasped. Her mind whirled with thoughts, reasons why someone would block the gate, and none of them were good. "Is there a way around it?"

"Not with a vehicle."

"He's trying to trap me here."

John nodded, his expression grim. "It looks that way."

Anger slowly began to overtake fear, and Olivia felt a flush start at her neck and move up her face. "Well, he's got another think coming if he thinks a tree is going to stop me from leaving."

"You can't drive through the tree and you can't call for backup, so he *has* effectively prevented you from leaving. At least for now."

"I'll walk. I'll take only my laptop, and I should still make it to Cypriere before dark. Surely, a phone works somewhere in that town."

John sighed. "Walk? You really think that the person who locked you in the tunnel and tried to kill me last night is going to let you stroll out of here? You wouldn't stand a chance against him in this swamp and he knows it."

Olivia slumped into a kitchen chair and clutched her face between her hands. This couldn't be happening. Not to her. At this house. First the tunnel and now this—for the second time in her life, Olivia was terrified while fully awake. "What chance do I stand here?" she asked, her voice cracking. "Even if I lock myself in the

back bedroom and nail the door shut, he could set the cottage on fire, or have another tree fall on it. For that matter, the walls are so old and thin that he'd probably have a good chance of taking me out just by randomly firing that gun of his into the cottage."

John stared down at her, the angst on his face clear, but he didn't argue with her words, nor did his expression change even slightly when she uttered them. She wasn't telling him anything he hadn't already thought of. Given his real job, he'd probably thought of at least ten more things that her mind hadn't yet gotten around to.

He kneeled beside her and placed his hand on her knee. "We'll take precautions…make sure both of us are as safe as possible."

"He tried to kill you last night. How can we make things safe if you can't even leave the cottage without the risk of being shot?"

"But I already left the cottage. If he'd wanted to kill me, he would have had a clear shot this morning."

Olivia shook her head. "Then why didn't he?"

"Maybe because we can't leave now."

"But as soon as we can call for help…"

John nodded. "We have to find him before that happens…turn the tables by stalking him."

"Go on the offensive? That's crazy."

"Not as crazy as sitting around waiting for his next move."

Olivia blew out a breath. "But how can we turn the tables on him when we don't know who he is, where he is, or what he wants from me? We're completely in the dark, literally and figuratively."

"Not exactly," John said and stood.

Olivia looked up at him, confused by his reply. He

glanced out the picture window at the main house, and a thought flashed through her mind. "The drywall dust—he left tracks?"

John nodded. "Faint, but they lead right into a brick wall."

Olivia smiled. "Sounds promising."

"In this case, yeah."

"Then what are you waiting for?" Olivia hopped up from her chair, her energy beginning to recharge, her hope beginning to rise.

"I was waiting on you. I know how you feel about me, and I don't blame you, but I need your help."

Olivia stared, taken aback at his admission, and then chided herself. He couldn't afford to leave her alone, and he had to find his sister. The only chance of doing that meant uncovering the intruder's secrets, and she was the key to it all. "Of course."

She took her laptop out of her backpack and sat it on the table then slung the backpack over her shoulder. "But this time I'm taking supplies. I'm not about to get caught in another small, dark space without backup."

He pulled her rain jacket from the coatrack and tossed it to her. "I found a sledgehammer in the tool-shed yesterday. It's coming with us. I have no trouble dismantling this place stone by stone if I have to."

He pulled on his own jacket and stepped out the front door and into the rain. Olivia zipped up her jacket and followed behind him, unable to keep from thinking that she was chasing the devil straight into hell.

JOHN PLACED THE lantern next to a brick wall in the basement, wishing the intruder hadn't stolen Olivia's spotlight. It would have made a big difference in the dim basement, and John had been unable to find anything

in the toolshed that compared. The lantern flame cast a dingy yellow shadow onto the walls, giving the space a grim look.

Focusing his attention on the faint steps that led to the wall, he erased the fanciful thoughts from his mind. Grim look. Damn, he was starting to sound like one of those novels Olivia wrote. Unfortunately, the word really fit the moment. They were trapped, being stalked by an unknown person or persons, his sister had now been missing for six days, and he'd been a damned fool and hurt the one person he'd ever felt anything for besides his mom and sister.

There was nothing to be done about it now. He looked down at the prints in front of the wall, studying them as he would those of any animal he tracked in the woods. Olivia crouched down for a closer look at the prints and ran her hand across the wall directly in front of the last two prints.

"I don't feel anything down here, and nothing sticks out as a possibility for a trigger point," Olivia said.

"I think it's on the top somewhere, maybe even the ceiling," John said.

Olivia rose up from the basement floor. "What makes you think that?"

John pointed at the footprints. "Look at the last prints. The toe is darker than the rest of them. Like he pushed his body weight up on his toes."

Olivia studied the footprints for a moment and nodded. "You're right. That's smart. I wouldn't have thought about it."

Despite the emotional wall between them, John still relished Olivia's appreciation for his ability. "You pick up a lot tracking. And I've read a lot of books."

Olivia nodded. "All the forensic investigative tech-

niques have really changed things in a good way. I've done a lot of research on forensics for my books. Talked to a lot of cops. But reading or even writing about it doesn't make you capable of practical application. That takes a level of talent."

John reached up and placed his hand on the ceiling above them. "Well, let's see if we can practically find that trigger switch. Otherwise, the only thing I'm applying to that wall is a sledgehammer." He ran his hand across the roof line in front of the brick wall, first directly against it, then moving back from it a bit at a time, testing the entire surface for bumps or indentations.

"We know something else about the intruder now," Olivia said.

"What's that?"

"He's shorter than you."

John paused for a moment, looked over at Olivia and smiled. "You're right. I can lay my hand flat on the ceiling without standing on tiptoe. Assuming the intruder only needs to press the spot with his finger, he could be three or more inches shorter than me."

Olivia frowned. "Which totally leaves out Tom Breaux, the cook. He's easily as tall as you. Damn, he was our best bet."

John shook his head. "I don't know about that. Tom may very well be doing something illegal that he doesn't want anyone to know about, but he's not more or less a suspect than anyone else. My bet is the old caretaker's not all that tall. He didn't have any tools stored on the top shelf in the toolshed. And then there's our friend the sheriff. He's a few inches shorter than me."

"I should be so lucky. That man really gets under my skin. I hate liars."

A flash of guilt passed through John at her last state-

ment, but then he couldn't really blame her. He hated liars, too, even though he'd deliberately chosen to become one. "I agree, he knows more than he's telling. He didn't look surprised in the least at your story, just annoyed."

"Maybe he's stealing the china, piece by piece."

John's fingers passed over a slight indentation in the ceiling and he paused. "I think I've got something here." He pressed his finger firmly into the indentation and a panel of bricks slid silently back, revealing a narrow walkway beyond.

Olivia's eyes widened. "Wow. I knew it had to be here, but do you realize what kind of engineering it took to make something as heavy as that wall work so quietly?"

John nodded and picked up the lantern from the shelf next to the opening. "Good engineering and a whole lot of WD-40. Someone's maintained these passages well, and I can't see any ethical reason why."

"What do you see?" Olivia stepped next to him and peered into the tunnel.

"Not much. All I can make out with this light is another solid wall ahead, so either the passage turns off somewhere that we can't see from the opening or there's another hidden door." He looked over at Olivia. "Are you sure you're ready for this?"

Olivia stared into the dim passageway and bit her lower lip. "We don't have a choice," she said finally. "I mean, I could stay behind but that's not exactly a great option, either."

"No, it's not."

She took a deep breath and blew it out slowly. "You're bringing the sledgehammer, right? I mean, just in case this closes and we can't get it back open."

"Absolutely. And I can do one better." He walked to a corner of the basement and picked up a piece of metal pipe. "This should do," he said and jammed the pipe at the bottom of the opening tight against the sliding panel.

"Unless someone moves the pipe."

"That's what the sledgehammer is for." He placed one hand on Olivia's shoulder. "I'm not leaving your side for a minute. You won't get trapped down here again. I promise."

Olivia nodded, but he could still see the apprehension in her expression. Not that he blamed her. The woman had been through more in the past couple of days than some cops saw in thirty years on the force. He lifted her backpack of supplies from the basement floor and wrapped the strap around the handle of the sledgehammer, then pulled the entire pack over one shoulder.

Olivia handed him the lantern and turned on her own handheld flashlight as he stepped into the passageway. He took a couple of steps, then glanced back to make sure Olivia was all right. Her face was drawn but she didn't look panicked. Lifting the lantern out in front of them, he continued down the narrow passage about twenty feet when it made a ninety-degree turn to the left. "There's a turn."

"That's good," Olivia said. "At least we don't have to figure out another trigger switch."

John nodded but didn't reply. The light from the lantern didn't extend far into the pitch-black tunnel, but from where he stood, he couldn't see an end. Continuing this way might leave them cornered deep in the basement with no alternate way out. He passed the lantern to Olivia and pulled his pistol from the waistband of his jeans. "Just in case," he said and took the lantern back. "You should check your own."

Olivia pulled her pistol from her waistband and checked the clip. "I've checked it at least five times since we left the cottage this morning." She gave John a grim smile. "I'm hoping I don't get to use it—this is awfully close quarters."

"Which is why we have to be very careful."

"Right, careful." She checked the safety on the pistol and stuck it back in her waistband.

John elected to keep his pistol firmly gripped in his shooting hand and started down the passageway, counting off his footsteps as he walked so he could get an idea of how long the passage was and where it might be located under the main house. He estimated they'd traveled thirty feet before they hit another wall.

"I am so sick of dead ends," Olivia said as she peered around him. "Someone had a serious obsession."

"Or was extremely paranoid."

"Well, I can't really say much about that. I think I bought a ticket on the paranoia train a while back."

John shook his head. "It's not paranoia if they're really out to get you."

"Thanks for reminding me that my impending death is not merely the work of my overactive imagination."

John handed Olivia the lantern and began a search on the ceiling with his hands. "Look at it this way—it'll make a great story once it's all over."

"No one would believe it. Fiction has to make sense even though real life often doesn't."

"Hold the lantern up a little higher, if you can," John said and looked over his shoulder at Olivia. "I feel a bump or something where my left hand is, just behind me. Can you make out what it is?"

Olivia raised the lantern up close to the ceiling, then let out a choked cry.

Chapter Fourteen

Before John could ask what was wrong, Olivia grabbed his arm with her free hand and yanked it down from the ceiling. Then she jumped back a foot from where she'd been standing, her eyes wide and still looking up. John looked up and saw black spiders running in all directions across the ceiling.

"It's a nest," Olivia said, her voice shaky. "You had your hand on a nest of spiders. I am officially freaked out."

John checked his hand to make sure he hadn't brought any of the creatures back down to visit. "At the risk of lowering my masculinity status, that was definitely not cool."

"If it makes you feel any better, they're not a poisonous breed."

"And you know that how?"

"Old houses have bugs. I make it a point to learn all the bugs and snakes of a region before I visit, so I can avoid the ones that may kill me."

John stared. Compared to the women he knew, Olivia Markham was a study in preparedness. Hell, he'd bet she even had most of the men he knew beat. "Well, then that does make me feel better."

"I wish I could say the same."

"I think it's safe to say that the trigger switch is not likely buried under a bed of spiders. I'm going to check the walls."

Olivia passed him the lantern. "Take a peek before you touch anything."

"Good idea. The next batch might be poisonous."

"Or a snake, and I gotta tell you, if you find a bed of snakes, I am out of here. I'll take my chances with the intruder."

"Duly noted," John said as he held the lantern up close to the wall on the left of the dead end and scanned for anything else living. "All that's here is some mildew."

He placed his hand in the top corner of the wall and ran it across the surface, then paused when his fingers dipped into the brick. He pressed into the dip and heard Olivia gasp. He turned around and saw Olivia pointing her flashlight into an opening on the opposite wall.

"It's a room," she said, "and it's not empty."

John stuck the lantern into the opening and it cast a dim glow around the room. It was small, maybe about twelve foot square, and bookcases lined every wall from floor to ceiling with books and boxes scattered among them. A long table sat in the center of the room, a pile of books in the center of the table and a single chair pulled up in front of it.

Olivia stepped inside the room and shone her flashlight along the shelves. "Looks like a library," she said, "like the one upstairs in the main house. Well, except for the two inches of dust and lack of windows and light."

John stepped up to one of the bookcases and held the lantern right up to the shelves. "Except it's not all dusty. Look. Some of the books have been dusted recently. They don't have a speck on them."

Olivia stepped over to the table and flashed her light on the stack of books. "It looks like journals." She flipped the first book open, then a couple more. John stepped beside her and placed the lantern on the desk to light up the table's surface.

"Unbelievable," Olivia said. "Some of these are over a hundred years old." She looked up at John. "Why would someone sneak around the house to read a bunch of old diaries? And why hide them in these tunnels?"

"I don't know, but I don't like it." John pulled one of the dusted books from the shelf behind them. "This one is an album, like the one you found upstairs."

He placed the album on the table and flipped through the pictures. The first couple of pages contained photos of laMalediction from years ago and while still under construction, but when he flipped over another page, Olivia gasped.

"It's Marilyn Borque," Olivia said. "Like the picture on my bed, remember?"

John studied the picture for a minute then looked at Olivia. "You really do look like her."

"What do you think this all means?"

"I don't know, but clearly someone has been re-searching the family and they must think you're con-nected."

"That's entirely possible, but that still doesn't mean anything to me. So what if I'm a distant relative of people who died a long time ago? I didn't know them or any of my family, for that matter. What difference could I possibly make to someone obsessed with them?"

John reached for one of the journals. "Maybe they think you know something. You do dream about this place. Maybe you were here at some time and the in-

truder knows it. Maybe he thinks you're here for a different reason than writing a book."

"Do you really think I could have memories from that young? Even if I did, it would be from the viewpoint of an infant."

John opened the hard cover of the journal and saw strips of paper sticking out the top. "Look at this." He pointed to the strips. "Someone was marking pages. Maybe this will tell us something." He flipped to the first marked page. Olivia leaned over to watch as he read the page out loud.

"February 11, 1862

Franklin got the word today from his father. He wants him to go to war. To uphold their community standing, the family must contribute to the cause and Franklin's brother is too young. Franklin took it as well as expected. His drunken rampage lasted well into the night and I had the marks to show for it. I took refuge with Sissy's cousin the voodoo woman, knowing it was the one place Franklin wouldn't come for me. She cast a spell for me—a spell of protection. I told her that with Franklin gone, I didn't need protection, but she insisted. She said the spirits spoke to her, that they told her I was in great peril. If it were anyone else but Sissy's cousin saying such things, I would dismiss them as the words of a madwoman, but I know better. I've seen her power. After all, I am her student."

"Oh, my God," Olivia said. "Whose diary is this?" John flipped the front cover open and located ini-

tials in the bottom right corner. He pointed them out to Olivia. M.B.

"Marilyn Borque," Olivia said. "It's got to be."

"The woman from the photos."

"Yeah. Is there anything else marked?"

John checked the top of the journal and flipped to the second scrap of paper. "Looks like three different spots. Let's see what this one says."

"February 23, 1862

Franklin left today. I made a big show at the train station because I knew he expected it, but I celebrated with Sissy when I returned home. You can almost feel the burden lifted off this home. The staff would never say anything, as it's not their place, but I can see the relief on their faces. I even convinced Sissy to drink a glass of champagne. She'd never had a drink before and it made her giggle.

 I'll send for him tomorrow. It's been so long that I wonder if he'll come to me again. Six long months of marriage to Franklin have not lessened my longing for him. I can only pray that he feels the same."

"Sounds like no one is sad ol' Franklin has gone off to war," John said.

Olivia nodded. "Since it also sounds like ol' Franklin liked to practice his backhand on his wife and probably the staff, I can't say that I blame them. But an affair? That's risky, especially in that day and time."

"Maybe they're banking on him not coming back."

"But we already know he did. He killed her, remember?"

John frowned. "Maybe we've found the reason why."

"True. He wouldn't be the first husband to kill his wife over another man. What about the last marker?"

John flipped the pages to the last marked entry.

"March 10, 1862

He came to me, my love. It's as if we were never apart. My heart sings with joy at the very sight of him and my body quakes with his every touch. I cannot get enough of him, even though we spend almost all our hours together.

If only I weren't tied to this dreadful house out in the middle of nowhere. I know well why Franklin built here, surrounding me with swamps and bayous. He knew if I were still in New Orleans, I could find a way to be happy, despite being married to him. But here, in this desolate place, an emptiness sometimes overcomes me, even when I am with my beloved.

Sissy's cousin says the house is lonely and it's tugging at my soul to fill it up. I know it's a thing of brick and mortar, but there are times when I'm certain I'm alone and I can still feel something watching. I will ask Sissy's cousin to cast a spell of protection for me. My sleep is troubled with dreams and I wake restless but unable to remember them with any clarity.

I sometimes wonder if I am afraid to remember."

Olivia crossed her arms across her chest and shuddered. "Okay, that's just creepy. She talks about this house like it's alive."

"Not exactly a stretch from a woman practicing voodoo."

"No, I guess it's not. I just… What in the world have I gotten in the middle of?"

"I don't know," he said, "but someone has been doing a lot of studying…a lot of research."

"On what? I'll give you those passages in the journal are fascinating just because of the subject matter, but what do they have to do with me? What purpose do they serve for the intruder? Why *those* particular passages?"

"I don't know, but I think we need to do some reading. There's got to be a link somewhere. Maybe we can find it." John stared down at the journal and frowned. "Why does she say 'Sissy's cousin' but she never gives the woman's name?"

"I can only guess that it's superstition. Writing her given name may give the spirits power over the cousin."

John stared. "Seriously?"

"I don't know for sure, but it wouldn't surprise me. A lot of the old cultures are centered around fear of spirits and being used as portals or gates for them to cross. I don't know that much about voodoo, so I'm just guessing."

"That makes as much sense as anything else, I guess. I think we should take these back with us to the cottage so we can read them thoroughly."

Olivia nodded. "There was a laundry basket on the washing machine. We could bring it back and load it up, but then he's going to know we were here." She lowered her eyes to the table. "And none of this helps find your sister. I'm…I'm afraid for her. If he finds out we were here."

John blew out a breath, considering her words, but he already knew she was right. If they took the books the intruder would know they'd found the tunnel, but they couldn't exactly set up shop in this room, either. Damn

it! Every step forward he took in locating the intruder seemed to be one more barrier to finding his sister, and after the shooting incident John had no doubt that the intruder would kill to get what he wanted.

He looked at Olivia, who was staring at him, probably hoping he'd come up with a solution. As she opened her mouth to speak, John heard an almost inaudible shuffle in the passage. He placed his finger over her lips and nodded toward the doorway. Olivia's eyes widened and her body went rigid.

Easing his pistol out of his waistband, John crept toward the doorway. He motioned to Olivia to duck down behind the table and she slid to the basement floor, the top of her head and her pistol the only things above the table's surface. He was only a couple of feet from the doorway when the door began to slide silently back into place.

He heard Olivia gasp as he dove for the closing wall of bricks, but he wasn't quick enough. The wall slid silently into place, closing them off completely from the passage. John slammed a fist into the wall in frustration, his heartbeat pounding in his ears. Always so close, but not within his grasp.

He ran his hands across the ceiling in front of the doorway, knowing already that it was pointless to hurry. The intruder had a huge advantage on disappearing and John knew he was long gone. Olivia stepped up beside him and silently began to search the wall next to the doorway. A couple of seconds later, she pressed a spot on the wall and the brick wall slid back. John lifted his pistol in ready position and moved quickly around the corner, but the passageway was empty.

He stepped back into the room and shook his head at Olivia. "He's gone."

Olivia glanced at the opening then back at John. "You're sure he was out there? I mean, there could be a delay on the door..."

John shook his head. "He was there. I heard him, just like I heard you that first night. He's good, but he's not a ghost."

"Well, I guess there's one positive thing."

"Really? And what in the world could that be?"

"He knows we found the room, so we can take all the books we want."

John sighed. "I suppose you're right. Do you want to go back and get the laundry basket now?"

"No," Olivia said as she gathered the books on the table and stuffed them in her backpack. "We need to keep looking for your sister. The books on the table are probably the most important ones. We can start with those."

John nodded, relieved that he wasn't going to have to choose between continuing to look for his sister and sticking close to Olivia. "Can you handle the backpack? I don't want to put additional strain on your ankle, but I'd like to be ready for action if needed."

"My ankle's barely sore, and I'd rather you had one hand wrapped around your gun and the other around the intruder's throat."

John lifted the lantern from the table and handed it to Olivia. "That can be arranged."

FIVE HOURS LATER, Olivia laid the backpack on the kitchen table in the caretaker's cottage and sank into the chair in front of it. She buried her head between her arms on the table and tried to choke back the disappointment she felt. Over six hours combing the tunnels in the basement, looking for secret doors and rooms,

avoiding spiders, and the library room was the only find they'd made.

She heard John open the refrigerator behind her, but she didn't even lift an eyebrow.

"You all right?" he asked.

"Yeah. I'm just too tired to move. I think I'll just sleep right here with my clothes on, okay?"

"You ought to take a hot shower while we still have power. That should make you feel better."

Olivia lifted her head as he slid into the chair across from her and pushed a beer across the table. "A shower would require taking off my shoes and clothes and then there's that ten-step walk from here to the bathroom. I'd have to turn the faucets on and off, and I gotta be quite honest, the thought of towel-drying makes me want to weep."

John smiled. "You writers aren't exactly a hardy bunch, are you?"

"Depends on what you call hardy. If you mean are we normally equipped to deal with stalkers and gunfire and being trapped in remote areas surrounded by numerous creatures that can kill you with no viable means of escape or contact with the outside world, then no, we're not hardy."

He raised one eyebrow. "But no shortage of words, I see."

"The day I have a shortage of words is the day I'm… Never mind." The last thing she needed to bring to the forefront of John's mind was death. She grabbed the beer and took a huge drink, wincing at the bitterness.

"More of a wine person?"

"Actually, I'm more of a coffee person. Even late at night. It doesn't keep me awake—the caffeine. I guess I'm just wired differently, but I drink it for the taste.

Or on a chilly night, I like to wrap my hands around a warm mug." She looked over at John, then down at the table. "Stupid, right?"

"No. I used to yell at my sister for taking the last cup of coffee. She doesn't even like coffee, but she used to say the same thing—that she liked the feel of the warm mug in her hands. And the smell. She loves the smell of coffee brewing."

Olivia could hear in John's voice how much he cared about his sister, and she couldn't help but wonder about this man who was such an enigma. "Tell me about her. I mean, if you want to."

"Rachel is beautiful, and smart, and hardheaded, like our mother. She's a grad student working on her master's thesis in architecture. That's why she came to laMalediction. It was on a list of houses she wanted to visit for her thesis." He gave Olivia a sad smile. "She'd like you, especially your knowledge of old homes."

"And your parents. You said she was your half sister—did your parents divorce?"

"No. My dad was a policeman. He was killed on the job when I was five."

A wave of sympathy washed over Olivia. "That's so sad. I sometimes think it's easier for me because I've never known what I was missing since I can't remember my parents. So your mother remarried. Is your stepfather nice? Is he a cop, too?"

"My stepfather was very nice. He was the attorney that handled my dad's will. I think Mom believed if she married a man who wore a suit to work and sat behind a desk, that she wouldn't lose him, but he died four years ago of a heart attack. We had no warning, and it hit my mom and sister hard."

Olivia felt her heart clench. "I can't imagine…to lose

not just one, but two men you loved. She must be remarkable to have held it together."

"She is remarkable, but everyone has their limit, and I'm afraid Rachel may be hers. Mom's in the hospital right now undergoing chemo. She's getting weaker every day, and I worry that if I don't find Rachel alive and soon that she'll give up."

"Oh, John, I am so sorry. How awful that must be for her and you. And you can't even contact her now to reassure her." Olivia bolted up in her seat. "The cell phones!" She reached for her cell phone that used to be attached to her laptop and realized the cord hung on the side of the table, her phone nowhere in sight.

"It's gone." She looked at John, unable to control the waver in her voice. "Please tell me you had your phone in your pocket."

John rushed into the bedroom and Olivia heard him curse. He walked back into the kitchen. "Stupid! I should have thought about the phones."

Olivia shook her head. "You're not stupid. You're just stressed and dealing with a huge unknown. I didn't think about it, either."

"But I should have. Why should we assume he hasn't gone through everything in this cottage?"

"It's pointless to blame yourself now, and with the way the rain is still coming down, we both know they would have been useless, anyway."

"Right now, maybe, but after the storm we could have called for backup. Damn it!" John slammed his hand on the table, causing Olivia's laptop to jump.

Olivia glanced at the useless computer and saw a piece of paper sticking out from the inside of the laptop. She pulled the laptop over to her and lifted the top.

A single piece of paper lay inside. Olivia sucked in a breath and John looked down at her.

"What's wrong?"

Olivia pointed to the paper. "That's not mine."

"Open it."

"Should I put on gloves first or something?"

John sighed. "Yeah, probably so. Hold on." He stepped into the bathroom, then returned with tweezers and grabbed a knife from the kitchen drawer. He pulled the note from her laptop onto the table, held one corner down with the knife and pulled the other side open with the tweezers. They both leaned over to read the handwritten message.

The time is now. Fulfill the prophecy and you can all leave.

Olivia's pulse quickened as she read the words, but her mind couldn't make anything of them. What prophecy? "I don't…I don't understand."

"He left the message in your laptop. It must mean something."

Olivia read the message over and over, her mind racing with the limited research information she'd gained on the history of laMalediction and its residents. "No. I swear. There's hardly any information on laMalediction available, and I'd definitely remember if I'd read about a prophecy. I have no idea what that could mean."

"Someone thinks you do."

"I don't care what they think. I ought to know what's in my own mind. Besides, I'd give him anything to leave here alive."

John pointed to the note. "See how he phrases this—'you can *all*'—it makes me think he's referring to more than just me and you."

Olivia looked up at him, barely able to make out his

face from the glow of the laptop. "You think he means your sister?"

"Maybe. Or maybe I'm looking for answers where there aren't any."

Olivia studied the words again. "Still, it's an odd way to phrase it if he only meant the two of us. But if he meant your sister, then he must know you're here looking for her." She sat up straight in her chair. "And that means he knows who you are. How can he know all that?"

"He probably went through our stuff when he took the phones. My badge is in my wallet."

"But all that would tell him is that you were a cop. If he thought you were looking for a missing person, wouldn't he expect you to drive in here with a search warrant, instead of posing as a caretaker?"

John shook his head, his expression grim. "I don't know."

"Do you think the cabin is bugged?" Olivia asked, the thought of the intruder listening to them the night before making her ill.

"At this point, anything's possible, but he'd have to be nearby or have a server to send the signal in order to listen, and with all these storms, I don't think it's possible—at least not often."

"Did you talk to anyone about your sister when it wasn't storming?"

John frowned. "Yeah, I think so. I mean, I talked to my partner on my cell in here, but I can't remember what I said exactly. I've talked to him in the main house, too." John looked out the window at the main house. "I suppose he could have overheard me. Those tunnels run everywhere and all it would take is a well-positioned vent to hear everything."

Olivia gazed out at laMalediction, and a chill came over her. "It's hard to wrap your mind around…that someone may have been watching me, listening to me… all this time. At times, it was almost like I could feel something, a presence, but I chalked it up to stress and nerves and being in such a remote location."

"Maybe it was intuition. Fear is a powerful emotion, and we spend too much of our lives ignoring the signals. Maybe we'd all be safer if we learned to listen to those feelings."

"Even if I think it's just paranoia?"

"*Especially* if you think it's just paranoia."

Chapter Fifteen

Olivia pulled on a T-shirt and shorts and towel-dried her hair by candlelight. The shower had worked out some of the stiffness she felt from all the activity of the past couple of days and even though she was tired, she was excited about reading the journals. She opened the bathroom door and the smell of freshly brewed coffee wafted by.

"You have no idea how happy I am that you have a Coleman burner. Even I didn't come prepared to make coffee with no electricity."

John looked up from the kitchen table. "I'd love to take all the credit, but the burner was in the cabinets when I got here. I figured out real quick why Aubrey kept it easily accessible. He probably spent a lot of time cooking on it with all these power outages."

"If Aubrey doesn't turn out to be the intruder, I owe him big." She took a cup down from the cabinet and filled it with the steamy liquid. "You should catch a shower while the water's still hot. No telling how long we'll be without power."

John placed the journal he was holding on the table and rose. "Yeah, I think I will. I sorted the journals we have by date with the oldest on the top of the stack. I

figured they may be easier to decipher in chronologi-
cal order."

Olivia nodded. "How do you want to approach the
research?"

"I don't know. I figured that was your area of exper-
tise, so I'd ask you."

"Were pages marked in any of the other journals?"

"No. That would be far too easy."

Olivia pulled a package of Post-its from her back-
pack. "I'll start scanning the first journal while you
shower. I'll mark anything that might be relevant, es-
pecially anything that refers to a prophecy. You can
read the marked passages and then we can divvy up
the rest of the journals and look for more entries that
might give us a clue."

"Sounds good," John said and headed to the bath-
room.

Olivia double-checked the dead bolt on the front door
and glanced over at the picture window, now completely
covered with a blanket from the bedroom. She eased
over to the window and lifted one end of the blanket to
peek out at the raging storm. The rain was coming down
harder now. Each flash of lightning exposed trees, bent
over from the winds. She dropped the blanket back in
place and slid into a chair at the table.

Despite the storm raging outside and the sound of
the shower running in the cabin, there was a stillness
in the air that unnerved her. She took a sip of her coffee
hoping to warm herself, but she knew that the chill she
felt didn't come from the night air. Whatever was out
there, she could feel it, and although she'd joked with
John earlier, she knew she wasn't paranoid. Someone
out there was watching…waiting…and she didn't have
any idea why.

She set down the coffee and pulled a journal off the top of the stack. Time to get some answers.

"July 5, 1861
Father told me today that I would be married in a month. I begged and pleaded, but he ignored my cries. Mother, as usual, deferred to him. In one month, I will become the final payment for a business transaction that gains Father the business he wished to acquire in New Orleans. Father assures me that Franklin is a gentleman, and I will have a big house with many servants. I find it ironic that a war is brewing over slavery, but the daughters of the wealthy are traded like cattle and expected to stay quiet."

Anger rose in Olivia and she gritted her teeth. No wonder Marilyn Borque had an affair. She was sold like a piece of property. What kind of man bought his wife? Olivia sighed and turned the page. Probably the same kind of man who beat his wife.

"July 19, 1861
My wedding day is two weeks away. It will be a huge event with champagne and extravagant food and happy people partying long into the night. Except for the bride. I barely know my husband, but I'm left with a bad feeling each time we are together. While his behavior is that of every other well-bred man, there's something just beneath the surface. Something wrong, and I'm afraid to find out what it is. He's building a house for us in the middle of the swamp. Even with a house full of

servants, I know I will be alone. I think that was
always his intention."

Olivia pushed the journal to the side and took a large
sip of coffee. Even tucked away in the caretaker's cot-
tage, she felt something closing in on her. Something
malevolent. Something that had been here for a long,
long time.

Something trying to break free.

JOHN SHUT OFF the water and grabbed the towel hang-
ing over the shower door. He'd been tempted to stand
under the hot water until it ran out, but he didn't want
Olivia out of his sight any longer than necessary. He'd
known that someone had easy access to the house and
that they'd been playing with Olivia and doing God
knows what else, but he hadn't really considered the
possibility that the intruder had been following their
every move, listening to every conversation.

More and more it seemed like that was the case.
Whoever was behind this had planned well and far in
advance, which led him right back around to the huge
gaping holes in the "why." Olivia didn't know more than
she was telling—he'd bet money on that—but every
instinct told him that everything going on at laMale-
diction centered around her past. Which left them in a
serious deficit when it came to motive.

He towel-dried his hair and ran one hand across the
three-day growth on his jaw. Since shaving wasn't any-
where on his priority list, he pulled on his jeans and a
T-shirt and tossed the towel in the laundry basket. A
long night stretched in front of them, but it had been
an even longer day.

He probably would have stubbornly continued

searching the tunnels, even though his focus wasn't what he needed it to be, but he could tell Olivia was ready to drop. He actually admired her for making it as long as she did. The stress of dealing with all those closed-in, dark spaces would have been enough to send most claustrophobics straight into a rubber room. He'd been surprised that she was in such good shape emotionally and physically given that her regular day consisted mostly of typing and reading.

At least they had the journals. If the intruder thought them important enough to read, then surely, there was a clue in those books that they could use to their advantage. Maybe something that would unlock a buried secret in Olivia's mind. It wouldn't be the first time an event or object had triggered a forgotten memory.

He looked at the closed bathroom door and blew out a breath, hoping the journals would take the edge off him and Olivia sharing such close quarters. The tension between them had diminished greatly from the night before, but it was still there. The regret he felt at hurting her needled him every time he looked at her, but it had been necessary.

He wasn't going to deny he had feelings for Olivia, or he'd be lying to himself. But he also knew that despite those feelings, caring for another person the way his mother had cared for both her husbands…the way she cared for his sister, wasn't an option for him. His work was dangerous and that was the way he wanted it to be. To form a relationship with someone would be putting them at daily risk for being a widow, and that was something he couldn't take.

His directives were simple—he needed to catch the intruder and stop him from accomplishing whatever he had in mind for Olivia. He needed to get Olivia away

from laMalediction and back into her normal life. He
needed to find his sister and return her to their mother.
And he needed to forget he'd ever felt anything for
Olivia Markham.

He strode into the kitchen, took one look at Olivia
and stopped short. Her expression was a mixture of fear
and anger, and he was afraid to ask what she'd found in
the journals. "Are you all right?"

Olivia looked up at him, her hands still clutching her
coffee cup. "No. I'm angry and sad and angry."

"You said angry twice."

"That's because I'm really, really angry." She gave
him a rundown of what she'd read in the first journal.

John felt his jaw clench when he considered that only
for the passage of time, she could have been describ-
ing his mother, his sister or Olivia. "I don't blame you.
That makes me angry, too."

"But I could be related to these people. Do you re-
alize that?"

"We don't know that for sure. And even if you are,
you look like Marilyn, not Franklin."

"Do you realize that the best option here is to de-
scend from a woman who was sold as chattel, had an
affair and practiced voodoo?" Olivia shook her head.
"What a mess. I mean, when I first saw the house and
realized it was the one from my dreams, I thought I
might get some of the answers I'd always wanted. Mari-
lyn's diaries make me rethink it on so many levels."

"We don't get to choose our family, but yeah, it's
definitely better sometimes not to know everything.
Still, all of this certainly explains the voodoo angle. It
was probably her last hope."

"What a miserable existence." Olivia blew out a
breath. "I didn't find anything in the first journal about

the passages or a prophecy…nothing that seemed relevant now."

John poured himself a cup of coffee and slid into the chair across from Olivia. "Pass me the next one. There's got to be something in these that we can use. He's looking for something."

Olivia passed him the next journal in the stack and took the one underneath for herself. "I hope we find whatever it is before he does."

John's back tightened at her words, not wanting to think about the outcome if the intruder got what he was looking for. He was afraid if that happened, laMalediction's history with occupants would be horrifically consistent.

IT WAS ALMOST midnight and two pots of coffee later when Olivia straightened up in her chair. "I think I found something." She pointed to one of the journals John had read earlier. "Find that post about the statue."

John opened the journal and flipped through the entries, looking for the passage Olivia wanted. "Here it is," he said and began to read.

"May 5, 1863
We held our first party since Franklin's return at the house tonight. Franklin was in all his glory, lording over his less successful cousins and their 'common' wives, as he puts it. I don't even want to think about the money spent on food and drink, but Franklin insisted on the top of the line for everything. He intends on displaying his new purchase for the first time. A statue from the Orient, with a purchase origin that he won't provide the details on. It's a plaster creature that favors a lion,

but with two breathtaking emeralds for eyes. Again, I can't even imagine the cost, or how he came by the statue, but my guess is it wasn't legal.

He's been obsessed with the thing ever since it entered the house, hiding it in his sleeping quarters and bolting the doors behind him every night. One night, after I'd performed my wifely duty, I made the mistake of touching it. He beat me with a candlestick and I couldn't walk well for days. Even though I know better than anyone what he's capable of, I've never seen him in such a state. It's like he's gone mad.

If he wasn't already mad before."

Olivia felt her excitement grow as John read the entry. "Listen to this," she said and picked up the journal she'd been reading.

"June 15, 1863
Sissy's cousin can no longer offer me protection from Franklin. He was already slipping into madness before the war. Now that he's returned and seen what I've done, I know my days on this earth are limited. At first opportunity, he will strike. His energy grows greater each day, despite my administering the potions from Sissy's cousin. She says he draws his energy from the statue—that the statue is the key to his madness.

I told Sissy's cousin I would destroy it, but she said the power in the statue could not be destroyed—it must be contained. I will drug Franklin's wine tonight and use the servant's passage to sneak into his room. I will bring Sissy's cousin the statue so she can bind the evil spirits inside."

"What in the world?" John asked.

"It gets better," Olivia said, then flipped a couple of pages and continued reading.

"June 16, 1863

I took the statue to Sissy's cousin tonight. She had a violent reaction to the piece as soon as she saw the eyes. The emeralds, she said, are cursed. She removed the emeralds from the statue and placed them in a pouch for safekeeping, then performed a spell on the statue to separate it from the evil in the stones. We then broke the statue and crushed the pieces until they were dust. We collected the dust in a jar and will fling it far into the bayou where the spirits that inhabit the water can prevent it from resurfacing. She will set the stones in metal to bind them and cast the spell two nights from now when the moon is full.

I know this is the only way, but I feel overwhelming guilt for the future I am creating for my ancestors. The stones will not remain bound forever. One day, the emeralds will call on those of my lineage to fulfill the prophecy that I have set in motion.

Even if it costs their life."

"Cursed emeralds, spirits in bayous…" John shook his head. "Do you think she'd gone crazy?"

"I don't know. I mean, she was sold to a wife beater, couldn't be with the man she loved and was locked away in this place from anyone who might have helped her, but that doesn't mean she was crazy. You have to remember the times. People didn't dismiss the paranormal as easily as they do today, and from reading these

journals it looks like she was under heavy influence from her maid's cousin."

"So you're saying she might have been perfectly sane and still believed the emeralds were cursed."

"Exactly."

John stared at her for a moment, then narrowed his eyes. "*You* don't believe in cursed emeralds, do you?"

Olivia took a deep breath and blew it out slowly, considering all the facets to his question. "On the surface, no, but I do believe there are plenty of things on this earth that can't be explained, so I try to keep an open mind. What I believe isn't relevant anyway. Obviously, the intruder believes it."

"And he thinks you're here to fulfill some prophecy. That's the only thing that makes sense."

"Maybe I am." She placed her elbows on the table and leaned toward John. "Maybe the dreams are the part that can't be explained with science or logic, assuming I'm a descendant of Marilyn Borque."

"You want me to believe that cursed emeralds are sending you nightmares as some sort of calling card? No wonder you write fiction."

"Maybe, or maybe Marilyn Borque's memories are buried somewhere in my genetic code and resurfacing in my conscience. Scientists still don't understand the extent that genetics has over our bodies and minds. It's not as far a stretch as you might imagine."

John raised his eyebrows and leaned back in his chair. "Okay, I'll give you that our understanding of the human body leaves much to be desired, but that's still a huge leap to make."

"But it's the only one that explains everything—my dreams, my resemblance to Marilyn Borque and most important, how the intruder knew to prepare for me.

Don't you see, if he believed the prophecy would be fulfilled, then he only had to wait for me to come. He didn't have to know who I was beforehand."

John sat upright. "But my sister came before you." He jumped up from his chair and paced the small room. "Man, that psycho probably thought she was the one. What if he killed her when you arrived and he realized he had the wrong woman?"

Olivia looked up at him. "I don't believe he killed her."

"Why wouldn't he?"

"It's too big a risk. Think about it. All these years no one's been to this estate and within a matter of days, two different women arrive...alone. I may resemble Marilyn Borque, but there's no way he can be certain that I'm the one. I think that's why the message on my computer referred to 'all' of us."

"You think he's holding my sister somewhere, waiting for what? You to find cursed emeralds so the sky can fall or hell can rise?"

"More likely, so he can steal them and make off with the money. Just because he believes in some bizarre voodoo spell doesn't mean he's not still a common criminal."

"Practical. I can appreciate that. So what's he waiting for?"

Olivia frowned. "My guess is a day. There's no reference to a future date in the journals, but he must have something in mind. Something soon for him to take a chance cutting down that tree and stealing our phones. He's got to figure that, risky or not, we're hiking out of here as soon as the storm breaks. I figure if the date was far off, he would have taken me hostage."

"And quite possibly killed me."

"I think that was his plan last night. Think about it. Earlier you convinced me to leave laMalediction. We had that conversation in the kitchen of the main house. He probably overheard the entire thing."

"And he thought killing me would be a good way to make you stay?"

"I think he thought killing you would leave one less person to manage if he had to chain me up and force me to cast spells to reveal emeralds, or whatever he thinks I'm supposed to do."

"Were there any more references to the prophecy in the journals?"

"No. And we've finished with what we brought from the library. Quite possibly there's more information in the other books, but it would take a while to go through them all. A lot more time than you want to spend."

John stopped pacing and blew out a breath. "I've failed everyone. My sister. My mother. You."

Olivia rose from her chair and placed one hand on his arm. "You didn't fail anyone. Your sister walked into a bad situation. Your mother knows you're doing everything you can to find her."

"And you?"

"You can't fail me. I'm not your responsibility."

"I hurt you. Intentionally."

"No, you lied intentionally. Yeah, it hurt at first, but I would have done the same thing if I were in your position."

John touched her face with one hand. "I need you to know that I didn't use you. Last night was special. It wasn't business."

Olivia felt her heart clench and she wondered for a split second how different things might have been if they'd met at another time. "It was special for me, too,

and I hope it's a memory I get to take with me for a long time to come."

John dropped his hand to his side. "Olivia...I... Never mind."

Olivia wanted to know what he was going to say, but she knew better than to ask. John Landry already had two full-time females depending on him, and it was clear to her that he didn't need a third. And Olivia didn't want anyone feeling responsible for her. She'd always called the shots, and including someone else in every aspect of her life wasn't something she was comfortable with. No one was allowed to get that close to her. That way, there was nothing to lose.

She dropped her hand from his arm and looked down at the floor, not certain how to say what she had to say. Finally, she blurted it out. "I'm not going to sit around here waiting for the final hatchet to fall. I'm leaving tomorrow on foot. I'd rather take my chances with the swamp creatures than a crazy man obsessed with cursed emeralds."

"You don't know anything about these swamps," John argued. "You're at a tremendous disadvantage, even if the storm subsides."

"I'm at a tremendous disadvantage here. Leaving is my only chance to get help. The main road back to town is too far, but I figured I can hike up to those cabins we discovered and see if someone has a way to call for help."

"And what if those cabins are occupied by the intruder or his family or friends?"

"It's a risk I have to take." She paused and bit her lower lip. "That risk could be lessened if you went with me."

John's jaw flexed and Olivia could tell that a mil-

lion thoughts, most of them unpleasant, were running through his mind. "And my sister? You think we should just go off and leave her here with a madman?"

"I'll help you search tomorrow for half a day. After that, I'm leaving whether you come with me or not. We need backup, John. With all your training, you have to know that. This is the Louisiana bayou horror version of Vietnam. We've been ambushed."

"Damn it. You're right. I know you're right, but the choices are all so wrong."

"I don't think he'll hurt her until the time has passed. If we can get help here, we can dismantle this place if need be. It might be her only chance."

"But you have no idea what date he has in mind."

"I have a guess." She pointed to a calendar on the kitchen wall. "Tomorrow night is a full moon."

Chapter Sixteen

The dream came again, unbidden as always, and Olivia felt her pulse increase as she drifted toward the house in the storm. She swooped down into the bedroom, but rather than seeing Marilyn Borque asleep on the bed, she was already dead, her eyes wide open in fright and staring blankly at the ceiling. Blood stained her pale, silk nightgown and spilled onto the stark white sheets.

Franklin stood above her, smiling at his work. He gently brushed a lock of her hair back from her face, then stepped away from the bed and left the room. As he walked down the hallway to the stairs, a door across the hall from the master bedroom opened just a crack. The young Creole woman waited until Franklin was downstairs before pushing the door open and rushing across the hall into the master bedroom.

She hurried to the bed and cried out when she saw what Franklin had done. "Mistress!" She gathered Marilyn's body in her arms and hugged it close to her, crying and repeating over and over "my friend, my lady." When Franklin's voice sounded from the courtyard, her body went rigid and she rose to look out the window.

He stood in the courtyard, in the midst of the storm yelling up at the night, "I want what is mine!" The Creole woman's face flushed with rage and she pulled open

the nightstand drawer. She drew a black candle and scissors from the drawer, then lit the candle with the lantern and placed it in the holder on the nightstand. She cut a lock from Marilyn's hair and held it in her hand above the candle.

She stared out at Franklin Borque, her eyes full of hatred, and started chanting. Her voice grew louder with each passage of thunder and she opened her hand to allow the strands of hair to fall over the flame of the candle. Olivia struggled to make out what the woman said, but it was lost in the roar of the storm and Franklin's continued cries. Finally, the last strand of hair wafted from her hand and drifted down onto the flame as if in slow motion.

"He took what was mine," the woman cried out. "Give him what he is due!"

As soon as the words left her mouth, a single bolt of lightning flashed down from the sky and struck Franklin Borque directly in the heart, sending him crumpling to the ground.

Olivia sat up straight in bed, her eyes wide open. She sucked in a huge breath of air, swaying as a wave of dizziness ran through her. A knock sounded on the bedroom door and she jumped. A second later, John peeked inside. She must have looked distressed because he took one glance at her then pushed immediately inside.

"What's wrong?" he asked. "Another dream?"

"Yeah," she said and recounted the dream to him with every detail. "The Creole woman must have been Sissy."

"She could have been anyone."

"She called Marilyn 'mistress' and clearly she was attached to her. Only Marilyn's personal servant would

have a room in the main house on the same level as the owners."

John sat down on the edge of the bed. "Olivia, you're assuming that what you dreamed is real. After everything we read last night, why won't you believe that your mind could have fabricated such a story? You're able to write stories interesting enough to publish when you're conscious. Don't you think your unconscious mind has the same level of creativity?"

Olivia shook her head. "It was real. I don't care how crazy it makes me sound. I believe the dreams."

John sighed. "Even if it's true, what good does it do us? The dream doesn't tell us anything useful. We need to find my sister or those emeralds, as I suppose the intruder would be quite happy to work out a trade."

"But we don't even know that the emeralds are at laMalediction. Sissy's cousin wove the spell in her home. There's never been any indication that the stones were hidden here."

"There's no indication in what we read," John pointed out. "But that library was full of books, and any one of them might refer to the return of the emeralds to laMalediction. The intruder must have had some reason to believe they're here, otherwise he wouldn't be doing this at all."

"That's true, but if the intruder's certain they're at laMalediction, and he hasn't found them yet, then they're not somewhere obvious."

"Of course not. Look at how elaborate that tunneling system is. Those people did not do things in halves. It seems they went out of the way to hide and cloister and secret away most everything. We could look for a decade and might never find those stones."

Olivia glanced over at the bedroom window, but with

the thick drapes drawn, she couldn't tell if the sun was up. "What time is it?"

"Almost seven. I want to get an early start."

"And if we don't find anything?"

John's jaw flexed. "If we don't find anything by noon, we'll leave."

JOHN PULLED A folded sheet of paper out of his pocket and placed it flat on the table in the underground library. He'd spent at least an hour the night before diagramming everything he could remember of the passages, making a concentrated effort to get the dimensions as close as he could to actuality.

"The black lines represent the sections of passages we covered yesterday," he explained to Olivia. "The red lines are where I think the house's ground-level structure doesn't jive with the underground structure. Now, certainly they don't have to. The basement area may not be as large as the house."

"Or it may be larger than the house, but that's not likely," Olivia said, studying the drawing. "At least the drawing gives us a good place to start looking again. This was smart, John."

John felt a small swell of pride at her approval, but knew he had much more to accomplish that day than a paper drawing. He pointed to a square section on the paper. "This is the library where we are now. By my estimates, it's beneath the center of the house, so passages or walls could extend beyond three walls, leaving out the one that the entry passage extends in front of."

Olivia nodded. "You're right. We followed all the passages yesterday, but never tried to locate another passageway in the library. If this room is central, it may be surrounded by other avenues of escape or storage."

"I'm hoping not, but yeah, this could just be one small rest area in a much larger maze."

Olivia scanned the room then looked back at John. "You know, I've always wanted to see one of those bookcase secret doors. Under different circumstances, I might be enjoying this."

"Under different circumstances, I might appreciate the creativity of the designer of this mess, but as it is, I'm mostly cursing him." He studied the set of bookshelves along one wall. "All the shelves have crown molding across the top that connects with the ceiling. If one of the bookcases moves, there would have to be a break somewhere in the molding, right?"

He walked the perimeter of the room, holding the lantern up to the top of the bookcases, checking every square inch of crown molding for a connection, but the only place it appeared to separate was at the corners. "Maybe I'm wrong." He looked over at Olivia, who'd pulled a chair over to one set of bookcases and was standing on top of it, studying the crown molding.

"Not exactly."

"What do you mean, not exactly? There's no break in the molding."

"But it doesn't have to. What if it's connected to all of the bookcases except for the one that moves?"

"Smart. You moonlight doing construction?"

Olivia blushed. "No. I saw it once in a movie, actually. But it makes sense. I mean from an I-have-secret-tunnels sort of perspective."

John held the lantern up to the top of the bookcase where Olivia stood and inspected the bottom of the molding that sat flush with the bookcase. "The only problem with that theory is if our carpenter is excel-

lent, then it will be almost impossible to detect the piece that's not attached to the bookcase itself."

He scanned the room again, trying to think of a faster way to accomplish their task. The stacks of books lining almost every shelf made it seem like even more of a task, until he remembered. "Look for places that aren't dusty. The trigger would have to be on the shelf itself, right? If he moved books to get to it, or touched it on a regular basis, there should be signs that the dust was disturbed."

"I'll start on this wall," Olivia said and jumped down from the chair.

John nodded and moved to the far wall. The first two bookcases appeared completely undisturbed, but on the third there were fine lines in the dust in front of one book. Like the book had been drawn back from its spot on the shelf. He pulled the book out from the shelf and felt the wall behind it. "I think I found something," he said as his fingers ran across an indentation in the bookcase.

Olivia abandoned her search and came to stand behind him. "Go for it."

He pressed the spot and the entire bookcase slid back from the wall. "Jackpot."

There was an opening on one side of the gap and a solid wall on the other. The opening was narrow, maybe two feet wide, and John glanced over at Olivia. "It looks pretty tight. Maybe you should stay here."

Olivia looked at the opening and frowned. "No. I'd rather be trapped in there with you than kidnapped and trapped in a room alone."

"Okay." John stuck the lantern into the opening and took one step inside. "I can only see about five feet in front of us, but there's not an end yet." He inched sev-

eral feet down the narrow passage, then glanced back to check on Olivia. She was only inches from him and her face was drawn, but her breathing seemed normal.

He continued another couple of feet. "I think I see an end," he said and continued to push forward until he came to a dead end. Holding the lantern up to the wall in front of him, he scanned the surface for any of those poisonous kind of creatures Olivia had warned him about, then placed his hand on the wall and began to search for a way to open it.

Olivia placed one hand on his arm and whispered, "Did you hear that?"

He stopped his search and glanced back at her. "Hear what?"

"I thought I heard voices."

He went still and listened, but only the faint sound of Olivia's breathing reached his ears. He was just about to chalk it up to stress and her imagination when he heard a noise, faint and muffled, but it could be human. He turned his head slowly in each direction, trying to determine the direction of the sound.

"I think it's coming from there," Olivia said and pointed to the wall in front of him.

He pressed the side of his head against the wall, hoping to hear better, and the noise grew a little louder. It was someone screaming—someone female. His pulse began to race, and he ran his hands over the wall, searching for the way to open it. Olivia stretched her arm around his side and searched the side wall of the tunnel.

"Got it," she cried and the wall in front of him began to slide back.

He passed her the lantern with one hand and pulled his pistol from his waistband with the other, then

stepped through the opening, Olivia right behind him. The light from the lantern spread through the tiny room, illuminating his sister and an old man tied to chairs in the center of the room.

Rachel stopped screaming the instant they stepped into the room and closed her eyes, probably because of the light. "Rachel," John said and rushed over to her, overwhelming relief passing over him at seeing his sister alive.

"John? Oh, my God, John, is that you?" She opened her eyes, blinking rapidly, then started crying. "I can't believe you found me."

John crouched down next to her and directed Olivia to check out the man tied to the next chair, who appeared to be unconscious. "Are you hurt?" He scanned her for injuries, but couldn't see anything obvious.

"No," Rachel replied. "I'm cold and hungry and scared to death, but he didn't hurt us."

A second wave of relief flooded through John and he placed his hands on his sister's cheeks and kissed her forehead. "Thank God."

His sister looked over at the man in the other chair. "I'm worried about Aubrey, though. He's been out for a while. I've been calling to him, but I haven't been able to wake him up."

John looked over at Olivia, who had her fingers on the man's neck. "Thank God, he's got a pulse," Olivia said, "but he needs medical care. He's probably dehydrated and who knows what else."

John moved behind Rachel's chair and tugged at the ropes that bound her wrists, and indicated that Olivia should do the same. "He must be the caretaker."

"That's what he told me," Rachel said.

"Who put you here? Did you see him?"

"I saw him when he caught me in the house, but he's always worn a mask since then."

John glanced over at Olivia who frowned, understanding the implication. "That means the man is someone Aubrey would recognize." John pulled the last knot out of the rope and removed it from Rachel's wrists.

"He's crazy, I know that." Rachel pulled her arms in front of her and rubbed her wrists, then rose slowly, her legs still a bit shaky. "He put a gun to my head and told me to tell him where the emeralds are. I couldn't convince him that I had no idea what he was talking about. So he said he was going to keep me locked in here until I talked."

Olivia pulled the ropes from Aubrey's wrists and looked over at John. "We were right. He's after the emeralds."

"You were right," John pointed out.

Aubrey stirred and Olivia moved around to the front of the chair to check on him. "Aubrey, can you hear me?"

"The prophecy," Aubrey said. He opened his eyes a bit and squinted at Olivia. "Marilyn? It's true. You returned for the jewels."

"I'm not Marilyn, but I'm here to help. Do you know who tied you up?"

Aubrey nodded. "He thought if he wore a mask I wouldn't know, but I've always known. Knew who he was the first time I saw him. Knew he'd be after the jewels. It was written, you know?"

John heard Olivia suck in a breath and he stared at Aubrey, waiting for an answer. Waiting for any reason to make sense out of this mess.

"It's that attorney," Aubrey said.

Olivia's eyes widened and she stared at Aubrey.

"Wheeler? Ross Wheeler is the one responsible for all this?"

"Wheeler may be what he calls himself, but I know what he is. He's the devil spawn of Franklin Borque is what he is. Been trying for years to get control of this property, but he can't until those emeralds is found. I've been here a long time. My people were here many years before me."

Olivia stared at him. "Aubrey, were you related to Sissy?"

Aubrey nodded. "She was my great-grandmother. I got her journals. Know all about the evil man that built this house."

"I think we better get out of here," John said. If Wheeler returned, they were in a bad position trying to move two weak people, one of them considerably old, through the tunnels.

"Can you walk?" Olivia asked Aubrey. She placed one hand under his arm to help lift and steady him. It took a bit to get him upright, and he was still shaky, but maybe he had enough in him to get out of the passages. If they could make it to the basement, John would gladly carry the man all the way to Cypriere if necessary.

"Ready?" he asked.

"Damn straight," Aubrey said. "Let's get the hell out of here before that evil comes back. He won't let us out of here alive...not without them emeralds."

The old man hurried into the passage at a faster clip than John would have thought possible. John motioned to Olivia to follow. She pulled her pistol from her waistband and slipped into the tunnel behind Aubrey. Rachel followed Olivia and John entered the passage behind them, his mind whirling with all the possible outcomes

and mentally trying to prepare a counterattack for the bad ones.

They made it down the passage to the narrow entry into the library. Aubrey passed through the bookcase opening with Olivia close behind, then Olivia screamed and John's blood ran cold. He squeezed by Rachel, who'd frozen in place in the tunnel, and he burst through the narrow opening into the library.

Wheeler stood at the other end of the room, clutching Olivia's arm with one hand and holding a gun to her head with the other. Aubrey was crumpled in the corner, no sign of life coming from him. "Put your gun on the table and slide it over to me," Wheeler said.

John hesitated, calculating his odds. He was a crack shot, but Wheeler had Olivia positioned in front of his body. Even if the shot hit its mark, Wheeler could still squeeze the trigger before dropping, and if John was off, even a half an inch…it was too risky. He gritted his teeth and placed his pistol on the table.

"Slide it this way," Wheeler repeated.

John pushed the pistol across the table and it stopped a few feet in front of Wheeler. The attorney pushed Olivia toward the table. Olivia's eyes flashed from the table to John and he knew she wanted to make a leap for the weapon, but he barely shook his head, warning her not to try. She wasn't trained for such a move and the possibility of it ending badly was high.

Wheeler reached around her and grabbed the gun, then tucked it into the back waistband of his jeans. "I hope you'll excuse me," he said, "but Olivia and I have some unfinished business to attend to."

He smiled and John felt his blood run cold. Olivia was right. He was mad.

John clenched his fists and watched helplessly as

Wheeler backed out of the library and into the passageway and then the wall slid silently shut behind him. He yelled for Rachel to come out of the passage and rushed over to the wall. He located the switch but the wall gave one small tremor and held in place.

"Why won't it move?" Rachel asked, her voice cracking with fear.

"He must have jammed something in it on the other side." John reached for the sledgehammer that still stood propped in the corner. "But he forgot to take my backup plan. Check on Aubrey."

He drew the hammer back over his shoulder and swung it as hard as he could into the wall. Brick and mortar splintered and flew in every direction. Before the final piece hit the floor, he drew the hammer back and hit the wall again. The wall crumbled on the third blow.

Rachel was kneeling beside Aubrey with her fingers on his neck. "He's got a pulse and he's breathing, but it's shallow."

"He needs a doctor. He's too weak. We're going to have to leave him here for now. There's no other way." He stepped into the passage and motioned for Rachel to follow him. When she stepped into the passage, he gripped her shoulders with both hands. "I need you to follow this passage out of here and into the basement. I'll prop the passage door open with something so you won't have to find the switch. Take the basement stairs up to the kitchen and leave the house by the back door, then run as fast as you can to the iron gate. That part of the lawn can only be seen from the kitchen windows, so you should be able to get away without being seen. Get back to Cypriere as fast as you can and get help."

Rachel's eyes widened. "I'm not going to leave you here."

"Yes, you are. You can't help me here and if things go wrong, someone has got to know what happened. Make sure they send a medic of some sort."

He drew his backup pistol from his ankle holster and ran down the passageway as fast as the narrow space allowed. Ross Wheeler had just made a fatal error.

Chapter Seventeen

Wheeler closed the door to the basement and locked it behind them. The butt of his gun pressed into the small of her back, removing any thoughts she may have had about running. Not that it would make a difference. If she couldn't give Wheeler the emeralds, and she couldn't, the end was likely all going to play out the same.

"I can't help you," she said as he pushed her through the sitting room into the front entry.

"You're the one," he said. "I'm sure of it. You're the one who will fulfill the prophecy. I've been waiting for you a long, long time and I've been very patient, but my patience has run out."

He shoved Olivia into the front entry and spun her around to face him. "Now, show me where the emeralds are."

"I swear I don't know," Olivia pleaded. "I'd never even heard of a prophecy or emeralds until I read those journals last night. Why can't you believe that?"

"I thought the other girl was the one, but then you came. I hid her away, just in case I was wrong, but when I set eyes on you, I knew. You're her descendant, the one who is supposed to break the curse and return the emeralds to their rightful owner."

"And what makes you think that's you?"

Wheeler smiled. "Unlike you, with your pathetic beginnings, I know my family. I am a direct descendant of Franklin Borque and his mistress—the woman who helped him steal the statue. Make no mistake. Those emeralds are rightfully mine."

"If you're the rightful heir, why can't you find them yourself?"

Wheeler frowned. "Because I didn't come from that whore, Marilyn. She's the one who cursed the stones and hid them. Only her descendant can break the curse."

"Marilyn didn't have children. I can't be a descendant of her."

Wheeler's face flushed red. "She had one child...a bastard. You came from him."

His words struck Olivia like a lightning strike. Could Marilyn have had a baby by her lover? If so, what had happened to the child?

"You're lying," Olivia said. "Marilyn Borque didn't have any children. I read her journals and she never mentioned him at all."

"Oh, she had one child—a bastard—conceived when Franklin was off fighting for this country. Fighting for despicable people like Marilyn."

"A bastard...like you?"

Wheeler lifted his hand and slapped Olivia across the face. "My great-grandmother should have been Franklin's wife. If he hadn't been forced to marry that pig, everything would have been different."

Olivia ran her tongue across her lips and tasted blood. "Nothing you say changes anything. I...I still don't know where the emeralds are," Olivia said, her hopes fading as she looked at the madman in front of her. She had no doubt he'd kill her if she didn't pro-

duce the stones, and that was something she simply couldn't do.

"If you know so much about me," she continued, "then you already know that I don't know anything about my family. I don't care about the emeralds, and would gladly give them to you, but I don't know where they are."

Wheeler studied her face; his eyes narrowed. After several seconds, his expression turned to one of disbelief. "That can't be. It was written that you would come and the stones would be revealed to you—the descendant of Marilyn Borque."

"What if there's another descendant? Maybe my being here is a coincidence. Granted, it would be the worst coincidence in the world, but maybe someone else is supposed to fulfill the prophecy."

Wheeler shook his head. "There's no way you coming here was chance. It's you. It has to be you, and you'd better figure it out, quickly. My patience is going, and I don't think I have to tell you what will happen to you and your friends if you don't produce the stones."

Olivia's pulse raced, her heart beating so hard in her head that she could barely think. She had to stall him, convince him she was looking for the stones. Maybe he'd make a mistake. Give her an opportunity to make a run for it as soon as she figured out which way to run. She was at a complete disadvantage in both the house and the surrounding swamp. Her only hope would be making it to those cabins and finding help.

She glanced out the front window at the raging storm, knowing that she had to convince Wheeler that the emeralds were outside. But where? The creative mind that had rewarded her so well in her books seemed to have disappeared, and she was left with nothing plausible.

"You're not going to find anything standing in the entry," Wheeler said. "Let's start in the library. You set up your office in there. Maybe the room was calling to you."

Not the library. Olivia's plans began to fall apart. The library was centrally located in the house. There was no way she could make it down the hall and out the door without him shooting her.

"Now!" Wheeler leveled the gun at her head.

Olivia took a deep breath and walked down the hall toward the library. Maybe she could figure out a way to stall him. She wanted to hope that John could figure a way out of the underground room, but Wheeler had jammed the door behind them. Even if he found another way out, it might take hours to find a way back into the main house.

And hours was something Olivia was certain she didn't have.

JOHN WATCHED OUT the kitchen window as Rachel ran into the woods toward the gate. The sky was dark and the rain came down so hard that he could barely see her cross the lawn. He prayed she didn't run into problems in the storm or on the road. They were probably going to need that medical team far more than he'd stressed to her.

He edged along the wall and looked into the sitting room, but there was no sign of Wheeler or Olivia. The faint sound of voices trickled behind him and he eased over to the hallway exit. He stopped just short of the doorway and held his breath, listening for a clue as to where they were.

Wheeler's voice sounded…louder this time and John could hear the anger and frustration in his tone. He

felt a tightness in his chest as he thought about Olivia, in the hands of that madman and with no way to give him what he wanted. He'd thought he didn't want the responsibility of another woman, but when faced with losing her forever he knew it was too late. He'd lost his heart to Olivia Markham, and damned if he was going to lose her now.

He peered around the corner and slowly let out his breath when he saw the hallway was clear. Three rooms had entries off the hallway before the hallway reached the entry and four more rooms beyond that. The voices were too faint to be in the first set of rooms, so they must be in one of the rooms past the front entry. The library. That had to be it.

He left the doorway and slipped through the sitting room into the entry. That got him halfway to the library without having to use the hallway. At the edge of the hallway, he stopped and listened. He'd been right. The voices were louder now and came from the left side of the hallway.

He slipped around the opening into the hallway and crept toward the library, with no idea of what to do once he got there. Exposing himself was risky without knowing where Wheeler and Olivia stood in the room. If John tried to peek into the library, Wheeler might see him straight off and that would give the attorney an opportunity to grab Olivia. If he jumped straight into the doorway, guns blazing, and Wheeler was already positioned behind Olivia, he could use her as a shield as he did in the underground room.

He drew up short at the library door. Decision time. He took a deep breath and slowly let it out, then gripped his pistol and whirled around the doorway, pistol pointed into the room.

Olivia was in between Wheeler and the doorway, the absolute worst place for her to be, and Wheeler was obviously on edge and ready for action. He reacted immediately to John's entrance by stepping completely behind Olivia and leveling the gun at her head.

"I would think twice if I were you," Wheeler said. "Although one has to admire your persistence."

Olivia stood stock-still behind the table, her fear evident. John felt his heart clench and he mentally cursed his inability to catch a break. This was the one situation he'd feared the most. "You can't get away with this," John said.

"Of course I can," Wheeler said. "Do you think this is the first time someone's disappeared from the estate?"

"There have been others?" John asked.

"I had a miscalculation several years ago and thought it was time. A minor problem with counting, really, but one that cost a couple of surveyors their lives."

"You killed the surveyors?" Olivia asked.

"Well, I could hardly let them leave when they didn't produce the emeralds. Besides, a little death every once in a while helps keep people away from this place. It wouldn't do to have many visitors."

"You're insane."

Wheeler smiled. "I'm not insane. I just want what's mine."

John's finger tightened on the trigger. He could make the shot, even over Olivia's shoulder, but it was risky. Even if he hit Wheeler right between the eyes, he could still squeeze off a round, even involuntarily. With the gun pointed directly at Olivia's head it would take a miracle for him to miss her.

"It seems," Wheeler said, "that I have the upper hand once more. It's a shame you let your personal feelings

get the best of you. This would be such an easy choice if you didn't care for her, wouldn't it? Women ruin everything."

He inched a bit closer to Olivia, bringing his gun even closer to her head. "Now, lower your weapon and place it on the table." He laughed. "It's like a repeat of downstairs, really. How sad. In your last moments on earth, you've become a cliché."

John gritted his teeth, his hands still clenched on the pistol. He was going to kill them, regardless. If he didn't take the shot now, there wasn't going to be another chance. He looked at Olivia. She stared him directly in the eyes, and he could tell she knew the score. She lowered her head a fraction of an inch then raised it back up.

He said a silent prayer and tightened his finger on the trigger. A huge bolt of lightning struck right outside the library and Olivia glanced outside and gasped.

"It's her," Olivia said and pointed out the window.

Outside the window in the center of the drive stood a woman in a long, white, flowing dress. Her long black hair whipped around her in the wind as another burst of lightning illuminated her face.

Marilyn Borque.

"No," Wheeler said. "It can't be. You're dead!"

The woman raised one arm and pointed directly at Wheeler. A bolt of lightning ripped through the sky and hit the window in the library, shattering it into a million pieces. Olivia dropped to the ground and John took his shot, hitting Wheeler in the center of the chest.

The attorney stumbled backward and crashed into a bookshelf, bringing a pile of books tumbling down upon him. His eyes were wild and he still stared out the window. "No!" he screamed and put his hands up in front of his face. "You can't take me."

The wind whipped through the window and another blast of lightning lit up the sky. Wheeler screamed and slumped to the floor, his dead eyes still staring out the window. A flash of white passed over him, but John blinked and it was gone.

Olivia bolted from the floor and ran into John's arms. He held her against him, afraid to ever let go. "I thought I'd lost you."

Olivia looked up at him. "Did you see her?"

"I saw something," John said, still not wanting to think about the apparition.

"It was her—Marilyn Borque. I saw her hover over him right before he died. He looked like he was scared to death."

"I think the cause of death was the bullet."

"But she distracted him...made lightning strike the window."

"Olivia, I...I don't know what to say. Maybe it was the storm playing tricks on our eyes. With all the stress and that crazy man ranting about emeralds..."

"I know what I saw, and you saw it, too. We did *not* share a hallucination."

John gave up trying to reason his way out of it and sighed. "I know, it's just...this is hard for me. I never imagined... I still don't know what to think or say."

"I think on the police report, you say that you shot a man who was holding a gun to my head—the same man who kidnapped your sister and the caretaker."

"You don't think I should mention that a ghost showed up and saved the day?"

"Not if you plan on working there much longer."

John smiled and placed his hand on her cheek. "Promise me you'll only stay in bed-and-breakfasts from now on."

Olivia smiled. "I don't know. Little old ladies fussing over breakfast croissants don't exactly lend themselves to great horror stories."

"Use your imagination," he said and lowered his lips to hers in a gentle kiss.

"Get a room." A familiar voice sounded from the hallway and John spun around to face his partner standing in the doorway, Rachel hovering behind.

"You're late as usual. I've done all the dirty work."

Rachel cried out in relief and rushed into the room to hug Olivia and him at the same time. She was soaking wet from the storm and giant tears rolled down her face. "I thought for sure he'd kill you both before I got help, then Brian's car came down the road and I almost cried."

"I wondered how you got here so fast," John said.

"When I couldn't raise you on the cell, I decided to make a visit. I had a bad feeling about all this. Apparently, I was right. Rachel told me some of it on the way here, but it looks like you two have a story to tell me later."

Sirens sounded in the distance and Rachel ran for the door. "I'm already soaked. I'll go meet them and take them to Aubrey in the basement."

"Oh, my God," Olivia gasped. "Is Aubrey all right?"

"Wheeler knocked him out, but he was breathing when we left. I'm sure he'll be fine with some rest and care."

Brian nodded. "I'll go help Rachel." He shot John a knowing grin and headed down the hall.

John turned to Olivia. "I know you don't trust me, and I have some things to make up to you. But if you give me the chance, I'd like to try."

Olivia's eyes filled with tears as the past few days

flashed through her mind, completely overwhelming her senses. She'd thought it impossible for her to have a normal relationship…to trust that someone could love her and stay with her, but maybe she'd been wrong. Maybe it was time to take that chance, especially as her heart had already made the leap. She looked up at John and smiled. "What if it takes you the rest of our lives?"

John gathered her in his arms again, knowing that he'd found the place he needed to be. "I hope it does."

One week later

AT THE SOUND of the front door, Olivia looked up from her laptop on the kitchen table and smiled at John as he entered his apartment. He set a cardboard box on the counter and leaned over to kiss her.

"How's the book going?"

"Despite terror week, I'm actually ahead of schedule now. I think my experience inspired me. My editor is thrilled with what I've sent her so far."

"As long as she knows that almost getting killed is not part of your preparation for any other books, she can be thrilled all she wants." He slid into the chair across from her. "I've got some information for you."

Olivia immediately shut her laptop and gave him her full attention. "About laMalediction?"

"Yeah. The cops turned Wheeler's home and office inside out. He had a file with the missing diary pages. He wasn't lying about the baby. It looks like Marilyn Borque had a child while Franklin was at war. Wheeler tracked the lineage from that child down the line until forty years ago, when he lost track of one of the descendants. There's a chance that descendant was your mother."

"Wow. I'm not even sure what I think about that."

"There's more. Apparently, Wheeler's been skimming from all his estate clients. The auditor has already uncovered two million worth of discrepancies and he expects he'll find more."

"Two million. Surely those emeralds couldn't be worth two million."

John shrugged. "With the historical significance, maybe, but that isn't why Wheeler wanted them so bad."

"So what, then?"

"That nut Franklin Borque tied the entire estate up in those stones. Until the stones are found, the estate can't be sold. The detectives found surveys in Wheeler's office and a family tree with supporting documentation that seems to prove Wheeler was a descendant of Franklin Borque. According to the surveys, the property is full of oil. I believe Wheeler wanted the emeralds so he could claim the property and sell it to an oil company. Then he could settle up the estate accounts he'd stolen from, and sit pretty and rich the rest of his miserable life."

"It's so unbelievable. So what will happen to the estate?"

"The prosecutor has some ideas about that and wanted me to run them by you."

Olivia sat up straight in her chair. "Me?"

"There's a good chance you're heir to the estate. There may be others, but at this point they're not identified."

"I don't see how I can help."

"He thought you might hire someone, courtesy of the estate bankroll, to do some research on the family tree and try to locate the emeralds." John rose from the table and opened the cardboard box on the counter.

He pulled out a dusty book and placed it on the table in front of her. "And I have a surprise from Aubrey. His great-grandmother's journals."

Olivia sucked in a breath and laid her hand on the book. "Sissy's journals?"

"Yeah, Aubrey claims that's how he knew about the prophecy and the emeralds. Ought to make for some interesting reading."

"How is Aubrey?"

"Ornery as hell. He said to tell you he doesn't want the journals back. He's leaving for Florida next week and wants to put laMalediction behind him. It will be the first time he's ever left the state."

Olivia smiled. "Good for Aubrey." She picked up the journal and looked up at John. "So I guess I've just got to find someone who's willing to move into a haunted house where several murders were committed, there's almost never any power and cable television and a decent cell phone connection are out of the question. Piece of cake."

John reached down to her and Olivia placed her hand in his. He pulled her gently into his arms and Olivia snuggled into his chest, still unable to believe how happy she was with this man. How content. She turned her face up to his and he lowered his lips to hers with a kiss that, for that moment, took all the troubles of the past away.

* * * * *

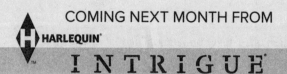
#1455 CHRISTMAS AT CARDWELL RANCH
by B.J. Daniels
Cardwell Ranch is a wonderland of winter beauty—until a body turns up in the snow. To find the killer, Tag Cardwell must work with Lily McCabe, a woman with a broken heart and a need for a cowboy just like Tag.

#1456 WOULD-BE CHRISTMAS WEDDING
Colby Agency: The Specialists • by Debra Webb
CIA agent Cecilia Manning has always chosen danger over playing it safe...in life *and* in love. And now Emmett Holt is her target.

#1457 RENEGADE GUARDIAN
The Marshals of Maverick County • by Delores Fossen
To save her child from a kidnapper, Maya Ellison must trust renegade marshal Slade Becker, even though he could cost her what she loves most—her son.

#1458 CATCH, RELEASE
Brothers in Arms: Fully Engaged • by Carol Ericson
When Deb Sinclair succumbed to the charms of a fellow spy for one night of passion, she never realized he would be both her nemesis and her salvation.

#1459 SPY IN THE SADDLE
HQ: Texas • by Dana Marton
FBI agent Lilly Tanner was once a thorn in his side. But Shep Lewis begins to rethink his stance when they're kidnapped together.

#1460 SCENE OF THE CRIME: RETURN TO BACHELOR MOON by Carla Cassidy
When FBI agent Gabriel Blakenship is dispatched to investigate a family's disappearance, the last thing he expects to find is a woman in danger and a desire he can't resist.

REQUEST YOUR FREE BOOKS!
2 FREE NOVELS PLUS 2 FREE GIFTS!

HARLEQUIN®
INTRIGUE®

BREATHTAKING ROMANTIC SUSPENSE

YES! Please send me 2 FREE Harlequin Intrigue® novels and my 2 FREE gifts (gifts are worth about $10). After receiving them, if I don't wish to receive any more books, I can return the shipping statement marked "cancel." If I don't cancel, I will receive 6 brand-new novels every month and be billed just $4.74 per book in the U.S. or $5.24 per book in Canada. That's a savings of at least 14% off the cover price! It's quite a bargain! Shipping and handling is just 50¢ per book in the U.S. and 75¢ per book in Canada.* I understand that accepting the 2 free books and gifts places me under no obligation to buy anything. I can always return a shipment and cancel at any time. Even if I never buy another book, the two free books and gifts are mine to keep forever.

182/382 HDN F42N

Name	(PLEASE PRINT)	
Address		Apt. #
City	State/Prov.	Zip/Postal Code

Signature (if under 18, a parent or guardian must sign)

Mail to the **Harlequin® Reader Service:**
IN U.S.A.: P.O. Box 1867, Buffalo, NY 14240-1867
IN CANADA: P.O. Box 609, Fort Erie, Ontario L2A 5X3

**Are you a subscriber to Harlequin Intrigue books
and want to receive the larger-print edition?
Call 1-800-873-8635 or visit www.ReaderService.com.**

* Terms and prices subject to change without notice. Prices do not include applicable taxes. Sales tax applicable in N.Y. Canadian residents will be charged applicable taxes. Offer not valid in Quebec. This offer is limited to one order per household. Not valid for current subscribers to Harlequin Intrigue books. All orders subject to credit approval. Credit or debit balances in a customer's account(s) may be offset by any other outstanding balance owed by or to the customer. Please allow 4 to 6 weeks for delivery. Offer available while quantities last.

Your Privacy—The Harlequin® Reader Service is committed to protecting your privacy. Our Privacy Policy is available online at www.ReaderService.com or upon request from the Harlequin Reader Service.

We make a portion of our mailing list available to reputable third parties that offer products we believe may interest you. If you prefer that we not exchange your name with third parties, or if you wish to clarify or modify your communication preferences, please visit us at www.ReaderService.com/consumerschoice or write to us at Harlequin Reader Service Preference Service, P.O. Box 9062, Buffalo, NY 14269. Include your complete name and address.

HI13R

SPECIAL EXCERPT FROM

 HARLEQUIN®

I N T R I G U E

Christmas in Montana is a winter wonderland...until a body turns up in the snow. Now it's up to Tag Cardwell and Lily McCabe to solve the icy murder.

Read on for an excerpt from
CHRISTMAS AT CARDWELL RANCH
by USA TODAY *bestselling author*
B.J. Daniels

"Lily, I have a bad feeling that the reason Mia's condo was ransacked and my father's, too, was that they were looking for this thumb drive."

"Then you should take it to the marshal," she said, handing it to him. "I have a copy of the letters on my computer, so I can keep working on the code."

He nodded, although he had no intention of taking it to the marshal. Not until he knew which side of the fence Hud Savage was on.

"Until we know what's really on this," he said, "I wouldn't mention it to anyone, all right?"

She nodded.

"I need to get to the hospital and see my father, but I don't like leaving you here snowed in alone."

She waved him off. "The plows should be along in the next hour or so if you want to take my SUV."

He wasn't about to leave her here without a vehicle even if he thought he could bust through the drifts. "Are those your brother's cross-country skis and boots by the door?

If you don't mind me borrowing them, I'll ski down to the road and hitch a ride. My brothers and I used to do that all the time when we were kids."

"If you're sure…" She turned back to the papers on the table. "I'll keep working on the code and let you know when I get it finished."

She sounded as if she would be glad when he left her at it. He was reminded that she also had plans to talk to her former fiancé today. He felt a hard knot form in his stomach. Jealousy? Heck yes.

Except he had nothing to be jealous about, right? Last night hadn't happened. At least that was the way Lily wanted it. He fought the urge to touch her hair, remembering the feel of it between his fingers.

"I want you to have this." He held out the pistol he'd taken from his father's place. "I need to know that you are safe."

She shook her head and pulled back. "I don't like guns."

"All you have to do is point it and shoot."

Lily held up both hands. "I don't want it. I could never…" She shook her head again.

"Just in case," Tag said as he laid it on the table, telling himself that if someone broke into her house and tried to hurt her, she would get over her fear of guns quickly. At least he hoped that was true.

Start your holidays with a bang!
Be sure to check out
CHRISTMAS AT CARDWELL RANCH
by USA TODAY *bestselling author B.J. Daniels*

Available October 22, only from Harlequin® Intrigue®.
Available wherever books and ebooks are sold.

HARLEQUIN®

INTRIGUE®

A MYSTERIOUS DISAPPEARANCE WILL FORCE AN FBI PROFILER TO FACE HIS PAST

There's an alarming vacancy at Bachelor Moon Bed-and-Breakfast. Now it's up to FBI profiler Gabriel Blankenship to investigate the sudden disappearance of the owner's entire family. But the steely agent finds it hard to do his job when distracted by the B and B's gorgeous blonde manager, Marlena Meyers. Damaged by his past, Gabriel has never loved and never wants to. But once Marlena's life is threatened, Gabriel is forced to reconsider his case *and* his emotions.

SCENE OF THE CRIME: RETURN TO BACHELOR MOUNTAIN

BY

NEW YORK TIMES BESTSELLING AUTHOR

CARLA CASSIDY

Available October 22, only from Harlequin® Intrigue®.

Love the Harlequin book you just read?

Your opinion matters.

Review this book on your favorite book site, review site, blog or your own social media properties and share your opinion with other readers!